THE PLAYROOM

BY THE SAME AUTHOR

A Question of Guilt
Shadows on the Mirror
Trial by Fire
(*All published under the name of
Frances Fyfield*)

THE PLAYROOM

FRANCES HEGARTY

HAMISH HAMILTON · LONDON

HAMISH HAMILTON LTD

Published by the Penguin Group
Penguin Books Ltd, 27 Wrights Lane, London W8 5TZ, England
Viking Penguin, a division of Penguin Books USA Inc.,
375 Hudson Street, New York, New York 10014, USA
Penguin Books Australia Ltd, Ringwood, Victoria, Australia
Penguin Books Canada Ltd, 2801 John Street, Markham, Ontario, Canada L3R 1B4
Penguin Books (NZ) Ltd, 182–190 Wairau Road, Auckland 10, New Zealand

Penguin Books Ltd, Registered Offices: Harmondsworth, Middlesex, England

First published 1991
1 3 5 7 9 10 8 6 4 2

Copyright © Frances Hegarty, 1991

The moral right of the author has been asserted

Printed in England by Clay's Ltd, St Ives plc

A CIP catalogue record for this book is available from the British Library

ISBN 0-241-13081-6

To Fanny Blake, Robin Blake, and the boys

Acknowledgement

My thanks to Jennifer Davies, tutor *par excellence*, for her wisdom, and the nursery rhymes.

PROLOGUE

The child woke, her face hot from the stab of sunshine arrowed through the window to her face. She turned on her stomach to avoid the glare, burrowed back among the clothes on the floor, attempting to restore the comfort of sleep but a buzzing at the window gradually disturbed her. She sat up and rubbed her eyes. Everything was silent apart from the buzzing and the tick-ticking made by the boiler in the cupboard outside the playroom door. Sometimes at night when the boiler gave a kind of whoosh, sign of life elsewhere in the house, someone running a bath and taxing the work of the gas flame, she could deceive herself that the very sound meant rescue, but nothing had ever followed. Now she was inured to the noise but the buzzing was different. There was a wasp at the window, grizzling at the pane, crawling upwards then dropping back; picking a nervous route round one frame, buzzing for a second, settling back again as if exhausted. Head hurt, I s'pose, she thought, trying to block out the noise, but her heart began to pound and in one automatic reaction, she began to crawl further away from the window. Progress would have been quicker if she had picked up the whole armoury of skirts, dresses and scarves with her, but the logic which had made her use them in the absence of any other cover defeated her now. Besides, she was weaker than she had been yesterday, more transfixed by the wasp than the hunger which had diminished. The wasp made her cringe more than the sight of her own vomit in the corner and the clawing pangs which had accompanied every other wakening.

Forgetting the wasp for a minute, she remembered she was

hot; too hot in the shroud of assorted clothes, hot and smelly although she could smell nothing, merely aware of being damp and flushed. She kicked away the shiny material which covered her, pushed up her T-shirt and with both hands, pulled down the cotton shorts to her knees, thought better of that and pulled them up again. She had some instincts of modesty, a clear memory of a voice saying, 'Don't do that, darling, please. She moved her legs listlessly, looked round the walls for the hundredth time. Pinned to one pastel surface was the legend, written large in red felt pen, 'I AM FOUR TODAY'; another poster, further down, 'TINKER TAILOR IS TWO'. Her own poster was tatty in one corner from where she had tried to chew it. The paper of the other was so shiny hard she had not tried the same tactic, while the satin dress was still wet with saliva on one long sleeve from where she had stuffed it into her mouth before going to sleep. She noticed idly how the stained shorts she wore seemed to have become larger almost overnight, slipping down with ease, moving round her middle when she moved, and she wriggled for a moment, enjoying the sensation of having nothing on her tiny person which restricted her at all. She examined her own, huge knee joints; they grew bigger by the hour. The sound of the wasp, some confused memory of winter birthdays and being cooler than this, brought the insect at the window back into focus. She sat up, a full six feet in between them giving her some feeling of security. Then she began to whimper, rubbed her eyes again, stared.

The sash window was open two inches at the bottom, held there by window locks in the side which prevented anyone of normal adult strength from pushing it beyond. The lower frame was scratched from where she had clawed after the early screaming had brought no response, episodes forgotten now. She remembered getting on a box and hitting the window with one of the metal toys, but neither angle nor strength had allowed any real impact until the toy broke. Jammed between the lower frame, sticking into the room, wearing a polythene sheet, guarded by the wasp, was a sandwich. She looked round wildly, dizzy with anticipation, the old fear of the wasp forgotten. Fear of things which buzzed and stung was a terror confirmed by the hideous shock of a striped bee once attached to her pink forearm administering a pain she could not begin to describe even in screams: in that other life of freedom she would shout at bees and wasps when she spotted them within ten feet, Go away, rotten thingy, go away. Or wheedle at them, Nice waspie thingy, go way please, eat someone else, please. Now the terrible sight of the wasp was irrelevant. She scrabbled to her feet, unsteady in step, pushed everything before her towards the window. Toys, dresses, boxes fell from below her bare feet as she scrabbled at the gap, reaching for the touch of polythene, feeling it between her fingers, her eyes suddenly level with the black and yellow of the wasp buzzing with businesslike fury next to her grasp. If it stung her in the eyes she would not care, falling back, watching the thing still at the window while she tore at the plastic with her teeth, spitting out bits, clutching the contents in one fist and stuffing bread into her mouth. She did not like the taste, beef, mustard, hot, grainy bread as dry as blotting paper with big lumps, all of it tasting of nothing but food, bolted without chewing until her throat was blocked and she began to choke. Coughing, she brought up most of the first half-slice, took stock, looked at it, put the mess back in her mouth and chewed more slowly, regarding the second sandwich jealously, keeping one hand across the bread in case it should move. Or the wasp should get there first. She shuffled back again, further from the window. She would eat the wasp too, and the single thought of that, the only thought since waking, all the rest action and reaction, made her grimace. Yuk.

The disciplines of her elders asserted something in her mind as one enormous gulp took down the substance of the crust. More left: she stared at the second slice, taking in with her eye the generous size of it, wanting to postpone the grief of finishing, closed her fingers round it and worked out how to prolong the pleasure. Sit still, eat slowly; don't show off, tastes better that way, as if taste mattered. Her lips felt dry with salt, the same taste on the fingers which had rubbed her eyes, sticky with the salt of dried tears, a saline crust which felt as if she could pick it off in lumps the size of crystals. She had done so more than once; the taste was similar to the sandwich, gritty, interesting. There could be no more discipline than this tiny

3

pause. Feeling inestimably good, so good she would have liked someone to have seen, she made herself tear the second sandwich into small pieces, dabbing at the crumbs to make sure none was lost, making herself take only a single piece into her mouth at a time although the succession of one after another was swift, growing swifter by the mouthful while she watched fixedly the shrinking pile of the remains, terrified they would escape. So swift, so soon, the grief of the empty space where food had been enormous. All gone, Granny, all gone, gone, gone. But a feeling of fullness, a marvellous gurgling as her tummy went into rebellion. Almost happiness, full of belief that more would follow.

Next, nothing, same old sleepiness, sun going down and the heat which had woken her into life receding into cold. She pulled up the satin dress, watching the last shaft of brilliant light from the window illuminate the vivid purple cloth, making it incandescent. Her hand stroked the cloth, loving the touch of the material, pulled towards her the lurex, goldy black shawl which she also liked, but which lacked the warmth of the heavier purple. If she warmed them now, they would be warm for later; they were cosy enough and the prospect of another night-time still distant.

Be good child, be good: can you remember what I told you yesterday? Sing to me, my lovely.

Who killed cock robin?
I, said the sparrow,
With my bow and arrow
I killed cock robin.

She could think of a room, full of comforting voices. Such as Silly, silly, silly; course the robin didn't die, 's only a song; don't go on so. All right, if you don't like that one, we'll do another, but I promise you, cock robin got better, they were only teasing, didn't have anything better to sing about, silly people. You like this one, don't you? Come on, remember? Like this . . . The child began to croon to herself, pulling the evening dress round her chin,

4

> Dance for your daddie
> My little laddie . . .

Wha's a laddie, I's a girlie: let a boy sing that one, not me. Don't be silly, he won't remember. Just go on with the next bit. Like this,

> You shall have a fishy,
> On a little dishy,
> You shall have a fishy,
> When the boat comes in.

'I don't like fishy,' the child murmured out loud in the empty room. 'I don't like it and I don't like Daddy.' She saw a familiar old face like a shadow on the wall, lingering above the birthday poster, shaking disapproval, fading away with the last shaft of sunlight, talking quietly. You mustn't say that, sweetie, really you mustn't. Let's sing another, my, you're difficult today. 'I don't like Daddy, don't like Daddy, let me out, please . . .'

The wasp hovered over her forehead. She felt too weak, too indifferent to brush it away. If stripy thing stung, she might scream, but could not prevent it. Her arms were heavy; she would not be able to flap it away. Sing then, nothing else but singing to the bassoon noises of her tummy.

Was a little girl who had a lickle curl . . . What came next? She was bad, that was it, no, good, that was it. Or maybe had a little lamb. And when she was good she was horrid.

Outside the door, the noise was slightly audible, the light drone of voice, words slurred, whole sound of deceptive content. There were scratches on the back paintwork on the inside of the door. The paintwork on the outside was perfect. The child was distracted by the marks, which her eyes turned into weird shapes like the patterns on her bedroom wallpaper. As the wasp landed and stung the hand which made no attempt to brush it away, the room beyond the door was silent. No one heard the muffled shriek, one tired little scream, but upstairs in the next house, quite unaccountably, another child began to cry.

5

I

Everything was going to be all right. Everything will be perfectly fine. She forced herself to stand still, raise her hands from her sides and take a few deep breaths until she was tired of taking deep breaths and forgetting to let go. That was the problem, forgetting halfway through. Concentration was not her strong point. They'd said so in all those schools. Mustn't get tense, always made things worse: must exercise control.

Katherine would have gone to the ends of the earth on any day of the week to avoid a row, and quarrels tended to follow whenever tension took the upper hand. Hence the deep breathing, which made her feel stupid as well as weak. Silly really: might be simpler to have the row and get it over with, but he was bound to win. What with his background and her own, quarrelling should have been anathema to him as it was to her, but was not. Rows were awful; she could not even see how he could risk them, but he did and there it was. Shouting for pleasure was all right and she sometimes did so, but never for any other reason and certainly not in anger.

Everything was going to be all right. There was just a ritual she had to go through now, just because the eggs for breakfast had been mislaid, sitting on some shop counter along with the soap (guilty, last-minute purchases these, from a corner shop where she liked to shop and chatter although David said their stock was as old as the hills). All that seemed small enough reason to be so angry, but she could not turn back and say you forget things too, you know, not often, but sometimes, it isn't the end of the world. She kept quiet instead. Anything for peace.

Not that silences were really peaceful: they were loaded, a pregnant silence throughout the house as David prepared to go off and see some client, taking Jeremy with him. That was another cause for insult if she had chosen to take the bait: he never left Jeremy alone with her, took him everywhere like a shadow as if he was bound to fall downstairs or cut a new tooth if left at home with his mother. A case of father love run riot: apparently the clients seemed to like it, made David look like a reliable sort of chap, she supposed without imagining for a minute he would take a baby with him for the sake of his image. There was no need, she thought, with a rush of affection: he is a reliable sort of a chap. Oh damn, damn, why had she forgotten those eggs, she was sure she had brought them home.

Very quiet; too quiet. For reasons or pastimes better left unquestioned, Jeanetta was in her own room, mimicking Mummy by tidying up while Mummy herself tidied with less heart but more efficiency in the master bedroom. Saturday, and a slight feeling of disorientation because there was no structure, a gap of a morning, and industry was certainly Katherine's second nature. Not always productive industry, but still work. What nonsense, thinking there was nothing to do: there was always plenty to do in this house and at some point, never certain, Sophie would be arriving. Lunch, tea, or both? David had not said, slyly arranging his appointment to coincide with a visit from his mother. Clever David.

Looking for some pleasant anticipation in order to stave off that sense of failure and the something like panic which made her so foolish whenever David was angry, Katherine smiled. Thank God, there was Sophie today, a thought which half reconciled her to his being out. They could get into a huddle, Sophie and she, with Jeanetta chirping on the sidelines. Sophie talked about nothing and everything, repeated the gossip of her friends and neighbours without ever giving a fig about the so-called more important issues of the world and her avid astonishment at the doings of all these people was only the same as Katherine's own. 'And do you know what her daughter did? The one I told you about? Well, she's only run off again . . .' 'No,' Katherine would breathe, chin in hand over the enth cup of tea, riveted to the chair in the telling of other ople's disasters, 'Never!' Sophie would adjust, sit back in triumph. 'Well, she did. Anyway, darling, what have you bought new since I saw you? Oh lovely, darling. Did I tell you about Mrs Major?' Oh go on, go on, Katherine would urge, craving gossip which only Sophie could provide. Old friends from pre-marriage days had all been abandoned, only now with regret, and the newer ones were too sophisticated for such indulgence most of the time and she was, without ever admitting it, a little short of gossip in a street like this. Difficult to chat over a garden wall when the walls were twelve feet high with the houses beyond so very large. Never mind; even with the isolation, she found the road in which they lived quite beautiful.

The thought of Sophie was temporary comfort, but only temporary. Katherine needed more than that to quell the feeling of reciprocal anger with him downstairs because the irritation was dangerous and he might think she was sulking, waiting for him to go. Which she was, in a manner of speaking, but not waiting and wanting. She needed something to bring back into focus the David she had known because life was quite unbearable without that man and all he brought with him. The day brightened. Early summer, sun streaming through the windows. Katherine shook the curtains and pulled them back. There was a smear on one of the panes which she rubbed with the inside of the curtain, another task circumvented for another day. The moss-green carpet where the sun lay was warm on her bare feet. Housework this morning would all be done thus, instead of wearing the favourite slippers, brown, fluffy slippers, which seemed, latterly, to have disappeared. David detested slippers, but any such footwear could well have been coveted by Jeanetta, who loved to put her small feet inside large shoes and hobble around like Granny. Idly, since there was no urgency in any task at the moment, Katherine took a look in the cupboard on the landing. Again, although she had looked before to see if she might spot these tasteless presents culled from one of Sophie's markets, those places of stalls, crowds, colours and cheap goods which Katherine secretly loved, treasuring the slippers accordingly. No longer. Oh dear, oh dear. Always losing things. You'll lose your head one day, my dear. Instead, the cupboard contained a jumble of other things, hidden by Jeanetta. Three toys which Katherine could not recognize. Oh God, not again. Now there really would be a row.

'Jeanetta?' she called. 'What are you doing?'

There was no reply other than the sound of shuffling and a slight cough. Probably the child hiding something else. Katherine did not persist, quickly covered the toys she did not recognize with Jeremy's clothes and scuttled back into the bedroom, reattempted the deep breathing and tried, desperately, to think entirely positive thoughts.

This involved sitting on the bed, just a bending at the slim waist for a moment, ready to smooth the rich cover when she rose, all such tidying motions automatic, giving self a lecture. Now come on . . . Whatever she lost or her daughter acquired with such habitual carelessness, there was still in this room a great number of things she could rightfully call her own. This quilted bedspread, for instance, well that always made her say, Katherine, you aren't as bad as all that: you were clever enough to make this. Scraps of silk from shops and stalls where she had worked, cut into identical shapes, fashioned into this multishaded, blue and green bedspread of such proportions. Katherine allowed herself a moment of self-praise. However was it, in the days of poverty, the half-finished courses for which she never had quite the right qualifications, the flat with Mary and the scrappy, short-lived jobs in arty shops where she liked the smell without being terribly good at the work, had she managed to find so much silk? You're like a little scavenger, Mary had said, not entirely disapproving: You're selective, but messy.

Something from nothing. All that work. Whether through half-baked education or scatter-brain or not, Katherine knew she was not possessed of an analytical mind, but as she sat on All That Work in the form of the bedspread she concluded with a shock that Something from Nothing was very much what she was this morning and if she died now, that could well be the sort of epitaph They might write on her gravestone. There was an oil painting in a gesso frame on the wall opposite,

9

showing a bowl bursting full of anemones: she had chosen that, how lucky she was, such choices, such lovely things to accompany her life. Made her humble, reminded her not to react against David being as removed as he had been with his impatience cutting at them like a whip. Only the prospect of duty visitors of any kind made him like that, darling David. But she still had to remind herself what he was, thinking of him as her darling David while stroking the silk to feel her own tiny stitches, reminding herself, non too subtly but timely, of what she was. 'I made you,' she said to the bedspread, 'and aren't you lovely?' Speaking out loud affection for objects loved was not strange for Katherine; merely an expression of delight and admiration although not an eccentricity everyone admired. The habit came from giving herself encouragement to make up for the fact that no one else did. I made you and David made me. No, that was wrong: she had been more like the painting, existing as it was, waiting to be chosen, perhaps pining a little for a good home. A princess waiting for the right courtier, but without any father to please. And all that unusual introspection triggered more of the memories, more of the gratitude. When David was coldly angry, like today, she often took refuge like this. It was hackneyed, it was sentimental: she knew it was, but the formula of romantic reminiscence still worked like a charm.

Thought of herself was what she did, sitting sewing at a trade stand five years ago, looking after the wares for a man with the improbable name of Claud who had imported all the silk fabric on display, herself clutching part of this very bedspread while looking pretty in front of an already pretty stand for the princely sum of two pounds an hour. Architects, interior designers, retailers large and small, tripping round and looking, not really buying, which was why Claud entrusted her with this task while he lunched, as gregarious, promiscuous Claud loved to lunch in the same way he liked to take unprotesting Katherine to bed and pretend to employ her. Katherine absorbed, working on the bedspread, ready to answer questions about the silks, her long hair framing her face. Then this man, bearing no resemblance to anyone else, tall, solid, dark, smiling and conservative in contrast to all the effete designers, the mere sight of him a glorious shock and the voice even better. 'Excuse me, I can't pretend I want to buy any of these ridiculously expensive silks, but when you've finished, I would like to buy that . . .' pointing to the bedspread. She had tucked the hair behind her ears, laughed the way she often laughed then despite all the complications of her life, a big laugh descending to an uncertain chuckle which revealed a clear skin and perfect teeth. 'You really want this?' her face twisted comically and one slender hand holding her work. Yes, yes, he had said, I really want this, looking straight down into her eyes. I want this for my house. I'll come back tomorrow, shall I? Oh yes, do, as Claud reeled back, claiming ownership of everything. Watching the back of the man as he walked away, remembering the words, I really want this. She had worked half the night in a fever but he had not come back until the last day. Talked about nothing, said he was an architect but only looking for things for himself. Pity the bedspread was not finished. She was mesmerized, helpless under Claud's jealous eyes to prevent the man walking away again, which he did, leaving only a card. Gone more than fifty agonizing yards when she saw his wallet left on the stand, got to her feet in her flowery summer pumps and orange taffeta skirt, grabbed that piece of warm leather and ran after him, pushing through the people, '. . . Stop, stop, you've left this,' not realizing in the crush that the dark head, so much taller than the rest, had actually heard and stopped until she cannoned into him. 'Whoa, what is it?' both of them facing and smiling, she holding out the wallet like an offering. Him laughing and all of a sudden catching her by the waist and swinging her round in that crowd, so her feet left the ground, a hug so extravagant and unexpected it left her breathless with surprise. Nothing clandestine here, no shame in him at all. Only a meeting at an otherwise unsuccessful trade fair. Guiltily she remembered the abandoning of Claud, so abrupt it was shocking, not deserving the generosity of his forgiveness. But then, he was married himself; no right to be jealous.

Oh get on, get on. Stop this, it has worked as it always works. Katherine put an end to the reverie. Turned off the switch on the picture of self five years before in long taffeta skirt and hoop earrings, rose off the bed, smoothing the cover, and hurried downstairs. A suggestion of his voice had floated up: a goodbye noise without contact and the sound of the door of the house slamming shut behind his Saturday bad mood. Suddenly she could not bear it and still in the bare feet with the door reverberating as she set out down the stairs, she reached the bottom two steps at a time to see his wallet on the walnut table in the hall. Never forgot anything, what a laugh: he'd be furious and naked without the only thing he ever did forget. Hateful, quite hateful when this ominous moodiness struck. Oh, David, don't go like this, please: what's the hurry? She opened the front door to the road, blinded by sunlight, took up the wallet and ran into the street after him. Please, David, don't, not without a proper goodbye, even for a few hours: I'm supposed to look after you. That was her job and her pride. Down the steps, pink feet twinkling, running after him ungracefully, catching up on the other side of the road with Jeremy just placed in the car. He looked up in surprise, aware before he heard the sound of her slight and flying figure, something comic in her urgency. Unexpectedly, blessedly, he smiled. Caught her in his arms and kissed her neck.

'Hey, hey, what's the matter? What's the rush?'

She put her hands on his shoulders, looked up delighted with the smiling response, the morning's anxiety swept away.

'You forgot your wallet.'

'Oh, clever girl. Running like that. Anyone would think you loved me.'

'I do. Oh, I do. You know I do . . . Don't be cross.'

'Shhhh.' Laughing still. 'I'm not really cross. The neighbours will hear.' The smile fading but not disappearing. 'Kath, you aren't wearing shoes on your feet and you've left the door open.'

Katherine was controlled now, mollified and happy. 'Yes, I know, I'm not staying. See you later.'

'Keep Mother happy. Bye, darling. Can you manage?'

'Course I can. Anything for you.'

Balance restored. Everything was going to be all right. Katherine guarded the open door, waved him away and heard the friendly toot of the car horn with pleasure, wriggling her toes which were cold from the pavement. Stayed where she was for a moment. This morning she was wearing a cream skirt, nothing as lurid as that orange taffeta which would never have been accompanied then by the tiny little diamond stud earrings she wore now. So lucky. Something from nothing, waving to a man who was soon coming back. Today and every day. She hugged her arms to her chest. Nothing to do with being cold.

When Susan Pearson Thorpe came out of her house, taking to her car her own logical mind and a bundle of goods for the ritual trip to the country, she had only managed a glimpse of that perfect skirt belonging to Beauty next door, noted with satisfaction the absence of shoes. Also noted, quite consciously, something she had regarded as the hallmark of the girl but not noticed in a while of brief exchanges, not that Susan noticed much first thing in the morning. Other people's capacity for happiness always amazed her. Katherine, she thought with slight sourness and a headache, had that. Look at her. How refined she had grown in the years she had lived here, but not beyond the point of standing on her own doorstep and yelling, 'What a lovely day,' as she was now. And really, I mean absolutely meaning it. Katherine always meant what she said. No, it was not *joie de vivre* she was witnessing, although Katherine was certainly capable of exhibiting that without being able to define it; nor was it spontaneity, because Katherine was really quite reserved, but what she found remarkable was this ability to throw oneself into things without always, at the same time, thinking of something else. Susan supposed that after shouting these formal greetings and remarks like what a lovely day, Katherine would go indoors and throw herself at the bloody housework since they didn't have any help, just like she'd thrown herself at the decorating of the house, only coming out of doors to glow with excitement, pregnant, talking about paintwork all the time. Such a girlish girl, really, and not what you might call worldly-wise, or not so's you'd notice from Susan's end of the spectrum.

'You off for the weekend?' Katherine yelled, still unnecessarily loud. She always spoke as if wanting to know. The same way she offered to help with something she could do, a nice eagerness, absolutely genuine. Dear Christ, thought Susan: there really are people like that. Cheerful and fit and healthy-looking. There must be a catch.

'Shall I help you with those bags? They look awfully heavy.'

'Awfully' was a word Katherine never used to say. Saying it now meant an approved addition to her accentless English, a sign of moving in the right circles, but there was never a hint of affectation.

'No, don't bother. Sebastian will do it and anyway, you've got not shoes on. There's some rather horrible-looking dirt on the pavement. Might even be our dog.'

'Oh,' said Katherine, grinning still, but slightly abashed. 'I didn't think of that.'

'Well, you should.' Susan had not meant to sound so severe, but Katherine's mood survived the reminder.

'Have a good time then. Bye.'

Katherine meant to go back inside and did indeed step back over her own threshold, listening with one ear for sounds from Jeanetta indoors, but still watching covertly the grumbling of the neighbours as they loaded their way into that huge Volvo of theirs which resembled a hearse, Susan just a little bit breathless, probably from nagging all the time and barking at her children. She was really too plump, poor thing, thought Katherine, remembering the days of being a little like that herself and actually pitying Susan for it, since being plump had been awful. Perhaps this didn't matter if you were like Susan, a bit of a feminist and a frightfully clever career woman, doing an important job (or so Susan always said in her condescending way) and earning stacks of money. Too clever and far too aggressive for easy communication between Katherine and herself, which one of them regretted. Katherine embraced friendship whenever it was offered: she would accept with wide-open arms.

None of this stopped her noticing that the progress of this up-market family into their up-market car was slightly funny, or from thinking that Susan Pearson Thorpe was, in her own intimidating way, a frightful snob and slightly ghastly, to use one of Susan's own favourite words, but she would have welcomed friendship all the same. Katherine giggled. Susan thought she was superior without hearing herself carping at her husband, sounding like a fishwife when she had been a bit pissed last time they came to supper. Calling her Sebastian a bore, which he was, rather, but still she should not have said so in public. I might not have those brains, Katherine thought, but I am nicer, and I'm glad I'll never look like that, all bouncy and bossy.

But laugh as she might, the fact that she was, somehow and all too often, clumsy in her dealings with others, was a feature those next door seemed to underline, together with many of the friends to whom she had been introduced. Mary had said something about it, in one of many lectures, long ago. You should be more selective, really you should, Kath. Don't expect everyone to like you just because you want to be liked, it doesn't work like that. David's advice, roughly similar, all of it bringing about a withdrawal from her previous habit of offering affection like a puppy. Between them, she had acquired as a wife the shy reserve of her manners, and from far earlier than that was learned the lesson Thou shalt not be a nuisance. Nor talk too much. Never.

The Volvo drove away, leaving the street empty apart from a vagrant pausing by the railing outside the opposite house. A new vagrant, whom Katherine noticed with a merely passing interest, poor things, common in these parts, but not at all disturbing today, though they sometimes were. She used to give them money if she had any, but other people said you shouldn't or you'd never get rid. Still hugging her arms across her chest, Katherine smiled at him. Not much wrong with the world. Everything was all right. Except for those toys upstairs, waiting to be missed.

2

Monday again, the first of the month. The three women sat at the table by the window, two facing out, the third facing in. Monica and Jenny had bustled to their seats, chirping triumph at securing the only table with an entertaining view of the street, while in the way which was now usual, Katherine hung back, precise in her movements but slower, armed with a heavier bag, slightly deferential. The other two were so brisk and so certain, seated with coats accommodated before Monica had asked, 'Did you want to sit this side, Katherine? I always want to call you Kate but you don't suit Kate. Would you like this seat? All you can see is us,' sitting comfortably in anticipation of refusal.

'No, no, of course not. I'm fine here, really.' She was cramped in the window against a dusty plant, looking gratefully towards her companions and the interior of Italian smells, pleased to sit still and pleased to see them. 'Is this place cheap, expensive, or middling?' she asked, merely conversational.

'Very reasonable,' said Monica. Reasonable by Monica's standards did not mean cheap. 'That's why we come here so often. Service sluggish, food excellent. But you must have been here before, haven't you, surely?'

'Must I?'

'Course you must. Come on, pass the cardboard. I'm starving.'

'Christ,' said Jenny, 'Pasta ... Oh no ... garlic bread, puddings ... Wine? One between three? None for you, you are strong-willed. Perrier again. What you eating, Katherine?'

'I'm not terribly hungry. Just the salad, I think.'

16

'What? Come on, come on . . .' Monica was the loudest, bossiest, largest of the three, a contrast to Katherine's slenderness, which she did not always envy, even with the interesting refinements of a pale face set off by high collar and beige cloth like paint with a dull, expensive sheen. Monica was wearing a cardigan which she called the dreamcoat, multicoloured, covered with birds and elephants cavorting together. 'The kids love it,' she explained. 'So does the office. Besides, it hides a multitude of sins.' Katherine loved it too. Jenny wore neat black trousers, pristine blouse slightly marred by egg stain on the cuff which she shuffled out of sight, an automatic reaction against Katherine's comparative elegance. Katherine had the knack of making her feel the unplucked eyebrows, bristly legs and clumsier shoes, since while Jenny always meant to be neat, the resolution rarely survived the early morning battle with two children. By that time nothing mattered as much but she always wondered how Katherine emerged so unscathed.

'Come on, come on. Oh, I say, Kate, did you manage to bring those samples? Jenny said you might be able . . .'

'I'm loaded,' said Katherine, smiling and gesturing the carpet bag beside her. 'One set each. One dozen pieces, one metre square. Awfully nice, I hope you think. Should be enough to make a few cushions, small table-cloth, that kind of thing. Anything else you want, you can use my account at the shop and I'll get you something off. Sort of discount.'

The two window-facing women looked at one another. 'Oh, you are an angel,' Monica almost shouted. 'Tell you what, lunch is on me.'

'No, no, I couldn't possibly . . .'

'Oh yes you could, you could, let's look . . . No, food first.'

'You paying for me as well?' asked Jenny.

'Not bloody likely. You don't carry bags of swag like good old Kate. Come on, come on, food. Only got an hour. Well, maybe a bit more. Where've you put your shopping, Jen, by the door? Don't know why you think no one would steal all that food. I sure as hell would.'

Monica was nice, Jenny thought, an irrelevant thought for a friend she had known for years. She ceased to think of them in terms of nice, nasty, clever, beautiful: they were simply there, totally acceptable, defensible against any outside criticism, or at least Monica was. They didn't discuss their own virtues much, save to dwell on how busy they were, or how guilty. Monica was there like a highly coloured rock, met over lunch or kitchen tables forever. No face swam into focus when she thought of Monica, no comments, except, nice, funny. But with Katherine, the newer recruit, picked up as Monica put it, via a successful husband, the face was still novel enough for scrutiny and words, such as fresh, pretty, elegant race-horse, pale and above all, sweet; the proportion of sugar unimportant and undecided. She watched Katherine in the act of leaning over the back of her chair, adjusting her handbag. Must be worried about someone pinching it, well brought up girl, rich enough to take care of money. They might all be bursting at the seams with mortgages, cars, school fees, nannies and the second house, but there were always those times when cash was short for lunch. Monica was paying today and as Jenny was also recipient of Katherine's bounty, she would share the cost. Jenny looked at Katherine. No, this one would never bear the description of good old Kate, wasn't the right dimensions for good old anything, somehow lacking in Monica's tousled sophistication, but sweet, very sweet.

'Katherine, where the devil did you get that dress? Wonderful, makes you look like a pencil.'

'She is like a pencil,' Monica shouted, peering over the menu.

'Oh . . . This dress?' Katherine flustered slightly, pointing to the high linen collar. Of course I meant this dress, what other dress would I mean, thought Jenny, mildly irritated, noticing for the first time how Katherine repeated like a parrot, the way she had when first met and even did in her own house.

'Oh, this? David bought it for me, actually.'

'Good of him,' said Monica. 'I wouldn't trust mine inside a clothes shop. He'd come out with a duster and anyway he'd never think of it. Your back, he says: you dress it. Not very well as it happens. Fancy having a chap like that. Must be wonderful.'

'Oh, it is nice,' said Katherine. 'He also buys food and cleans up a lot.' She'd been thinking such mean and disloyal thoughts about David, she felt bound to do him justice and praise him out loud. Thinking kind thoughts was often necessary to make her actually feel them. Jenny did a check to see if her carrier bags by the door were still in place.

'Good God. You're wedded to a paragon. I suppose he feeds the baby too?'

'Well, yes, he likes things like that.'

She looked awkward when the other two burst into short, comfortable laughter. Monica touched her arm, a gesture of apology. 'Sorry, Kath, we aren't laughing at you. He's only doing what they're supposed to do, but only ever do once in a while, to say the least. And he's so big. I like to think of him like that, big, handsome David, in a pinny in the middle of the night with the Johnson's baby powder. Wonderful.'

Oh, dear, this was hardly giving David a good image either. There must be a better way to describe him without making him seem such a sissy. A line of magazine script swam across Katherine's mind and her brow cleared.

'He's the new man, then. The modern man.'

'In that case,' said Monica, snapping shut the menu and waving vigorously towards one disinterested waiter who sensed the presence of three women as the beginning of small, weight-conscious orders and no tips, 'mine is out of the ark.'

'What do you mean, out of the ark? Doesn't he do the dishes?'

'You mean put them in the machine? No. Sometimes. He pretends not to know how it works.'

Does he, Katherine wanted to ask, require everything to be polished, to throw away toys before they cease to be favourites? Or have an appetite for love-making which required daily relief? She wanted to know, wished Monica would say. Katherine wanted either of them to moan or recite the problems of their daily existence so she could sympathize, add her own and find they were the same. She supposed they were, without being sure. But neither ever wanted to play this game: Monica was never in the mood for secrets. Husband bashing as she called it.

'Now listen, people. We are not forgathered to discuss the better half. May mine remain a mystery, even to me. Come on,

Katherine, show us the means to beautify our houses. I can't wait till after, really I can't.'

Katherine's back against the window was uncomfortably warm. She was shading them from the sunlight while they looked beyond her into the street. She looked into the restaurant, disheartened by the deliberate quelling of intimacy since it would have been so comforting to compare notes, but still exhilarated to be free for an hour or two, with the help of a lie or two, perhaps longer, sitting with her peers, accepted and even popular, the fifth time they'd asked her towards their warmth. The announcement of the strictish lunch timetable was a disappointment because she could have sat here for hours, even alone. She liked to sit. In a moment, rushing by the irrelevancy of food, which Monica ate quickly, Susan diligently and Katherine hardly at all, their corner of the room would become her emporium. Sample bag off the floor, swatches of material displayed; she would please them and it was a joy to please. Mr Isaacs, David's friend and her employer in his temple of interior design, would not approve of Katherine's gathering of the remnants of stock for her wealthy but bargain-seeking friends. No windfalls here, darling, he would say if he knew. And besides, what did twenty-four separate metres matter when he ordered by the ton. Swatches from Italy, luxurious covering for otherwise undistinguished windows and ever improving lives. Women, he said, spend more on this even than clothes, I ask you, even more than clothes and that's saying something. Why not, Katherine had said; what better could they do? They were spending more on Katherine's area of expertise, her pride and joy. Over the materials dumped on the table she smiled in benediction.

'God, these are gorgeous.' Monica speaking in tones of reverence. After children, she had become almost aggressively lacking in vanity for her appearance, hopelessly acquisitive for her house, comforted by the fact that Jenny and other comtemporaries were even worse as if all of them had decided simultaneously that household fabrics were more endurable than flesh. 'How do you choose? You are clever, Katherine: what do you reckon for the bathroom? I can see the place now, welcoming this little lot with open arms.' So can I, thought

Jenny, amused by the sight of Katherine's flushed face, tinged with embarrassment in the knowledge of pleasing, basking in their approval; oh dear, I hope she doesn't think we're using her for what we can get. No, she wouldn't think that surely, not really true. She folded the material, ready to stuff it into the bag of more mundane shopping acquired *en route* from the office, her guilt lessened by her share of the lunch bill and another peek at Katherine's glorious dress, still sitting neatly below the gazelle-like face. Remembered to ask, 'How the kids, Katherine?' 'Fine, absolutely fine.' Asked as an after-thought, answered vaguely, although again, Katherine wanted to elaborate. Only this time, like Monica on the subject of husbands, it seemed disloyal to parade her own concern in front of two mothers who were so successful with their off-spring while she knew she was not. Biting back questions, she held her tongue, afraid to show ignorance. Jenny forgot that she and Monica had talked of little else, houses, new food, décor, but always back to the children. Re-embarked now, the mere mention of the word bringing forth a flood of un-discovered news. Permissible if not mandatory themes as soon as all those round the table were similarly blessed or afflicted, depending on the mood, nothing more fascinating, assumed to be more riveting than What does he eat? Katherine had remained silent, nodding understanding, not contributing, pic-turing the two of her own, the thought of them making her mouth dry and the food taste of nothing but sand.

Monica's Italian designs lay on the table, very flat. They had not captivated so entirely after all. Katherine shifted slightly while she sipped coffee with more decorum than the other two, smiled. Georgiana, Antigiano, Monteverni, Romana, she knew them all. Such colours, Alexia, Veneta, names like glamorous women, against white walls and muted carpets, granting a lift and a dignity to a thing, exquisite. The sun streamed on to blue and gold, green and pink, blessed them, while Katherine smiled and smiled, leant forward and picked from the grubby cloth one of her own golden hairs, frowned at it, examined it, twitched it between her fingers, knotted it, twisted it and finally placed it beneath the table while the others talked. Both of them competitive where she

was not, one a company administrator, one directing an adver-
tising agency, Katherine vague as to where and how, supposed
she ought to have know, but they would still have liked to go
home for the afternoon. In that respect, Katherine considered
her own plans preferable. She could have postponed going
home for a long time.

So they parted. Bumping between tables. Christ, late again,
Monica muttered, squinting at the open air. Taxi? Only a
couple of quid, looking for a sharer to accompany her own
direction; such profligacy. Other way for me, said Katherine,
taking on board the lovely to see yous with a flush of pink
pleasure, standing back while they lurched away the short
distance back to their desks.

Remaining on the pavement, self-consciously shading her
examination from passers-by and as a preliminary to taking a taxi
herself, Katherine was free to examine the contents of her purse.
She walked a few steps, puzzled. There was so much less in there
than she remembered: Thank Heavens Monica had paid for the
lunch; the thought of such embarrassment made Katherine
blush. She couldn't have borne to look like the sponging friend,
even less to have been one, couldn't have borrowed casually, the
way they sometimes did. Having enough was a matter of acute
pride. Ah well, the richer the house, the lesser the cashflow, or so
she had read, and the lack of coinage was only a reflection; hadn't
that often been a subject of conversation between them? Let
them taxi: she walked, one mile and another mile to the door of
the health club. Three o'clock class, duty and pleasure, possibly
even more conversation before and after the mid-afternoon,
mid-classes housewives' sweat. Must keep your figure, David had
said, and paid for the subscription. She checked in the bag again.
Towel from home, shampoo siphoned into small container from
large economy one, track suit old, worn and clingy, but still a nice
colour, pink, and a good foil for her blonde hair.

She had closed the bag, so automatic was the check, before
she realized the track suit was not actually there, stopped
again. Gone. These two reminders of rotten, irresponsible
memory, at war with her own, clear recollection of placing the
kit in the bag and the money in the purse, were horribly
disturbing, but the sun shone and she shrugged them away.

Borrow left-over stuff at the gym, get going. Call yourself an efficient housewife, standing on the pavement, doing nothing: get going, before anyone notices you looking silly.

Not enough food in her very slightly swollen stomach to interfere with the purpose, although her comfort was more the changing room than the shining floor of the studio gym. A room full of half-dressed women, thriving in all sizes, groaning, joking and laughing. 'Spent all day trying to talk myself out of this,' said one. 'You never,' said another. 'Hallo, Katherine. What a great dress . . .' Hallo, hallo, her best, beatific smile of great affection for the regulars escaping from other furious disciplines to subdue the irregular body to the torture of exercise, then titivate the hair, straighten the crumpled clothes to wear them better, emerge office-bound or home-bound, newish women. But no intimacies here either. Something I do wrong, Katherine had once wondered, dismissing the thought behind her own pleasure in being part of the camaraderie. Perhaps I'm too thin, too streamlined, too smartly dressed for this lumpy, bumpy crew, and that thought was not displeasing. She had never mastered the art of dressing down; emerged either polished perfect, like the house, or nothing, with no untidy edges either way. And none could doubt the dedication of Katherine Allendale, whom no one ever called Kate. She stood midway through the class, thin and strong as a ballerina, no surplus flesh to quiver even when she ran, which she did with effortless determination until the perspiration gleamed on her long throat and disappeared into the crevice of her small cleavage. Teachers were puzzled and delighted with a pupil like Katherine, at once enthusiastic and so absolutely literal. If you shouted, 'Jump higher! Go on, pull! Come on, squeeze those buttocks,' she did as commanded as if her life depended on it. If you said, 'Reach for the ceiling,' she really tried to touch, stretching her fingers and extending her slender arms for a quite extraordinary distance, while the others aimed for halfway and never beyond pain. Nicer for never pretending it was easy or saying it was natural. No problems about borrowing Katherine's towel, brush, comb, etc., she even waters the ferns in the foyer. Can never persuade her to buy a new leotard, though. She fingers them on the stand, likes the touch and look of them, but never ever buys. Hair slicked back into a thick mane, Katherine stretched and pulled, deferring her favourite place in the classroom to another who simply stood there. Let her: it wasn't important. Everyone liked her.

Four o'clock. High and low point of a regular enough kind of day. Katherine sat in the café on the corner behind the gym, relaxed for the first time. The afternoon was dying; the sunshine from far away lunchtime gone to bed behind cloud which sent gobs of rain splodging on the windows. Steam had begun to fog the inside of the glass. She began to drink her tea laced with sugar, savouring it as the most delicious thing to be had in any afternoon. Katherine adored cafés like this, not cafés à la bentwood chairs, espressos, croissants, but caffs with large, cheap cups of tea, tables occupied by one, a slight fug and smells of overused fat, bacon and toast. The caffs of her childhood and adolescence, where no one noticed when she sat alone; being thus almost *de rigueur* in the wasteland of late afternoon. Neither was it assumed you could afford to eat, the lack of cash a common denominator, comfort almost free and conversation an optional extra. She felt utterly at home, wrapped in the smell of baked beans, writing on a scrap of paper her order of preparation for the evening meal at home. Things so tight on one hand, so luxurious on the other, symptoms she had come slowly to recognize as such odd features of so many of the lives she knew. She had read that in a magazine too. All about how the bigger the house, the less money in it to pay the milkman. Nothing abnormal in hers after all.

Cheered by that particular thought, Katherine wrote, 'Avocado mousse; defrost. Halibut? With wild rice?' The thought of rice being wild made her smile: odder juxtapositions of words often did that to her. 'Mousse au chocolat' for pudding. No, not two mousses, or was it mice in plural? she smiled again. Sorbet then, fresh from the freezer. The slight sickness which always followed an hour's strenuous exercise had by now receded, came back again with unabsorbed lunchtime lettuce. She looked at her list of tasks. Dinner on the go by half past eight, children first. Screams and yells when she dragged Jeanetta away from next door's Mrs Harrison, who always made it seem as if she was doing them a favour, instead of the more simple arrangement of being paid. Both carried home to be fed with sludge in the big kitchen. Jeremy's was sludge food, Jeanetta turned hers into sludge before devouring it. Katherine thought wistfully of an egg and bacon sandwich, baked potato with butter, popcorn. Anything sniffing of fat, sugar, starch. Uncurled her long spine from the plastic-covered bench, prepared to leave for home. She wished she looked forward to seeing her children, but she did not.

From the opposite end of the caff, with a cold radiator at his back, John Mills regarded her sourly and wondered what she was smiling about, probably the laughable vision of himself, or more probably the joke just practised on him. As he turned in his pocket the plastic card which identified him as charity worker for Child Action Volunteers, he could not dismiss the vision of his wasted, humiliating afternoon and imagined everyone knew. Knocking politely on a door, meeting an old lady who was shapeless and malevolent, poking her head out like an angry cockerel.

'What you want?' Even the arms of her had quivered, the head moving back and forth as if revolving by remote control from a massive neck.

'Oh, I hope you don't mind, Mrs Harrison . . .'

'I'm not Mrs Harrison, I'm Mrs Jones.'

'Of course you are. Well anyway, Mrs Jones, I hope you don't mind . . .' putting on his best lopsided, half-concerned grin, '. . . but a friend of yours asked me to call and see if by any chance you need some help with the children . . .'

'Oh yes, which friend was that?' 'Friend' was spat and Mrs Jones's arms snapped shut across her chest.

'I forget the name, she's a neighbour of yours.' He pretended to look in his pockets, at the same time darting glances round her to peer through the basement doorway beyond, looking for clues. The search distracted him: he did not notice at first that she was laughing, the fleshy bulk shuddering with the arms on the chest moving fractionally on a soft bed of bosom. 'Ooooh, Aaaagh . . . she's really done it this time, have to give her top marks. What a liberty, scraping the bottom of the barrel that is, setting the NSPCC on to me . . .'

'I'm not the NSPCC,' he started.

'Same bloody thing, I bet and I don't give a sod what you are. Encylopedia salesman one day, social services last month and the RSPCA last week, she sent. That was more like it, at least I've got a cat.'

'About the children,' he started again. 'Children?' she shrieked. 'Children? You silly git. Wanna come in and look? You can take my old man to the knacker's yard if you want but children? You must be joking.' She thrust a huge face towards his. 'I'm seventy-four, you silly fool. And you've been had.'

John Mills squirmed at the memory. He should have been beyond the anguish of this shame, but it still afflicted him as he stared into his watery coffee, feeling quite capable of hitting that slender woman opposite for the mere fact of her beautiful clothes and her unselfconscious smiling. Katherine rose to go.

Six o'clock. Monica crashed through the door of her own house, the shopping on either side doubling her own width and making her feel fat. She'd been thinking on the way home how she really ought to go to that gym place Katherine Allendale had mentioned. No, don't really want to, no time and God alone knows I ought to be fit, climbing stairs, humping this lot about, cleaning, cooking, fighting, gardening even. Whatever the money there never seemed anyone else to do the work. Buys the groceries, does he, David Allendale? What a joke. Must tell Colin that; also about David buying dresses. The same David Allendale who was about to supervise the construction of a conservatory for Monica's own house, something akin to one she had spied elsewhere, but nothing to approximate to Katherine's kitchen. Not only was Katherine thin with a gorgeous house, but the man indoors did most of the shopping while she remained untroubled and generous. Monica manoeuvred round the door, only slightly angered by such transient thoughts, conscious as soon as she entered of who was in and who was not. Husband a few miles off, discussing plans with David Allendale, plenty of discussing the way he liked. At least she knew where he was, which was something of a luxury. Guess who would, after all the discussions, clean up the sawdust, brick dust and any other kind of dust while the children rolled. Shit. 'Mummy, Mummy, Mummeee . . .' shrieks from the corner of the stairs facing the front door, howls of joy and argument from above. The first of two boys launched himself towards her from the landing, head first, like a human sledge across the carpeted treads, braking with his hands, slithering down at horrible speed in a series of bumps. A new turn, this, designed to bring heart to mouth. She did not pause for breath, expelled her opening shout even as her bags hit the floor.

'For Christ's sake! How often do I have to say, Don't do that!' He was at her feet, undeterred, face upturned in a grin, trousers descended across bottom through contact with the carpet. 'Hallo, hallo.'

'You little blackmailer,' she said, scooping him up and cuffing him lightly. 'You gorgeous little sod.'

Jenny's house was like Monica's, four miles to the north-west of the Allendales', comfortably close for dinner. All their houses formed a triangle with the Allendales' at the spiritual centre, Jenny's and Monica's, of course, less grand and half the size, but still substantial, and though neither of them would have countenanced such a description, comfortably rich, as they were themselves. Jenny had thought once, noticing the cast of the furniture, how much her house resembled Monica's, with similar ideas, sofas, chairs of roughly the same shape, the same type of kitchen made to look as if it belonged in a country mansion. She shrugged off the slight annoyance which afflicted her at the thought of being so influenced by an old friend, stared at the conclusion reasonably and told herself, yes she was, and why not. Besides, they all influenced one another, were never as individualistic as they seemed, all went the same sort of directions in pursuit of style, shopping carefully, only sometimes rashly, led by the nose and the credit cards in pursuit of some image of excellence; of course they would have similar things.

Only difference in her house setting it apart from Monica's and far removed from Katherine's, was the mess. Jenny could not control the mess, while Monica, who emerged dressed like a tribeswoman, expensive ethnic festooned with tassels, colours and swinging earrings, put her house under strict orders not to follow suit, and it more or less obeyed. Jenny's was clean of course, but without a single clear floor or surface and whatever she did, *objets* and objects crept out of hiding places and became a kind of universal litter. All to do with design, David Allendale had said. With the greatest of respect, nothing in your living room is in the right place. There is never a cupboard within easy reach where you do not have to cross a floor to open the door: no wonder you don't. And don't range your furniture round the walls like sentinels, of which you have too many, by the way, and as for your kitchen, it is fashioned to impede rather than assist. He had been generous with free advice when he and Katherine had sat over dinner, nibbling at collapsed meringue after over-seasoned casserole, not a well-matched menu either. She supposed she would come to copy Monica in the end, and one day soon. Let the man in to do his worst.

Jenny's house was silent, not a scene of devastation exactly, but bearing the traces of two daughters about the same age as Monica's brood. Copycat, I am, thought Jenny. I'd like a house like Katherine's really, would I: one where I opened the door to the vague fragrance of pot-pourri in every room like hers without any spilled on the floor. Daughters were not in evidence. She had forgotten: they were staying overnight with grand-mother: she should have remembered their being wild with excitement at the very idea as though it had never happened before and by tomorrow, doting grandma would be on her knees silly with exhaustion but still game for more. Jenny had looked forward to the break, actually craved the time while saying, Are you Sure, are you really sure, but now, quite perversely, she already missed them, wanted an armful of child in the way she might have wanted food. Yearned for the feeling of small bones on her lap with fingers smearing egg on her collar, could almost have called out for them. The feeling passed like a flush, but for a moment, if she had thought they would not be back for the space of a week, she would have screamed. Silence. She shouted upstairs for her husband even while knowing he was out and in any event no substitute. Anything to dispel the calm, the dreadful vacuum of their absence.

*

Katherine let herself in to blissful silence. Her house was bigger and better than either of the other two, with its proximity, through a series of grand and leafy avenues, to the edge of Hyde Park giving different perspective. The other advantages of Katherine's house were several decades of age behind the other two modern versions of success, less utilitarianism and far more waste of space, each room infinitely bigger and better and every ceiling higher. The street outside had the benefit of large, mature chestnut trees, the pride of the road, celebrating a century of growth. She and David had always occupied this house, he first, she following, thrilled to enter such a castle, such sublime safety. Since then David had refined the house, altered it, polished it, indoctrinated Katherine in every aspect of every corner. Theirs was designed to be a house inviting admiration since if it failed to do so, those wealthy clients would not talk of it as they did now, or consult David with such regularity in the hope of achieving comparable effects in their own. The house managed to be unpretentious, clever was all, with a way of seeming endless. Give a place a vista, Monica had joked, standing in a kitchen all wood and Italian tiles, but with armchairs rather than ordinary chairs, covered in fabric more vibrant than the dreamcoat. That's the bit defeats me, Monica had said: I'd never have thought of handsome armchairs for a kitchen, seems sinful somehow. There were elegant French windows to the broad back garden, and neatly placed at the end of the kitchen, fully viewable from the cooker, sink or table, an alcove playroom where the sun shone through. Jeanetta's playroom, soon to be shared by baby Jeremy, who already crawled in that direction as he did towards anything new. At one stage before the life of this kitchen, there had been three small rooms in the same space, which was half the huge ground floor. The playroom had been either scullery or maid's room in halcyon days, while the business end of the kitchen now incorporated machinery behind wooden doors which somehow deadened the sound, leaving the alcove room for childish recreation. David, with David's natural economy, had preserved all the original doors, told Katherine he would find a use for them, like everything else she was clearly instructed not to reject. She had obeyed faithfully, discarding nothing at all, miserly even with rubbish. Odd earrings beads from broken necklaces, broken bangles, laddered tights, worn-out clothes, her own and the children's, filled drawers and cupboards, neatly folded and stacked until he had said, 'Not everything, darling: I meant anything of use.' He had taken away the pile of broken jewellery and had it set into one long necklace, earrings and beads fashioned together into a rope, a talking piece with such history and an act of such imaginative kindness she was tearful on receipt, it was so beautiful. David's generostiy could feature such inventive flair, and then, as often, she loved him to distraction. The baby clothes and her redundant garments had been shipped to Oxfam with less ceremony, apart from the evening things left in the playroom for Jeanetta to dress up.

Katherine thought of this as she went upstairs to her dressing room, took off the beige creation, donned wool slacks, cashmere sweater, the necklace and flat shoes, a swift operation carried out in silence, but not without thought. On her way in, she had seen the vagrant again, lolling against the car, and she had not told him to move, as David would certainly have done. She took off the sweater, feeling the softness of it with great, ever renewable pleasure. Then put on another sweater, the ribbed, tight-fitting one David liked better. I am so lucky, she thought, so terribly lucky. Change one cashmere sweater for another and I might never have owned the one. In a place where Katherine had endured part of her early childhood, all clothes had been pooled, never owned, but savagely laundered into brittle, scentless cleanliness, scraping against the skin, and now this wool, soft as down against her face. She never forgot the contrast.

Above her head she could hear David talking in the second-floor room which served as his studio and office. Mercifully large, this house; ample room for three bedrooms and two bathrooms first floor, David's suite and the children's quarters on the second. Beyond that, there was the underdeveloped attic floor, skylight constructed as the first step towards an alternative sitting room, the smaller room next door still without a light. David wanted to turn his genius towards this space when his plans were sanctioned. As it was, the top floor was bare and swept, but unwelcoming, the only part of the house of which she was faintly ashamed, and because of the bare darkness, slightly nervous, imagining as she fell to sleep, the sound of footsteps and scurrying insects on the empty boards.

Nearly six o'clock. Collect the kids from next door in fifteen minutes. Jeremy would be tired, a long day for him, even in the unlikely event of Jeanetta behaving herself and allowing him to sleep. Katherine thought how lovely it would be if Mrs Harrison had given them something to eat, bathed them, so that all she had to do was dump them into bed. Neat and trim, even taking neat steps, hair loosened from the headband which had subdued it in the gym, smelling sweetly of her own perfume which David chose, Katherine went upstairs and knocked on the door, entered in the same movement, an intrusion only allowed with advance permission by long-standing tradition. 'If I'm still in the studio at six,' he had said 'come and knock at the door. Colin Neill will have gone on about the plans for his extension long enough by then. Wish he'd send his wife, what's her name, Monica? Much more sensible and to the point. Her man has more money than sense, never wants to spend it.' By this time, he had been talking to himself over the breakfast crumbs, simultaneously clucking Jeremy under the chin and glaring at Jeanetta. 'That child needs her hair trimmed, it looks awful. Anyway, come in and save me if he's still there at six, OK?' 'OK,' she had agreed, complying with the directive as the grandfather clock on the ground floor struck four chimes out of six, entering David's room with the happy stride acquired through the pleasures of her afternoon.

The studio ran the length of the house, light pouring from gracious windows at either end. From the back, David could see into the south-facing garden, look down towards the steps which swept from the kitchen windows to the lawn, and there stood his drawing board, a device he could move to the other end of the room if the light was better. A room designed for work rather than comfort, but like all the rooms, welcoming. There were pale rattan blinds to maximize the light, the pragmatism of the place softened again by the shape and fabric of two enormous chesterfields angled round a Persian carpet at the street end, beautiful, slightly worn fabrics for both as if they had been the priceless possession of a gentleman's club, forming an area where people sat and never wanted to rise. With a division of labour which had become a familiar hallmark, David had provided the symmetry of design for this room, while Katherine provided the colour. She noticed the plants cascading on to the floor from the walnut table which stood over the rug and saw they were in need of a little attention. One of the trailing stems was beginning to go brown. David's client, feeling every inch the guest, was touching the healthy leaves. The glance he gave in her direction turned from one of brief and familiar admiration into a broad smile. What a nice man, she thought. Under David's protection, she thoroughly enjoyed male appreciation, preened a little.

'Would you two workers like a drink? Come on, don't talk so hard.'

Monica Neill's husband leapt to his feet, approached with hand extended, shook hers and held it a fraction longer than necessary for someone who needed no introduction. David sat where he was, using Katherine's arrival to begin a casual rolling of the plans in front of him.

'Hallo, hallo! How well you look, Katherine. Good God, is that the time? David,' turning to him, 'I'm so sorry, I've kept you. Monica will berate me.' Katherine could not imagine what form the berating would take, but understood the general picture, smiled and shook her head.

'Gather you girls had lunch today?' said Colin heartily.

'Yes, we did. It was lovely.' The response was warm although Colin stumbled over the words, thinking as he spoke of how Monica would react to the description 'you girls': probably slap him for the suggestion of condescension. Katherine would never think like that. 'Meantime,' said David lazily, 'yes, these boys would like a drink, I think. Gin, Colin? Go on, to wrap up business?'

David was so good at this; no one knew when they were being given twenty minutes' notice to leave. Katherine recognized the talent, admired it while she was frozen before awkward visitors like an animal in headlamps unless he helped her. Otherwise the dislike would show on her face. 'By the way,' David added, as Katherine turned her graceful back on them towards the inconspicuous kitchenette, 'don't worry about the kids. Mrs Harrison phoned. They've all been out to the zoo or something, Jeanetta got filthy and was dunked in the bath, and now she's feeding them all. Probably in rather the same fashion as the lions. Says she'll bring them round at half six.'

'Oh,' said Katherine. 'Oh, lovely, how very kind of her.' Her face brightened further in the promise of an evening without conflict, no kids' food, no rows. Colin Neill absorbed without realizing the cue to leave before 6.30. It occurred to him fleetingly how no one appeared to come to this house without express invitation, no doorbell ringing of casual callers; how nice. Wondered if it was his imagination which saw in her shoulders a great shrug of relief when told about the children. He would not have blamed her since he always thought Monica fussed too much. Children could be a pain. They stopped a wife being a wife, and Katherine was a real wife. He watched her tranquil progress with envy.

3

My name is Susan Pearson Thorpe, but actually, we usually drop the second bit and leave the name as Pearson. I live next door (left, second house from the junction) to the beautiful Allendales, but I do have other claims to fame, thank you. The houses are roughly similar, but I'm never quite sure about our house and I'm never entirely certain if I like this street; so vulgar living among all these foreigners and *nouveaux riches*. Not that I think about it much: there simply isn't time. It's basically the right kind of house, though miles smaller, of course, to the one where I grew up. Sebastian, too, although I'm afraid his family is not quite the same calibre as mine. Seb and Sue, sounds so common, sort of thing printed on the front of a really naff car. Anyway, this house, this street. I'm always surprised at people's reactions when I give the address, but they're just very big houses and frankly, a bit short of ground. That's the trouble, they all seem out of scale. Houses this size should have half an acre around them and not be glued to the one next door. Here we sit, with our big, broad frontages straight on to the street, inches away from the neighbours with no more than a pocket handkerchief at the back. Hardly enough for a cat. Speaking of which, the Allendales abhor cats and they're a little vulgar too.

They use their garden as a kind of ornamental extension of the house; you know, the bit you look at from the French windows, backdrop for a room, rather like a lovely picture. I like something to stomp around in, can't get over a perverse desire to grow vegetables since that's the purpose of a garden, really, but our patch is a bit of a wasteland. Oh, trees, and bushes and things sort of thrown about, but the children have worn away the lawn and since the thing disappoints me so much, I can't be bothered to have it repaired, although I'm quite sure the Allendales would be able to refer me to an expensive cure. No joy sitting in a place anyway if it isn't strictly private and this one can never be that. For one thing, there's the Harrisons in the basement who do rather regard it as their own territory, and then there's the Allendales next door. He can look straight at our grass from the window of his studio and although we've got a fence thing, more like a trellis with creepers above the wall separating their garden from ours, it's hardly foolproof. Even in summer you could peer between the leaves without the other side seeing you at all. Not that they would, of course. Far too polite, especially her. She'd feel guilty, unlike Mrs Harrison or I, and anyway I know she knows I know how she puts down those pellet things to keep out our cat. The cheek! Still, she's very sweet, Katherine, both of them extremely pleasant, very hospitable and friendly without being nosy. I always tell people we're very lucky in our neighbours, they have a great respect for privacy and they're equally keen on their own, more than us, if anything, and there's always the country most weekends.

That time already? Time for a drink.

I suppose there's only weekends I get to see much of the children. Some people might feel guilty about that, but frankly, there's no need. We were both brought up to boarding school from the age of six and look at us, certainly hasn't done me any harm and proving my point, our two are as happy as sparrows. There's another thing about this house I resent though. Here it is, gracious and spacious, but the children spend most of their lives in the basement amongst Mrs Harrison's gewgaws. This is a splendid arrangement which keeps them out of my hair since in my view they ought to be seen and not heard, but it does strike me as odd that while we have enough space above stairs for an army, the one place they want to be is downstairs in the clutter of those little rooms, all squashed in with the Allendales' pair. Don't know how or why it is Mrs Harrison loves it so much, but that's another reason why having the Allendales next door is such a blessing. Couldn't be better.

David pays half of Mrs Harrison's wages for having the kids five days a week, sometimes weekends too when we're away; I've worked out it saves me £3,561. 56 per annum, thus I get a bargain and Mrs Harrison is as happy as a pig in shit. The more the merrier, she says when she's in a good mood, and oh, my feet are killing me when she isn't. Not that sharing's strictly necessary, but I was brought up to economize wherever possible, which is why I'm a tax consultant rather than a housewife, with figures having the same effect on me as children do on her downstairs.

Thinking of which, I wonder where the Allendales are thinking of sending Jeanetta to school? High time, come to think of it; she's got to be nearly five, looks more, of course, with her size. Don't really want theirs alongside mine: I mean, absolutely OK for now, but not for ever.

Damn, I've left the tonic downstairs. I really should keep it up here, in my study. Sebastian and I have a study each to maintain mutual independence, though Christ alone knows what he does in his, I don't like to ask. His faces the back, with a small window. I face the front to avoid the updrift of all those stories and rhymes from the basement and because I bagged the bigger room so I can walk up and down, look out of the window between turns and see what gives in the road. Not a lot, usually. There are thirty-three houses in this street, usually forty cars with about one foot between each, makes the street approx. four hundred feet long, that can't be right . . . I must stop counting, most annoying, really. Other times, I lean right out of the window, elbows on the ledge, staring up and down, thinking quite inconsequential things, like what a funny basement area the Allendales have, uphill from ours, iron railings like ours with no room at the bottom for the biggish flat the Harrisons have got here. The Allendales only have space for storage and some kind of workroom, I think, and if I don't stop leaning out, people will think I'm a bit touched or something, not that I give a tuppenny damn about what people think. People are either stupid or boring, most of the time.

Tuppenny rice, half a pound of . . . They were singing that in the garden earlier, all the children. Tuppenny rice, chance would be a fine thing this day and age. I need a break from figures and right on cue we have footsteps on the stairs, knock on the door. You can tell by the wheezing how this stair climber is old Harrison. Couldn't possibly be my workaholic Sebastian who never sees his own home before nine o'clock and looks like a bat in daylight even then, zonked by work and usually monosyllabic. 'Come in,' I yell, glad to be found at the desk instead of by the window, hiding the neat gin, waiting for the ponderous opening of the door. There they are, framed like a picture. Harrison and dog, equally decrepit.

'Evening, Mrs Pearson. Eileen's got the babes downstairs in the kitchen. Ready for bed, I reckon.'

'But it's only 6.30.'

'Time for a bit of Tee Vee, then,' he says doggedly, about as subtle as margarine. The dog ambles over, able to manage five steps without sitting down.

'You mean it's time the mob were out of your hair?'

He shuffles a bit: that's exactly what he means, poor old Harrison, five times a grandfather, never reckoned to be living at his age in a basement, something he always sees as a bit of a disgrace, surrounded by someone else's children, but he can't go yet since there's no one else to do the chores round here and it isn't going to be me. Housework bores me rigid and one did not battle with a career to clean bloody pans and nursemaid children. He shuffles again, smiles slowly.

'Course I don't mean that, Mrs Pearson. Eileen'd like a word with you, though.' Oh God, I bet she would.

Downstairs, me fast, Harrison professionally slow in all his movements in case anyone should think he could go quicker, dog clattering behind. There in the kitchen, surprisingly pink, clean and glad to see me, my children, kept under starter's orders.

'Mummy, Mummy, Mummy . . . Look at me!'

Cannoning from table to chair in her red pyjamas, four-year-old Samantha holds a yoghurt pot in her teeth with the rim of it balanced on the end of her nose, draws attention to this as well as her new slippers. Mickey Mouse with long whiskers appliquéd to the front of these, making her feet look extra large and ridiculous, and I guess Mrs Harrison chose them since I did not. Sammy has dark curly hair, very piercing eyes, a definite face. I am not a sentimentalist by any manner of means, but this second of my children, born by mistake in my fortieth year, is a creature I could find almost edible, supposing I had the time. She squirms on to my lap and holds each foot over my eyes for inspection and I wish I had a fraction of that agility. Meanwhile, Mark, a sterner creature in the wisdom of his seven years, consents to stand within the circle of my other arm, but only briefly. Mrs Harrison (I never get used to calling her Eileen) hovers portentously but this, too, is quite normal. Both she and Harrison are more at home in my kitchen than I.

'Had a good day?' I ask, heart sinking slightly as it always does before the ritual recitation of ritual moans. She disapproves of me more than slightly, working mothers remaining the mystery of her universe, but she cannot say so because she doesn't dare.

'Not so bad,' she says. 'Took the lot to Regent's Park, didn't we? Seen all the animals, didn't we just?' She turns to the children for confirmation. They nod, and Mark takes up the story.

'We saw lions,' he said. 'Very very, big.' 'The biggest in the world,' adds Samantha. '. . . And one of them got out of its cage,' said Mark, pushing her aside in rising excitement. '. . . And ate a boy', she interrupted, stealing his thunder. 'Everything but his shoes,' Mark finished. '. . . And they give whole cows and horses to the crocodiles,' he began again, almost shouting. 'No, they don't,' scoffed Samantha. 'Only pigs and chickens. I saw.'

'Do they really do that?' I ask doubtfully, looking at Mrs Harrison over the heads. She shrugs and smiles.

'Do, do, do,' shrieks Samantha, wriggling on my lap, still admiring her feet. 'Dogs as well,' said Mark, determined on the last word. 'For breakfast?' I tease. 'No,' he mumbles, ever so slightly ashamed of himself in the realization of what I may and may not know, 'only for lunch, silly,' he finishes lamely. I frown at him: he really shouldn't fib like that.

At least he knows when he exaggerates. Samantha, being younger and more prone to it, doesn't. I once heard her telling the postman he couldn't come in because there were spiders in the kitchen. As big as pans, she said, lots of them, so the postman imagines we have cockroaches. She also told a decorator there were snakes behind the walls which poked their heads out of the light bulbs after dark. Marvellous, but much as I love these tales (which often involve their own daring and lion-taming in our insignificant garden), I'm not sure if I entirely like the tendency. God alone knows what stories Mrs H tells them; frightfully lurid, I expect, but since I've abdicated the care of both of them to her so comprehensively, I've decided not to ask although I'm aware of it all the same. Tall stories and nursery rhymes; she knows them all and I know not to believe my children, even now. The hovering has changed into a fidget. Mr Harrison will be waiting for his tea. Probably sick of the sound of tuppenny rice and wanting to eat it.

'Well, and how were the Allendales today?'

Samantha giggled. 'Jeanetta went in the duck pond. She nearly drownded'.

'Did she?' I ask Mrs H. 'She did indeed, Mrs Pearson. Go into the pond, I mean,' she adds, seeing my glance. 'She's a handful, Mrs Pearson, really she is. Had my work cut out, I can tell you, what with these two and baby Jeremy in his pushchair. Getting them home was a problem.'

'She was all covered in slime,' chants Mark, 'like a lizard, all green and things . . .'

'So she was, wasn't she, my pet,' agrees Mrs Harrison. 'She certainly was. Put it all over everybody, shrieking fit to bust . . .'

'She liked it though,' said Samantha earnestly, quick to reassure me. 'Jeanetta loves getting dirty.'

'And that's what I wanted to ask you, Mrs Pearson,' said Mrs H, before the two of them dragged her from the point of the story which obviously had purposes other than illustrating both the traumas of her day. '. . . Wondered if you'd speak to Mrs Allendale? I don't like to, not for me to do, really. Oh I suppose I could when she comes to collect, but it'd be better coming from you, if you see what I mean. Would be much better coming from you.'

'What would?' I ask, feeling the familiar threat of irritation.

These children are her concern; why can't she bloody talk to next door, and if she thinks Katherine Allendale is too high a cut above her for familiar speech, she's way off beam.

'Would be better you speaking to Mrs Allendale about Jeanetta's clothes, if you could Mrs Pearson.' Eileen Harrison's voice has sunk to a conspiratorial whisper which is designed to exclude the children, but only ensures their ears are pinned back for maximum input.

'. . . Her clothes, you see, Jeanetta's. When she comes here, bless her, she nearly always needs a change of clothes, never has them. Fact, what she does have on her back are a disgrace if you ask me. Worn and thin and always too small. A disgrace, I say, don't know what the woman thinks of . . .'

'That will do, Mrs Harrison,' I interrupt. I cannot have her criticizing Katherine Allendale, especially in front of the children. I can criticize: Mrs Harrison cannot. 'No wonder the child always grizzles,' she finishes haughtily, very aware of the reproach. 'Jeanetta's very fat, Mrs Harrison.' This is meant to conciliate, get us back to even ground.

'Plump, well yes, she is, a bit bonny, but she must have more clothes. I usually wash whatever she's got and half the time, like this evening, she's running around in Mark's pyjamas, 'cos I've nothing else to fit her. Can't you tell her, Mrs Allendale, I mean? It's a disgrace, I have to say it is.'

'I don't mind her having my pyjamas.' This was Mark's contribution. Exceptionally kind little boy, my son. 'I really don't mind at all.'

He might not mind, but I do. They may be very nice et cetera, and the arrangement convenient, but I do not like next door's lump running round in my son's pyjamas, don't want her inside his trousers, not at any stage, thank you, including now. 'Yes,' I tell Mrs Harrison. 'Don't worry, I'll mention it. When I get the chance. And thanks so much for the zoo trip. Jolly noble of you, I must say.' Christ, I'm a hypocrite sometimes: so what if she has a hard life. She's paid, isn't she? Mollified, she collects Eric, who was clearing the kitchen sink meanwhile, and they both toddle off downstairs. Within seconds, I hear the muted sound of their television announcing the soap opera which is the staple diet of their entertainment;

no wonder she exaggerates. I'm glad they've gone: one has to have servants and I can't imagine how or why next door manage without, but God, they're a trial.

Look at these bairns, as Harrison calls them; I mean I love them and all that, but not all day and every day, oh no. They'll sleep early tonight, so I whisk them off without much complaint after a bit of telly, read a story to Samantha and encourage Mark to read his own. Really, Sebastian ought to do more of this even if he does double duty weekends, when they treat him like all the saints rolled into one, very, very irritating. Wish he was home sooner, just once in a while you'd think he could make the effort. Even though it's usually easier to ignore him and the male of the species is always hankering after food while all I want is the superior interest of drink, just a large one please. I'll stop after this. Or maybe not. Food's an understated pastime in this household anyway, what with me never really wanting much more than a sandwich and quite disinclined to cook, and Sebastian grabbing his sustenance on the run like the wandering tribes of Egypt, quite prepared to eat the plague of locusts on toast. He might prefer another regime, but too bloody bad. Gin makes me feel stronger, occasionally very much crosser if I'm cross already, and come to think of it, has that effect now. The washing machine is rumbling in the corner, making an irritating domestic sound which makes me crosser still. And reminds me . . .

Bugger Katherine Allendale. What does she mean, sending Jeanetta round here to romp in my son's pyjamas? They've got money, haven't they? Rather a lot in fact if that isn't too vulgar a thing to mention. I know kids' clothes are a terrible waste of that commodity, but she can surely find her way to any old department store; it doesn't have to be Harrods for God's sake. Look, I might be a somewhat distant mother, don't believe in all this bonding stuff and letting them into bed, but at least I know when they need bloody clothes, because someone bloody tells me.

Right: all quiet; I'll go round and have a word with her straight away, no time like the present. Kids will be fine for a few minutes. Mark's pyjamas, be damned, does she think we're made of pyjamas?

Out in the street, everything looks larger, very clear once I pick myself up from the step where I've tripped, always falling over these bloody steps. Whoops. So inhospitable, large and impersonal, sort of bleak, thirty-three houses in this street. Golly, thoughts do race a bit after a drink or four. I can feel them coursing round as soon as I hit the fresh air, walking up the road to their front door, hope I don't smell.

Golly, again. Look at those houses opposite, very shut indeed, windows like sleepy eyelids, closing all the time. We need the bloody Allendales for parties and they need Mark's pyjamas . . . Shhhh . . . Very, very quiet indeed, rather cold, as if everything was already over until morning. White stucco houses, curtsying goodnight, gleaming rich with their own haloes, goodnight all of you, a few big trees, full of summer leaves, sheltering the white fronts or dripping sticky stuff on the cars. Everything so still you could hear the leaves drop but never a voice. Bit sobering if you see what I mean, everything so much bigger than it looks from the window. Don't like being on ground level.

Here we are. Our ground floor is raised, so you can't peer in, which suits me well enough. The Allendales, slightly uphill from us, have their kitchen facing the road, just about low enough to see inside. The room glows, perhaps intended to be admired from the street, which I do, of course, both room and contents, people included. The two of them are dining at their splendid table, opposite one another: they have bowls and plates which look suspiciously like Crown Derby from here, one superb large salad bowl, and they eat with a kind of ceremony. She glows a little like the room glows, casual and rather perfect with that hair of hers like a well-controlled roan mane, hanging down her back. Eating like royalty without servants. Looks like they're having fish: no wonder she's slim as a reed, fish and salad, oh dear. David Allendale gets up to fetch something, glances towards the window, comes back with another lovely bowl, places a hand on her shoulder as he passes. She smiles up at him, continues eating, rather more delicate in this art than her daughter, I can tell you. How strange their children should be so disparate, the boy so sallow, like him, the girl a blonde tank, pink of skin, paler by far than her mother's lovely colours; probably designed their children to complement each other like they do themselves. I'm sure he's seen me, refuses to look; I know he loathes unsolicited visitors after all. Beyond them in that long, wide room, I can see the window to the garden and the annexe at the end they use as a playroom. Not a sign of a toy.

No, since you ask me, I don't think I shall, go in, I mean. Not in the workday suit I forgot to take off, so that they can ask me to sit on the edge of their feast and take water and wine at their altar of health, and anyway they might think I'm lonely or something silly, which of course, I am definitely not. They took so contented, him so solicitous, patting her arm and all that, everything so stylish. I can see the flowers at the window end of the table, so frightfully vivid in front of her fawn-coloured clothes, an enormous wodge of overripe sweet peas nestling in a clever little terracotta trough. I suppose he brought them home. Bet she smells fragrant, and the gin on me would be spotted a mile off. Another time, then. Did I shut the door quietly, this is a respectable street and I've got slippers on my feet, slippers and a suit, I ask you. Dear Katherine, would you like to come over tomorrow and transform my house, taking in my life while you're about it? Make it perfect and me a pretty little miss like you? Sebastian would approve.

I think, after all, I'd better go home, I'm not nearly as angry as I was.

As Susan Pearson Thorpe shuffled back towards her own kitchen, the tableau in the kitchen of her neighbour broke abruptly, as if at the end of a play. Passing her chair, David had stroked Katherine's long hair, sat facing her, offering more wine. No thank you, murmured with a rueful grin; one glass is enough: you know it makes me silly.

'Fine thing for husband to say to wife, darling, but you do look well.' She smiled under his careful regard, happy in the flattery, slightly embarrassed at the formality of words, as if he was a stranger.

'Thank you, kind sir. Should I bow?'

'I think old Colin Neill fancies you.'

43

'Oh, rubbish.' Nice to know all the same. She stored that observation for future reference. Not as a bargaining power, simply a pleasant fact to be looked at from time to time, like a child's valuable toy, too good to use, always lovely to be admired. David kept on looking at her, so keenly she felt very slightly uncomfortable. One glass of wine went a long way: three was the sickening minimum before she lost inhibition. Cheap drunk, she told people and they laughed about it.

'You'd look lovelier still with a softer haircut. Your face is so thin, the way you do it now, there's a risk of looking severe . . .'

'Oh.' She was absurdly disappointed. He was looking at her the way he looked at things, evaluating people's kitchens, their styles, just like he looked at this house, coolly, while she looked with a kind of passion. 'Well I don't want to change it.'

'Of course not, if you don't want. I was thinking of wonderful, shortish, you know curls. Lots of lovely curls.'

She was thinking of her headband, worn home from the gym, left off when she went upstairs before the children were delivered home in a merciful state of amenable fatigue. One yellow headband another thing lost. Rather like cutlery: you started with eight and always ended with half. No one ever knew where the things went. Oh, the joy of reading that in a magazine too.

'Well, I like it like this. Easy to keep.'

'Lovely,' David murmured. 'Isn't it nice, having a husband who notices such things?' She beamed back at him. It was, as it happened. What had Monica said? Your back, you dress it? David wasn't like that. Something to be proud of, even if there were times when it became, well, awkward.

Then Jeremy's chortled crying was transferred down to the kitchen through the little electronic device on the wall. He could easily get downstairs, Katherine thought resentfully; he'd done so before on his little nappied bottom, but he rarely had the chance since father leapt up the stairs two at a time on the merest signal of the merest whimper. Seconds after his footsteps had receded and the crackling from the intercom faded, the other one appeared. Jeanetta in all her glory, trailing after her one elongated teddy bear which Katherine recognized as having been, very lately, one of Jeremy's favourites. Damn.

'Hungry, Mummy.'

'No you aren't. You can't be hungry.'

'I am, I am.'

David's romantic mood, fading in front of her eyes, the sound of the intercom ominously still. Jeanetta pretending to cry, damn, damn, damn. She was fiddling with the cupboard door, where had she put those biscuits, not here, not there, something had magicked them away, she said, still looking, aware from the lighter steps that he had come back into the room, materializng from the nether regions like a genie.

'I want a word with you, young lady.'

Jeanetta stopped crying. Any attention was better than none and Mummy was not really trying. Katherine got up from her knees and went over to her daughter.

'She's only whining, darling, take no notice. She's over-tired.'

'Tired? Why tired? She's plenty of energy for taking things which aren't hers. That's Jeremy's teddy she's got there. And a few other things not hers upstairs as well. And look at the state of her. She's got something stuck in her hair.'

'David, please. She's only four. How should she know? Jeremy must have given her the teddy and Mrs Harrison gives her things. She doesn't just take them . . .'

'What's this eh?' He seemed to have leapt to Jeanetta's side, playfully. Picked up a hank of her straggly, thick hair, held it aloft. She looked at him hopefully, sensing a lightening in the tone, ready for a game.

'Don't shout, David.'

'I'm not shouting. I simply raised my voice.'

True. He never shouted, just as she never argued. She knew very well how bits and pieces of other children's toys came into the house, pushed down the side of Jeremy's chair, secreted by Jeanetta and amusingly, recovered later. Katherine thought it was really a bit of a joke, nobody minded really. She wouldn't have minded either, like all these things they had, wonderful, but giving away the surplus didn't matter. You're welcome to old toys, she would have said, but he was still holding on to Jeanetta's hair, and she wished he wouldn't.

'Chewing gum,' he said finally in tones of enormous disgust.

The child did not flinch. She beamed instead. David's movements had become swifter, horribly efficient. He pulled her gently and she followed willingly towards the kitchen sink where lay the kitchen scissors, still sticky from cutting the slivers of cooked bacon he had added to the salad. Jeanetta still smiled when the blades of the scissors cut cleanly and noisily through her hair, shearing off a whole pony-tail of sticky curls. Only when the tangled mass hit the floor and she raised one uncertain hand to her head to feel the shorn reminder, did the smile waver. Katherine felt the sound of the scissors champing as if they had been applied directly to her own skull. Jeanetta's only pretension to beauty, her crowning glory, lay on the kitchen floor, and still she smiled. In some instinct, Katherine smiled too, grinned desperate encouragement at her daughter while protectively, her own hand flew to her own head.

'Me tomorrow,' she said, suddenly inspired to say the right thing. 'Oh, it does look nice. Does if feel nice?'

Jeanetta shook her head violently. A drift of stray hair joined the hideous, dead-looking clump on the floor. The puckered face did not know whether to weep, smile or laugh out loud, looked for guidance. How could you, Katherine wanted to shout: How could you do that, why, why, why? She wanted to spit and scratch at him for such a piece of strange, quixotic violence, but he was smiling too, quite unperturbed, like someone looking at a job well done, while she felt like the onlooker at a scene of rape, her own eyes smarting with tears. But another line of magazine script came floating by, something suggesting, if you make a fuss, they make a fuss: cool down emotional situations. Anything for peace. And maybe she was wrong herself to find this barbering obscene. Katherine was never sure of being right, so she kept the encouraging grin affixed to her own face, and slowly, slowly, the little girl copied, smiled back, still uncertain, looking the picture of stoicism. All this passed within a minute.

'Biscuits?' Jeanetta asked hopefully.

'Daddy's getting them.' The words were a challenge, not accompanied by a look. Jeanetta staggered towards mama. They turned their backs on him. Biscuits were produced and even in the task of hugging her daughter without making the occasion seem important enough to warrant extravagant gestures, Katherine wondered where the biscuits had been found.

'We could trim it nicely, round a pudding basin,' David's voice suggested from behind her head. His hand came on to the table between them, bearing a dish of biscuits, although these were placed on the polish of the table somewhat abruptly.

'No, I don't think so.' She was watching Jeanetta. 'Time for bed, darling. You shouldn't have got up.' The last words were heartfelt, her only hint of hostility. Child nodded, still smiling with her mouth full, grabbing three biscuits and ambling towards the hall. She was unusually good at going back to bed on her own. 'Sleep tight,' Katherine called. Uncoordinated feet fell into silence. Katherine slumped back into her chair without looking round.

'Have we finished the wine, darling?'

'Plenty more.'

He sounded cheerful. She could not bear to look as he swept away curling locks from the pristine marble tiles of their cooking floor. There was the sound of the tap as he rinsed the scissors, while her scalp waited for the same shearing sound of her own hair, the noise of it still resounding through each ear. A fresh glass, full of bubbling white, appeared for himself, while he hummed a tune she did not recognize, filled the dishwashing machine which always confused her, not for the mechanics, simply because she could never see quite why it worked. Sounds of domestic harmony: no trace of the curls. She breathed deeply, glad of these household noises which hid her own subterfuge, mind latching on to one thing, two things, three things. Such as why she had not been quick enough to stop him; gratitude for the fact her own hair remained untouched; relief in his evident playfulness which somehow made everything normal. Don't fight, she told herself: he wouldn't take it seriously and he always wins. She looked at the wine, drank a large gulp. Some kind of oblivion, any kind. Please.

He passed by the chair again, stroked her hair again and they were back as before. Katherine breathed deeply. Everything was going to be all right.

*

47

Sebastian Pearson Thorpe came home, pulled up his Mercedes across the frontage of the Allendales', led by the light in their kitchen and disappointed to see it go out. He really must tell Susan one of these days about David Allendale, little bit of family history which might amuse her. If he ever could amuse her, or find her awake. He wished the house next door was still alive, a beacon in the road which encouraged him home. There were no signs of life in his own house, which he entered slowly, perspiring in the muggy heat of the early night.

After he had gone indoors, taking off his city jacket *en route*, the small, sallow-skinned vagrant shot out from the tree opposite and huddled close to the warm bonnet of the car. To his own damp forehead, sweating in a mild fever while the rest of him was cold, watching the lights go off, one by one, it was not warm at all. But everything was going to be all right. Summer had come, he had heard on a radio in the park. So everything was all right: survival was assured.

4

Mornings had an unpredictable momentum. Katherine found the less she thought about them, the less they mattered and the better they were. Mornings and the prospect of getting away from the house, much as she loved these cool interiors, well, mornings appealed. She felt sane in the mornings. Jeremy's docility always amazed her: she had no idea babies could be like that and he seemed prepared to make his transition to little boyhood in the same spirit. Good child from birth, born all sweetness and light with a cry of surprise rather than anger although the act of it nearly killed his mother, a fact she could never quite forget. She could guess that he was not always so sweet when she did not see him, which she had to admit was most of the time; also that he played to the gallery of his father, hardly cunning enough at twenty-three months to act out a constant, favourable contrast to Jeanetta, but doing it all the same. Katherine looked at Jeremy's goodness occasionally with guilty irritation. He was so easy to love, but on behalf of his sister and herself, she resented him.

Jeanetta, on the other hand, was pulled into clothes half an hour before breakfast, screaming throughout. She had not wanted to relinquish the flannelette pyjamas in which she had been delivered home: they were roomy and comfortable although the length of leg impeded progress, perfectly adequate wear for a warm, early summer day, and even without such conclusions in her small mind, she could see no reason whatever to transfer her fat little body into anything else less amenable. The elastic of her own cotton trousers bit into the rolls of her stomach and the knees were worn thin. Her T-shirt

49

rode up over her waist, carrying the vest beneath it and adding to her bulk. The head shoved through the neck of the shirt was haloed by ash-blonde curls, short, horribly uneven, but still unmistakably hers and the face beneath was already pink and mottled, the translucent skin no disguise for the morning's extreme emotions.

'Do your teeth, darling, please, just for Mummy, Please.' There was a pact they were honouring so far. Everything as normal, even with half the hair.

'Won't . . . Why? Why can't I have my pyjamas?'

'They aren't *my* pyjamas, I mean your pyjamas, they're Mark's pyjamas . . .'

'He said I could have them.'

'No, darling, his mummy doesn't think so, now do your teeth. Nice breakfast in a minute.'

Nice breakfast the battle ground to follow. Katherine looked at Jeanetta with a mixture of perplexity and panic, uncomfortably aware that the pyjamas, which Jeanetta would now insist came to breakfast as a talisman before personal return to their owner, were one of three such pairs, to say nothing of the toys treated in the same way. Clearly no good: the child would have to have more clothes before anyone else saw fit to mention it. What with these clothes and the shorn hair, she looked like a product of a refugee camp even though sheer weight denied any notion of want.

'Come on, come on . . .' Then a cunning threat, 'You'll miss cornflakes if you don't hurry.' Jeanetta sulked into action, pretending a sloth she could never quite maintain in the face of food; then propelled herself downstairs with a force and a shout which made Katherine wince. The banister rail was polished mahogany transported from another house at vast expense. Once a week Katherine restored the nicks and scratches inflicted by Jeanetta's progress and once a month shampooed the carpet where Jeanetta's tracks took chocolate, gummy sweets and left-over meals, Katherine powerless to stop her. Jeremy had been carried down by his father, chattering in his make-believe words, the two dark heads together discussing their breakfast in calm, orderly tones, David's full of amusement, Jeremy economical with his few real syllables.

50

'Onge, Daddy?' He meant juice. 'No, yellow Daddy. Isn't Daddy silly?' David's chuckle rose up with this reply of his own to greet the other two.

Father and son were well ensconced in the kitchen, David with his padding acolyte stotting round at his heels, chuntering like a train, understanding nothing of Thomas the Tank Engine which David read to him, but imitating the noise in lieu of words, a sound quietly expressive of contentment. He was tall for his age, promising the height of his six-foot-tall papa, the uncanny resemblance between them prominent in all other features from skin colour to the mutual texture of their thick hair. Somehow Jeremy had missed on the plump stage of babyhood, the bulge of his nappy remaining the only protuberance carried behind with a kind of pomp, while Jeanetta had always resembled a statue of Buddha. She sat on her own chair at the refectory table, raised to the height of it by cushions under her ample bottom, looking like one big cushion with her chest absorbed into her tummy which settled on to thighs resembling diminutive tree trunks. Her chin merged with the moon of her pale face; there were two pink spots on her cheeks, the skin elsewhere white. Katherine quickly brushed the truncated golden curls while the child was half captive in the chair. To do so otherwise, when Jeanetta was free to kick as well as grab and memory of last night's outrage came back to roost, was out of the question, bringing into Katherine's morning mind the knowledge of her own hopelessness. Child had inherited from the paternal side a will of iron, a love of confrontations from the day of her birth and every single day since, rendering her mother weak with frustration.

'Want yogot.'

'Want yoghurt, Please.'

'Please c'n I yave yogot?' She had picked up intonations of speech from the Harrisons in her years of daily existence with them. They seemed to suit her and at least Mrs Harrison, or was it Mr, distilled in her some beginnings of manners. 'You got to fight with them Ps and Qs, Mrs All'dale,' she said to Katherine when thanked for her efforts. 'Never comes natural in any child, you know. Not even ones who don't say boo to gooses.' Meaning of course, Jeanetta boos everything. Guilty

51

Katherine had taken in the hint of criticism implied by the tone although it had been no more than an observation, one of Mrs Harrison's vain attempts to engage conversation, but she had remembered the Ps and Qs later. Now she corrected most of Jeanetta's words and found to her surprise that the ploy occasionally worked. Especially if the bribe was edible. Nothing else about her inept, panic-stricken mothering seemed to succeed.

David fed Jeremy, who sat in his high chair consuming a smooth white mixture with minimum fuss, David scooping the surplus from the chin with each withdrawal of the spoon while the child frowned in concentration. Jeanetta mixed straw-berry yoghurt with her favourite cornflakes, spilling the sugar she added with a look of defiance at her mother. Mummy did not like sugar, but did not prevent daughter. She had not forgotten the cutting of the curls, felt she was owed. With sweet taste in mouth, Jeanetta was as happy as she had been as a baby with sugar in the bottle. So tempting to give her what she wanted, even while knowing better. 'You've given that child a problem for life,' Mary had bawled, reading straight from a text book. 'How can you say that, she loves it,' Katherine had said, furiously resentful. Leave me alone; if I take anyone's advice it won't be yours. But Jeanetta still loved sugar; sugar was peace at breakfast, withdrawal the opposite. Apart from the noisy business of crushing cornflakes into yoghurt to make a concoction of psychedelic colours, all was serene.

'You look a bit tired, darling. Are you going to work?'

Katherine looked up in surprise. 'Yes, of course. I'm expected. Ten o'clock as usual. Why?'

'Just wondered.'

It irritated her, this almost daily litany. Of course she was going to work, but the mere question made it seem as if work was a movable feast, not a commitment of any importance to be avoided whenever inconvenient as soon as he voiced his preference for her to stay at home. Katherine took work seriously even though it was only three hours per day watching Mr Isaacs' exclusive shop, talking nicely to the customers, displaying rich wares to the rich, losing herself in the window displays as she stood watching the world pass by. The shop was another world, full of the things she loved, but of course it would have been better if Mr Isaacs had not been a friend and customer of David, so that by some strange quid pro quo arrangement she had to accept while not understanding why, payment for her services went into David's account rather than directly to herself. Better for tax, he said, handing back to her the approximation of her earnings. Why, she had asked, closing her fist round a pathetically small bundle of notes. 'Listen, darling, trust me, you know what you're like with the stuff, this is the best way, OK?' Then kissed her lightly, smoothing the long hair back over her shoulders, rewarding her agreement in advance with one of his seductive smiles. She had smiled back, OK. All for the best, he was probably right although she was sick of smiling. Difficult to answer while she knew how money slid through her hands like water, leaving no trace. Extravagance; impossible to explain where it went; she never quite knew and the knowledge of that was acutely uncomfortable.

While she sat now at the breakfast table, avoiding a view of the hair, she caught sight of Jeanetta's T-shirt again, rucked up to show pale, round stomach. The child leered at her, pink cereal mixture displayed on white teeth. Jeanetta's star performance, showing them exactly what she was eating. Clothes for Jeanetta, Oh bloody, bloody hell. Jeanetta turned her multi-coloured mouth to display to David. He neither smiled nor reacted. 'Don't do that, darling, please,' Katherine murmured, reaching for the coffee. Jeanetta tried once more, turning her wide-open jaws towards Jeremy, who rewarded her with a stare of blank astonishment. Disappointed, she turned back to the mixture, snorting loudly and clattering the spoon violently in the bowl. Splatters of pink fell on to the polished wood. Automatically, Katherine wiped them with a cloth held in the opposite hand to her coffee cup. She ate nothing.

'And after work?' David continued.

'What? Oh, gym, I expect, as usual.' Such a good excuse for doing nothing, wandering round. 'I'll be back quite early. We've got the Neills this evening, haven't we, and the Loreans and Fosters coming in for a drink? Wait a minute, not so early.

I've got to meet my sister, just for an hour. About four o'clock, have to check my diary, shouldn't take long.'

'Why don't you get her to come here?'

'I thought you didn't like her coming here.'

'Whatever gave you that idea? I don't mind at all. I'll be working anyway so I'm not likely to notice. Don't you mean she doesn't like coming here?'

Katherine was immediately confused as to what she did think, distracted by Jeanetta's head. At this point she did not wish to say that actually, Mary liked coming here, rather too much. Well worth the ducking and diving to meet Mary on neutral territory. She only had to look at the cream walls, the rich kitchen and the armchairs to remind herself why. 'Another new chair then?' Mary would say. 'Why do you need that?' and Katherine would feel her own skin tingle. There was enough to feel guilty about without adding a tyrant like Mary, charity director, great preacher of the virtues of poverty. And then there was the business of always having to feel grateful to Mary. Everyone said Mary had been so good to her, but long before she had married and escaped the spartan flat they had shared, Katherine had been sick to death of Mary being good to her. Mary always knows best, nag, nag, nag, and hadn't she shown her. 'Mary's so kind to you,' David reminded. So horribly true. Armed with a small inheritance from her own adoptive parents, conscious of having done better in their lottery of life, ever prudent Mary had bought a flat and plucked her sixteen-year-old sister from the last of many messy hostels after the last of four sets of foster parents. Terrific. Gratitude, which Katherine was hard pressed to feel was as corrosive as the accusation that it had all been her fault, something she felt without suggestion. So getting married had a lot going for it, including showing two fingers to Mary and all that worthiness. Mary always knows everything, always knows best, but I don't need you any more, I'm the king of the castle, la da di da da. All that. Mary in this house might spot the cracks on the fabric, wheedle her way through and Katherine could not bear that. Mary was everything she had left behind and she hid from prying Mary.

'No,' she said to David, 'I can't change the appointment

now. She wouldn't like it even if I could reach her, you know what she's like, busy, busy, busy. We'll meet in town, it's quicker.' As well as safer.

He nodded. 'OK, darling. As long as you know she's welcome. Everyone's welcome.'

That is not true, Katherine thought. Then remembered not to be disloyal. Once you started being disloyal you went on. Another women's magazine. Jeanetta stuck her fingers in the sugar bowl, withdrew them covered in white grains, transferred the sticky paw to her mouth with great smacking sounds. They both chose to ignore her.

The house ran like a machine on the days when everything worked. Open the front door by 8.45 to spill out the mistress, Jeremy in chair, Jeanetta trailing pyjamas, wailing for the toy she had left behind, refusing to move, then following, curious for the day despite herself, keen to reach Mrs Harrison and the prospect of another breakfast. They bumped down three or four wide steps, Come on, come on, Jeremy beaming and squinting at the world, turned left, downhill four steps, up the next steeper steps, all of them slightly anxious to effect the day's first transition. Mrs Harrison at the door, taking in the posse of them with a smile which faded slightly when she saw the pyjamas, dusty from the brief journey and clutched to Jeanetta's chest like an offering. 'When you've got a minute, Mrs A,' she intoned, the face suddenly stern, 'Mrs Pearson'd like a word with you,' gesturing back into the house as if to call up a giant. This sounded ominous; so ominous, Katherine, unable to face another confrontation, muttered something along the lines of yes, yes, of course, this evening, ever so late, and with a bright grin which embraced everything in sight, fled down the street, waving back towards them. Mrs Harrison watched shaking her head. Off to work with a spare dress in her bag: the world was mad. Jeanetta pressed inside without a backward glanced, dropping the pyjamas to the floor along with the red cloak she had grabbed at the last minute from the playroom alcove, while Jeremy raised his arms to be embraced.

'Look at her, she's like someone escaping,' Mrs Harrison

remarked out loud, tutting under her breath. She remained at the doorstep, holding the boy in her arms and watching Katherine skipping out of sight. After a minute, he wriggled to be free and she put him down. He waddled into the house where Mr Harrison ushered him down the stairs at the end of the hallway into their flat. He liked the children in the morning although afternoons saw an imperceptible slackening of his patience. Already Jeanetta would have been scooped up for kiss and cuddle and hallo, my lovely, how you been then, a brief embrace because of her weight and his arthritis, but mutually enjoyed all the same, she returned affection with aggressive warmth first thing in the morning. Then transferred her adoring attention to Mark Pearson if he was home from school, her condescension to Mark's sister when he was not. School holidays rendered Jeanetta easier to please.

This point in the morning was bliss to Mrs Harrison. She still wore her slippers, slouched against the door frame admiring the street, feeling in her pocket for the ever present packet of fags. It enlivened her, this first interlude of the morning after Mr and Mrs had departed and the house was her own. She didn't want the house, wouldn't have the foggiest idea what to do with all those rooms to which Harrison administered his daily lick and promise, but she liked the occasional feeling of being the only one in control. Just for a while. The sun was shining, the birds audible in the chestnut tree opposite the house. She could always have sat in the garden, but the garden was quiet and she liked a bit of noise. Besides, this was about the only time in this road when anything happened much. Big cars passed, people walked up and down: she wasn't going to miss the sights or the chance of gossip. Eileen sat on the second of the four steps, pleased to find her view unobscured, lit her first cigarette.

Not a friendly neighbourhood, but not bad when the nobs had gone out to work, such of them who did. Then there were the nannies and babies and passers-by going places. Out of the corner of her eye she saw Mr Mills turning into the street, strolling down the left hand of the road towards her as if he had all the time in the world. Well, it was a nice day, she thought lazily: why should he hurry; worked something called flexi hours, he'd informed her, which seemed a funny term for always being late. Talked a bit funny too, Mr Mills, told her once this was his stroll through civilization, the only bit of it he ever saw all day. Oh yes? Well he was a friendly enough chap and she'd talk to anyone, whatever rubbish they said.

His clothes were as odd as the conversation. In summer, as now, he wore the same heavy cords as winter, only his feet finished in sandals with whitish socks, a sight irritating Mrs Harrison beyond belief. Waist to neck was covered in a creased Indian cotton shirt, identical usually to yesterday's and the day before's, while his face was always festooned with a bit of fuzz, which Mrs Harrison longed to attack with scissors since it looked as if he had forgotten, and on top of that, like a final decoration, a pair of granny glasses of the kind old Harrison had given up wearing long ago. Really.

'Hallo, Mr Mills,' she called as he drew level. 'Not seen you in ages. Been on your hols, then?'

He stopped in surprise, thoughts obviously elsewhere. Or maybe he just didn't fancy a chat this morning, and if so, that was too bad, since she did. An awkward posture for John Mills, involving him crossing his ankles, standing on the outer side of his feet with his knees pressed tight, hands in pockets and thin torso leaning forward, looking like an anxious bird.

'Oh no, no no,' he said, 'Holidays? What are they when they're at home? We workers, Mrs Harrison, we workers . . .'

She chuckled. 'Speak for yourself. Thought you'd gone for ever.'

'Alas, no, on a course . . . Went away for a few days, but now I'm back. On the treadmill.'

'Poor old you. Still looking after them kiddies, are you?' She had the half-idea he did something of the kind, he'd said so and she saw him, with his slight effeminacy, as some breed of teacher, all of whom she imagined to be pansies if they were male. Or something on the local council, for all that stuff he said. Talking politics as soon as they'd said hallo, Fancy; so unexpected he must be paid for talking like that; it wasn't natural. No one else had ever spouted that kind of stuff to Mrs Harrison: she found it faintly gratifying, but slightly indecent.

'You housekeep,' he had said, ten minutes into the initial

conversation six months ago, when it was winter and she had more time, 'and they own all this,' waving his arms about. '. . . And another house too, I expect. It's disgraceful, absolutely disgraceful. No one should be allowed to own so much.'

'Why not, then?'

'Because it's wicked, that's why. It should all be shared. Look, there's room for four families in here. Places where I work, they come from four to a cupboard.'

'Well,' she had said, slightly offended by a view of her employers which seemed to include her as a conspirator, 'don't bring any spares up here then, will you?'

'I might,' he had said darkly, 'bring half of them up to squat in this street.' 'Now, now,' Mrs Harrison had answered, laughing. 'Cruel world, Mr Mills, but don't you go thinking you can change it. Think that, you'll go mad.'

These days, and particularly when passing through these delicious extremes of Bayswater, he privately wondered if going mad was not a preferable option to pretending to remain sane, doing as he supposed Mrs Harrison did, and simply making shift with a bad lot. John Mills had been hippy, poet and preacher, teaching the gospel of revolution to which he still clung like a dying man to a raft which all others had abandoned. He had stopped and spoken to Mrs Harrison in the way he did with anyone so clearly a member of the proletariat, which she did not even have the wisdom to resent. Most people didn't. They were mad too. He looked up at the window, saw a cat sitting in state. Those up there paid part of his wages he supposed, by putting their bloody loose change in some charity box, but it did not endear them to him. Lovely houses, very nice: he could not resist this street while wanting to bomb it out of the water. Submerged in these houses would be everything wrong with the world, wrongs he felt like acne on the skin.

'Lovely day,' Mrs Harrison said.

He was full of it this morning, up to the gunwales. The morning before, his first back at work, he had been in a filthy room in a street two miles and several light years from where he stood now and the contrast was no balm to a shattered conscience and uneasy nerves. He said nothing of course, and

Mrs Harrison simply thought him odd. She saw his present vacancy, sensed in him a vague desire to be off, but not to move. He looked paler than ever, still talked with his whole body rocking to and fro as if he could not trust any part of him to stay still, telling her how the roof had fallen in on his office, domestic details she relished with Ohs and Ahs, and It Never Dids. From behind her, Patsy the dog ambled down the steps, shuffled for position on the warm stone and flopped her large Labrador body down with a grunt. Behind her, Jeanetta appeared, silent for once.

'She looks like the dog,' Mills observed out loud, pointing at both of them. Mrs Harrison laughed. She did too, didn't she, blonde and fat, with the same kind of eyes only surrounded by pink. My, my wasn't Mr Mills twitchy this morning, the dog so placid in elderly contrast. She was suddenly bored and ready for the great indoors, the cigarette at an end. She flicked the stub on to the pavement, her deliberate contribution to a litter-free street.

'Mustn't keep you, Mr M. Nice to see you again. Sure you don't want a cuppa?' She hadn't offered one at the outset but found his usefulness as a five-minute distraction over. He untangled his feet, bent to pat the dog and walked away. There was a peculiar lack of dignity in his walk, almost comic.

'Isn't he a bloody fool, then?' said Mrs Harrison to Patsy. 'Always so bloody miserable and nervous. Isn't he just that, sweetheart?' turning to Jeanetta, commencing the hours of endless chatter which so mollified the child. 'Don't know,' muttered Jeanetta, stroking Patsy with rapt concentration, her chest and stomach balanced on her fat knees, the smooth flesh of her back exposed. 'And when's your mummy going to get you some new things then?' asked Mrs Harrison, pulling down the T-shirt. Jeanetta giggled at the tickle of the touch. 'Pyjam-as,' she said. 'Oh, I don't know,' sighed Mrs Harrison, 'I really don't. What shall we do today, pet?'

Jeanetta beamed and clapped her hands. 'Pat a Cake?' she asked.

'This one?' Eileen said. 'Pat a Cake, pat a Cake, Baker's man, Bake me a cake as fast as you can . . .' The child joined in and the sound of her tentative singing followed John on his way to work.

*

59

Katherine always knew when she was cutting it fine and the urgency of the errand made it exhausting. She arrived, slightly breathless, looking at her watch, which was always fast in a vain attempt to kid herself into being early. Fifteen minutes to spare, not quite enough after the queue for the showers and hairdriers at the gym. She was back to base, three doors down from Mr Isaacs' emporium in fashionable Marble Street, outside David's favourite dress shop. She had explained this place to Mary once, pointing it out since they tended to meet at the other end. 'What! Does he wear dresses, then?' Mary had asked, deliberately obtuse. 'No, for me, silly. He likes the things in there for me.' 'You mean a bit like dressing a racehorse in your own colours,' said Mary tartly. 'He has you wearing his.' 'Well, no,' said Katherine, flustered, deciding not to expand on the subject. Mary always did this, cut her down to size, but then Mary was at her tartest when envious. This was, in a way, a very satisfying equation for the time being.

Katherine never knew whether to dress down for meetings with her sister in order to avoid the 'That's nice, must have cost a packet' remark, or dress up in order to feel confident and enjoy the slight *frisson* of jealousy and underline her own emancipation. There was usually little enough choice. She dressed immaculately, knew no other way of taking pride in her appearance, and if David's choices, as well as Mr Isaacs' preferences for his shopfront, were the shapes of West End designer fabrics, then so be it. Today, Katherine was wearing the same tailored beige as the day before, offset with different earrings, brooch and shoes, very sleek indeed. The rope of the bag she carried bit into the palm of one hot hand as she slowed her steps to a dignified walk, entered the shop with a nonchalance she did not feel. Today was complicated: no time for the lingering and dreaming she preferred.

'Oh, Mrs Allendale, what a shame, but never mind; Mr Allendale was so sure it would suit you. What would you like to try instead? That one. Really? Not entirely silk, you understand, and not the very top of the range' (this accompanied by a small curling of the lip). 'A slight difference in the price. Yes, I'm sure we could give you the difference on the dress. Cash?

Madam would like cash?' eyebrows arched towards the sky as if articulating a very dirty word.

Crunching of tissue paper, bad-tempered. Be nice to the customers, cooperation at all times. Especially if they were notable for extravagance like young Mrs Allendale. How strange of her to prefer a cheaper suit in that colour. Her husband buys them all for her, you know. Why? Well between you and me, she can't be trusted with a charge card. So I was given to understand, in confidence, of course. Katherine worked in a shop herself, dealt with the same kind of customers, knew how to flirt with them or pander to them and she could hear what this manageress was thinking. Never knows the value of money, no idea. So one hears. Well, bother her, the stuck-up cow. Katherine emerged, flushed and triumphant. The suit didn't matter: what counted was the fifty pounds change which made her feel rich, free and generous.

She was now more than two minutes late for the coffee shop at the other end, cantering up the pavement in tiny Italian shoes, relief apparent in the step. Sitting at a table, looking at her huge manly wristwatch, Mary saw Katherine's smiling approach, and considered smugly that her younger sister was actually pleased to see her. The thought put her into a mood of great sweetness. She straightened her spine, patted her very short haircut, pulled down her plain black sweater. Less attractive than her sibling, but by no means lacking in the same raw material, her own slim neatness deliberately unadorned and her face only blemished by a hungry look. Mary was always prompt, early in fact for every appointment, and only the shimmering glance of her younger sister could excuse a lapse of two minutes in the timetable, although earliness was far more normal. 'I taught her that: she never used to be like that,' she had once explained to David, who approved of such punctuality. Amazing how Katherine was slipping these days. What had happened to the time when she would always be fifteen minutes early, quite content to circle the block in pouring rain, looking at shop windows or standing in doorways to pass the time, anything rather than be late? In all those respects, Katherine was not entirely beyond hope, but in the pursuit of long-term redemption, sister Mary did not really rate her chances. Not if being a consumer sent you to Hell.

Their meetings roughly once a week were entirely at Mary's instigation, a state of affairs and a duty she never resented any more than she noticed the monosyllables which were Katherine's more frequent responses. Well, she had to make allowances. Little sister was several years younger and she had been pushed from pillar to post through a series of foster homes, never mind about that, better to gloss over the cruelty of parting them in the first place; social workers did not do that now. Mary had been luckier, adopted by parents now conveniently deceased, donors of some kind of education. Katherine had always preferred colours and pictures. Juvenile, thought Mary: Frozen in adolescence when she still liked comics; give her those and a paint-box and she's happy. Rather apt when she came to think of it, and she did think of it rather cattily, since Katherine's life was a bit like a kit for painting by numbers. All those little blank areas with a number on each; fill in with the paint of the corresponding colour, and presto, a woman. No, no, this would not do: this was her sister, her only kin, whom after a fashion, she loved, even though the responsibility was one she had been grateful to shed. It might have been a liberal regime she imposed, but Katherine had been, well, wilful. And still, charmingly and irritatingly, was.

'Well, well, well . . . What have we here, Kate's late.'

Katherine beamed and Mary softened, watching her sister flop into a cane chair, shrug off the little black jacket which Mary craved, grab the menu card.

'What about pastries? I'm paying today, anything you like. Oh, Lord, look at the price of this stuff,' all remarks which Mary welcomed as the Katherine she knew.

'No,' she said kindly, 'we'll go Dutch. And we'll just have croissants. Tell me the news.'

As if she did not know. Same news as last week. Katherine would have been to work in her chichi shop, kept her rigorous fitness routine, gone to lunch with friends and bought something new, which Mary could have told in advance from the sight of the bag on the floor. All over in two sentences. Then Mary would recite hers in more detail, a life of duty. Went to committee meetings for Oxfam, Mencap, some offshoot of the Royal Society for the Protection of Children, discussed fund raising for buses for the handicapped over coffee and cakes far inferior to these, received phone calls, wrote letters in three offices, scattered information with great precision, studied reports for the improvement of facilities here and there, and was paid a modest stipend for being regarded as an authority. Mary worked assiduously for a charity information service, was a professional trustee for charitable funds, a self-styled and now indispensable expert on who did what, and the scourge of many; all of which made Katherine very bored. Also, Mary's determined visiting of her own mother-in-law, a badly kept secret, irritated her with its possessive overtones. Before she had learned to keep silent, little sister had been known to call big sister a bloody Girl Guide. Now she listened politely. Always easier to pretend to listen.

'Honestly, people are so inefficient, Katherine, you've no idea. Why don't you come and help? You need to do something useful.'

The words came out the same every time and every time Katherine demurred. It was always so condescending, as if she had nothing to do. 'I might like company,' she had tried to explain, 'but I don't like people as a whole, not your way, never.' And I should not criticize my sister in the married state, Mary thought: a vast improvement on what had gone on before. But Katherine was not listening. She often stopped listening. Mary sighed. Nothing different in this either. Kath had always been a dreamer, forever escaping the worst, so easily read it was like taking down a favourite book.

'Mary,' said Katherine, as if embarking on a theme of vast importance, 'do you remember those pyjama things we had when we were little?'

'When?' Mary was puzzled by a question which was so out of the blue she was taken completely by surprise.

'You know. We must have been, what? About four, no, me four, you ten, or so. That first school place. Where we woke up, in those flannelette pyjama things. Sort of tough flannelette, plain colours, not very comfortable for bed. Would've been better for playing in. You remember?'

'No.' But she did remember. Always presumed and hoped Katherine did not. Her hand froze on the teacup, startled by the memory. Herself and Katherine, removed from the dark coal cellar of a house where either by accident or design, their parents had left them, door shut on blackness, and simply moved on. Mary had sometimes wanted the history of whatever drug-induced traumas had brought this about, decided against it. She would not have been helped by knowing how she and Katherine came to be fainting with the effort of screaming; once seeing light, waking up in another place swathed in carbolic and that harsh cotton. She remembered, and firmly suppressed the memory. In one fell moment of clarity, Mary could see in some weird kind of perspective why she herself had adopted her life of charitable causes while Katherine had gone hell for leather after a life of comfort. But that perspective drifted by like a swift shadow; so much had intervened since. Mary believed past was past; not something ever to be used or discussed to excuse the present. She felt so strongly about the sheer wastefulness of such thoughts, she would have liked to deny Katherine's recollections altogether, dismiss them as fantasy, but could not go quite as far as that, even after years of telling Katherine not to think.

'Why on earth do you want to know about those beastly cotton pyjamas?'

Katherine, too, was staring into the far distance of memory, shook herself and laughed.

'Seems silly, but I just thought of them. Jeanetta has this things about pyjamas. Boys' pyjamas.'

'She's got a lot in common with her mother, then,' Mary interrupted rudely, made sharp by the shock of the images Katherine had brought to mind. Katherine's face was unperturbed.

'. . . So, I was just wondering where I could get something of the kind. To play in, not to sleep in. Cord ties round the middle you see, they're always baggy, might be able to get some to fit the waist without her tripping over the feet. She has to have something roomy which doesn't restrict her and she hates track suits. How ever will she lose weight if she can't move? And she seems to have run out of clothes all of a sudden. You know, the same way light bulbs all seem to go at once.'

Well that was fine if that was all it was. Mary enjoyed a practical problem, felt slightly bitchy for having been frightened.

'You could go to Oxfam. Or one of those other charity shops. They have them even in the West End, you know. You wouldn't even need to get on a bus. Or,' she continued, warming to her theme, 'you could go to a very trendy kiddies' shop, of which I'm sure you'll know several, and buy a rather fetching Chinese outfit, you know, those sort of trousers and jackets Chinese children wear in pictures with Chairman Mao in the background. Look very practical to me, as long as you don't buy them in silk and don't bind her feet to go with it.' She laughed at the thought; fat Jeanetta Allendale in oriental multi-colours with trotters below. Katherine looked interested.

'Oxfam?' she queried.

'Katherine, you must know about Oxfam. Don't pretend you don't. There were years when you lived out of Oxfam shops, when you were a student. You cut down all their clothes and very clever you were too, looked terrific. You only got your half-baked diploma on the basis of a project called how to make something out of nothing.'

Katherine's turn to shudder. She could remember the musty smell of those things, sweaty and rancid with poverty, herself fishing amongst the rails for a colour, reaching alongside equally smelly, horribly poor old ladies who had revolted her. 'Yes, I know. But I can't recall anything for children. And I'm not going back there, ever.' This was said with savagery and Mary was alarmed to see Katherine's fingers were white. The croissant she had been breaking was reduced to messy flakes spilling over the side of the plate.

'Course not, why do you never know when I'm kidding you, silly creature. What on earth's the problem anyway? David'll buy Jeanetta's wardrobe surely? He buys yours.'

The face Katherine turned on her was so bleak, Mary's heart came towards her mouth for the second time in the afternoon, recognizing that familiar blankness, irritating and frightening in equal parts as it had always been. 'Buck up, Katherine,' she said briskly. 'Leave it all to good old David.'

'I can't,' said Katherine softly, and then with a voice

emergeing like a hiccup, 'David doesn't think that Jeanetta's his baby, you see. He really thinks Jeanetta came into me from someone else.'

The crumbs on the white cloth were so far spread they looked like confetti round the plate. Mary sat very still, picturing the confetti of Katherine's wedding, the dearth of relatives just as well bearing in mind the slight bulge to the front of the cream dress the bride had worn in preference to white. You aren't qualified to wear white, not by anyone's standards, her sister had shouted. Christ, you are so lucky to have found a champion all-pedigree male like David who loves you to pieces, but don't wear white. Even if you're going to shine with virtue from now on, and not go bouncing from bed to bed because you simply can't stand an evening alone, about as self-sufficient as a new-born puppy, nuzzling to anything, doing anything including swinging from the chandeliers in one mad scrabble to be touched. Even after David had arrived on scene, the knight in white armour, besotted with the very fair maiden, you couldn't bloody stop. Katherine had slept with David on the first night; Mary remembered the sounds through the wall despite her own hands in her ears. But then Katherine rarely paused for thought in these matters, her life one long collision course. Mary had been the one who collected up the pieces. Sometimes the men moved on to Mary's bed, finding it less congenial but more predictable, but she could hardly tell Katherine that. Including the last man before the quest for Katherine's husband was finally over. Her brow cleared. All alarums ceased. She picked up her coffee cup.

'Katherine, that is absolute nonsense.'

'Yes,' said Katherine, visibly regretting the gulp of words, shuffling for departure and hiding behind a bending to one side of the table with a curtain of hair shielding her face. 'Yes it is.' Repeating Mary's words loudly, extremely angry with herself. How many times had she vowed not to tell anything to Mary, never again to admit any weakness and let her get her foot back in. 'Absolute nonsense.' It had taken years to break Mary's hold on her life: she wasn't going to regress now. And Mary was not coming near their house until that golden hair had grown, so there. They could do without Mary, so there.

66

She straightened up, picked up her cup. The other hand carefully plucked the flakes of pastry from the table and put them back on the plate, one by one.

5

Absolutely bloody extraordinary, is all I can say, the whole bloody thing. Halfway through the afternoon I remembered one or two things, shot out of work early, watching their faces glad to see me go. I built my career; now it runs by itself. Snap, snap, snap all day, the result of a headache and the eyes I couldn't find on the pillow this morning. (Ha, ha, they were there somewhere.) Tried to do some shopping and found I couldn't. Such a bloody bore, but the evening after was rather jolly, or not jolly, at least, not jolly really, but jolly interesting. Better than shopping anyhow like a silly housewife, but then, most things are.

A great sort of evening in fact, for a slightly nosy neighbour like me. I caught her, you see, Katherine Allendale, cantering up the street on her way to collect the kids, armed with bags of shopping (now there's a woman who loves to shop: a tour round their house is like an expedition through furniture boutiques in Europe). Wee Katherine tends to make off a bit sharpish if she collects the kids, but I wasn't going to let her get away even if I had failed to bite the bullet the evening before. 'Aha!' I said to her. 'There you are. Come in for a drink.' She looked at me as if I was giving her an order.

Not that she's the drinking type, our Mrs Allendale, but she's such a princess. She sat on a stool in the kitchen looking like an umpire at Wimbledon and though I've always felt older and wiser, with her perched there, all of us drinking our tea, I only felt older. She does have that effect on me.

'Well,' I said, 'been shopping?'

As if I needed to ask; she's always been shopping, but this

had the makings of a very subtle ploy to lead in to a remark about how pricey clothes were these days, even for children, a gambit suggested by the label on the jacket she had thrown over a chair, but she beat me to it.

'Yes,' she said. 'Yes I have been shopping as a matter of fact. I bought presents.'

She pushed along the table to Mrs H a box of ultra-expensive chocs, something she does quite often, very shyly but not predictably. Very sweet of her but it doesn't half show me up and I take a grim satisfaction in the knowledge that Mrs H only likes cheap chocs anyway. Then dear Katherine steals my thunder yet again.

'I'm really terribly sorry about Jeanetta borrowing Mark's pyjamas. We've been so busy recently, I only noticed this morning how low she was on clothes. So I managed to get some and she'll be round tomorrow in a new wardrobe, won't you, Jeanetta darling?'

Jeanetta darling, I noticed with a start, had an awful haircut like a convict and didn't seem to care about new clothes. My God, what had they done to her? She was edging towards the pantry, a move I gather she uses often at going-home time, both to suggest that a little grub wouldn't go amiss and secondly as a place to hide behind the door in the hope she'll be forgotten. I hear screams as often as not when Jeanetta goes home, frightful screams, the spoiled little blighter, but in this instance, the reluctance was silent and the expression on Mrs Harrison's back as she bent to pick up some toy which had nearly broken her neck, was eloquent. But then the relief of the news was temporary, because just at that moment, sweet little Jeremy, rocking in his high chair, began to totter dangerously.

'Christ!' I yelled. 'Catch him!'

The chair caught against the edge of the table and went down in slow motion, toppling him out in a gentle enough fashion from less than half the table's height, but still delivering him to the floor with a pretty decisive crack. We are all in a state of paralysis, the way one is, Mrs Harrison halfway off her knees at the time, sinking back on them before making for him at a fast crawl. I leapt up and bashed my hip on the table while blundering in the same direction. Jeanetta shot from the pantry like a bullet from a gun and got there first, humped him into a sitting position rather clumsily but effectively, and put her arms round him. 'Don't be silly, Jemmy,' she instructed rather loudly, slightly rough but tremendously gentle, and he stopped crying at once, like a tap turned off, even though I could see the symptoms of a lovely bump in the middle of his forehead. By that time we were all around him with oohs and aahs and who's a brave boy then, that sort of thing. Mrs Harrison picked him up: I picked up the chair, dusted us down and the whole set was reassembled, Mrs Harrison clucking a bit about how on earth could that happen, was the leg of the chair loose or something? Jeanetta sidled back towards the pantry.

It was only then I noticed how Katherine hadn't moved at all, not a muscle. Quite amazing. Sat there, just as she was while we all flapped. Looked at him as if he'd just said something unfortunate and it served him right. Odder still, he never looked towards her, as if expecting rescue from that quarter least of all. I might not know much about the nauseating details of motherhood, but I tell you, I was perplexed. She might not be the brain of Britain, but I always thought she was competent.

'Yes,' Katherine said, smiling at us all as we went back to the tea mugs. 'Yes . . . I managed to do a bit of shopping on the way home. Things are so expensive these days, aren't they?' There wasn't a lot I could add apart from two sentences in vague agreement. 'Humpty Dumpy sat on a wall, Humpy Dumpy humpy,' Samantha intoned, quite unable to remember what came next but realizing it was apposite. I was a bit shaken, bloody glad when the whole entourage left.

But there was more of course, from two sources. Back down to the kitchen to congratulate Mrs H on a timely hint and I found her looking triumphant. 'Those clothes, Mrs Pearson,' she hissed. 'That stuff for Jeanetta. You'll never guess where she got them.'

'Where she got the clothes?' I questioned, stupidly.

'Well,' said Mrs Harrison, settling down to make a story of it. 'Well, this afternoon I took the girls out for a walk, left the boys with Harrison, and on the way back, we decided to go up the market.' (I love the way she makes it sound as if the four-year-olds took a vote and the whole decision was democratic.) '... Anyway, we cut through the back, down that grotty end of Church Street where all the winos go, where they have the really cheap stalls, and there she was. Mrs Allendale, I ask you. Buying kiddies' clothes at a stall, not only on the market but on that end of the market, all stolen goods down there, dirt cheap and probably fallen off the back of a lorry. Only others go there are the Pakis and blacks buying things at fifty pence top whack until a bobby comes along and they all close up shop. Honest, Mrs Pearson, I'd never buy anything there, so why should she?' You don't know where it's been.'

She leant forward like a plotter. 'And you know what? I think I saw her put something in her bag. Without paying.'

To tell the truth, I was more amused than shocked. The funniest things shock Mrs Harrison, and while I was quite delighted to have a piece of insight into my dear neighbour, I can't pretend it changed my opinion of her, and I couldn't see why Mrs Harrison found it so exciting to discover Katherine Allendale with her domestic knickers down. I didn't believe for a minute that Katherine had pinched something from a stall: there's just no need. Mrs Harrison would have picked this up from the front page of her horrible newspaper, you know the sort of headline, 'Duchess found shoplifting', and translated it to fit someone nearer home because I've heard her tell so many of these transposed stories before. Everything's always happened to someone she knows and half her relatives are dying of cancer or mugging. What tickled me about Mrs Harrison's shock horror revelations was the notion of our Katy stepping over the rotting cabbage leaves in filthy Church Street market while wearing those marvellous Italian shoes.

'Well,' I say to Mrs Harrison, failing to give the story of theft the benefit of any comment, 'she can shop where she wants, of course, nice to know someone economizes.' Couldn't let her know I really was surprised.

Gossip does make for a good mood, I can't help it, so when Sebastian came home at a semi-decent hour, we actually had a conversation. God alone knows, this is rare enough, since we don't usually get beyond the point of him saying, 'Anything to eat?' and me saying, 'Get it yourself.' But I must have been influenced by the Allendale mould, so grudgingly helped him cobble together steak and something out of the freezer, all the food showing signs of carelessness and age. Then I told him about Mark's pyjamas, and to my amazement, he was actually interested, but then it did have some faint bearing on his son and heir, which usually sparks a modicum of awareness. He loves his children with a passion, even at one remove, far better acquainted with all the minutiae of their lives than I am. Poor Sebastian, he fell to musing. Probably considering the Allendale family tree because of the mention of Jeanetta in Mark's pyjamas and getting them married off already. My husband is such a careful man, he could plan himself to death, but whatever the reason, he was thinking about the neighbours.

'Knew a chap once,' began my own Sebastian, who knows a lot of chaps, '. . . who knew Allendale's father.'

'You never told me.' He looked at me strangely, as if to underline the fact that I'd never asked.

'You never tell me anything interesting.'

He shrugged, resigned to my constant criticism. Resigned, I supposed, to my shrugging him away in the early hours of the morning when he feels affectionate. I had a sudden vision of them next door, into their ritual eating by now, while we chewed manfully and I drank the whole bottle of wine.

'He had an empire, Allendale Senior. Floated on the stock exchange. Then went in for shady dealing, looted the firm, went bankrupt and lost everything. David must have been a boy. Good family, went to ruin.'

'How?'

'Don't know the details.'

'Oh, for God's sake, why not?'

'Only gossip. Papa Allendale went to prison, but David rose from the ashes, made a small fortune for himself, you know. Became an architect while playing the stock exchange. Acquired a chain of shops and sold them at vast profit. He doesn't really need to work now, but he does.' He was still thinking of Mark's marital prospects. 'Very sound, David,' he added.

'Not like his father, then?'

'Oh, no, not at all. Do you really need another glass of wine, dear?'

'Don't be so stuffy and mind your own business.' He was silent, knows not to argue.

'I think I'll go to bed.'

'Suit yourself.'

I don't really want him to go on, you see: having finished that bit, Sebastian will want to talk, about children, about work and I really can't be bothered to listen. Think I'll just take a quick gin in the study since clearly old face-ache is not going to broach another bottle of wine. Just a little nightcap, add a dash of tonic . . . Oh, Sebastian can be a bore. Truth is, though, only admitted to *alter ego*, I've always rather fancied nice David Allendale, and all this information really fired me up. Rolled him up in my estimation, if you see what I mean. Always did like a fighter, not a man of mere patient endurance like Sebastian. Yes, quite a fighter with a background like that; I can't imagine what it must be like to lose all your money and have to start again in the teeth of a daddy in clink. Wow. It all made me like him so much better. Solid, gentle, brave chap, no wonder he has to be so organized. With a bit of a, you know, dicky wife.

Sorry, Katherine, I shouldn't even have thought that. Ha, ha, ha: people might say the same thing about me.

Of course they wouldn't. Would they?

6

One of those evenings defined by a sense of hopelessness. Even the minor thought of meeting at dinner people whom she actually liked did nothing to relieve a feeling of resignation, mixed with a sensation of panic, like a child waiting for a slap from teacher. She had looked a fool in the boutique, let herself down with Mary and shown next door she could not even control her own children. The triumph Katherine had felt in buying Jeanetta's clothes evaporated when she approached her own house and imagined emptiness inside, acknowledged in one single instinct of alarm as soon as she tried the door. The paint surrounding the lock was scuffed and her key refused to work. On the sixth attempt the key bent, and in an awareness blunted by the knowledge of being late, in possession of a guilty parcel, and also of being very tired, she realized she must have the wrong key. A key to another house entirely, perhaps. Katherine looked at it in perplexity, the same key as yesterday which refused to work today, licked the metal, tried again in the clear knowledge the endeavour was hopeless. She considered going back to Mrs Harrison, decided not, for the shame of it; imagined the doorbell beneath her finger sounding into emptiness as she had known it would, and the usual feeling of panic assailed the back of her neck, moving her mind forward like the button on a tape machine into a dreadful scenario for the evening ahead. A space of hours in which she stood with the snivelling children on her own doorstep, marooned by being unable to move, smiling at the guests due to arrive for drinks within an hour as preamble to the barbecue at Monica's. Four of them to be disgorged from cars only to be told I do not have the wherewithal to refresh you, but would you like to sit down on the step: My husband has left me.

The fact of David being somehow delayed, traffic-jammed at the tail-end of an appointment, injured somehow, or simply failing to watch the time, did not occur to her, especially the last, with the other possibilities too remote for consideration. Perhaps she could take the children and sit in the car but the car was not visible, parked each day in a different place, and she could not begin to look inside her bag for another key. It would not be there, and he had gone, left, fled the nest: the house beyond the door would never again contain him; she would be on her own, penniless, explaining his absence as yet another but easily the greatest of all her failures.

Jeanetta's screams had ceased when faced with the inevitability of entering home for the indignity of bed, the same way her voice ceased when the audience was clearly preoccupied. The whingeing which replaced the howling stopped too as soon as Jeremy's began, the one voice dying away on the rising cadence of the other like a duo without harmony. Jeanetta flumped on the doorstep, looking at Jeremy in silent perplexity as he screamed Dada, Dada, the most used of his small repertoire of words, pulling his mother's skirt with one, none too clean hand, while Katherine herself felt a similar, childish scream rise in her own throat. Not for Dada, only for David; where was he, in this whole city, other than here? But as the scream died stillborn with Jeremy's commencement of the second stanza, the door opened and there he was, Papa to them all, dishevelled and slightly puzzled by the row. In one moment, there was a unison of smiles. David moved forward and took Jeremy deftly into his arms.

'What on earth are you all doing out here?'

Everything was subsumed in relief. 'The door was locked,' she said.

'Of course it was. Like always, I mean when isn't it locked? The new lock, since two days ago. The old one broke, remember?'

She pushed the hair out of her eyes, instinctively aware of the rearrangement caused by bending and twisting, speaking physical persuasion to the key, coaxing it to work with the

75

whole of herself. 'I don't remember. You've let me in before. Yesterday and the day before . . .'

'As I would have done today if only you'd rung the bell, silly.' The grin with the words was pure affection.

She thought she had, pictured her finger on the bell, relief still making her smile. Don't argue now. Jeremy and David beamed at the world below them from their enormous height, the child at head level with his father, the way he liked. 'Don't just stand there, you sillies,' said David, addressing Katherine and Jeanetta, who drooped like a fat tulip, turning her sideways grin at him as if the angle increased the chance of attention. 'You live here. Come in.' Katherine compressed the market carrier bags more firmly inside the boutique bag, lifted both and stepped over the entrance. She was home. It was the home she had searched for all her life. Without it she knew she would wither and die, but lately, it seemed vulnerable.

John Mills turned the lock on the outer door and went upstairs, home at last, but without any sense of relief, always amazed that the first key would work on a door so warped and disfigured by graffiti and thumps. He had lived here for more years than he could remember, watching the scenery shift around him with indifference to anything but the establishment of the takeaway food shop on the ground floor. He had not even resented the presence of the bus stop and the traffic lights near the living-room window which meant that he could find himself eating a meal in the full gaze of thirty top-deck passengers sitting at the same height as himself and taking in every detail of his diet as well as the kitchen beyond. A room with a view, he had joked, pointing to the clinic for sexually transmitted diseases, no longer approached with discretion and clearly revealed when a double-decker bus was not obscuring either its frontage or the employment agency above. There might have been splendour to the left and right of the Edgware Road, but no prosperity had spread to this particular patch, which remained shaken by traffic, stirred by change in a way which was not the same as improvement. Beginning London life in this flat simply because there was nothing else to be had, he stayed here now out of obstinacy. To move away would be weakening in the face of the capitalism of his landlord.

Gurjat Singh had managed, by dint of various manipulations and a friend in the planning department, to install down below a distant relative on a short lease, whose cooking might shift the upstairs partnership while turning in a profit at the same time. When John opened the downstairs door, the early-warning smells of onion and spices, never quite definable as left from yesterday or begun today, hit his nostrils with force, diminishing only slightly as he trod up the battered linoleum stairs to the second door, where another fumble with keys gave entry. The number of keys was impressive and represented a large investment in locks, a barrier against the landlord on the one hand and the several episodes of burglary on the other, although in his worst persecution mould, John did not consider the two enemies entirely unconnected. No self-respecting burglar would deign to enter here, since the height, the smell, the stairs and the ultimate rewards would be scarcely worthwhile. The burglars did not listen.

He opened the door to the flat in three manoeuvres, one for the Yale lock, two for the bolts top and bottom, both placed slightly too close to the frame and therefore skinning his knuckles each time. On the third turn of the key, he could hear Kat yowling beyond, scratching away at the last of the paint. Kat was a once off. He or she was called Kat on account of a rapacious appetite for Kit-e-kat, nothing else but. Not Whiskas, remains from tasty human meals, steamed fish or any other morsel, only Kit-e-kat, fresh from the tin or three days old, didn't matter. Kat liked only the scent of this particular food, fungus and all. 'Just like the takeaway meals,' grumbled Matil-da Mills. Don't be silly, said John, aware how much she disliked Kat, not for being what Kat was, but simply for being symptomatic of a failed life in a demoralized house.

Even before they had discovered the secret to her health, they had christened the wizened thing Kat with a K because she resembled no real cat, especially not a fat cat, inherited as an aggressive, half-starved kitten with a short tail and a look of malevolence towards human kind. Matilda's choice, subject of an argument which she won as part of many concessions, but abandoned soon after when Kat, with uncanny feline instinct,

77

aimed all her attentions towards the one in the household who had not chosen her, but was burdened with the greater conscience, namely John. Half-wild Kat would not respond to Matilda's advances: she sensed instead the crippling compassion of the man of the house, who had not wanted her at all, laid her catlike bets on him rather than fuss and attention. Kat's premonitions were sound; Matilda could have kicked the animal downstairs after three weeks in a flat so unsuitable for such an inhabitant. So could John, but being himself and unlike Matilda, did not, and saved ugly Kat from those who would. He had twice climbed on to the roof to rescue Kat terrified by intruders, and whilst not exactly loving her in any sense he recognized, was stuck with her.

Mrs Matilda Mills felt roughly the same way about John. Stuck with him, roughened by pity and disappointment while desperately looking for an excuse to leave.

Of that fact, John was dimly and hopelessly aware, but put it to the back of his mind. Matilda, with whom he had once shared politics and pop concerts, but could not provide now with whatever it was she wanted, was late again. Never mind: there was always Kat. John scrubbed at the surface of the enamel sink and felt Kat weaving in and out of his legs. He remembered seeing an immaculate Persian version sitting in the window of the house he passed most days, the one where he spoke to the old lady, what was her name, Harrison. 'Now you wouldn't do that, would you?' he said to his own poorer specimen. 'You wouldn't sit yourself in the window behaving like someone's potted plant, would you? Course you wouldn't.' Strange to think how devastated he had been when Kat had gone missing over the rooftops. He looked down. Her movements were frenetic and the bowl of food was untouched. 'Now what on earth's the matter with you? Mad at the mention of some other beauty, are we?'

She scratched at the floor, turned in circles, then skittered towards the wooden box in the corner of the kitchen in which he stored old newspapers and any periodical which supported his point of view. Then she strode back, circled his legs twice more, turned her head upwards, miaowing in the fashion of extreme hunger, a series of beseeching yells straight from the chest, repeated as she wove back towards the box, arching her back with her tail straight in the air. John looked at her exposed behind turned to him in fury, wondered quite inconsequentially if they had ever determined Kat's sex or simply assumed she was a She. Then in a dawn of amazement he could see Kat's rear end was heaving, and in one more turn through his legs, felt the bulge of her flanks and realized everything at once. Bending to touch her, swearing at his own blindness, he was consumed with anxiety. She was yowling and squirming as he felt her sharp nipples, withdrew his fingers with haste and clapped a hand to his forehead.

'Oh, poor Kat,' he murmured. 'How can you bear such ignorant people as owners? Here, here, here . . .' He squatted by the wooden box, picking out papers and throwing them on to the floor, rocked back for a moment, perplexed. The wooden box would not do: the sides were too high for Kat to come and go with ease. Wild by now, he rushed back to the kitchen, found a shallow cardboard container, piled newspaper into it followed by three clean dusters. Kat watched and interrupted, her movements and noises a constant protest, but as soon as the nest was prepared, she jumped in and scratched around, then lay on one side, stretched with her abdomen moving violently.

'There, there,' John crooned. 'Is that a good place for kittens then? Oh Kat, I am sorry, I should have seen. Bit of milk, shall we? No?' She did not want milk. When he left her to fetch it she raised her head in anxiety, howling after him and starting to scramble out in order to follow. She wants me, John thought in wonder: she wants me standing by and stroking her head like any woman in labour; how absolutely, enthrallingly, unbelievably marvellous.

A fluffy kitten twisted and turned on the still warm paving stones of Monica Neill's patio. The kitten lay on its back, pale underbelly exposed, paws at right angles, the upper half still and lower end wriggling. Katherine watched, fascinated by the sheer abandonment of the pose, secretly slightly shocked. The patio was full of people and she was dreadfully concerned that someone might step on the thing and squash that naked underbelly. She shuddered and nudged the kitten very gently with her foot, reluctant to touch but wanting it to move, hearing in her mind the snap of the frail backbone.

'Oh kitten, you idiot brute. No bloody shame at all.' Monica put down the carafe of wine she was holding, scooped the kitten into her arms and blew into its face. She handled the animal with affectionate ease: having kissed the pink nose, she threw kitten off the patio on to the lawn. There was nothing savage in this hurling from waist height, the legs of the kitten unfolding to land within three feet, but the movement staggered Katherine. She recoiled slightly from Monica, who had recovered the wine carafe in the same stoop as abandoning the cat. Katherine envied that bossiness while finding it irritating. 'Stupid puss,' Monica shouted after it fondly, then turned to Katherine, waving the wine. 'More wine, Katy, come on, do. Last orders before food. Don't you like cats? I would have thought you would.'

'Yes I do,' Katherine smiled, gritting her teeth on 'Katy', which she hated. 'David doesn't though.'

'Katherine, that's nonsense. I don't mind them at all,' David interrupted, laying an arm around her shoulders.

'David puts pellets down in the garden to poison next door's cat,' Katherine continued. The hand round her shoulder moved: she felt her ear pinched hard and looked at him in surprise. Monica barked with laughter.

'That's not true at all,' David said, joining in the laughter. 'Katherine puts down pellets to preserve her precious flowers, and the stuff isn't poison: just drives off felines, the smell or something. I like cats. That one's particularly beautiful, but they are difficult to keep. Katherine wouldn't like the mess.'

She twisted out of his arms, shrugging him off crossly, looking sulky. I bet she wouldn't like the mess, Monica thought, warming more than usual to David's vivid smile and noticing the fur on her own cotton skirt, absent from Katherine's pristine slacks. Monica was not disposed to be critical of her guests or question any of their remarks since she was so pleased to see them standing on the floodlit patio (soon to become a conservatory if only David and Colin could agree how). David would do a good job because he had the right kind of hands. She liked David's hands and the sight of them distracted her from the surprise on Katherine's face. They were strong brown hands with the stubby fingers of a craftsman. By comparison, Katherine's hands were very long and pale, pointing at the cat which had resumed its exercise on the grass. Look at me, I'm so pretty. They might both have used the same words.

'Well,' said Monica, winking at David in some sort of understanding, 'if you want a cat, you can have one. We've three spare. Inside there,' she gestured towards the house, 'there is a mother cat still in disgrace. She's a thoroughbred something or other, cost a fortune, so I put her on the pill.'

Katherine laughed. 'Oh no, not really . . .'

'So what does pussy do?' Monica demanded, turning her attention to David, who had not heard the story before. 'She spits out the pills and goes off frolicking with some mangy tabby, comes back pregnant. So we now have three surplus kittens, like that one, all more or less housetrained, no pedigree at all.' She turned back to Katherine. 'What do you think?'

'I'd love one,' said Katherine enthusiastically. She could see its little feet and imagined a tiny animal to hold. 'Jeanetta would love it too . . .'

'No pedigree?' murmured David, shaking his head.

'Definitely not,' Monica beamed, waving her arm to include more of the gathering around her into the conversation. 'Anyone want a kitten? Come on, come on, lovely kittens going spare. No pedigree but sweet natures and probably a mother's tendency to randiness. Any offers?'

'Nothing wrong with a bastard after all,' said David lightly, his mouth near Katherine's ear. 'Every house should have one.'

In the erratic, expensive floodlighting of the patio, Katherine blenched and the hand holding her glass trembled. David moved away, busied himself at the buffet table, helping Monica, who was helping the help. Katherine turned to watch the kitten, hiding her eyes from David's brown hands touching the capable fingers of his hostess as he took plates from her grasp. Colin Neill, ever champion of fair ladies, thought Katherine looked pale and went to the rescue, a pleasure, he was sure. Jenny, sitting lazily with her back to the wall, talked to the Neills' neighbours and noticed nothing at all, until out of the corner of her eye she saw Colin pick up the kitten. He had his hands under the kitten's chin and showed Katherine the china-blue eyes. 'Look,' he was saying, 'she likes you.' Katherine's trembling ceased. Her face opened into a smile whilst she touched the kitten's ears with tentative fingers. The eyes which faced Colin Neill's were full of artless admiration, shimmering with a smile. 'She's so soft,' said Katherine in wonder. 'Yes,' said Colin, his eyes fixed on hers. 'Yes, He is. As it happens. I think you should have him.'

Jenny turned back to the Neill neighbours, slightly fazed, more than a little disturbed. 'What do they eat?' Katherine was asking Colin. 'Sugar and spice and all things nice. Same diet as you.'

She stroked the kitten with growing confidence. Her loud laugh of nervous pleasure struck into the back of the dozen surrounding the food.

David heard her, smiled at Monica, touched her bare arm.

'Wonderful food, Monica. How on earth do you manage, all this, the job, I don't know.'

Monica liked to be admired and was frequently perturbed by the fact that her husband had the habit of admiring others. Her full bosom strained against her cerise silk shirt. Despite the large sums both she and Colin earned, she spent most of her days struggling to keep up with her own timetable, but was more than content for the impression to be the opposite.

'Oh I can always find time for the things I want to do. It's the duties are such a bore.'

'Perhaps you'll find time to discuss your new conservatory then,' David queried quietly. 'Your husband can't make up his mind on the details. No disrespect intended, but you're probably better equipped to make decisions.'

Monica's eye wandered to the sweet tableau of Katherine, the kitten and her very own husband. She saw Jenny's face pointing in the same direction, like a gun dog after a scent of trouble. They both knew Colin well. By contrast, David was impeccable, his loyalties beyond doubt.

'Yes,' she said brightly. 'I'm very decisive. Perhaps we could meet one lunchtime next week?'

Parties like these merged in Katherine's mind, the triumphs of her calendar. They were committed to a whole high summer of them following a cold winter where the same sort of thing occurred. She moved over to the women. Basically the same women every time, and the same degree of houses, with the addition of the odd itinerants like the American couple who drifted round the edges of this circle, full of admiration before planning the best party of all. The Allendales entertained the Neills and the Fosters and their own neighbours roughly once every three months: the Fosters and the Neills did the same and by the time everyone had taken a turn, there was some sort of gathering most weeks of the year, all becoming steadily more competitive. David's fortieth birthday party, to which he would invite some of those present, was going to beat the lot for food. This evening they forgathered here from Hampstead, St John's Wood, Totteridge and even the duskier slopes of Surrey, all of them respectably rich and as David put it, seeking protection in one another's company from those who weren't. These were not remarks Katherine understood. Her own pleasure in entertaining was quite without reservation, a joy to show off, especially when visitors such as the Americans admired her home. Compliments which others took lightly, were personal tributes, granting a marvellous sense of achievement, only ever marred by David's occasional cynicism. At the moment, she was angry with David, even as she watched him, being admired as the guru of houses, herself respected as a kind of lesser guru of taste.

'You never criticize,' Monica had teased. 'You always admire, you're great for the ego.'

'There isn't much point, criticizing,' Katherine had said, watching them shake their heads and laugh. 'People don't like it.' Standing in the kitchen and discussing with the American wife the whys and wherefores of Italian ceramics and how to buy them at a discount outside Italy, Katherine would not have dreamt of remarking, even in confidence, how ugly the kitchen really was. You could think so, but not say so: let people have what made them happy. Monica's house, the best in a small estate of half-timbered mansionettes, resembled Monica, she thought, big, attractive, full of energy and no taste at all, while like Monica, it longed to be small and chintzy. There were obvious, if few, signs of children. David would not like that and even Monica could see Katherine's slight wrinkle of distaste at the presence of toys on the floor. Jenny caught Katherine's eye and laughed, putting an arm round her. Part of this was relief that Katherine was so soon detached from the adoring gaze of her best friend's husband, part of it genuine admiration.

'Isn't Katherine's house perfect?' Jenny said teasingly to the American wife. 'Is there ever any clutter?'

'No,' said Katherine, slightly puzzled as to why there should be. If there was ever clutter, it was imperative to clear it, otherwise everything slipped out of control. She wanted to say, look, nothing is ever perfect; sometimes there is a mess, but succumbed instead to the constant need for praise.

'We must have lunch soon.'

'Oh yes please,' Katherine said.

'Can I come to your shop, honey? So you can help me with a few things?' asked the American wife. 'Of course,' Katherine replied. She was in demand, felt herself appreciated, and that was heaven.

But the mention of lunch occurred to her when she went to the bathroom to smooth her already perfect hair, which remained long, reapply lipstick, prepare herself for the buffet which the others had already attacked. She opened her handbag to check the contents in a manner which had become second nature as an antidote to her own, chronic carelessness. The house key was the final straw and the checking of the bag became an obsession. She fingered her purse in the privacy of the bathroom, wondering in the meantime how anyone with money could have chosen such terrible wallpaper, then froze in horror. The twenty-five pounds change from the dress shop remaining after her trip to the market, was gone. She had lost it, the way she lost everything without ever knowing how. There would be nothing for a taxi, nothing for tea. Then she opened the coin wallet at the back of her bag and found five one-pound coins twinkling like chocolate pennies. She snapped the bag closed, squeezed her eyes open and shut several times to forestall a desire to cry, then pushed herself back into control. She had better go and eat. Tomorrow could be a hungry day.

The table was groaning with food fit for twice the number present, a typically Monica overloading on which Katherine gazed with greedy pleasure. Hunger was sharpened by the night chill which had caused a gravitation towards the kitchen begun by the women in the thinnest clothes. Katherine found David at a small table, his empty plate beside him. Her own carried salad niçoise, Parma ham skewered in rolls between fat bites of melon, three large slices of delicately smoked turkey breast, salad of mange-touts and baby corn, and on the edge of that, a slice of perfect Brie. He bent forward and took the plate from her hands.

'Katherine, you are silly,' he said softly, the voice a plea, Monica noticed in passing. He picked at the plate with a fork, showing her her folly. 'You know very well olives make you sick. As well as anchovies and Brie, for heaven's sake, worst of all. You know how ill you were with Jeremy. Don't want anything like that again, do we?'

She shuddered at the thought of morning sickness run riot, so that even water had made her vomit for fourteen weeks, ending in hospital with fluid being dripped into her arm, thin as a stick-insect with the belly growing on, regardless.

'Here,' he said, proffering the cocktail stick with the melon and ham. 'Eat this. I'm sure it's safe.' His voice implied criticism of so much surplus, both on the table outside and on the bodies of the women who ate it. Katherine took the large morsel and ate obediently, no longer able to afford anger after what she had found in the bathroom. He was right of course, she thought, desperately: David was always right, she was often sick; needed his guiding hand in everything. The plate with the rest of the supper stayed on the floor. After a while, a large Persian cat crept in from the garden and swallowed the white turkey.

Matilda Mills wobbled off the bus at half past nine and found her way to the bottom door of the flat with difficulty. Despite the warmth of the evening, the takeaway, selling its own version of heat (two onion bhajis and chips, please), was doing a roaring trade. Matilda knew this by the smell and the ragged-looking queue, as well as the fact that someone was being ill outside. Right. They would leave, move. They had to go: John was going to have to listen to her this time. She'd command his attention once and for all, kick that damned cat downstairs and pack her own bag if he would not pack his. In the throes of one and a half bottles of wine with a few friends from work, she felt she could do anything. Tackled the door at the top of the stairs, mistakenly fumbling with all three locks before she remembered he was indoors and would let her in if she knocked, rapped on the woodwork instead. Light showed below the door but there was no response. Furious, she turned the key in the Yale lock and stormed inside.

He was at the far end of the kitchen, reached by crossing the hall and living room. There was a stench, something which reminded her of her own menstrual blood, a fecund, rotten, but still sweet smell. John was bent over a cardboard box and she could see that one hand holding the side was sticky with blood. For a moment, she panicked. This time he must have gone entirely mad.

'Who's a clever girl then, what a clever, clever, cat . . .' He reached down and picked out one damp, pink object from the box, a sight so disgusting Matilda blenched. He held the moving thing in his hand as he looked closely at a tiny mouth moving next to his own, impervious to the remnant of umbilical cord still trailing from the belly of the kitten. 'Oh,' he crooned. 'You little darlings, you marvellous little darlings. Daddy'll look after you, promise, you wonderful, wonderful, little darlings.'

His pale face was transfixed with love as he turned to greet her, presenting the pink skinned thing in his hand, as triumphant as a midwife.

Matilda thought she was going to be sick.

7

'Sod you, Claud.'

  'I didn't mean . . .'

  'Yes you did.'

  'I wasn't making comparisons, for God's sake, it's years since . . .'

  'But you do see her?'

He hesitated before the lie. Not in the way she meant he didn't. 'No,' he said.

What a fool to relax with Mary. He could not imagine how any man could relax with Mary, even when she was as naked as the day she was born. Mary with whom he coupled on Saturday afternoons, commitments of marriage allowing, who was like the memory of her sister, slender, strong, passionate in her own undemonstrative way without any of Katherine's raw sensitivity or touching desire to please. Claud admired her. They had simply inherited one another, a pragmatic arrangement, occurring rather to his surprise. Mary took what she needed from men, like eating a meal. The only difference was that, within the limits of an extremely selfish arrangement, he had liked Katherine, even loved her sometimes. Hence the wistful inquiry after her health and his habit of gazing, unseen, into the window of Mr Isaacs' shop. No, don't make comparisons, say nothing out of turn. Mary had curled away from him, gripping the pillow on her own side of the bed until he began to stroke her neck, the only erogenous zone apart from the very obvious. Then she turned towards him, threw off the sheet which covered them both, wound herself round him and bit his neck lightly. He hoped she had left no mark. 'Come on then,' she taunted, holding his shoulders and looking down without smiling. He took her while she crouched astride him and the Saturday afternoon sun filtered through the cotton curtains behind the bed to warm her buttocks. The window was open, curtains fluttering slightly in the breeze. He was touching her as she rode him, bossy even now, always in control, she making peculiar little animal sounds which contained no endearments, gripping him in the vice of her thighs, thinking at the same time, Christ, even those bloody curtains are Katherine's left-overs. Then she came over him with violence, collapsed almost immediately into a five-minute slumber. Afterwards, with their mutual and predictable sleep almost pre-timed, he would be fretting to dress and leave. Mary never resented these abrupt departures since quite apart from her understanding that he had reached the natural end of his alibi time, there was so little to say.

'You off then?'

'Yes, I thought I would . . .'

'OK, love, see you next week.' Only the briskness betrayed her. He tiptoed out, as if she was asleep.

But after he had gone, dammit, dammit, up and about and knocking over the furniture, clearing up like a dervish, changing the towels, the sheet and even the bathroom rug, all done, all traces of him gone in ten minutes flat. Because she really did need him, knew he still hankered after Katherine and she could not help feeling resentful. Not for the wife: bugger the wife; that betrayal was Claud's own concern, but obscurely about her only relative, a little emotional worry buzzing in the ears she was not disposed to analyse. All this emotional baggage was not for Mary, none of it. She would step around such messes the way she sidestepped traces of dog on the pavement. Ugh. And practically ran round her flat, looking for some task to fill the vacuum of late Saturday afternoon with no one to see, or failing a task in this pristine place, a good deed. It was all Katherine's fault. She had become so self-sufficient after she had left, hurtful, rarely asking Mary round to see her, but leaving a mess in her wake. Mary had tidied up a lover as well as all the rest, even now, longed for more useful tasks, grateful for Katherine's success, but still seeing it as a kind of defection, wanting someone who would rely on her and needing to be needed. Post-coital sadness, a feeling of loss, made her desperate for some activity, some sort of contact, a perverse wish to talk. Inspiration followed resentment. She would go and see Sophie Allendale. Not exactly a substitute mother: but Mary managing to grab for herself a do-gooding share in the welfare of Mrs Allendale Senior, which gave her, at one remove, a small part in Katherine's life. David Allendale did not know of this: Katherine scarcely knew, but the regular visit gave Mary some obscure role, and importance, in the Allendales' lives.

This was not quite an arrangement to suit Sophie Allendale's taste, but this did not mean she was ungrateful for any kind of company at all, especially as she pottered up the road to the Hampstead Mews house which David had provided and for which she was also grateful, most of the time. Honestly, she was prepared to say to the one neighbour who seemed to acknowledge her existence, I didn't expect to be home so soon today. What a horrible afternoon: I would have been better going to the shops. Lunch with her son, daughter-in-law and the children had turned out to be the opposite of a treat. Katherine all over the place, muttering about not being able to find things, such as a new suit or even the stuff in the huge wooden cupboards in the kitchen: David, preoccupied by making the playroom alcove at the end into a proper room with a door. Not even a new door, but one of the old panelled doors from the basement, monstrous. Only plasterboard, whatever that was, he said, to keep in the mess. Well there was a mess, with Jeanetta dragging out things to play, what did they expect? Katherine saying he had put locks on all the doors in the house and she didn't know why. Obvious, wasn't it? He was trying to keep people out, but even so, putting them on kitchen cupboards was a bit extreme. There, there, David knows best. Only there were times when Sophie, muddled as she was, wondered. And lunch, terrible, terrible. She had looked at them both, bewildered, happy to be with them, miserable at the same time. Never darling David's fault, of course, this prickly atmosphere, but difficult to believe what he said as he saw her down the road. About Katherine not wanting her there and only pretending she did.

By the time Mary arrived, Sophie was feeling a little better, softened out of anxiety by the prospect of tea and chocolate biscuits, but still relieved to see through the peephole in her door the sight of a human face. Even if that meant unbolting all the bolts and unlocking all the locks, placed there by a loving son in pursuit of a familiar Allendale neurosis. Mother and son knew what they were keeping out, even if no one else did. Burglars and bailiffs and Daddy. Sophie had refined the fears down to burglars, who loomed extra large in her imagination. Daddy was dead.

Very dead. Sophie looked every day through all her papers, all her documentary mementoes of married life, all the court documents, to check if Daddy was really dead. And he was.

Mary breezed through the door as if there had been no delay, ostensibly ignoring the sheen of tears in Sophie's eyes, but noting them all the same. 'Hallo, Granny,' she said in that condescending voice which other of her old folks, unbeknown to her, detested but Granny Allendale seemed to appreciate. 'Howzabout a nice cup of tea?' Mary was aware of having a full two hours to kill. Sophie brightened visibly. The perfect hairdressing of her scalp twitched in artificially brown curls with grey peeping through as she shook her head and made for her seat in the living room. This was an afternoon for being eighty. Mary could make the tea. Uncomfortable suspicions were distracting Sophie from her indifferent role of hostess and even from the biscuits.

'Did you go to Katherine's?' Mary was so bright you could see the polish on her, clanking down the best tea-service in a manner which irritated Sophie so much she could scream. She had hidden that tea-set in a dozen cupboards in order to preserve it and as it was, there were only three cups left. Oh dearie, dearie me. She remembered how some of the bailiffs had been nicer than others. The room was full of ornaments: ornaments were easier to hide. You stick them down the sleeves of a coat or something. Or in the cistern of the loo if Daddy was about to pawn them. No wonder all David's school cups needed a polish. Antimacassars, chintz curtains, perfect linen napkins and flowery curtains had been easier. No one wanted them. To Mary's eye, the room was hopelessly overcrowded, full of froth, decorated with lace, which was Sophie's favourite thing. Each was thinking that the other was really perfectly silly. The one thing Sophie could well understand about Mary was nobody wanting to marry her.

'What's the matter, sweetheart? Was lunch awful, or something?'

'Yes,' said Sophie with an exaggerated shudder, 'it was, rather.'

'Babies acting up?' Mary cooed.

'Oh no, everything was fine.'

She ate a biscuit with feverish haste. Something dreadful had occurred to her. David with all those locks, not again, surely not. She ate another biscuit.

'When do you think I'll get burgled here?' she asked to change the direction of her thinking.

'Never,' said Mary flatly, thinking of the locks, the bolts, the peephole on the door and the windows so firmly braced against summer.

'Oh Good. David's so worried about it.' Sophie wanted the company and at the same time wanted Mary to go. So she could look again at the papers in the top drawer of the cheap little bureau and again, ensure that Daddy was really dead. She had read the hidden certificate which said so hundreds of times.

'. . . Well, everybody does, don't they? Get burgled, I mean. I was only thinking about that when Katherine was flouncing about today saying all the cupboards had been changed round or locked or something, which was nonsense, of course. Quite the prima donna, such an awkward, spoiled girl a lot of the time. Oh, it was awful: she wasn't nice to me at all. Said she was tired, did Katherine. What've you got to be tired about, I asked her. Well, she doesn't do much, does she?' Sophie was gabbling. Mary could not really follow, pretended she could and nodded.

'Jeanetta had nice new clothes too, but I don't know what they've done to her hair. A yellow top with pink dots, just her colours, and I said to David, she's just like you, you know.'

'Is she?' said Mary doubtfully. There was no resemblance she had ever been able to see herself.

'Oh yes. Daddy was blond, you know, but I think he went grey before David was born. He was very handsome once, you know, but he did get very fat.'

'Tell me about Daddy. You never have.'

Sophie was silent. Not likely. She did not know how much Mary knew about Daddy. Daddy was a secret shared with David and not even discussed with him. Daddy was a liar and a thief and a violent bully who had married her out of her own expensive private school in the days when she thought florid-looking pirates were glamorous. The locks reminded her of Daddy. Daddy had put locks on all the doors to keep out the bailiffs that last time. And then David had locked him in, after he came out of prison and started again. She could remember the fight and Daddy falling downstairs. Falling. Drunk, they had said, but he wasn't. Hadn't had anything to eat, never mind drink, in days.

'Oh well, Daddy was strange. He sold all David's things, David went spare. Twice.'

'Why?'

'We had no money. Never mind why.' Or exactly how he died either, thank you, mind your own business. 'Do you want some more tea?'

'No thanks.'

Sophie could not quite maintain the silence which followed.

'I do hope David's not putting locks on the doors because he's expecting the bailiffs.'

Mary laughed out loud and the sound was balm to Sophie's ears. 'Silly Granny, of course not. They have such lovely things, they have to keep out burglars.'

'Of course,' said Sophie. It was the explanation she had wanted to hear: she was comforted.

Mary moved behind her chair and patted the old woman's back absently, looking round the room with distaste. The wallpaper was chintzy, large moss roses, only some of them toning with the blush of the carpet. There were three nests of side tables, spread out and each covered with a lace doily similar to the one on the tea tray which had lain ever ready in the kitchen, holding the pot with its decoration of buds. The curtains at the window sprouted multicoloured blossom, while the inner frame carried swags of lace to hide the iron security gates pulled across the double-glazed panes. There were pie frills at the collar and cuffs of Sophie's white blouse. Every-thing, including Sophie's face, was in an advanced state of preservation. Today, Mary found the room stultifying, an overblown funeral parlour, with Mrs Allendale Senior resem-bling a relic of a spoiled past. Stories of hard times were difficult to believe and she only took on board the suggestion that Life in the Allendale household was not as easy as it seemed. That was obscurely satisfying.

'Not an easy life,' John said to the caretaker in the office. No, Mr Mills, don't know why you do it. John was not obliged to work on Saturdays, but he had always chosen to do so and old habits died hard. His labours for the Child Action Volunteers had always been thus, never distinguishing the end of the week from the body of it, one of Matilda's complaints until she had taken to avoiding the conflict by not minding and simply going out. But as John approached the top floor of an old mansion block awaiting council repair, puffing slightly from the stone stairs, he had the feeling he should not have worked today after all. In other years he had clambered up steps like these *en route* to grimy premises like these, on fire with his own anger, curiosity, energy, all qualities which gave him powers of tact, courageous cunning which he lacked in other areas of his existence. Third visit today, himself exploited for the gentle touch which allowed him behind doors and encouraged the group to send him as a kind of front runner. Another complaint from some neighbours, John: Mrs Singh, 41B, says the child screams all the time/is silent all day, never goes out and the house is a mess; Somebody ought to do Something. There were not so many variations of theme. Mob handed raids on suspect families required such certainty of evidence supporting an alleged abuse of a child that they often came too late. John's role was to call first, without portfolio, like one inviting himself to tea, smiling, innocuous, bearded and unofficial, carrying sweeties for the children. If the family would not allow him inside, there was no choice but to go away, although five times out of ten, he was able to put his foot in the door and persuade them to open up further. Once inside, his eyes, made cunning by long experience, registered false alarm or real trouble. All he did was talk, listen and watch, suffering in silence long diatribes of abuse, and invective, nodding throughout, histories of stupidities far more common than wickedness.

We should never have children, he had told Matilda: so unfair to drag them into a world as rotten as this. He was sorry now she had believed him.

John knocked at the door, composing his anxious smile. The paint was scuffed, and inside a dog began to bark. A baby began to cry in response to the barking. He knocked again while the even-pitched crying continued, until a voice sounded in his ear, so close he was startled. 'What you want, man?' a rumbling echo he first thought to have begun from a throat immediately beyond the door on which his own hand still rested. Blows to one ear, inflicted on visits like this, had left John partially deaf to the left, never very acute to the right.

'What the fuck you want, man?' said the voice again, and an enormous hand descended on to his shoulder and wrenched him upright. He was transfixed with surprise, turned to face a large male individual, huge of chest and deep of voice, about thirty. John always found himself registering details for a future report, because the excellence of his reports either shoved into action the rumbling of the whole quasi-legal machinery or stopped it altogether, leaving him the uncanny burden of great trust. The man was taller than himself by a foot, dressed in a boiler suit of stained blue denim, his hair grizzled red as if he had used an unsuccessful dye. More noticeable, but not for the report, was an expression of calm fury, a face kept deliberately still and a sweetish, sickly smell which reminded John of Kat as it poured from the man in waves, surrounding them both in heat. The eyes beneath the grizzled head were pink and hostile; the hands held by his sides clenched. John began in his conciliatory tone, full of a sudden sense of hopelessness and the sense of fear to which he had once been immune, but which was now his daily affliction. He stuttered as he spoke. 'I'm not from the council, I'm not from the police and I'm not from the social . . .' he began, a time-worn spiel which sounded unconvincing even to his own ears, but the voice interrupted. 'What you want then, man?' John continued on a rising note of desperation.

'Oh, nothing really – it was just, well someone told me your baby was a bit sick, not well, I mean, so I thought I'd come by and see if there was anything I could do to help . . .'

'Our baby. Not your fucking business.' The fingers on the hands curled and uncurled like a pianist stretching knuckles and wrist before beginning to play. John looked into the man's face, faltering before the gaze of the bulbous eyes. The sky beyond them, seen over the balustrade of the sixth floor, was beginning to grow dark. Please believe me, I am here to help, not to condemn; useless entreaties left unspoken. Instead he said, 'Could I step inside, do you think, say hallo to your wife? I've brought . . .' patting the pocket of his loose jacket to show the presence of the sweeties and the absence of either warrant, summons or anything smacking of officialdom, but he knew as he did, there was no use in the gesture.

'You the tenth one today, man,' said the voice wearily.

'Really?' John answered, his voice high and clipped, showing the well-disguised signs of an educated background he had despised as long as he could remember. 'If I could just come inside for a minute . . .' Sweeties for juvenile mothers and hapless children, himself as welcome as a salesman or a debt collector, thinking on that theme when the man hit him straight in the jaw with one clenched fist. A blow landing with the force of surprise, John staggering while dimly aware of the breaking tooth and the sudden spurt of blood into his mouth, tasting like iron filings. 'The tenth today, man, the fucking tenth . . . interfering cunt . . .' 'No need,' John mumbled as he fell against the wall, '. . . Really no need for this, 's all right really, no need . . .' 'Tenth today,' the man repeated. 'Thu social and thu neighbours and thu rent man and thu priest and her mother and thu polis. Coupla others. Fucking leave us alone.' With each syllable, he struck; accurate blows delivered in a way which was both tired and systematic, one to each eye with the right fist as he held John's inconspicuous, unofficial jacket with the left, then changing hands to haul him up and slap him again, harder. When silence fell apart from the hum of distant traffic, even the dog behind the door silent, the man

95

hauled John to the balustrade, took the seat of his trousers and the back of his shirt and hoisted him halfway across. John lay, his eyes half closed, still for a minute, looking down from a dizzy height at his own blood dripping on to the balcony below, chest compressed by the iron rail, himself, hanging there, held only by his assailant, thinking of nothing at all, but full of deathly calm, pain and a clarity which reminded him to slump, act dead weight, far too unimportant now to kill in one last gesture of such easy, drunken strength. He felt himself slide off the balcony, his left cheek grazing the concrete on the inside as he slid clumsily to the ground, free of grasping claws, his chest heaving. 'Fuck off,' said a disembodied voice. 'Why don't you just fuck off?' In a parody of humility, he felt rather than saw himself wave one hand in surrender, began to crawl towards the stairwell, a bag of sweets in the pocket of his jacket bumping against his hip. After a minute of watching John's slow progress, the man turned back and knocked on the door of the flat. Light flooded out on to the terrace. John stayed gasping in the darkness of the stairwell. Then he began to go down.

The sweets in the pocket were crunching against his hip bone. Kittens, hungry kittens. All he could see were their eyes. Must get home.

Mary spent her evening usefully, annotated another report, 'Incentives for Unqualified Charity Workers', thinking as she did so, how cynical it was, even the title. 'At a time when self-help for the community is vital and the role of the low-paid or unpaid volunteer becomes essential, this Report suggests a system of rewards, in the form of public recognition by this Body for those who have made conspicuous contributions . . .' Answer to that, Mary thought, simple; pay them more. '. . . It is proposed to confine these rewards to the unqualified who do so much, since the qualified receive awards under a different system . . . A list is appended below of those to whom a preliminary letter of encouragement/congratulation could be sent . . .' BALLS, Mary wrote in the margin.

'What's the matter? Why aren't you asleep? You were making a noise.'

'Singing, Mummy, Mummy. Tell me a story.'

'I don't know any stories.' Katherine tucked the duvet round Jeanetta's fat legs.

'Mrs Harrison knows lots of stories. And singings.'

'Songs,' Katherine corrected. 'Sing me this one, then,' Jeanetta requested. 'It goes, Three blind mice, three blind mice . . . Cut off their tails with a carving knife . . . And see how they run . . .'

She was crooning softly, words without a tune, the same droning sound which had drawn Katherine to her room. 'I don't know that one,' Katherine said, moving to the door, fingering the new lock which was so flush with the wood to be scarcely obvious. Then she looked round the door into the corridor to see if David was still downstairs. Looked back at Jeanetta, finding herself sad and entranced, still irritated and made guilty at the sight of the child. She had let Jeanetta be rude to Sophie, put the child into a temper by lying to Sophie herself about the haircut. Jeanetta never behaved when told to shut up. She, Katherine, had allowed the lie to prevent David taking it out on her by brooding silence afterwards. Which meant she had caused the upset when Jeanetta, made rebellious by a sharp command to silence, spattered mayonnaise-covered salmon all down her clean clothes. Then smashed raspberries and cream into highly coloured pap and smeared it on her bare legs. Uproar: the same legs stinging where Katherine slapped her. Oh God, she had let all that happen, why did the silly child forgive her: just as she had let Sophie leave the house without ceremony before they had a chance to talk.

Katherine sat on the bed, guilt rising like indigestion, making her edgy and uncomfortable. I cannot even sit with my own child: I'm embarrassed to be with her looking at me, trusting me: I can't even sing to her. I'm such a failure as a mother, never wanted them in the first place, it just happened. Things have never been the same and now everything seems to shift around me. Motherhood is supposed to be instinctive, but I don't even know how it's done: I can't learn, no one told me how. She was a little frightened of Jeanetta, not now, but sometimes. When Jeanetta seemed to need her, she shrank. The child had such willpower. In a way, Katherine was grateful for that. It absolved her from worrying too much. A child like Jeanetta could survive anything, including earthquake. She felt more fragile herself, still wanted to say she was sorry for being so useless.

'Poor Mummy doesn't know any singing, do you, Mummy?'

'No,' said Katherine, 'I'm afraid I don't.'

'What did your mummy sing?'

'She didn't sing, darling.' Katherine touched Jeanetta's cropped head. That hair had been her only saving grace. She examined the face beneath her hand. Was there a hint of Claud in those soft features? Surely, no certainly not.

'Never singing?' Jeanetta insisted.

'What? Oh no, never.' This telling to herself how she did not know what to do with either of them because she had no memory, no first-hand knowledge of cherishing, worked as an excuse. She could always say, I have no memory of being that age other than dark rooms, being hungry and trying to be good: why can't this little monster be more like me and learn that being good and quiet is the answer? And since nobody showed me what to do as a child, how should I know what to do now? But Katherine knew as excuses went, these were thinner than the paper of all those magazines she read for unintelligible instructions. Guilt grew, along with annoyance, wanting to stay with the child, but also wanting to be away.

'Mummy's not very good at singing. Never knew any nursery rhymes either, silly Mummy,' she murmured, her heart contracting with pity and self-pity combined. Jeanetta's store of these strange fragmented lines puzzled her, such refinements in the child, all missing from her own experience, which included no one singing or telling stories outside the television which had been an intermittent, heavily rationed companion. Patting the soft hair, she smiled, looked back to the door. David was waiting somewhere downstairs, seeing to Jeremy, good as gold, pious-faced little Jeremy who never needed her at all. Jeanetta's crooning was calming, made her feel sleepy.

'I can't sing proply.'

'Yes you can. Sing it again for Mummy. I like it. Please,'

Katherine said, watching Jeanetta shrugging further down the bed, warm, absolved from everything, blissfully irresponsible.

How wonderful it would be to be a child again. She would like to be a child again.

8

. . . Foul summer, foul city, foul everything. Sticky heatwave, thumping head, the whole place quite unbearable and everybody else under this sun a bloody fool. My blouse, which was ugly to start with, feels like toilet paper: I'm home again early because if you must know I couldn't cope at work and no one needs me. I feel like that beggar who seems to be sitting by our roadside most evenings and I can see why he doesn't move off. I hate him, both of us turning up and down the road with nothing to do. Did I say that? Course I've got plenty to do. Nor am I lonely or worried. I have a home to go to.

It's only the cat being sick which has got to me, nothing else really. Poor thing. (Sebastian says I care more about animals than people.) Does Katherine put down strychnine or something in her garden, damn her? I can't challenge them of course: our pussy goes into more back gardens than theirs. Maybe too much feline sex, ha ha, chance would be nice, I suppose, but not in this heat. I can't remember the last time with Sebastian, only remember pushing him off.

Christ, I hate summer. Summer is claustrophobia, restlessness, boredom and constantly wishing to be somewhere else. Couldn't help it, you know. The only event of the day was a card pushed through the door inviting us to David Allendale's birthday party, some weeks hence, made me feel worse. Beauty incorporated, next door, a mere boy he is at forty, but the thought of nice David raised a smile all the way to my eyes. He's the only thing I've liked in quite a while. So when I met him in the street, there didn't seem anything wrong in letting him know, but of course I got it wrong.

Whole conversation wrong-footed from the start. I'm not subtle: no small talk: Sebastian says I should have been a chap, but I never could flirt.

'How's tricks and isn't it hot?' I say. 'Thanks for the invite to the birthday party, forty again, are we? I thought you were older than that, letting us know so far in advance.' Men aren't supposed to be sensitive about those kinds of things, but in retrospect, perhaps David was. 'No, forty for the first time,' he says, 'and not for a little while yet. How are you, then. Where's Seb?' I must have looked a bit surprised at that, assuming everyone knows dear Sebastian acts like a lodger except for first thing in the morning when if he was paying rent, he would be seen taking liberties with the landlady and not much of that recently either. 'Oh,' I said, 'he's in a meeting somewhere, often is up to eight or nine at night, jolly good thing actually.' Don't know why I said that really; sounded peevish, but he was looking right through me, not really listening at all. Where's Katherine, I asked, wondering if he was going to tell me she was out back, putting down poison for our cat. 'Oh,' he says, 'she's indoors getting a meal while himself and I take a little walk.' I didn't even see he had Jeremy with him in a pushchair, this godly parent, but it seemed as if he was suggesting I should be indoors doing the same as his wife. 'Hallo, poppet,' I said to the child, who scowled at me and tugged his father's trousers. Even he didn't want to know me.

'I think they like it round with Mrs Harrison.' My bright remark. 'They seem very happy from what she tells me.'

'Yes,' he said, giving me an indifferent look and a forced smile, 'yes I'm sure they are.' Jeremy suddenly noticed the dog standing like a baked statue next to me, pulled towards her with a squeal of joy, then sneezed. David took his hand to stop him touching. For some reason, I found this terribly irritating. Frightful little patsy of a child, likely to grow up a real wimp. 'They do seem to love the Harrison discipline,' I purred; 'she's a natural with kids, our Mrs Harrison, but the only trouble is they have such a good time, they never want to go home.' I hate people looking through me like that: he'd bloody well offended me, hadn't even said I looked well or any of the usual courtesies I bloody well wanted and I wanted to needle him.

David frowned. 'You would think,' I went on, '. . . that the end of the world had come some days, Mr Harrison tells me. Something wrong in your house, David my dear, makes them so reluctant to go back into it? They never want to go home, do they? What do you do, beat them, ha, ha?'

Oh, very funny. His look was like a thundercloud passing over the sun: my little, gin inspired barb had gone home, but how dare he keep his boy away from my dog. The dog was sniffing round the pushchair: this time David didn't stop him.

'You can never work out kids' preferences,' he said. 'Jeanetta screams before she sets out in the morning. Must be any kind of change she dislikes, there's no telling. She just screams, full stop.' The old ease of manner was returning, but I could sense he was angry. 'Don't know how Sebastian can stick working in the City, weather like this,' he went on. 'I certainly couldn't. Where do they have all these early evening meetings then? In the pub, I should think.'

'I don't know.' I shrugged, acting the ignorant little woman.

David's smile was very lazy. 'In the dim and distant days when I knew the City,' he says, 'before the City chucked me out, being in a meeting was a euphemism for everything. Late afternoon, evening meetings even more suspect for the married men. Not that any of that applies to Seb of course.'

Touché.

Jeremy started to cry, and we made our goodbyes, both cross with the other. So much for the flirting I had planned, but if I had put the wind up him, he'd certainly managed to do the same to me. Damn him: what was it he'd said about meetings? Hadn't I seen him, wandering up the road with Monica Thing, that friend of theirs I met at their last party? Meetings aren't fictions, at least mine aren't. I felt I'd been given a rap on the knuckles and my knuckles ached to punch something, the way they do after a rap. Was there something I was missing with Sebastian, something he was trying to tell me?

I went back inside to check the brood: 7.45 and only Mark somnolent in front of his own TV, hopelessly tired after an early rising. Sparrow-fart start, buzzing he was at six this morning in his repossessed pyjamas. I ambled into the garden, found it had not grown any larger, so strode back through the house again, crashing down the steps in a straight line for the park. Looking for water for no particular reason except a dim and silly memory of some other lakeside where Sebastian and I had gone courting at a time only just inside the scale of my memory. In the days when the sight of my well-proportioned bosom poking out of a T-shirt was enough to render the average man incoherent, even my husband. Something ailed me at the time: I didn't know what, but something; something terribly wrong with their house next door, and ours, but I'm never good on analysis: I just blunder on.

I adore the park, although the place is so unreal, cosmopolitan Hyde Park, lush Kensington Gardens. I'd cantered half the length of the Serpentine before I slowed down, transformed by that place into a quieter animal myself. There were weeping willows grazing the water by the first bridge beyond the Fountains. Two old men sat near the Lido, looking like gnomes with folds of mahogany flesh hanging shamelessly over shorts, a tribute to their daily dip in the murky water. Further back, I passed inanimate Peter Pan, polished by the hands of children, watched another old man holding up his hand like a signal while he waited for the sparrows to clutch his knuckles and take out the offered crumb from between his thumb and first finger. I was mesmerized, stopped to look. 'They like that,' I said to the man stupidly. 'Course they do'; his reply was scornful. 'Everyone likes biscuits.' How straightforward a place is the world for some, but amongst them I had nowhere to go. David had disconcerted me horribly.

But the breath was removed from my body by all I could see. I had to sit, watching the contrasts. First a beautiful blond boy feeding nuts to a squirrel through a railing, a boy like my own Mark, whom I have never, ever, brought to the park and I suddenly wondered why; then, by way of the opposite, an elderly crone sitting on the bank of the lake, so old you wondered how she could still be alive, with her nylons rolled down over fat and mottled ankles, her grey bra-strap looped over one elbow and her crotch displayed to the ducks. The ducks were in concert, such sounds, such squabbling, deep basso profundo honking, comic squawking, deafening yells, bursts of a terrible humanity in their raucous arguments. I watched the last of the rowing boats turning to shore, confused things creaking slowly for home while the haze seemed to thicken over the water.

Then, on a seat further down, where the lake disappeared beneath the tunnel of a bridge, sitting pathetically slumped, I saw Sebastian.

He was sitting in his shirt sleeves, this man who so rarely takes off a winter jacket, the slight red of his hair catching the last of the sun, pale forehead on fire with it. Sitting alone, staring fixedly at the ducks. Sebastian has always craved water, wanted a house by the sea, but I wouldn't let him. From the other direction, beyond him, I saw a blonde girl walking away, couldn't tell if she had walked from the same seat or if, in my squinting vision, I imagined she may have done so. I could see her, had I turned one second before, trailing her long hair across his broad shoulders, one hand now pushing golden strands behind her ears and adjusting her bag to her shoulder as she walked. She was very slim, like a reed, beige coloured in a short dress which fitted like a dream, walked as she walked, made for a shape like hers. Sebastian, in a meeting.

Oddly enough, since I cannot see why, I was more distressed to consider him sitting there alone than I was to contemplate the prospect of that possible companion. A man sitting by himself and watching ducks is one without purpose, a creature without a home, all dignity lost except for the kind of pathos peculiar to a lonely child. So I got up and walked down the path, my sandalled feet scraping in the hurry with the thong over one toe suddenly sore, my heart in my feet, pounding discomfort. But when I came near, coughing my own familiar cough as a signal for him to compose himself, he remained as immobile as that statue of Peter Pan which promises such movement while remaining still. When I asked him, what time is it, please, I heard a voice removed from the body of this man on the bench; a man with a coarse face, reddish hair, a headless patrician, a stomach more often assaulted by beer and less by exercise than that of my own spouse. A coarser version, not my

Sebastian ever, a heavy, disgusting, grimy at the edges stranger was all, with a suit so cheap the creases shone like his skin shone, paler eyes looking through me with complete indifference as he consulted a watch of astonishing vulgarity. I thanked, I began to mumble, I shuffled on, so dizzy with relief I almost fell, feeling an utter and complete fool. Sebastians on benches, looking at ducks, wouldn't be seen dead, would he, never. And my own reflection in the water, dusty, faded, plump, with all those dun-coloured, frayed clothes, more in common with the crone without knickers I had seen with her rolled-down nylons than the woman whose bosom was the talk of Oxford and the hazard of another lakeside. Christ, I needed a drink, badly.

I should not have moved, of course: should have stayed inside my own study with a calculator rather than go out into the world where nothing is predictable at all. I should not have spoken to David. I went home, holding on to my own wrists, embracing myself with my arms across my untidy chest for reassurance. I kept on forgetting that it had not been Sebastian on the bench, not him at all, but another of similar build and different persona, not my own man, Oh no, not him, but the turmoil his image caused was unforgivable; for the way I was walking with those stupid tears cutting lines in the back of my eyes, it may as well have been him. Nor need it have been Katherine Allendale I had seen walking away from the man who was not my husband, but her image was as firmly stuck, wedged like a dart. That slim beige dress tiptoeing into the distance, at home with the splendours of the park, beckoning men like some sort of shy goddess. If she were the siren on the rocks, I wanted her covered in oil slick.

No Sebastian at home. A meeting with Japanese clients, he had said. I wanted to talk, even to Mrs Harrison, but old habits die hard. My life, you understand, my rational thoughts, were in the grip of some kind of paranoia. Which is why I went into his study via the garden, a circuitous route to say the least, but for reasons I cannot be bothered to explain and certainly cannot rationalize, I wanted to see from the opposite way up exactly what he could see from his infrequently used eyrie of the garden next door, but it was darkening by then. I could see no more than an orb of light from the playroom end of their kitchen, a dimmer light upstairs in David's studio, no sound but the gurgling of a drain, strange, urban music.

My husband's study was dusty and bare. On his desk was an address book containing particulars of people I had never known. There were dead flowers in a vase by the window, and a wasp buzzing and crawling round the perimeter of one pane, dozy but angry, literally dying to be free. I tried to kill it, but I was tired and it would not die. In the back wall mirror, I caught a sight of myself, flapping at the wasp, trapping the wings in the Indian silk scarf from round my neck, pinning it against the pane but unable to press hard enough to hear that little crunch which would have signalled disablement, they are so slow to perish. In the end, I opened the window and dropped out the scarf, hoping the insect was inside. Both of them fluttered down to the garden, the scarf a flag of no known nation, floating slowly. I felt so unutterably hopeless, so incompetent, so fat, so inept, slumped on the sill, watching nothing, crying like a baby.

'Whassa matter, Mummy, wotcha doing, whassa matter?'

'You're supposed to be asleep, child . . . I thought you were asleep!'

'Well, I'm not,' Mark said logically enough, standing there in the door of the study, rubbing his eyes, looking like a little blind hedgehog, quite unsure what to do with all the paws. 'I'm not asleep. Whotcha doin'?'

'Killing a wasp.'

'Ugh. Well, that's nothing to cry about. Can I have a biscuit?' The adult composure, the matter of factness, is really rather marvellous: I looked at him as I might have done a stranger. 'And some milk,' he added. 'Don't cry Mummy.' He shivered with great exaggeration. 'Cold in here anyway. Wasps is horrible, I think, anyway. You can have a drink if I have a biscuit. Two biscuits?'

'Everyone likes biscuits,' I said, remembering the old man in the park. 'No they don't, not all of the time, but I do,' he said, pulling up his pyjamas which were spreading like a fan around his feet. 'Biscuits are all right really. Very all right. Are you coming downstairs now?'

I let him lead me, moving our disappointing vantage point from the death of the wasp and the uncomfortable barrenness of father's study, went downstairs and looked out of another window facing the road. 'I often look,' Mark explained to me. 'Mark, that's naughty. Mustn't be Nosy Parker ...' 'Why not?' he asked, the logicality foremost, knowing I could not answer. 'Everyone likes to look all the time.' 'Some of the time,' I corrected. 'Shh,' he said, 'look, there's that man.' We watched the vagrant I had seen in the street before, shuffling up the road out of sight. 'I tried to talk to him,' Mark told me, 'but he can't.'

'Mustn't talk to strangers, sweetheart.'

'Why not?'

'They sometimes bite.'

'Mummy, why were you crying?'

'I wasn't,' I lied. I was slightly affected by the vision of the vagrant moving off down the street, a displaced person alone at night, up to mischief.

'All right,' Mark said, looking at me with totally unselfconscious curiosity, willing to believe what he wanted to hear. 'But you should ask me next time. I'll sort out the wasps for you, honestly.'

Enough, I said, enough, enough, enough. You may have three biscuits for that.

9

The high summer social calendar was a blessing to some.

'Tum ti tum tum . . . Tra la lari lee . . .'

Mrs Sophie Allendale was babysitting and as ruler of the mansion found her sudden elevation perfectly heavenly. So much so, mid-pirouette, the idea crossed her mind to pick up the phone and invite round the posse of Hampstead widows who were both distressed and genteel enough to qualify for her own social circle. Until she remembered how either David or Katherine had been overheard to refer to these cronies as Granny's coven. Who had spoken this description was a matter Granny had forgotten, but she believed the culprit was Katherine, and in memory of the words, which she imagined she could hear in Katherine's voice, did not phone. Which was a pity since she was certain she could have prevailed upon the coven to descend in entirety, twittering with curiosity to see herself play hostess with David's alcohol supply. She could have summonsed her grandchildren for display by way of extra aperitif; then given her guests a guided tour provided the poor old dears, none of whom boasted a surviving relative as comfortable as her own, could manage the stairs. The plan was stillborn because Sophie had been quite unable to find the kind of foods she required to complement the drink. Smoked oysters, home-made cheese straws and small pieces of anchovy toast, things she would have served as a girl, would have done nicely except she was not sure of the etiquette of serving anchovy toast at any other time than tea. To hell with the details: they would have fetched up by the charabanc load for coffee and biscuits never mind vermouth and gin, but she could not find sufficient supplies of the former either. The whole kitchen seemed to have undergone yet more comprehensive alterations since her last visit, forgotten after a couple of phone calls, and most of the food cupboards were now locked; Granny proofed, she thought with irritation, until she remembered the locks were more towards burglary prevention with herself only as an afterthought; David's calculation, such a clever son. Granny's own delicious meal was laid out delicately, salad and half-bottle of wine in the fridge, dear, plus access to a limited number of biscuits in a china barrel. She had already eaten half the meal, skipping round the dining table in the process, moving the plate from one end to the other to try herself out in various seats, saving the wine for later but making some progress with the very dry sherry although not exactly to her sweet taste. The nibbling progress was interrupted by a visit to the garden and a long conversation with the flowers.

'Ooooh, you are a beautiful one, aren't you just? Does my boy look after you then? Look at you, you spoilsport, all closed up for the night. . .' Then humming, 'Boys and girls come out to play, the moon doth shine as bright as day . . . ' before bidding the blooms goodnight; ' . . . Night-night, sleep tight, mind the bugs don't bite,' tittering at her own wit.

Sophie had done all that long before the onset of darkness provoked the desire for company along with the first star in the sky. She played with the radio in the kitchen until she had filled the room with loud music, then sat in the window, ready to incline her head like royalty towards passers-by, disappointed to find a certain lack of young men willing to tug the forelock in her direction. So she telephoned Mary Allendale, not unduly distressed, since there was plenty of time, to receive the dismissal of the answerphone. Later would do, dear, really: the house was hers for most of the night and Jeanetta was bound to wake up soon. The cork lifted out of the sherry bottle as if by magic. 'What sort of sound was that you made?' she asked it. 'A thlunk, I think.' She giggled a trifle wildly.

Out in the square, John Mills paused and looked towards the grandeur of the kitchen, arrested by the bright lights and the vision of a porcelain old lady, frothing lace at her pink throat, grinning at him over the rim of her sherry glass, winking roguishly. Despite himself and the twitching of one eye, which had become permanent in the last two weeks, he smiled back because she looked so nicely ridiculous. 'Silly me,' Sophie cooed to herself, patting her hair into place, 'could have been a burglar.' The thought passed on. There were no burglars near her son's house; they would never dare intrude on such hallow ground. And Daddy was dead.

The champagne had entered Katherine's bloodstream bypassing the digestive system on a straight route to her head, giving a dangerously emotional glint to her eye. Drink did that; her head was like a sponge. She knew exactly what she looked like: could see it in the eyes of the women, three of whom had kissed her cheek without once remarking she looked nice. Looking nice was important, gave her presence and confidence, was absolutely vital to any pleasure in the whole thing; knowing she was not up to standard was the potential ruin of an evening and she felt a freak. Catching sight of herself in a mirror, she saw the brick-red tube of a frock, clinging jersey above the knees, fitting snugly over the bosom, not quite the right side of modesty. There were suggestive and useless bootlace straps over her bare shoulders: the large earrings worn to distract from the total effect did the opposite, the whole image tarty. I can't believe I ever chose this dress, but David said I did: I can't remember when; could I ever have liked myself in this? Common, expensively vulgar, reflecting a predatory glimmer in the eyes of the men. Humiliation, discomfort and a desire to disappear were all being saturated in alcohol, rising heat and the immense puzzlement of why he should do this to her. You bought it, darling; you can't be so extravagant for nothing, you have to wear it now. Teetering on the brink of confidence, less and less sure of her own mind, tense before any party, she felt all the excitement ebb away in the knowledge of her exposure.

The American couple had excelled themselves in a feat of planning which had been shrouded in secrecy in order for Mrs Holmes Junior to reward and totally upstage the friends and acquaintances who had offered her hospitality in the past. The assistance of the heatwave had been beyond her capabilities, but she had organized the hire of a huge room at Kenwood House where the guests could spill out to a gracious balcony commanding the sculptured landscape which Mr Holmes Junior considered the finest view in London town; nothing better, with everything in his sight, including every single one of the guests, looking mighty pretty, some of them prettier than others, oh boy, but a fine sight all the same. They could dance inside if they wished, gawp at paintings, grin at the sweating musicians, stroll in the grounds or get drunk at his expense. Some of the invitees, Mr Holmes noticed with the satisfaction of a generous man, were embracing all those options. He did not mind being the only one wearing a tuxedo, but then he was the host. Mrs Holmes was the only one whose skirt reached the ground in a confection resembling a waterfall, but she likewise took hosting seriously. Both of them were very happy indeed.

So was Monica, passing the reflection of herself in a long mirror, liking what she saw. She was still too big, hardly fat, but busty, a Victorian hourglass figure currently dressed with extravagant expense in a dress with a shot-silk skirt of emerald and black stripes, high black bodice and emerald belt to offset the narrowness of her waist. She had copied Katherine's devotion to shops without price labels, but added her own passion for high colour. Dressed as she was, she hoped David Allendale would admire her as an extravagant and good-natured peacock in comparison to his own paler, if classier, hen, currently dressed like a street walker. Monica did not even try to kid herself as to whose approval it was she sought. There was an element of revenge in this. If, in the days intervening since their own gathering, Colin Neill had opened his mouth once more in praise of dear Kate's ethereal appearance, Monica would have screamed. Even two clandestine lunches with the husband of this paragon, assignations with the innocent purpose of discussing the new conservatory, but nevertheless not confessed at home or abroad, had done nothing to relieve the irritation.

The music waltzed for the people rather than the other way round while the American host, hoping things might loosen up a little round here, went looking for his favourite guests, failing to find at least one. Katherine had gone to the ladies purely in order to cry. Where Jenny found her and blamed the champagne.

'What's wrong, Katherine, oh don't cry, please don't ... What on earth's the matter?' If there was an edge of impatience to her voice, she hid it well, but elements of Monica's aggressive common sense were uppermost and this was not the way, or the place, where Jenny had wanted to spend any part of her evening. Katherine was a man's woman, after all, not receptive to comfort from her own sex, and anyhow, in Jenny's view, when people in tears are asked whatever is the matter, they are rarely able to tell the truth, but tell you something else. It would not really matter what she said in return, so she fussed in Katherine's handbag for a comb, waited for a reply.

'I hate, loathe and despise this dress,' Katherine said slowly and finally with so much hesitation that Jenny decided not to believe this was the reason for visible grief, while being irritated that such a superficial explanation should be quoted at all, especially when it was wasting her time and her ready sympathy, and even though she knew how much the wrong dress could kill stone dead any feeling of self-worth.

'You look perfectly wonderful, Katherine, you always do. Here, borrow my mascara and do your eyes. The dress is fine, doesn't David like it? Is that the problem?' She was remembering Katherine's desire to please, hints heard of the autocracy of the household, which she privately began to consider necessary for a wife who had so much to spend but time to weep over a dress. 'Doesn't David like it?' she repeated, noticing with relief the way Katherine had begun to repair the damage to her face, grief dissolving in the tissue paper with which she scraped her cheeks. 'Yes,' said Katherine, 'I mean no, it isn't the problem. He does like it. He made me wear it. I took something back, you see. If ever I do that I have to put on something he knows I hate. He's hidden all the rest.'

Jenny was confused, handed another tissue, impatience growing despite a natural kindness. 'Made you wear it?' she laughed, 'Oh come on, Katherine, you make it sound as if he put the thing over your head.' 'He did,' said Katherine simply. 'That's exactly what he did.' 'Well,' Jenny was soothing but completely incredulous, 'he must have seen what you don't. Absolute cracker of a dress. Everyone says so and I'm so jealous I could die. Come on now, mirrors tells fibs, but I wouldn't. I'm your friend, remember?'

'Are you?' said Katherine, the voice still tremulous. 'Are you really?' At the moment, having a friend could make all the difference.

'Course I am,' said Jenny embarrassed. 'Tell me all about it next week.' The pale face nodded, so transfixed with gratitude Jenny made a mental resolution never again to lunch with Katherine alone. Not even if she supplied a bale of material. There were demands implicit in this gratitude, all of them regrettable. She had no room in her life for anything like that: everything else was far too complicated. The children were sickening, her husband argumentative and the car had failed to start, while on arrival she had sought the comfort of Monica, not for a shoulder to cry upon but one to laugh against, found her mentor dressed like a flamingo feather and hell-bent on some strange distraction of her own. Katherine would never understand such a feeling of rejection: no one could possibly reject Katherine, but Jenny patted her bare arm, spoke with conviction.

'Hey, come on: Stay with me, we'll go and eat. Or not, whatever you like. All men are bastards, just treat them as spoiled babies, I do. Go and flirt like mad; we'll talk tomorrow, eh?' Katherine nodded absurdly comforted but slightly querulous in a way which made Jenny feel even guiltier.

'Flirt?'

'Go on, knock 'em dead.'

Jenny forgot the guilt as soon as they emerged and Katherine began to bestow smiles like scattered confetti. Katherine forgot too. She could take a morsel of comfort and turn it into a meal.

Knock 'em dead. Flirting suddenly OK; Jenny had said so. Be a girl, be yourself, be admired. Bother David and to hell with everything. The music was quite suddenly delightful; the cheap, palm-court themes reminiscent of a kind of glamour which had been some stepmother's hallmark, a woman Katherine had tried to copy for the short while they had spoiled her, and now she wanted to dance. The American host launched forward and seized Katherine by the hand, ready to shuffle round the floor, dancing some indeterminate, unknown step which she followed with ease, laughing loudly in response to the flow of his slow and clumsy compliments, forgetting to look round. When he relinquished her to Colin Neill, Katherine's smile was as wide as the view from the balcony.

He had seen the tears, the departure and return, because he had been watching all the time, noticing as well as his own wife's preening, catching everything with the talent of a gossip. Colin knew he was prone to confuse female signals, always imagined there was a code to them he might one day crack like a difficult phrase of music after several rehearsals. He could see that Katherine was as high now as she had been low thirty minutes before, while the messages relayed by the dress, the inviting glance and the suggestion of abandonment, all conflicted with the hesitation he recognized rather better. More champagne might aid the ambivalence: he fetched another glass when she had drunk his own. They paused in the silent tippling, watching without concern for their spouses who were seen engrossed in conversation. Katherine followed his eyes, listened and nodded when Colin suggested they stroll in the grounds, lightening the hackneyed invitation with a laugh, 'Very warm . . . Leave the clever ones together and look at the flowers, hmm?'

Jenny watched, always watching, hurt in her own abandonment. Maybe, in a little while, a word in David's ear.

Sophie Allendale's boredom with the scant attention received from the street set her off on a cruise round her borrowed domain. In the course of her perambulations, creaking from floor to floor, marvelling at the number of locks on doors, she managed to wake Jeanetta accidentally on purpose. Conscience forced her to make a few grandmotherly sounds encouraging the child back to sleep, but these efforts were half-hearted since she really wanted company and was in any event, no proof against another's superior willpower. The two of them descended to the kitchen where the door to the garden stood open and the music still blared from the radio. First they picked some precious old-fashioned roses and stuck them in a milk bottle without water. Then they danced a little, both of them chatting throughout between one two three, one two three, turn now, darling, neither making any sense to one another but understanding perfectly all the same. Then Jeanetta dragged Granny to the playroom, where the brand-new door, creating a room out of what had once been an alcove, remained unlocked. Inside the playroom (which Jeanetta displayed with some pride), both of them began to rummage in a large chest, flinging out the contents on to the kitchen floor. Sophie fell on a dress of purple taffeta, one of Katherine's rejects, so bright it pre-dated any acquaintance with David, but perfectly suited the more flamboyant taste of her mother-in-law. Jeanetta found a shimmering shawl made of black and gold lurex with a long fringe she stuck in her mouth to test before wrapping the cloth round her little fat body, helped by Sophie. They sat back and rocked with mirth. 'Sweetheart, light of my life, you look gorgeous. Whatever shall we do next?' Jeanetta had no hesitation. 'Biscuits?' she said hopefully. Sophie nodded. 'Everyone likes biscuits,' she agreed like a wise old owl. Jeanetta agreed with nods more vehement. 'But there aren't many left.'

They shuffled into the business end of the kitchen, Jeanetta half in, half out of a pair of oversized high heels, teetering dangerously but highly pleased with herself. When an exploration of the fridge yielded no more than raw fish, live yoghurt, skimmed milk and fruit juice, all in copious quantity but nothing fit for addicts of carbohydrate, Sophie borrowed one of the high heels and tried to insert it into a lock on a cupboard which promised food, led by her granddaughter's eloquent gestures. She hammered first, while Jeanetta kicked at the door. 'Just like burglars,' Mrs Allendale giggled, pausing for breath. She gave Jeanetta the last contents of the biscuit barrel as an incentive to further effort, took another swig of sherry while considering if a wire coat-hanger might not be more effective on the door. The whole enterprise was obviously going to take some time.

Seductions, Colin Neill concluded, can often take time. The

seduction of Katherine Allendale, a fantasy in mind for the whole year or more he had known her, was one he always imagined would occur in the slow lane. He loved the reverberating tone of the very word seduction and in his experience, the whole operation was either fast or slow, with him greatly preferring the latter, even if there was no real end-result at all. Promise was often far better than performance. So the fact that Katherine Allendale was panting slightly in the bushes, allowing him to kiss her and run his hands over the smooth upholstery of her bosom, was unnerving without being particularly pleasant, since he was still enough of a romantic to prefer his conquests to confide. I mean a chap has to know whether she likes you or not. He detached her gently.

'Here, here, my darling Katherine, you like old Colin then, do you? Well, fancy that, lucky old me, here, sit down, it's dry here, really it is, do sit for a minute . . . '

'Can I have a cigarette?'

'Course, course, anything you like.'

She took the proffered light and drew on the cigarette with a hungry lack of expertise, similar to a teenager with the first. The bubble had burst. A sense of her own ugliness was back.

'I haven't upset you, have I?' he asked anxiously.

'No.' She sounded surprised as if pawing in the bushes from the husband of a friend was par for the course.

'But you were a bit upset earlier on, I noticed. Tell me all about it.'

Katherine was behaving like a child, sitting on a lap, confiding. 'David's cross with me,' she mumbled, slurring the words slightly. 'Very cross.' She sounded like someone complaining about a teacher. 'Oh dear,' said Colin placatingly.

'He won't let me have Jeremy or my own clothes or any money. I don't have a single thing of my own and he hates Jeanetta.'

'No,' said Colin, 'I'm sure not . . . '

'Yes,' Katherine continued. 'She's very bad, you see. She won't act like he expects and he thinks she isn't his. She won't do anything he tells her, you see. Everything has to be his. And under orders. Nothing moves without orders.' She hiccuped.

'Not his?' Colin was confused, the near warmth of Katherine and the Dutch courage coursing through his head making him enjoy the conversation less and less. He inserted one hand easily down the side of the elastic dress, finding that she was quite unmoved by the touch, hardly noticing. The liberty he was being given was almost offensive. 'What else is not David's?' he asked for something to say.

'What?' She had already lost the thread of the conversation.

'Surely there are things in your house which belong to you? All your lovely things, the ones you choose, they belong to both of you, not just him.'

'Everything belongs to David. Everything pretty. He won't have anything ugly. He couldn't stand it otherwise. He had such a horrible time as a child, you see, never allowed to keep anything nice. Just like me; that's why I loved him so much. We were the same, you see.' She sounded injured by his failure to see the logic.

Colin no longer knew what to say. Most of this was nonsense. He wanted talk to centre on themselves and what they were going to do about this mutual attraction, an intimacy *à deux* to give spice to the other, not an exposé of a crazy-sounding life nor any silly talk of who the hell owned what. Having considered her temperament perfectly OK for a bit on the side, beautiful without complexities, rather like his secretary, he was a trifle out of depth, concentrated on kisses made moister by her passive response, conscious of a sense of danger and the need to return to the music. As his lips met the curve of one round breast rising from the dress, he saw, from beyond the circle of weeping willow which hid them, a pair of dark-clad feet walking away.

Granny was becoming a little exhausted, while Jeanetta, fortified by five chocolate Olivers and a nap earlier in the day, was feeling sick but still energetic, her movements becoming slower like a clockwork toy winding down. The sherry was finished. 'I do wish they'd buy the sweet stuff,' Granny confided. They sat at the kitchen table, drawing on the surface with wax crayons, having been quite unable to supply themselves with paper, despite a foray in the direction of David's studio, which they had found locked. Jeanetta had been worried about drawing on the table, but Granny brushed the worries aside along with the crumbs. 'It'll surely scrub off, darling; Mummy can do that, she's good at it.'

One worry led to another. 'Ooh, should we go and look if Jemmy's all right?' Jeanetta's anxious tones. 'We might have woke him.'

'Why?' asked Granny. 'Mummy put him to bed, didn't she?' Jeanetta shook her head. 'No Daddy does. Mummy not allowed to touch him, nor me,' she said. 'Only Daddy.' 'Well really, I must say, honestly,' said Sophie. 'Well, I can't go back up all those stairs, you go. You're nearly five after all. Go on, I'll wait at the bottom.' Jeanetta, taking the directive as a dare and a rare chance to touch the adored Jeremy, scrabbled upstairs, still in the lurex shawl but without shoes, disappeared for a matter of three minutes while Sophie waited impatiently. ''S OK,' she announced on her breathless return. 'Alive?' Sophie asked caustically. 'Sleeping,' said Jeanetta. 'I'se put back on his cover and give him Teddy.' Upstairs, Jeremy slumbered with the coverlet over his ears, a teddy bear thrust against his nose, making breathing perfectly possible, but stertorously noisy. Granny and granddaughter returned to the kitchen. One of them was in the act of shredding rose petals, for pot-pourri, Granny explained, the other crayoning a copy on to the table surface, when David, soft footed and too quiet with the insertion of his key in the oiled lock of the front door, returned to find them.

He took one look at the faces turned towards his in benign surprise, transformed to welcome, quickly in the case of Sophie, slowly for Jeanetta, who suddenly saw the tableau of their presence with some dim understanding of the way he might see the same, scuttled beneath the table. David turned from the kitchen and ran upstairs, found Jeremy breathing like a pug-dog, half smothered in blanket, his breath a harmless rasp and his body overwarm. At the door of the room were a couple of rose petals, and part of the detached fringe of the shawl Jeanetta had been wearing. David threw Teddy out of the cot, pulled back the duvet and added to the boy's unconscious comfort, trembling with rage. Descending to the kitchen, he was still speechless as Jeanetta's head poked above the table. He pointed at her as if he could not bear to have touched, then stabbed his finger in the direction of the stairs.

'I'm not telling you twice, you little bastard. Go to bed.'

'Lost my 'jamas . . . '

'Go to bed.' His hand was raised. She slid away under his arm, ducking as she went and traversed the stairs on her hands and knees at a fast crawl without any attempt to say goodnight. Granny looked once in her direction, then, as soon as the child was out of sight, forgot her; fixed on her only son one radiant glance of adoration.

'David, darling, we've had such fun . . . '

'So I see.'

There were three dismembered coat-hangers on the floor against the open cupboard. Biscuits for cheese, chocolate versions, wrappers of cellophane and a few tins of something lay in a heap. The floor was otherwise littered with taffeta cloth, shoes, toys, crayons and two bread rolls trodden into crumbs. Mrs Allendale was wearing a tiara and the music still played.

'And where's Katherine, dear? Did you have a nice time? Tell me do, was there real dancing?'

'Katherine stayed at the party. She must have known what she'd find here. I'll get you a cab, Mother.'

Sophie's face fell. 'But I thought I was staying the night.' Her smile lit on the carnage which was once the kitchen, noting for the first time, but shrugging away. His speech was low and clipped as he dialled from a phone on the wall. 'This was your last chance, Mother. Katherine anticipated something of the kind. I'm sorry if I seem so fussy, but I must do as she asks. This mess will kill her. Hallo? Yes, please, yes, Hampstead village, on my account. As soon as possible, thank you.' Such mild politeness, betrayed only to himself by shaking fingers. He gave his name and address, replaced the receiver and turned to her.

'You've had it, Ma. And you mustn't ever come here again unless Katherine asks you. Which may not be for some time, if ever at all.'

Sophie got the message in a sharp way, taking the meaning without understanding, wailing, 'Why, darling, why? What did I do so wrong? Only playing, me and your daughter, playing, that kind of thing, what's wrong?'

'You're a bloody conspiracy,' he said calmly. 'All of you. You can never do as you're damn well told. You shouldn't disobey me. I gave you strict instructions. Anyway, the last thing you should do is give that child food.' The doorbell rang: he collected Granny's handbag, all her small luggage of nightie and toothbrush inside. 'Here's your cab. Get out. Don't forget to tell him where you live.'

She looked at him, her eyes blank with hurt. 'Just like Daddy,' she said in a whisper. He spun round to face her, shouting, 'Get out.'

Get out, get out, get out. He calmed himself by repeating the words like a litany chanted over his own rage until he was under control, no longer at risk from his own violence when the engine of Sophie's cab echoed away down the street. Then he began to tidy the room, re-establishing order in the dry-food store, folding the evening clothes, wiping the table, loading the dishwasher, rearranging furniture with swift, two-handed efficiency until he had got the whole thing straight enough to be recognizable as the kitchen he had made. He polished the table until the mahogany shone, stroked it sensuously with the back of his hand; stood back and admired his room. He did a survey of the rest of his house, switching on lights, checking and smiling as if the possessions might respond. Mine all mine: all things in their places, beautiful and ordered. Then he went out into the garden, examined the blooms, tutting over three rose stems where the branches had been cruelly broken, smoothed out the soil where Jeanetta's footsteps were prevalent, picking up the dead leaves scattered by his mother's progress, seeing only Jeanetta's progress. Then he adopted the nightly ritual, put down the pellets against the cats she encouraged into the garden, supplied by the pet-hating chemist who promised them as lethal to cat life, benign to vegetation. Garden tidied, kitchen restored to final discipline with the floor shining again, he began to feel calm, his passions sated for a moment. They would all learn: some were slower than others was all.

David consulted his watch. She should be home soon, any

time now. The anger was ice cold. He supposed he had better wait for her. As an afterthought he checked Jeremy again, found his breathing quieter. After that, he slid the bolt in the front door. Let her knock. Unnecessary act even as he thought of it. He was the only one with a key.

Get out, get out, get out. She had loved the sensation of being driven home in the car, a feeling, aided by alcohol, of hiding away. Their car, David's car, seemed huge; she never remembered the type, but an all-singing all-dancing car with electric windows, automatic locks and gears, an engine of smooth-sounding power. Progress through the dark streets, the odd, erratic illumination casting shadows over her face, was making her feel part of a capsule travelling through time, watertight, airtight, permanently warm. Despite the heat of the night and a feeling of safety, Katherine had been loath to open a window, disliking the feeling of a draught of fresher air to disturb this hermetically sealed safety. She was not unduly worried by the silence of his driving, felt she had been rather clever, not worried by anything, floating without alarm since David seemed to have enjoyed his evening and anything she had failed to do had not been registered by any single word or gesture of his since she had returned to the light of the party, combed, restored to good grooming under Colin's direction. Well somebody liked her, nobody cared what she did and flirting was all right. A short sojourn it had been, very short indeed, with nothing happening, and all of it already fading into memory apart from the lingering and treacherous smell of her cigarette smoke which she was too drunk to conceal. Drunk and defensive and smiling into the darkness, listening to the radio, tra, la, la. Soon they would be home and she could take off this hideous dress.

In Kilburn the darkness was more sinister and more interesting, the light more irregular. The desertion of the pavements was intermittent, groups stood in conversation, debating which of many moves underground for entertainment, everything spoiling for trouble. Multicoloured youth lurked on each corner, waiting for Saturday night to start on Sunday. Pretty view from the window of the car. Pretty woman, soon home, regarding them like exhibits in a gallery, some sub-species forming part of the view while they waited for the dealer, watched by a wife in a big car who shuddered a little at the dim spectacle of all those other lives.

That was where he stopped the vehicle to one side of the road opposite a small group drunk with argument or quarrelling drunk, same difference. He had walked round to her side of the car, opened the door and pulled her by the arm. 'Get out,' he said, 'get out, get out – you walk from here.' They watched her, the youths, Hey man, get that, celebrating the fall of midnight. 'Get out,' he said again.

David heated skimmed milk in the kitchen, laid the table for breakfast. Three places, father, mother, son. While Katherine was running, a stumbling flight somewhere near the Edgware Road, sense of direction half functioning, clutching her bare arms, sweating, but chilled with cold. She had walked slowly from the car, watching ahead, but the first of the youths had stopped her after a hundred yards. ''Scuse me, you got the time, lady?' Looking up to see him, black and glistening, his face hanging back. Automatically, she extended her wrist to look at the gold dial, saw another face move in behind the first. She pushed past both and began to walk faster, conscious of the third man in pursuit, unprepared for the shove which sent her sprawling to the ground. Instinct made her roll on to her stomach, clutching her handbag to her chest: there was a searing pain in the wrist which had broken her fall. She felt a blow to her head, punch or kick she could not tell, a wrenching of her back to force her to turn. She was pulled over, legs spreadeagled, hands clawing at her chest to free the bounty while she twisted her head from side to side, the scream in her throat prevented by an arm across her neck: panting in the darkness, her watch torn away from a clenched hand. The pressure eased: her opening eyes could see nothing but blackness and for a moment she thought she was blind, but within a second she could identify a muscular body tensed over her own, smell the stench of dirt and excitement. 'Run, man, run . . .' an urgent voice, one set of feet pattering away, but another breathing deep, waiting. Above her head there appeared an orb of black features, pink eyes like a ferret holding her own, but vacant while the crouched man patted her supine body, frisking but pausing. A small, impersonal grin appeared at the edges of his full mouth, revealing yellow bared teeth as one hand thrust down the dress squeezed the nipple beneath with such ferocity she cried out in pain. 'Leave her, man,' words almost shouted, ' . . . For fuck's sake leave . . . '

But he wrenched her to her feet from behind; with one arm locked round her throat, the other pinning her waist against the ominous bulge of his groin, half dragged, half pulled her back from the central pavement, her feet scrabbling for purchase, one shoe lost, feeling the sweat on his skin. 'Leave her man, leave,' the voice becoming a hiss of urgent command, the shuffling, cursing continuing many more steps until they ceased. Her half-open eyes registered boxes, dustbins, bottles around their feet, something like the enclave of a pub's back yard, full of the odour of rubbish and stale beer. Then a sudden silence apart from thunderous breathing, lights visible at the end of the alleyway to the street. In the near distance, there was an insistent rhythm of music, while nearer at hand a long low whistle.

'See what you mean, man,' another face swimming into focus. 'Oh yeah, pretty lady.' One hand mounting her thigh, digging into her crotch with fingers of steel, vicious, bruising jabs, the dress tearing, screams suffocated by the arm across her throat. 'Oh yeah, man, put her down, put her down on the floor . . . ' A scrabbling at her pants, fingers yanking the dress down to reveal the small bosom. She gouged her fingernails into the forearm as it relaxed, felt the nails penetrate flesh, a temporary release. She sprang up, one athletic movement learned in the gym, pulled off the remaining shoe and ran for the light of the street, one of them reaching for her hair, pulling her back. She swung wildly with the stiletto end of the shoe, blind and repeated striking, felt connection with the bone of forehead, a short scream following, stopped suddenly, the sound of a siren wailing closer and closer with shrill urgency. Then she was lying still, kicked in passing, one arm imprinted with the mark of a trampling shoe in their haste to move, footsteps padding away into the dark, back down the alley away from the bins into the distance. The engine carrying the siren flew swiftly on, following the call to another destination, screaming past her in a blur of blue light as she reached the pavement and beckoned vainly towards it.

She began to stumble down the road in the same direction, one breast bouncing free from the red dress. Katherine was familiar with running away, but the childish running had been a game, played in the confidence of someone finding her; not like this.

The doorstep was icy cold. The knocking on the door and leaning against the bell had continued for what felt a longer eternity than all the time she had walked, pausing to hide in doorways, shoulders wrapped in a piece of filthy polythene which had drifted against her legs and made her scream. Utterly exposed, harlot, tart, alone again, gasping, oh please, please, anyone, please . . . When he finally opened the door, the heat from within hit her like a blast from an oven.

'Good of you to call,' said David. 'I suppose you think you're going to come in.'

She nodded dumbly.

'Well I don't know about that, darling. Did you have fun?'

Katherine looked up, searching for his face. The light behind reduced his features to one enormous silhouette. She willed herself not to cry, thinking quite out of sequence how there had been neither money nor keys in the bag she had lost.

'Found a couple of fans out there, did we, sweetheart? I can see you did. No one else's business of course, but what a surprise. No one in their right mind would want a fat little tramp like you. No one short of a faggot like Colin Neill. Was he gentle, darling, was he? Better than the others? Sweet and kind and flattering, come on, you can tell me.'

She raised her face, waiting for the slap of his palm to ring against her temple, felt her head jerk sideways. Then she began to cry, crouched at his feet on the front steps, pressing her hands against her ears. 'I'm sorry, I'm sorry, I'm sorry. Please, don't send me away . . . '

'Hush, darling, hush . . . Darling Katherine, good girl, oh don't cry, hush now . . . my lovely.' He drew her up into his arms, her face sobbing against his chest, and carried her gently inside. 'Hush, darling: I'm sorry too; you're home now. Here, here, carefully, come on now . . .'

His face in the hall mirror smiled, although his eyes, like hers, shone with tears. Katherine felt the tears she did not see. Order was established.

IO

As a little girl, I said, 'I want', rather often; and somewhere down the line, more usually sooner rather than later, I got. You become cunning about these things as a child, I seem to remember, particularly in my case because one's will had to be translated to so many people, all of whom required a different approach. No good tackling Nanny in the same way you would seduce Mama, and most of them drove a hard bargain anyway. You can have a bicycle if . . . You can go to that school if . . . Posing in the wake of their promises the kind of obligations which make the labours of Hercules seem like ten cents. Where grown-ups were being outstandingly dense, complex manoeuvres were required, such as being quiet and ostentatiously good, or making them think it was their idea in the first place and applying their own logic, e.g., this will be cheaper in the end. Either way, one usually won, so much so I simply can't remember the failures. I acquired the animals, the clothes, the school, the career and finally the chap I wanted at the time. What I don't understand is when the process ceased to be successful.

Because it damn well isn't at the moment, at least not in any way which is helpful. I've taken to looking in the mirror and quite clearly something is out of control. There's nothing wrong of course: everything's wonderful really, but I don't like myself as much any more; the flesh swells while the mind of me stinks. All this self-torture began after I'd seen the Sebastian look-alike on the park bench haunted by the ghost of Katherine Allendale, but don't think it has anything to do with him, because it doesn't. Sebastian wouldn't stray in a month of

Sundays and I wouldn't give a monkey's if he bloody well did, but he really isn't like that honestly. I just need to tidy up the litter in my life, get everything straight, including the person. Then everything will be absolutely fine.

So there it was, staring me in the boxer-like face with the pink eyes and the throbbing head several days hence. The naked and knackered truth behind a revolutionary resolution, Susan Pearson Thorpe about to embark on a course of self-improvement, a complete physical overhaul of skin, clothes and hair. (Reminds me of a joke about an old lady going streaking. Did you see that, one old man asked another; what was she wearing? Don't know, said the other, but whatever it was it needed ironing. I used to find that one funny. Ha ha.)

Which is how I got to the subject of willpower. I imagined the emergence of butterfly from chrysalis was simply a matter of applying will, but you've got to be joking; the whole thing is unbelievably complicated. Having seen Katherine Allendale fold herself into the car wearing a red dress which must have been poured on her, I was inspired while wondering how ever she had the time to do all the preparation, which is actually quite numbingly, ballbreakingly, hideously boring. Nothing daunted, I started on the black hole of Calcutta otherwise known as the wardrobe, full of garments of similar dark colours complete with the wear, tear and fungus of rather too many seasons. I never thought clothes mattered, but I suspect they do. I beat a few of the shoes into submission, but my feet appear to have grown. There was little for it but to slop the whole lot back into the black hole and make for the shops. I meant business, you see: shops, no booze and a regime of exercise at Katherine Allendale's club. In deep secret, on a clandestine day off work, of course. Christ Almighty.

Now I am well aware, and may have said so before, that going to the shops is a thrill for some people who are slightly soft in the head, viz. Katherine Allendale, Mrs Harrison and almost anyone else they might count as friend: even Sebastian when pointed in the right direction for buying no more than one thing at a time, but this is not for me, oh dear me no; the whole thing is as thrilling as toothache.

Ever tried West End shops in midsummer, pursuing a dress

fit for the greenhouse effect, plus trousers or skirts designed to minimize a lumpen figure; something to send one back into the throng a transfigured and cooler self? There are, I remarked icily to one of those ultra-female masks laughingly known as assistants, many more people around living comfortably at size sixteen: we may even be the majority, but there would appear to be a conspiracy to pretend otherwise. Looking down a street I do not see a vista of twiggy persons: I see women of larger sizes, many generous indeed, and as for you, you frozen little size-ten waif, why don't you smile at me while you still have teeth, because if you bring me one more dress with a straight skirt, you won't be keeping them. By the time I was slumped over the fourth sugarless black coffee eyeing the kind of pastry forbidden on the most rudimentary self-improvement course, I was beyond depression and into nausea.

So I changed tack and went off in pursuit of lotions for the face; tonics, I'd been told by someone, or was it a magazine read in the doctor's, reverse the effect of ageing, some such thing, very clever, describing stuffs infinitely superior to the little tub of cold cream which is my whole repertoire along with Christmas-present soap and water. Soap and water, madam, repeated back at me as though I had confessed to a nightly ritual with paint-stripper. Then she shook herself, firmed up, pressed her flawless forehead with nails like talons to check the absence of wrinkles before moving into her routine. What madam should do to ensure youthful skin is as follows; here goes. First you clean your face with blue gunk at fifteen pounds per bottle, then you clean it again with yellow tonique (most unlike the sort I prefer, but she pronounced the word with aplomb) at seven pounds ninety-five a bottle; then you lightly smooth over face and neck this corn-coloured slop at thirty pounds per jar, finishing off the whole process with this translucent eye balm at twenty pounds per tube. I said wouldn't it be cheaper to have my head cut off or the whole lot lifted to make room for total replacement, since this activity was going to take twenty-four hours a day even before you've embarked on whatever it was you had to do in the morning, such as waking at 5.00 a.m. to unscrew the jars or wallow in mountain dew. But then, dammit, whatever happened to the person I once knew, bossy and immune to nonsense? Silenced by her own eyebags, and did she have anything else to make them re-emerge from behind the gin folds? Punny punny, ha ha, I was taken to the cleaners. Yes OK, fine, terrific, have the lot.

Then the sodding health club. The final stage of the self-improvement course, which on a stinking hot afternoon was beginning to tax my willpower more than anything else. So easy just going home, but what would I do at home, out of work creature that I am in my own house, waiting to be displaced by Mrs Harrison, ignored by the children, who have better things to do, and no prospect of seeing the spouse until after dark. Besides I was committed: I had phoned, made an appointment for this exercise class in this health club Katherine had once described as the answer to a woman's prayer. So, with the vision of a forbidden gin before my eyes like a mirage, I was crossing the park, trying to look as if this was something I did all the days of the week instead of the first time in what seemed, just then, a very long lifetime indeed. Not, however, as long as that class. There has never been an hour in any afternoon, not even the ones spent in thrall to labour pains, as long as the hour it took to endure that class. Shall I begin at the beginning, such as the way I ballooned into the foyer of this place with my clanking parcels, or describe these functional changing rooms, where a group of comfortingly ordinary-looking women without a single sequin on the leotards proved friendly to a plump and, by this time, irritatingly nervous stranger? The whole experiment going so well, even my ancient track suit in place, until the door opened on Katherine Allendale, looking rather strained as she came in, but on sight of me, leaping forward with little squeals of friendliness like a small puppy left alone for five minutes: and with one lurch of heart, watching her undress (so modestly, under a towel), right down to her thin ribs, even though she left this odd, flannel choker round her neck, I immediately wondered why on earth I was bothering.

The room used for the class was full of mirrors. Glass on three of four sides, I ask you, all the better to catch the reflection at every ghastly angle, an exercise in humiliation.

'We'll start slowly,' said teacher with relish, 'just a gentle warm-up, ladies, then a little jog, not much because it's so hot, then a bit of work on the bum and tum . . .' Promises, promises. The warm-up consisted of flinging arms over one's head in opposite directions, squatting on one's haunches and moving slowly up and down so that the thighs felt as if they were igniting; but dear God, that was just the beginning, a mere introduction to the real pain. Ghastly music, everyone running on the spot. 'Now kick higher, higher . . . another twenty . . . Star jumps, one, a two, a three, ten more, girls, good, good, back to can-can kicks . . .' And between all this, teacher emitting strange little whoops of encouragement which no one appeared to need since none of them was even breathless. Katherine Allendale could kick her leg as high as something from the *Folies Bergère*: her face was pale as ever, despite more *maquillage* than usual, transfixed with strange pleasure. I thought I was going to die, and in that moment, even forgetting her double walking away from my husband on graceful pins as long as hers, I hated her. She watched for me; she helped me as she might have done some little geriatric, and I hated her more.

Some of them laughed at my look of sublime disbelief when asked to put my head between my knees or attempt to push my ample chest towards the floor as we sat with out legs spread-eagled, but Katherine did not laugh: she was distressed. It should have made me like her, this obvious concern for my discomfiture, but it did not, just as thereafter, her kind solicitude, pressing on me all the stuff such as shampoo, talcum powder, towel, all of which impedimenta I had forgotten entirely, did not make me like her either. I walked round the changing room like a film version of old John Wayne walking down the street of the OK Corral, my legs fixed at peculiar angles and the knees unlikely ever to touch again, irritated by her concern, that naïve niceness. She emerged from the shower never quite showing herself naked, always modestly swathed, perhaps out of some sort of deference to me, chatting like a sparrow issuing platitudes.

'Don't worry, Susan, you did ever so well, really marvellous, and it does get easier each time, I promise. Specially when you know what to do, because half the effort goes into concentration, you know? Once you know the routine, it's so much simpler, you won't believe.'

No, I didn't believe, and as this chatter accompanied me all the way home in a taxi I paid for, to her patent delight, there settled on me the most monumental depression. 'Always makes me feel great, these classes.' Katherine, talking far harder and faster than usual – was it guilt? – but looking as healthy as she clearly felt, leaning forward with her hands' span waist on show while I could only imagine the demolition of three loaves of bread washed down by a pint of pure spirit. She so wanted to be friends: in her own way, she has always wanted that, but by the time we reached her door and mine, I could only excuse myself with a briskness which might well have amounted to rudeness. For nothing, I think now, nothing at all: for her being nice: for being the double of someone else, for being so clearly in control of her life while I felt my own was slipping away.

She took her children, leaving me with mine. I looked at them with wonder, thumb-sucking, rapt with attention, not needing me at all. Nobody needs me. I've made myself redundant.

> Mary Mary, quite contrary,
> How does your garden grow?
> With little bells and cockle shells
> And pretty birds all in a row . . .

Samantha squirmed in an orgasm of sleepy delight: I watched her, wanted her, felt desperately shy of her, went away to contemplate the effects of my day, undo those parcels, review the reflection of this brave new self.

Was there a difference? Yes, there bloody well was. Removed from the horrors of the shops where they were found, the two new frocks were a revelation, floral prints of subdued colours but fresher than anything I owned, the face above them clearer now the puce colours worn in the gymnasium had died down. Stiffness was setting in throughout every limb, but never mind: in that pain there was the pride of survival, a wonderful promise of improvement, and by dint of breathing in, holding my face up high and away from the light, I could see what I might become. Or return towards, or make for, whatever stupid thing it was I wanted; to be loved, perhaps. Or even loving. This is pure silliness: I did not say that then: I did not know it: my ignorance was so profound: I never have been able to see what I was doing wrong. I could not admit any need.

Downstairs again, with good grace. Any messages, Mrs Harrison, before I repossess my brains? No, none, she said, stiff with sulks, but Mr Thorpe came home earlier, says he left you a note in his study, something about tonight, I don't know what. No hurry then: I looked at the new dress again on the way downstairs from the children, puzzled over all the multi-language instructions which accompanied my ludicrous face-creams, all of me sober as a judge, wanting to be seen. Remembered this note in Sebastian's study, strange practice for him, what's got into the man with all this coming in and going out, went to look, thinking, well, my dear, I am even going to cook a meal, aren't you the lucky one. Maybe you'll notice me for once, or, more properly, I you. Let's see if you see the difference.

Sebastian thought otherwise. The note covered one side of paper. The words of it I cannot remember since I tore the sheet in shreds. The paragraphs were redolent with apologies and regrets, suggestions of meetings, none of them capable of obscuring the bottom line of this missive. My husband was leaving me. Susan Pearson Thorpe was being abandoned.

I did not cry as I shredded the paper. There was no outrage, no surprise, not even sorrow, only a blow far duller than shock. I looked out of the window of his study into the garden next door, thinking of the wasp which had buzzed at the window. Katherine and David Allendale were sitting sweetly in their garden. I knew such anger at the sight of them I could scarcely breathe.

Then I went down and found the bottle of gin. One whole bottle, plus one wide straw.

I I

'They will grow, you know,' Matilda snapped. 'They won't stay little and tiny and sweet. You'll have to find homes for them soon before they lose their good looks. If you don't mind. Kat's disgusting enough on her own, but five duplicates? And they will grow,' she repeated. 'They're bloody growing by the second, can't you see?'

She noticed John's hand was shaking slightly, his face turned from the kitchen table where he had begun work early, eyes constantly astray in the direction of the cardboard box from which Kat purred like an engine. There was still an obvious lack of coordination between hand and eye, which persuaded him to write at home rather than work where everyone could see. The mere suggestion of seeking treatment had been spurned. He would not even try to make himself better.

'Please, Mattie, no; I'll be fine, not the first time after all, is it?' The width of the smile translated as a desperate plea for peace. Certainly not the first time he had suffered injury, but she was not sure if this was simply the worst or taken the worst, not even sure of the difference. 'Why don't you tell the police?' she had screamed, incoherent in the face of his placid acceptance. 'Because . . .' he paused in a manner which only increased irritation, '. . . because blows are struck out of desperation, reactions against oppression, victims can't choose. He's a victim, I'm a victim, and I'm never going to put some poor chap in the hands of the police.'

'Why can't policemen also be victims – because of the uniform? What about some of the good ones who've helped, eh? Such as the chap who brought you home?'

'They,' said John, turning his gaze back to the kittens in the box, 'are only the exceptions proving the rule. Authority corrupts, like money, and so do uniforms.'

Matilda gave up, threw her cereal bowl into the kitchen sink, which smelt subtly of Kat's Kit-e-kat, a lingering smell she could never understand since the tins were wrapped in polythene before being placed in further, different-coloured polythene at her behest inside the rubbish bin. Perhaps it was the lingering smell of the only kind of meatstuff which was allowed to cross these portals. Typical of John, she thought bitterly: John in all his bloody-minded inconsistency, being illuminated into such devotion for a carnivore which was as horrible as it was voracious. Matilda had a sudden craving for forbidden fruits, and a vitriolic hatred for animal life.

'They're thinking of giving me an award,' John said casually, nodding towards a letter on the table, 'for outstanding devotion to duty.'

'Thinking of it? After this long, still thinking? After all the cases you've brought to light? Why simply think of it, why not just do it?' She snatched the paper. '. . . You are being considered for . . . Like free gifts with soap powder. Anyway,' she added, throwing down the letter, 'you don't believe in public honours. Only self-motivation counts, you said, any kind of recognition is so random it's bound to be unfair.'

'Quite right,' he said calmly, only the nerve beneath one eye twitching, the rest of him perfectly still. 'But I'd like it all the same.' He flashed on her one of those rare wide smiles which could be so disconcerting, huge and anxious, transfiguring his intense face into boyishness. Reluctantly, hating herself for the first sign of melting, she half smiled back, but he had already turned his head towards the kittens' box, missing her response.

'Here, kitty, kitty, here, here . . .' The largest stumbled out of the box, rolled in a somersault and made for John's outstretched finger on little drunken legs, the stump of tail in the air like an upturned rudder failing to give balance. 'This one swanks like a model.' John said. 'Look at her, I'm going to call her Cleopatra,' gesturing the furry bottom pointing towards the ceiling. The kitten's china-blue eyes were full of purpose, the scrabbling paws stopped for a moment in sudden concentration while a tiny pool of urine appeared on the floor, trickling downhill on the uneven surface. Matilda moaned softly and fled for the door. John smiled wider, tutting at the kitten more in admiration than rebuke, 'Oh you clever girl, or is it boy? Naughty, naughty, naughty little thing. Who's a clever one, then, but you shouldn't do that, you really shouldn't.' The kitten deliberated, looked at him, sat down in the puddle. He clutched the tiny damp body, kissed the nose, his smile wide and his face in a twitch of joy.

As Matilda exited at speed, the Indian man from the takeaway, whom she normally avoided, was entering through his own side door, the method always used when the shop was closed, forcing them to collide sometimes in the narrow hall where his face crinkled the welcoming grin he bestowed without choice. 'Nice day,' he said. As either greeting or goodbye this formula of words seemed to work while Matilda's nostrils twitched: if her nose was not filled with Kat or kittens, she was subject to further assault, spices, burnt oil, the rancid smell of foreign diets issuing from Mr Singh's kitchen as she brushed past him.

'You wouldn't like a kitten, would you?' she asked, venomously eyeing the loaded bags he brought with him, imagining kittens squirming inside, turning her head in distaste for his breath as she spoke, a minuscule gesture which he nevertheless noticed and ignored.

'Pardon?'

'A kitten. Or three.'

'Oh no, missis. We got a Rottweiler.' Looking at her, perplexed by the subject of this rare conversation.

'A what?' From the height of her own five feet eight to his mere five foot, she gazed down in disbelief, wondering if she had heard correctly, seeing some strange picture of a man with a dog twice his weight. 'Where do you keep that?'

'At home, now,' he said, still puzzled by this sudden interest in his life expressed by the upstairs lady who clearly despised him. 'Only we are bringing him here, Rotty, at the weekends. In the back yard,' he pointed to the side entrance, 'through the kitchen, in there.' He grinned. 'You didn't know? He is never barking, this dog, very nice nature, but if we are having many drunks in the shop, we are bringing him out for a walk. To stop ourselves from being beaten up. This happens, you see.' The chuckle which followed was slightly obscene. 'He no biting, this dog, only scary. Big balls,' he explained.

'Oh' said Matilda faintly. 'Oh, really?'

Bugger, Jenny thought, Bugger, I'm stuck. Why don't I act like Monica, definite, I mean, conscience free, quite able at the last minute to get on the blower and leave me with Katherine at the last minute, cancelling lunch with some excuse she simply expects me to believe, even though I know her regime always allows lunch since there is no one to talk to at lunch. Leaving me with Katherine, for reasons I'll tell you, Monica said: can't stop now, an edge of gaiety in the voice which was profoundly suspicious, a carelessness slightly insulting in the whole insinuation. You'll understand, Jenny, I'm sure you will. Meet you tomorrow, Jen darling, promise and don't be cross, please, I can't handle that: tell Kate I'm sorry, see her soon. I'm sorry too, Jenny grumbled, what do you want to happen, me listening to Kate confess, which I promise you, she's on the brink of doing, something profound, like she doesn't like her dresses or any of those boring old restrictions which at least we don't really have, such as being the truly kept woman whose better earning half buys the clothes. But in threading through the traffic from Bloomsbury to Bond Street, she was cheered by the prospect of food if not by the prospect of conversation with Katherine, which was ever so slightly stilted with Monica absent, and amused by the thought of what was Monica up to, so silent in the last fortnight, the only explanation being contagious disease. Once inside the fussy wine bar where the waiters looked welcoming and the tables half empty, her mind half detached to the thought of shopping later for children's clothes, the vision of a sweet dress in a window along with the vaguest suggestion that Katherine might bring her something, all somehow redressing the balance of resentment, so that by the time she saw that cool blonde head arrived before her, she was capable of enthusiasm. Noting in the meantime Katherine's crisp linen blouse with the high

136

Nehru collar, offsetting the oddness of Katherine's more than usual make-up, such an aberration for high summer, such an indication of tiny slips in the usual perfection, the sight cheered Jenny enough to make her smile in relief. She never meant to be unkind. Lunch would be perfectly palatable after all, with a little wine to oil the wheels, a little something to thin the varnish.

But it was Katherine who broke the ice, speaking with jerky conviction. 'Sorry I was so silly at the Holmes's party,' she said, breaking bread with delicate fingers. 'Time of the month, I expect. I do get so het up over little things sometimes, David says. Hope you didn't mind. Where's Monica?'

There was an edge Jenny chose to ignore. Katherine had been practising this speech, determined on self-control.

'Monica can't make it, sends apologies.'

'Oh what a shame,' said Katherine. 'Only I've brought a couple of rugs from the shop, surplus to requirements, actually far too cheap for his usual stock.' She was ferreting round in a bag, finally flourishing two small rugs, recognized by Jenny as Indian numdahs, but exquisite examples of their kind, pinks, greens and blues against a warm but impractical cream background, looking more like embroidered material than covering for a floor. Katherine relaxed slightly as she produced the colours. Colours soothed her. So did the survival of Jenny's scrutiny. That was another thing she had read somewhere in a magazine. About how if you show people you need them, they run away.

'Do they wash?' Jenny asked, knowing they did not, but looking temptation in the face. Numdah rugs were relatively cheap, but never so cheap they would go free and she had a dreadful suspicion they were not surplus to requirements. 'If they don't wash, they won't be much good in our house.' Katherine's face fell, and Jenny was aware of sounding brusque. 'But Katherine,' she said more gently, 'they're far too nice to give away. Couldn't you use them?' She stroked the rough wool; very superior numdah rugs. Katherine was still one step behind, listening to the previous response. 'Put them some place where the children don't go,' she suggested blithely. Jenny was reflecting how in her whole, large house, there was no such place, thinking also of how much she always wanted these offerings of Katherine's, seeing the pastel colours in her bedroom, one each side of the bed, two for herself and none for Monica. Serve Monica right. 'Thank you very much,' was all she said, remembered to establish the fact that she would be paying for lunch, knowing it was cheap at the price, thinking how this, too, had become a ritual, and without further thought, settled to talk of nothing.

If I say something, Katherine thought: if I tell her what happened, she won't believe me. She'll think it was me: she'll stop smiling and stop liking me. I can't. She let Jenny set the pace.

Mary Allendale had chosen to lunch in the same place, or at least the same street. Latterly she had decided to extend the number of treats she allowed herself, increasing the range from expensive teas to the occasional frugal lunch in expensive surroundings. The fact that she approached most of these venues by bicycle somehow made all indulgences perfectly OK, even after careful examination of her bank account had given her several moments of shame. She was actually very much better off than she cared to admit: the discovery of this fact coincided with the need for treats. While she had kept her expenditure constant for the last few years, her salary had bounded and a nest-egg accumulated. Wonderful to contemplate over a solitary lunch. Katherine and I, she thought, how we hated being poor, but I must not grow like my little sister, never quite, if I can help it, such an addict of the opposite, but the money excited her, made her understand a little of the sense of power it could bring, at a time when she was desperately in need of some distraction.

A strange kind of panic had begun to take hold, a creeping paralysis which was affecting all her efforts to be useful. Those who worked with her, seeing a person always determined to maintain control, analysed the condition as loneliness, a sense of isolation which had increased ever since she had lost Katherine. Didn't have anyone else, poor soul: probably wanted a baby at her age, but Mary would have defied any such accurate guesses as rubbish; stated that all she needed was good food and fresh air. And maybe, just maybe, the reassurance of a lover. Claud was under her skin more than she had ever known, and Claud had disappeared. She pretended not to mind, but she did mind, very much, moving about in a state of hurting which was unbelievably acute, taking to Bond Street for today's cure. Bond Street always brought about some kind of recovery because the sheer extravagance of the place made her so furious. As well as self-indulgently jealous.

Modus Shoes, Fenwicks Designer Range, New Bond Street silversmiths, galleries replete with Old Master paintings entirely free of price indications; she paused before each display without really looking at the goods, only considering the monumental waste implicit in all these things. She also looked with the eye of a Robin Hood. Perhaps Bond Street was a place for collecting tins; maybe she could persuade these effete establishments to canvass their customers for charity. No, they wouldn't do that, nothing so obvious, but how beautiful it was. Small windows, perfectly dressed, a series of exquisite still-lifes. This was the sort of place where Katherine often came in her spare afternoons. She felt a stab of envy for Katherine's security and a surge of grief in the realization that her sister had not telephoned in ages. Mary could see why that wayward child would like to linger here. Looking at silver, gold, silk and paintings was like looking at stars.

Mary was standing enthralled, admiring a window rich with Persian carpets, when she spotted him across the street. The dark background of the display made the window a perfect mirror, his pale-blond head catching her eye as he sauntered past on the opposite pavement, pausing himself in front of a similar display, obscured for a minute by a car in the narrow road, revealed again in all his glory, Claud, the lover of Saturday afternoons or some early evening in the week, a regular tryst in her flat, one of Katherine's souvenirs, the last of the many partners. Mary's lover, still resorting to the same flat, Mary's flat, same place for the same exercise as he had done for years, but not for the last two weeks, so the shock of seeing him was so palpable Mary began to tremble. Holidays, she had been told: no alibi from family and wife in the South of France; see you when I get back, but here, untanned, large as life unless this still handsome vision was a ghost, the same gambling man. Mary kept her eyes fixed on the window until he passed, then looked after him, recognizing the contours of his shoulders, the all too substantial flesh, and in confirming her own identification, confirmed the fact of his lies. A man sauntering through a familiar route, rubbing more salt into her own wounds with each step.

Mary shook herself, moved down the pavement, walked into Modus Shoes and purchased one pair of frivolous red sandals she was most unlikely to wear, paying by credit card and wanting nothing more than to sit for a minute, rationalize, put away that great gulp of emotion which afflicted her. Don't lie to me, she had said: I am not my sister: I know my limitations, but don't lie to me. I'm not asking anything but that. When the shoes were brought back to her in brilliant green paper the colour of envy, she accepted them dumbly, and moved towards lunch. Food was her own first aid for hurt.

Anywhere would suffice although sheer hunger had faded, anything accompanied by a drink to restore the equilibrium of the day. The wine bar she had earmarked earlier was twenty yards north: she walked briskly in the same direction he had taken, scolding herself, dazzled by the sunshine, slightly restored. Then sidled between the tables, blinded by the contrast of the half-dark interior, and with eyes still refocusing, saw Katherine at the back of the room. Outstanding little sister who had lain with the man in the street who never failed to ask after her with such carefully disguised feeling, the same girl in luminous white blouse, the eyes surrounded by kohl, the hair swept back off the forehead like a horse's mane, her long hands flicking through a magazine and the legs below the short skirt elegantly, but tightly crossed. An attitude of nervous waiting, tense body below over made-up face, was all Mary comprehended as she turned on her heel and moved deftly back to the door before her sister could see her. Katherine just had to be waiting for Claud, early as usual for every appointment, he just as consistently late. From beyond the grave, the huge good fortune of marriage, Katherine was reclaiming her territory. The presence of them both in the same twenty yards had no other explanation, nor did his lies. After all, it was they who were at home in this kind of world, familiar with this incessant trade in luxuries, while it was Mary who was an interloper: who felt as if her face had been held, and carefully scraped with sandpaper.

'Of course,' Jenny said, returning from the loo, pointing to the magazine Katherine had been showing to her and still held, 'of course I see what you mean. That's the kind of conservatory David builds, like he's going to do for Monica? No good for us, though. We need a loft extension, something to use as a playroom for the kids,' she added wistfully. 'So we can keep the place tidier.' Katherine beamed. 'Oh David'll do that for you,' she said. 'He knows all about those because he's just done some plans for his.'
    Not ours, Jenny noticed; His. She stirred uncomfortably. 'Going to make it into a flat,' Katherine explained. 'For what?' Jenny asked, anxious to keep the conversation neutral. 'For Granny, I hope. She's sweet, David's mother.' Jenny laughed, gathering up her rugs. 'There's probably room up there for both your mothers.' Katherine's face assumed that bleak look Jenny recognized from the ladies' lavatory at the Kenwood party, the look which presaged self-revelation and imminent need.
    'As a matter of fact,' she began with a deep breath, her voice wobbling ominously.
    'Goodness!' Jenny said. 'Look at the time. I really must fly.'

'I should go back to work,' Monica murmured, the reluctance poorly concealed in the businesslike words. 'But this has been lovely, delicious, in fact. Excellent, for a man.' The attempt at teasing was out of place, Monica out of her depth. David was equally delectable, she found, her body lazy in the summer light of the sunny Allendale kitchen, and all of her warm towards him. So lacking in self-pity he was for such an awkward life, revealed piecemeal in two hours of hints and stories indicative less of the desire for attention than the desire to amuse, but all the same there were telling jokes about a terrible childhood, a history which turned him into something courageous. He had made all this, he explained, together with one small fortune, with his own bare hands, his own inventive genius and no assistance from his peers, no nepotism, no silver spoon; quite the opposite. And not about to let any of it go, she imagined, seeing in all his words a fierce possessiveness. But his marriage, dear God, his marriage: he was treating the fiasco of that, all Katherine's understated irresponsibility, with the nobility of a saint, mentioned difficulties and impossible behaviour without elaborating. 'I'm so pleased you're all friends,' David had said, referring to herself, Katherine and Jenny, but Monica herself was no longer so sure about that, not in Katherine's case at least, now she had some idea of what he had to tolerate. Oh, poor, brave man. Monica knew no more powerful aphrodisiacs than pity or wine and she was well supplied with both.

'Don't go yet, please,' David said. He came and stood at the back of her chair, touched her lightly on the shoulder, inviting no response. She had half expected the touch, slightly disappointed to find anything of the kind so absent from the other two meetings, her conscience dying now. 'Katherine won't be back before five,' he added inconsequentially. 'Come and see my studio.'

She walked upstairs to the studio as if this was no more than the guided tour she had been given on other, public visits to this house, content to be led, making remarks about how beautiful it was while admiring his back and pretending herself as serene as these surroundings, never stopping to pause or examine as she would had she been that kind of tourist. His unlocking of the door of his studio puzzled her since she could not see why it should be locked, but she forgot to ask for reasons, dazed by the colours of the room, light from both windows dimmed by the blinds making the whole interior richer, like landscapes seen through tinted sunglasses, more luxurious than anyone could ever require for the discipline of work.

'We could take a post-prandial here,' David suggested. Monica sat obediently on one of the chesterfields, watching him open doors in the small kitchenette at the far end, thought of the squealing of children, the total lack of privacy of her own house, sighed with pleasure. 'I think,' she said, 'I would like to live here. Just in this little bit. I wish I could work at home and be left alone . . .' aware she was gabbling slightly, a sudden sweat of nerves like blood to the head, the waist of her skirt tight, her hands sticky as she pushed back her hair, acutely conscious, as she was for every minute with him, of her own appearance, pulling down her skirt, crossing her legs, adjusting her low-necked cerise blouse where the top button seemed to have come undone of its own volition, aware of being watched in her own self-betrayal, flattered by his appreciation, but more by his confidences and the sheer physical power of a large, dark man. Her own was small and fair, streamlined Colin whom she saw in her mind's eye fluttering among the women at parties like a butterfly, all golden, and oh what was she doing here, the faithful wife taking revenge, wallowing in it. David sat next to her, his weight as heavy as her own wanting, so when he kissed her, she could not resist, did not even object as the next kiss drew the wine-laden breath out of her mouth and his fingers slid beneath the buttons of the blouse. 'Katherine,' she muttered, 'what about Katherine?' her mind full of questions and late starting guilt. 'Out,' he murmured back. 'Out for hours, I told you. Plenty of time. Darling Monica, how strong, how lovely you are.' They were sliding from the chesterfield towards the thick carpet of the floor, and her cerise blouse began to slip down from one shoulder. He cradled her head in one arm, very tenderly, pushed back the material and freed one large breast from the confines of a lacy brassière, bent and took the nipple into his mouth. One hand of hers fluttered the merest protest, then came to rest on the back of his head, fingers lost in the thickness of soft hair, pulling him towards her. The pupils of his eyes were as black as ink. 'Plenty of time,' he murmured, 'plenty of time.' Somewhere from another corner of the room, a radio was playing softly, some innocent concerto. Monica heard snatched, harmonic sound between her own breathing and the sensation of his tongue.

Katherine knew she would have to go home. The lingering bruises around her neck and eyes had lost the power to hurt, but somehow added to the lassitude of heat already made worse by her one glass of wine to Jenny's three. She peered at herself in the mirror of Selfridges ladies' conveniences, hating the quantity of eye make-up the psychedelic yellow of her eyelids made so necessary. She could only remember blows to one eye from the muggers, but the emergence of two small sets of bruises had seemed somehow just while granting a kind of symmetry to an attack which she knew now was entirely her own fault. Retiring to hidden corners like this became more frequent as the days went on, her steps taking her in the direction of the nearest privacy whenever she saw dark faces in the street, the sight of them gripping her with waking nightmares and a trembling she could not control. 'You brought it all on yourself,' David had said, sadly. 'You must learn to be responsible, but we won't tell anyone. You know what? They'd laugh at you, darling, laugh themselves sick. Go out and prove you've grown up. Be normal.' She was trying to be what she perceived as normal, the illusion slipping, every action one of will.

The crowds had lost their power to embrace. Go home, go home, then. There was no energy whatever today for the gym and absolutely no money in her purse. If only Jenny had offered her five pounds for the rugs, she might have stayed out longer, but it had not been offered and she could not have asked, not even to relieve the penury which was her daily affliction. All these ploys to get money: changing the dresses David bought, bargaining for lunches with pieces of material, cheating the customer who would never notice, combing the shops for bargains when sent out on one of David's errands, whilst he, with systematic thoroughness, searched her pockets, her handbags, found every other little cache in the house where she hid her pathetic savings, all except for Jeanetta's room where there were several one-pound coins remaining secreted in an old rattle. She never discovered him in any of the searches, never realized for a long time what he did, and because she was still not entirely sure, never challenged the practice any more than she could have challenged the constant changing of the rooms, the alterations in the kitchen and bathroom which so disorientated her, or the arbitrary removal of disliked garments from her wardrobe which she might so well have thrown away herself. All for your own good, darling: I must have order in this house. Perhaps he never did any of these things: when she pictured herself explaining she could see how ridiculous it was.

Madness beckoned slowly, but there was still, and always, her home, full of colour and comfort. Outside there was darkness, black faces, screaming hatred. Running down a street, half naked: that had shown what really lay beyond her own front door.

But in the panic which assailed her now, the fear of David and the love for him which dominated even the greater dread of the dark outside, she could still feel a moment of triumph, force herself to the optimism which was her second nature, her survival line. She had been mad and bad, but now she was good, he said; forgiven, he said, so that after weeks of begging, she had in her possession a key to the front door, and although the concession (so unexpected after all the knocking to gain entry) had been surprising, she regarded it as a hopeful gift. Everything was going to be all right. From now on.

All the locks worked in silence: he could not bear to have around him anything which did not work with immaculate efficiency, responsive to the first instruction. The house was built for discretion with the silence of a nunnery, thick carpets delicious on naked feet. Once inside, Katherine wanted to see him, establish her presence in case she was needed and also show her ability with the new key, hesitated. There was no sound: the kitchen bore untidy traces of luncheon which did not worry her, showed he had left her a task, and she breathed a sigh of relief that the house should smell so of absence. Then she thought of the money hidden in Jeanetta's room, the possible pleasure of tea in a café, walked quietly upstairs.

The door of the studio was slightly ajar as she approached in bare feet, the Italian shoes kicked to one side at the foot of the stairs in the belief she would have ample time to put them away. Katherine paused at the door, arrested by the sound and curiosity to find it unsecured, listened intently to the slight scrabblings she could hear from the landing, unobscured by the tinkle of the radio, sounds like small animals, inhuman noises. Pushing the door open two more inches, she saw a flash of bright colour at the other end of the room, a brilliant cerise cloth draped over the sofa, and on the floor, pale and glowing in the minimal light, two bodies intertwined. Her eyes focused on the cerise, Monica's favourite colour, Monica unrecognizable on the floor, her head obscured by David's own, the sounds emanating from her face while her hands were clutching at his buttocks which rose and fell rhythmically. Katherine could smell a suggestion of perspiration, Monica's perfume sneaking towards her, a slight scent of brandy drawn by the draught from the window, stopped herself walking forwards. Then David raised his head, met and recognized the eyes at the door in one blank challenge, held her gaze for a second. The figure below him, large bosom shuddering, began to moan softly. He ignored the white face of his wife, bent over the rosy skin pinned by his weight, moving with renewed energy. To the sound of louder cries of pleasure, soft but deafening in the silence, Katherine fled downstairs, picked up her shoes and ran out of the house, remembering to close the door quietly behind her. There was an instinct to spit, run, fly as fast as she could. Back to Mary, to anyone; the thought checked by the blackness of the sky, the thought of treacherous Jenny, who would know of all this, the total lack of friends. How could Monica, how could she? Laughing at her, lunching with her, all of them . . . The sky was dark, thunder looming.

Mrs Harrison was coming up the street, flanked by Jeanetta and Samantha. She was chatting to them in the same way she chatted to adults, telling them all the gossip, grumbling, asking their opinions on the state of the world regardless of whether they listened or not. 'Well I don't know what to make of all this,' she was telling Jeanetta, who listened with rapt attention, quite addicted to the sound of any voice. 'I don't know at all. Mr Pearson Thorpe not coming home although Mrs Pearson Thorpe pretends he does, but we know better, don't we, my pet?' Jeanetta nodded, eyes scanning the street. 'Are you talking 'bout Mummy?' Samantha asked, disinterested, taking in the mention of her own surname among the chatter. 'No, sweetheart, I'm not; I'm talking about someone entirely different, and really I should stop talking to myself, little things like you have big ears. Only,' she continued, addressing herself to

Jeanetta, favourite of all charges, '. . . I can't get my old man to listen, see? He only says, mind your own business, you big fat busybody, nothing makes any difference as long as we're paid.'

'Big fat, biddybody,' Jeanetta giggled, suddenly helpless with mirth. Jeremy was in a pushchair brandished in front of Mrs Harrison, pushed at erratic speed. 'Never knew a child have a trolley quite as posh as this,' Mrs Harrison remarked. 'Quite a Little Lord Fauntleroy, aren't you?' He twisted round and smiled at her, his hearing acute, the smile interrupted by a spasm of sneezing. 'Sharp little bugger as well, your brother,' she continued under her breath. 'And I'll bet I know who's favourite in your house. And it isn't you, darling, is it? But then again, all the women round here daft as brushes if you ask me. Save myself, of course.' She laughed. 'Wait a minute, Jetty my girl, there's your mum, early, isn't she? Only four o'clock. Got to get in before it rains.'

Jeanetta broke from the posse of the pram and ran forwards up the pavement, shrieking loudly, 'It's Mummy, Mummy, it's Mummy, Mummy, Mummy.' 'So it bloody is,' Mrs Harrison addressed Samantha, who had fallen behind but now drew level. 'And look whose mummy looks like death warmed up. Bet the silly cow's locked herself out again. Eh, isn't she like her daughter?' Raising her voice to a yell as they drew nearer, Jeanetta scampering ahead to jump at Mummy like a puppy, Mrs Harrison shouted in a sudden effluxion of friendliness, 'You want to come in for a cuppa tea, Mrs Allendale? Only you're early.'

Katherine had been standing on the step, completely indecisive, holding on to the railings, breathing deeply. She had been planning which way to run but found she could not move, wondered if she could bear to go back into the house, grab the few pounds from Jeanetta's rattle, maybe even find some clothes, then realized, in her haste, she had left the key on the kitchen table along with her handbag, and a sense of profound helplessness crashed like a wave around her head. She blinked, finding the sound of the road deafening. Mrs Harrison thought her neighbour a dreamer, squinting at dark cloud as if she was afraid of it: Katherine was temporarily blind, mesmerized by the vision of the key she had left behind, the knowledge of how foolish she was. Then Jeanetta cannoned into her and she knew there was more than one reason not to leave the house after all. She gripped the child by the shoulders, then tried to lift her, but the fat body squirmed, tickles, Mummy, tickles, and the weight was too much. Rare affection inspiring her, showing off, Jeanetta buried her head into Mummy's waist, was embraced with a fierce gesture she did not understand, dragged her back towards the next house. Greeting Mummy was not quite the same prospect as going home. She liked the one but not the other. Together they moved back down the road.

'You'll never guess, Mrs Harrison,' Katherine said with a gaiety which seemed laboured to her own ears, her words emerging with desperate slowness. 'I've forgotten the key.'

Monica was drowsy but she knew he had moved away. Not in any way she could have called perfunctory, but so soon after she felt immediately uncomfortable. She must have slept for a matter of seconds: the waking was ominous. His naked figure was framed against the window, looking down into the street. She sat up so suddenly her head swam. There was a distant sound of yelling from the road outside, very distant.

'What is it? Oh God, not Katherine . . . She hasn't come in, has she? Oh God . . .'

He moved back beside her, cradled her in his arms, nuzzled the back of her neck which was damp with sweat. 'Oh no, no, no. We'd better move though, I'm afraid. But she couldn't have come in here.' Monica looked across the room to the door. He followed the movement of her eyes.

'Don't worry,' he whispered. 'The door was locked, all the time.'

12

'Get off, you bastard. Why don't you fuck off? Go, shoo. Piss off. Oh, there you are. Begging your pardon, Mrs Allendale, bugger off now, go on.'

Commotion, shouting, as Mrs Harrison's posse reached the door of the Pearson Thorpe household, an explosion from the handsome entrance into the street with old man Harrison patently relieved to see them, while flapping before him a thin, dark-featured man, the street vagrant, who was stumbling down the steps, trying to run, uncoordinated by shock. Mr Harrison was framed by the stucco white of the house, the hallway a black hole behind him, in which Mark stood indecisive.

'I seen you before, I seen you. I seen him going down the street.' He was pointing at the man, who stared back wildly, beginning to mumble.

'Go on, dirty bastard, get on out of it,' Mr Harrison was shouting.

'Not really dirty,' observed Jeanetta, breaking ranks from the startled group which surrounded Mrs Harrison. 'He isn't really dirty. Not all over.' She grinned at the man, who regarded the crowd before him in panic. He stepped sideways, then back, looked up and down the street and pushed past Samantha, who screamed. On the outside of the huddle, Katherine hung back with Jeremy in the pushchair. The thin man crashed towards them both, stumbled over the pushchair, thrust his hands down the sides in an attempt to correct his balance, looked round once more, fixed Katherine with a glance of wild despair and ran on. They all rushed towards the boy, then turned in unison to watch the fugitive scampering up the street on spiky legs in dirty khaki trousers, his sweater torn at the back.

'Well,' said Mrs Harrison. 'Well, I never.'

'I seen him, I seen him,' Mark sang, enchanted with his recognition. 'I seen him the other night. He won't talk.'

'Oh do be quiet. Don't make such a fuss. We all seen him.' Mrs Harrison was the first to recover. 'What the bloody hell . . .?' turning to Harrison, her whole body one intimidating question mark, then remembering the group behind. 'Oh come on in, Mrs Allendale, let's put the kettle on. What a fuss, I ask you.' She faced her husband, full of accusation. 'You ask someone else in for tea as well, did you, you daft git you?'

'No,' Harrison mumbled. 'Cleaning the step, I was. Went for some water downstairs, found him in the hallway. Said he was looking for a job. My eye.'

'Sod it,' said Mrs Harrison, only slightly mollified. 'Didn't get further than the hallway, did he?'

'Not as I know,' Harrison said carefully. 'I wasn't long gone. Oh do come in, will you? Afternoon, Mrs Allendale. You're early.'

Katherine hesitated on the step, looking back down the road, haunted by the brown and desperate eyes of the running, stumbling man whom she, too, had seen before. As they went downstairs inside the house towards the basement quarters, respect for Katherine not requiring the china cups of the drawing room or even her mistress's kitchen, Mrs Harrison chattered over her shoulder explanations half lost in the clatter of footsteps on the stairs. Each of them moved at a different pace. 'It's them beggars, see? Drunks,' she hissed, as if the word were too rude to repeat in front of the children. 'Down and outs. Might have had good jobs once but they take to drink, see, hard stuff. Then their families chuck them out, no wonder, and where do they go? Nowhere. You read about them in the paper and we always have one or two. Disgusting.'

'Poor, poor man,' said Katherine, utterly distracted by the fear on the face of the refugee. There was a certain hostile and pathetic face to those deemed homeless; she had seen it before, felt its expression. The institutions of her past had given her close acquaintance with that look, gummed to the teeth of child or adult, almost ferocious. Mrs Harrison did not want to see the desperation of it.

'Poor nothing. They just don't want to work.'

'They can't work. He won't know where to go.'

'Looked like a criminal to me. Probably sacked for thieving.'

Katherine did not want to persist. On sight of the vagrant, she simply wanted to go back indoors. He was too poignant for words, but temporarily forgotten in the clutter of the basement where she had only been twice before, rare indulgences on the part of these hosts who were proud and jealous of their domain. She gazed wistfully at the cooking range, a small and battered contraption, with the shelf above it decorated with lurid jugs from holiday resorts, all announcing their origin in black letters; the windows festooned with plants, making the whole effect even darker. In the comfort of this cave, tea was produced from a simmering pot, stewed black and brackish, laced with sugar before any preference was suggested. 'He likes it so the spoon stands up by itself,' Mrs Harrison chuckled, mistress in her own kitchen. Mark had disappeared upstairs, Jeanetta out to the garden. Samantha stayed, clutching a furry elephant of hideous colour, gazing at the neighbour as if she was a freak. The old Labrador circled Jeremy, who sneezed continuously.

'Pity he's allergic to that dog,' Mrs Harrison remarked cheerfully. 'He loves it so. More tea?'

'Please.'

Silence fell on the gathering while Mr Harrison took to a chair, deciding like his wife that undue respect was not required for this particular visitor, not if she shopped in Church Street market. It was a comfortable silence but one Mrs Harrison was determined to punctuate. Her invitation indoors was purposeful since she wanted two things. First, to establish whether Katherine was better informed than herself on the subject of Mr Pearson Thorpe's defection, and second, dependent on the first, to impart to her neighbour some concern for the defector's wife. Harrison had pieced information together from the torn-up letter the master had left, but anyway, Mrs H had guessed the imminence of the event for some time. Mrs Pearson never took any notice of him, see?

Never took any notice of anyone but herself. Crossing her mind as she spoke, inspired by Katherine's look of vacancy, was the swifter thought that this girl neither knew nor cared, was only shaking herself into politeness with difficulty. Mrs Harrison could see she was going to have to be straightforward, a technique she loathed. Most subjects when spoken of to any person of employer status, were approached by a crablike route.

'Listen, Mrs A, we're a bit worried, Harrison and me. Oh, go and play Samantha, take Heffelump in the garden . . . Well, as I said, worried, we are. About Mrs Pearson. We think her hubby's left her for some reason or other, and well . . . well not to put too fine a point on it, she's been taking to the bottle.'

'Oh no,' said Katherine. 'You can't be right, she can't have done. She came to my gym last week, she was absolutely fine . . .'

'Yes,' said Mrs Harrison patiently. 'That might be so, but that was last week, not this.'

Katherine's brilliant smile flashed radiant. 'But he's such a nice man. I'm sure he hasn't really gone anywhere, she would have said. What would she do?'

'Drink,' said Harrison darkly from the depths of his chair. 'Drink and be lonely. Nothing different.'

'Shut up, Eric, just shut up.'

'He'll come back, you'll see,' said Katherine firmly. 'He's only away for a few days: he'll be back and everything'll be all right again, you'll see.' She suddenly could not bear the tenor of the conversation.

'And we must go. Thanks for the tea.' Embarrassment showed in a frown of disapproval, her leave-taking a rude dismissal. She watched herself from a great distance, repeating the lessons learned at lunchtime, operating a verbal barrier against any intimacy or unwelcome knowledge, none of which she could face. Reflected back from the old range she could see the challenge in David's eyes, and shutting out that vision, she could see the darker eyes of the desperate little vagrant crashing into the pushchair. Saw more closely than anything else, Susan Pearson Thorpe, whom she had always tried to befriend, stumbling round the gym like a giant bluebottle. There was a trio of them dancing, beggarman, deserted wife, herself in danger of the same, all of it so wretched it seemed better to blank her mind against any further information. Jeanetta's face appeared from the door to the garden, hopeful of reprieve, the forehead creasing into a cry when she saw the shufflings of departure with all the vibrations of awkwardness. Mrs Harrison was deeply hurt and offended. Katherine had refused her trust and was ticking her off. She knocked around teacups with a deafening noise.

'Thanks for that, it was really lovely.' Repeated echoes from Katherine of a polite child, very chilly.

''S all right,' answered Mrs Harrison, stiff with resentment. 'Perfectly all right, y're welcome.' They watched her leave.

'Snob,' muttered Mrs Harrison, 'stuck-up tart.' 'No, love, no,' he protested.

'Yes she is. Stuck-up tart.'

Better to pretend she had imagined everything, put all this in the same bag as childhood memories: scenes of abandonment, two illustrations in twenty minutes, dogging her steps with nightmares as she dragged up the street to her own door, ringing the bell, nothing worse than being left, go home, cling to it: there is nothing outside. Jeremy back in the pushchair, Jeanetta walking behind: David at the door, urbane in glorious welcome. 'Hallo, darling, you look wonderful. Did you forget the key?'

He kissed her lightly, plucked Jeremy out of the pushchair and turned indoors, holding out the other hand to Jeanetta. When she ignored it, he placed his arm round the shoulders of his wife and drew her in. He smelt sharply of the shower, expensive soap, conspicuous cleanliness: there was about him the aura of physical power which had drawn her always, pleasure to see her so obvious, along with concern. 'What's the matter, darling? You look tired?'

'Nothing,' she answered, smiling back, swallowing hard. 'Nothing at all.'

Monica found the sanctuary of home, the grey nanny and the hyperactive children in the middle of a row, everything the same as usual. All the way back in the tube, she had been conscious of the smell of sex, that pungent odour of sweat mixed with gluey scent of the male, clinging to her, the sweet taste of brandy still in her mouth. Drew herself to herself in the crush, aware of dampness showing beneath the armpits of the cerise blouse, a stickiness between the thighs, imagining that the guilt of her assignation was stamped on her forehead, visible to all who could see the corner of an eye. But no one pointed a finger and the children did not react: the nanny's sullen resentment was consistent; nothing had altered save the pace of her own heartbeat. Monica breathed in and out the same way as ever; adultery was easy after all. She pushed all her clothes in the laundry box and stood beneath the shower, glowing with triumph, bursting to tell. She would have to tell: she would absolutely have to tell: there was no discretion about her. Besides the little matter of the invitation in today's post. David's fortieth birthday party. Distant yes, but what was distant now would soon be soon. Throughout the fury of thoughts, she kept catching herself smiling.

The vagrant had nowhere to go and nowhere he wanted to go. His knowledge of the geography of even this part of London was fairly scant, the ignorance his downfall. Weeks since, he had been swept up like municipal rubbish, moved on when his bedding-place in the West End, down by Charing Cross, had turned overnight into a quagmire of a building site. Seeking its familiarity, he had blundered back one night, hit his head on a piece of scaffold, spied none of his quarrelsome fellows, but a security man with a dog, both of them barking. So he had walked away from the restaurants and the copious cardboard boxes and the downtown hostels he had always despised. But the effort was a dislocation with all known memories, the alteration in habits merely a shift but in practice a monumental change. This was not home: the quotient of pity so much less in these richer, quieter streets.

So. His activities had not always been honest and honesty had become irrelevant: he loved pretty things to the extent that he was often tempted to take them, but somehow forgiveness was forthcoming, although he feared the police and most others he encountered. Taking things was not natural, but inevitable to bargain for the billet at the end of the road where one surly acquaintance slept by day in order to wander by night; from ten in the evening the vagrant man took over the bed. The other occupant occasionally shared dyspeptic food gleaned from a restaurant he would not reveal in return for whatever the other had brought. Only these days the vagrant could not always find his way back to the billet, the sense of direction, like his command of speech, disintegrating.

The sun warmed his stomach as he sat in the park and watched the women, leering without any real intent, beyond all that, none of it even real any more. But the fair woman had been nice, baby nice. The thought of the little child in the pushchair made his palms sweat. Dimly he realized that he had been very nimble that afternoon, might never be as lucky again, especially his hands, but stepping inside that house had been suicidal. Thank God for the child in the carriage. He raised one grubby wrist and slapped at it with the other hand. Naughty. Hungry.

Katherine was preparing a meal. She had cooked salt beef at the weekend, a long slow broiling left to cool, for consumption now with warm potato salad. Mayonnaise to be blended, chives taken from a corner of the rose garden to be chopped, new Jersey potatoes little bigger than marbles, boiling merrily. Before all this there would be a delicate cocktail, pink grape-fruit segments combined with prawns and a dash of single cream, the remainder of the cream, minimal amounts to be used thereafter for strawberries, frozen but luscious. Concen-trating hard to block thoughts, she had checked the supplies of high-baked water biscuits and cheese, for David, not herself, but found supplies low. He must have eaten at lunch, in quantity, and she did not want to contemplate that.

Jeanetta was dressed for bed but claiming hunger which her mother conceded as genuine. Katherine set a place at the table – oh let her eat after such a tiring day – and besides, even with all the ineptitude of her clumsy maternal instinct, Katherine wanted her daughter to stay where she was, wanted with her in this kitchen something of her own. David's mood had been so

155

benign he would make an exception to the usual impatience and Jeanetta seemed disposed to be good. Not my child, he had said so often: not mine; ugly and ungainly . . . Look at her. And while Katherine had been reassured by Mary saying nonsense, comforted by infinitesimal David-like resemblances she imagined she had seen, she was, in her very heart of hearts, wretchedly unsure. There had been Claud, and Claud had been very persistent; she could never say no to Claud: confrontation made her sick. But latterly David's stabbing remarks on the subject had eased a little, his kindness following the Americans' party had been prevalent and when he was gentle, she was optimistic. She remembered that and deliberately tidied away all the images of the afternoon, bent over the food with deft but nervous fingers translating to the ingredients her own aesthetic passion for the finished result. Everything was going to be all right provided she kept control. Jeanetta played on the floor, singing broken rhymes to a large doll which was placed in Jeremy's pushchair like a throne. Katherine could not guess where the doll had come from since neither she nor David had provided it.

'Mummy, Mummy, look!'

'What darling?' She could not look immediately since the state of the mayonnaise was crucial. She kept her eyes fixed for the next few seconds, then looked. Jeanetta had been holding aloft a necklace and then in the face of her mother's indifference, rammed it over the head of the doll which had belonged to a Harrison child, a battered doll with an old-fashioned face, blue eyes and thin blonde hair. The necklace hung across one of the eyes, heavy gold links, every third link decorated with sparkle in an understated brilliance which twinkled for the eye rather than blinded. A non-garish, beautiful necklace.

Katherine dropped her spoon and went to look. 'Mine,' said Jeanetta, trying to snatch the gold out of her mother's hands. 'Mine, I found it.'

'Where?'

'In Jeremy's chair. Down the side.'

'Did you put it there?'

'Course not. Why?'

156

The necklace shone heavily in the palm of her hand and she held the heaviness of it to the light. As a voyeur of pretty things, devotee of jewellers' windows, her instinct had her looking immediately for the hallmarks, surmising how the diamonds, in all their careful lack of ostentation, were perfectly real. 'Where?' she repeated to Jeanetta 'Where?'

'Pushychair,' Jeanetta bellowed. 'I said.'

Katherine sank to the floor beside her daughter. 'Did you take it?'

'No, no, no.' She was puzzled, affected by the rising note of alarm in her mother's voice. 'Don't really like it, much,' she offered by way of further proof. Katherine panicked, some great tide of guilt rising up in her throat, still holding the thing in fingers which burned. Worse than all the toys Jeanetta had 'found', far worse.

'We'd better hide it,' she said. 'Don't tell Daddy . . .'

'Don't tell Daddy what?'

She jumped at the sound of his voice from behind her neck, began to stuff the necklace into the pocket of her slacks, but he held her wrist gently, withdrew the gold, examining it carefully.

'I think,' he said, 'our esteemed neighbour, Mrs Susan Pearson Thorpe, is going to miss this. In due course. She wore it, remember, last time she was here. Nice little bauble.'

'It was in the pushchair,' Katherine gabbled, 'Jeremy's chair. Down the side, I think, Jeanetta just found it. Someone must have put it there.'

'Yes, I expect someone did.' David looked at her sorrowfully. 'Oh, darling, what shall I do with you both? Like mother, like daughter.' He had heard, recited by them all, the outline narrative of the vagrant intruder, also heard Katherine's rendition of Mrs Harrison's story of the Pearson departure, and the wife's affection for the solace of alcohol, absorbed all this information giving licence for exaggeration, but only seemed to remember Katherine going into the house for tea.

'Don't be silly, saying someone must have put it there. Either you, or this little monster took it. You've both been in the house with Susan Pearson out. Perfectly obvious to me.

157

First time you've been right inside there for a fortnight and that has to be the day a necklace walks out with you.'

'But I only went into the basement . . .'

'Not a single trip to the loo? Nothing of the kind?'

'I don't remember,' she said, faltering. Memory was something she could never trust. She did not know, could not remember any more what she had done.

'Probably not, darling. You can't help it, can you? Or Jeanetta can't, not fussy about whose dolls or whose pyjamas. What do you want me to do, call the police? Or take this round next door without delay and see who'll believe you there?'

There was silence. Katherine remembered the icy displeasure of her departure, Mrs Harrison's look of acute disappointment. David placed the necklace on the chopping board where it glittered with subdued richness against the vivid green of the chives. 'Is she . . .' he nodded in Jeanetta's direction, '. . . staying up?'

'She hasn't eaten.'

After all the accusations against him which had passed through her mind Katherine was now completely defensive, almost whining. 'OK,' he sighed. 'Shall I finish this?' He chopped the chives with the efficiency of a chef, the knife flashing next to the golden links. As an afterthought, he placed the necklace in his own pocket with an absent gesture, and continued chopping. Katherine drained the potatoes, added a dash of cream and a smaller dash of alcohol to the prawns. Jeanetta hauled herself up to the table, adjusted her cushions and waited in mulish silence.

'I think it will be better if the children don't go next door any more,' David said, stirring mayonnaise and chives into the potatoes. 'Not after this. And not if the mistress of the house is on the bottle, living without a man. Anyway, the dog makes Jeremy sneeze.'

'But he loves it so,' Katherine protested, echoing Mrs Harrison.

'That has nothing to do with anything.'

She was defeated: her hands were slowing to a standstill over the food, watching him do everything so much faster than herself. The hunger which had dogged her day through a half-eaten lunch when she had been trying all the time to speak, was sunk to a hollow ache. Guilt about Jeanetta, confusion and guilt about everything else, filled her bones.

'Who'll look after them, then?' she managed to question through the lump in her throat and rising anger which she knew she was not going to be able to express.

'You for Jeanetta, me for Jeremy. Very democratic. Oh and nursery school. All fixed. I'll tell Susan Pearson tomorrow, after they come home. Mr Isaacs phoned, by the way.'

'Who?' Katherine's reactions had reached an all-time low as they sat at the table. A small portion of prawns sat on Jeanetta's Peter Rabbit plate accompanied by brown bread and butter. She looked unconvinced by the spectacle.

'Mr Isaacs. Katherine, are you listening? He phoned about certain things missing from the shop, darling. Rugs, pieces of fabric, you know, a few things like that.' David spoke in the same even tone, no accusation whatever. 'Don't worry, darling. We won't talk about it now. I managed to calm him down so he won't go rushing to the police, but he doesn't want you back. So everything's worked out very nicely, after a fashion. I never liked you at work anyway: I like you here. Do eat, darling: you've been getting rather thin and these are quite delicious.'

Jeanetta collected the food on to her spoon, put it all into her mouth and chewed slowly until the bitter taste of grapefruit hit the back of her throat. David was on her left, Mummy opposite. She leant over the plate and without much delicacy, inclining slightly towards her father, let the whole mixture drop back out of her mouth and on to Peter Rabbit. Occasional fragments of pink prawn and yellow grapefruit hit the cloth placed carefully to protect the table. 'Yuk,' said Jeanetta, 'yukkie, yukkie, yukkie.'

'Eat it, Jeanetta,' David ordered. 'Just eat. Good for you.'

'She doesn't like this sort of food, I shouldn't have . . . I never know what to give her,' Katherine watched, words trailing away. '. . . Eat the bread, darling.'

'No, eat the grapefruit,' David repeated. Jeanetta's blue eyes went from one to the other, looking for support, finding none. Slowly she picked up two fragments of prawn, then put her fingers into the plate, pushed three segments of fruit into her mouth. Katherine relaxed a fraction and began to eat her own. Then Jeanetta spat the new mouthful in David's direction, showering the table, settled back with a grin of triumph. 'Can I have a bikky, Mummy. Can I, can I, want bikky.' Then seeing the faces, added, 'Please.'

David took a sip of his wine, pushed back his chair without a word, came round to Jeanetta and from behind her stiff back, wiped her dirty chin roughly with his napkin. She cried out in pain. 'You eat what we eat, you little bastard, or you eat nothing.' She bit at his hand and he flicked the napkin across her face. Then he plucked her from the chair, scattering the cushions, carried her the length of the room, her legs still curled in the position she had sat in, dumped her on the floor of the playroom alcove, throwing after her the necklace from his pocket and her sweater grabbed from the back of the pushchair. Astonishment prevented screams until he closed the door. As she came alive and began to shriek, he fished in the other pocket, pulled out a key and turned it in the lock, returning the key to his trousers. By the time Jeanetta began to scream and hammer on the inside of the door, David was back at the table, finishing the appetizer with quick, controlled mouthfuls. Katherine was frozen. 'Let's have some music on, shall we?' he suggested. 'I really can't stand that noise.'

Monica sat with Colin at the kitchen table. They rarely occupied the splendour of the dining room unless they were entertaining, which was frequent but not as often as Colin would have liked. He was never bored with Monica: that was not the point, but he loved her diluted in company rather better. Alone together, she had the tendency to cross-examine and although he practised deceit like an art form, the repetition of half-truth being second nature, he blushed in the stating of fully formed lies. Today he found her surprisingly serene, remembered some mumble of the morning about lunch with the girls, risked a casual inquiry.

'How's our Jenny then? Did you meet?'

'Nope. I had to cancel. I'll see her tomorrow.' Monica's intellect was quicker than Colin's and she had learned sooner, by his reverse example, how much easier to lie if the bulk of what one said happened to be the truth. 'Poor you,' Colin sympathized. 'No lunch then?' 'Oh you know me,' Monica said airily. 'I always manage to eat. Want some more?'

She pointed to the dish of haddock mornay, fresh from freezer to microwave and thence to table. 'No thanks,' he said, 'I'm not very keen on fish.' Normally she would have snorted, said something faintly feminist along the lines of well you do the shopping since we don't seem able to find anyone who will, but this evening she grinned, positively devilish towards him, smiling sweet and smelling sweeter. 'You should eat it. Fish is good for you. Stiffens the sinews.'

'Stiffens what sinews?' He grinned back, forgetting questions about lunch since there would clearly be no mention of Katherine. 'All of them,' she said lightly, 'I hope.'

The telephone rang, an Edwardian reproduction perched on the stand of the reproduction Edwardian table in the hall. Monica moved from table to receiver with speed, remembering in time to slow down a little and thinking as she lifted the mouthpiece, how much David would have hated the thing.

'Hiya, Monica, how did it go?'

Monica's heart leapt into her mouth.

'What do you mean, how did what go?'

'Your business lunch, whatever it was so important for you to cancel me, again, remember?' said Jenny, puzzled on the other end of the line.

'Oh, that? Fine, perfectly fine. Tell you tomorrow.' She turned her back to the kitchen to prevent Colin seeing her smiling. 'Usual place?'

'Surely. Look, I must talk to you a bit about Katherine, not now, tomorrow, I mean. On the phone if you don't get there,' she added pointedly. 'I've been slightly worried, a bit guilty really . . .' The mention of Katherine's name, alongside the word 'guilt', brought another lurch, subsiding this time within a breath. 'Worried? Why should you be worried? Or me, for that matter, or any of us? What did she say to make you worried?'

'Nothing really,' Monica slumped. 'Only I think she's got some problems and I couldn't bring myself to listen. She brought me some rugs, you missed out there, but she's on my conscience a bit ... I don't know, think we ought to do something, only I don't know what ...'

Monica thought fast and hard of Katherine flirting with Colin, of all the anecdotes she had heard over her own lunch, and all the horrors. She could not afford too close an acquaintance with this particular life.

'Katherine Allendale,' she said firmly, 'is quite capable of looking after herself.'

Colin pretended not to hear this last remark as he busied himself with the removal of the dishes, domesticated to that degree, but looking for the port to go with the cheese, fetching a glass for his wife in the hope of extending the existing mellowness. But the mood needed no massage, continued sublime without any assistance. The house was quiet, late evening, children asleep, no interruptions. He passed her chair and deposited a kiss on her neck. 'Early night?' he asked, the lightest suggestion in his voice. She nodded vigorously.

'Leave the dishes; the pans are done. Tomorrow will do, don't fuss so, darling, I'll do them.' David sat back and lit a small cigar.

'How can you be so calm,' Katherine whispered, 'with all that racket?'

'All what, oh that.' He did not turn his head in the direction of the playroom door, which vibrated very slightly in the increasing hysteria of Jeanetta's kicks. 'Only temper. She'll have to learn, Katherine: we all have to learn. Her manners are dreadful. Listen, even her noises are ugly. You know I loathe anything ugly. She just has to learn, that's all, if she wants to live here.'

'I hate it when you put her in there. Does she have to learn like this?'

'Yes. Like this.'

'I'll put her to bed now,' said Katherine, making for the playroom door.

'You'll do no such thing. She can stay in there. She won't even be cold.'

'No, David; no, please.'

He shoved a brimming glass of wine in her direction across

the table. 'Drink this, darling, go on, you look pale.' Katherine grasped the stem of the glass and drank it in one long draught the way she had seen men drink beer. The noises behind the playroom door diminished as if Jeanetta were drawing breath. 'There, she's fine,' he said cheerfully, kneading Katherine's tense shoulders. He put his arms round her neck and spoke into her ear. 'Come to bed, darling, come on . . .' She followed him upstairs.

Mr and Mrs Harrison were watching television. Above the row, since Harrison in particular preferred the volume on maximum, Eileen Harrison could hear the faint sounds of perambulating footsteps above her head in the Pearsons' kitchen. She looked knowingly towards Eric, but he was fixed on the sports programme which followed the news. Since there was a good piece of drama to follow, a nice, hospital soap, Mrs Harrison was willing to tolerate the sport and continue knitting a purple cardigan, a clever gift for her daughter-in-law, who would not be seen dead in any such colour but would have to wear it all the same, every time they visited. Good. Harrison got so excited about the cricket: she could never see why.

'That blighter never could play. Will you look at that score, will you? Daft sod was in the pub instead of out training, should have seen him this afternoon, got wooden legs, he has. You can say what you like, but the only good cricketers we've got left are all darkies, every single one of 'em. Bloody cripples, the rest.'

A shining light was working on Mrs Harrison's brain, illuminating a series of ideas. She had been slightly worried by something about him ever since she had seen him so active on the step when they all came home. Being bored by the cardigan and bored by the news made her more than usually astute. She put down her knitting, turned on him. He quailed.

'Eric, you were lying, you were bloody well lying, weren't you? Oh don't bother to deny it, I know you were. When you said this afternoon about how you only went downstairs for some water for the step, so that drunk, that beggar, couldn't have done more than admire the paintwork on the door frame before you found him . . . No time to have got in, you said. Oh I should have known. Where was the bucket of water, then? I know what you were doing, you were down here while I was out with all the others. Leaving the front door open, watching telly, you were, this bloody cricket, that's exactly what you were doing, tell me, tell me. Or I'll ask young Mark in the morning. You'll have told him what he missed'

He shrank further back on the worn moquette of the sofa. 'Wasn't long,' he said, 'not long at all. Just a few minutes, only a couple, not long. Three balls . . .'

'You what? Don't you be rude,' she shrieked.

'I mean, like I said, just a few minutes. Not much good at that,' he added.

She settled back, knowing truth when she saw it.

'Right. Just a few minutes? Long enough for him to go upstairs and downstairs, he could have murdered you. Or put a bomb in the lavatory.'

'Why would he want to do that?'

'Oh I don't know, I really don't. But he could have pinched something.'

Harrison was angry now, as angry as he knew how, which was not particularly furious. He had always found something to distract himself before anything as disturbing had a chance to set in. 'Well so what if he has? Taken something? Didn't look like it. I did check.'

'If he's stole anything, my man, this job's on the line. And I don't know about you, but I like it here, I even like her, really. But she won't let past anything as sloppy as you, nor anyone getting into her bloody house while you're cleaning the step. She,' gesturing her head to the footsteps upstairs, 'couldn't give a tinker's curse about the step. But she will bloody care about something valuable. Even in her state.'

Harrison settled further back. The dramatic music of the hospital drama began to play and Mrs Harrison's eyes went to the screen, began to glaze over, no longer looking at him in accusation.

'Well,' she said comfortably, 'if he did take anything, I dare say we'll be able to find another reason. About how it went, whatever it is. Or was. You talk to Mark in the morning. No reason for him to bother his mother with anything about a little old beggar. All right?'

'All right,' Harrison said. His eyes began to close.

'We had enough people in the house today without mentioning vagrants, right?' she persisted.

'Right.' His eyes began to close.

13

A standing prick has no conscience . . . Who said that, I don't know and don't care; some chap in the Navy with Daddy, but I do think it's frightfully funny, ha ha ha. Daddy had another one too, meaning a fellow who's really made a hash. What was it he'd say? 'That fellow's really put his cock in the custard this time.' I like that, I really do; Daddy's vulgar phrasebook surfacing on the lips of deserted daughter like some gunk coming up with the tide. Well, the two phrases certainly apply to dear Sebastian, who has clearly put his great guilty organ in the porridge. He can go flashing on the beach; I doubt they'll all fall back in amazement. Mother always said I should never have married him. Oh, I've just thought of another. 'All conscience is soluble in alcohol.' So, a standing prick has none – it is soluble in alcohol. What is it? How about that for a question in a family quiz show? Speaking of which, of alcohol, do you know what, I think I'll have another drink. Just a large one, steady on the rocks.

Harrison looked at me oddly the other day when I came home from work and said, Do be a darling and go to the off-licence for me. Silly old bugger can keep his opinions to himself: what does he think I wanted it for, bathing? Only needed a snort or two and there's nothing more natural than that, especially now. Not that I'm unduly upset, of course: for God's sake, this isn't the end of the world and everything's thoroughly under control. I'm not a Pearson for nothing, you know. Tough stuff, us lot. Once you've bullied your way through a couple of wars with a bit of rape and pillage in between, getting left in the domestic lurch is nothing more than a little local difficulty. After you get used to the idea.

I've been to see him of course. We met for a drink after work, his suggestion. I'd phoned him once and said, You blithering idiot, what the hell's this about, don't be such a silly arse, which met with a pained response his end. Pained, who does he think he is to be pained, sneaking off like a thief with a note of apology, sorry I took the family silver but I might be back for the rest? Not the only thief around here either, but I'll come on to that. 'Listen, Susan,' he said in his most pompous voice, 'I'm not meaning to leave the children . . .' 'Only me,' I snap back. Oh No, No: in his language, leaving home is not the same thing as abandonment, must have read his dictionary upside down or maybe has illogical thoughts when he's jumping up and down on top of whatever floozie he's run off with. There is one of course: I have her taped in my mind, small, slim, blonde and . . . Another drink, thank you.

I mustn't bang on about him; he's only a man and they've always struck me as congenitally stupid, what little brain normally resident in their trousers. Anyway, we met in a city wine bar, somewhere near Bank where all the wine bars look the same to me, subterranean, authentic sawdust on the floor, must be hell to sweep, old-fashioned, freshly faded lettering on the barrels to make it look as if they still serve port by the pint; the whole place deliberately gloomy to hide all the ghastly assignations between secretaries and middle-aged men: that phrase about conscience being soluble ought to be in lights over the door. Of course I have no conscience at all: why should I? Sebastian's to blame for everything, but all I can say is when I saw him sitting at a table by himself it was I who felt guilty, which made me crosser than ever. Men look so pathetic sitting alone: I remembered him, sorry, not him, someone else, sitting on that park bench like the end of a sad play. Then I remembered what the silly bugger was up to, mid-life crisis, imagined his thing practically sticking out of his pocket all points north, south or east. (Reminds me of another joke, you know the one. Man goes to cinema with pet duck down trousers since they won't let him in with the thing on a lead. Duck gets restless, which severely disturbs girl in next seat, who complains to blasé boyfriend on other side about how the gent on her left is exposing himself to her. Don't worry, says blasé boyfriend. They're all the same. No they're not, she says: this one's eating my crisps . . . I knew you'd like it, ha, ha, ha.)

But he did look sad, Sebastian, all contrived of course. He asked about Mark, wanted to come and see them. Well you either live with us or not, I said: you want to come back as a visitor, not likely: you should have thought of that before you left.

I did, he said: I thought very carefully; I almost went mad, thinking.

The place was beginning to get noisier: echoed yaw-yaws from city types, cockney accents and bellowed intimacies, whoever would imagine a romantic tryst down here without the world knowing the colour of your underwear. So dear Sebastian was explaining himself in either stage whispers or shouts, leaning across the table towards me while I leaned back to make it more difficult. Things hadn't been right between us for ages, he was saying. The house was bare, we never spent time together; no affection, no comfort, you don't even notice my presence provided you get driven down to the country every weekend to count cattle or play on a calculator: I thought you'd hardly notice if I left, no difference. There's one difference, like less laundry, I snapped. You never do laundry, he said: you never do anything as if you don't really belong, even with the kids: the whole domestic scene bores you rigid. We've all the money we need and as you well know, you far more of the stuff than me, but all you do is work all the time, and snap, and drink and push me away. Only thing has animated you in weeks, months even, was all that gossip about David Allendale. The house is cold: I'm superfluous with you. I worked longer and longer because there was nothing for me at home.

Well if that didn't beat everything. All true, all that stuff we debated long ago in school before I cut domestic science out of the curriculum in deference to economics on a wider scale: all true about how all man wants of woman is creature comforts, slippers before the fire and a wee wifie wearing transparent pinny when he comes home after hunting, loving hands to press his loin cloth: I wouldn't have believed it. Why didn't you marry a bimbo? I never married you to be a housekeeper, we pay one of those, I yelled at Sebastian above the wine-bar din. I know, I know, he said, looking round, a trifle embarrassed, but I did want a woman on the other side of a brain, old girl. And I do need to be noticed. Sometimes, not often, but sometimes.

All right then, I said: Less of this rubbish. Who is she?

There has to be someone, doesn't there? Always is, men as self-sufficient as babies. Always someone, some frightful little cow aged about twelve, who understands. I once told Seb (I bet she calls him Sebby) another joke. The one about the Italian in the surgery, saying Doctor, Doctor, there's something wrong with my wife. What's wrong with your wife, she's a nuclear physicist? Yes, but she don't cook my pasta ... Sebastian hadn't laughed then: he wasn't laughing now. What did I mean, She, he asked, there isn't a She; I just needed time to think ...

'Oh, Fuck off!' My voice fell into one of those sudden silences, a sort of universal lull which falls on a crowd of drinkers as if they'd all raised their glasses at the same time. 'Who is She?' I hissed at him, taking his glass and draining it back. He looked at my hand, hopelessly, then at my mouth, didn't speak. Then went for another bottle of wine.

Oh God. Of course there's a bloody she. OK, down the hatch, must get another bottle, sneak it in in the briefcase. The Harrisons are all eyes and ears, but I decided from the beginning to say absolutely nothing, not to my parents, his father, the children, or the bloody housekeepers. Having my husband cheat on me is no one else's business: fob-off stories such as Daddy's had to rush off on business will have to do for now: he can explain his own dilemma to whoever he wants, including his son, I'm not going to do it. There is a fiction abroad that he has some crisis at work, may be true for all I know, but that will do very well. Everything's perfectly fine; just a little local difficulty. Meantime I shall quell the already quiet libido with a little more gin and address a few more pressing problems.

Such as, I seem to be losing things. Don't know why, this evening, for lack of anything better to do (so much daylight: I do wish it would get dark sooner and then I could just go to bed), I started to resume going through things, something I began last night, a sort of inventory if you like. When I started yesterday, back from the sodding wine bar, I was somehow moved to take a raincheck on all those things about me which are durable. Such as jewellery, for instance, diamonds being a girl's best friend and all that. Yesterday I fished out the shoebox in which various items have always resided, got fed up with the whole idea and shoved it in the study on the desk on my way downstairs to greet Harrison *en route* back with the booze. Either yesterday or the day before, can't recall, doesn't matter. Funny how I used to use all the earrings, such a palaver, turning them all out and never finding one to match the other, and when I could never find a damn thing to match the nicest necklace, I gave up trying. My father, good old Daddy, gave me the necklace when I married, a little thing to weigh down my neck with impending responsibilities. Remember, darling, he said: You can always come home if it doesn't work out, but he must have lied since he and Mummy would be perfectly appalled if I did that now. I suppose all promises have a shelf-life, like about two minutes; odd how we keep on making them all the same. But anyway, about the necklace which graced my throat to quite a few dances until I discovered quite how much it had cost, at which point I kept it in the bank for a bit, then after one more outing, couldn't be bothered, and gravitation to the shoebox occurred along with everything else. There it has lain for about a decade, and now lies there no longer.

Someone once told me that alcohol makes the memory go: I have to concede an element of accuracy in this, but I never forget things, or the price of them, or whether, on some super-efficient day, I took them back to the bank or not. The shoebox was overturned on the desk where I had left it and that bloody necklace was gone, nothing else, just the necklace. Takes a little gin to make me focus, but I'm focused now. What time is it? I couldn't give a damn about the loss, but I want to know who. Who is screwing my Sebby husband and who has got my necklace? If they are one and the same I shall sever her head: she can have the one, but not the other.

'Harrison!' A little yell down the stairwell. Whoops. Silly me, the man's at the door, acting butler with ill grace, forgetting he doesn't have working hours as such, supposed to be on guard, here, twenty-four hours a day or he's out on his bloody ear. 'Harrison!' What's he doing at the front door, dammit, I want him here. Materializing like a genie, the sort of servant you'd have in a Hammer horror film, murmuring, Mr Allendale to see you, Mrs Pearson: Shall I bring him up or will you come down? As if he was going to yank the body upstairs on a pulley.

Up, not down: let the others use their legs. I pushed a cushion over the shoebox with insufficient time to wonder what all this was in aid of, callers in this eccentric house to enliven my endless evenings. Especially some visitor flown hence from the planet of Happy Marriage to look at me through a periscope.

But I still liked David Allendale, as I said, at least he's a decent volume of man, and when he called on this errand, I might well have told him all about the state of affairs in our house because the ache to tell had grown and grown, along with the shameful knowledge that the act of telling could make me collapse. Oddly, with a lack of women friends, I did think of Katherine as the one to tell; I remembered her kindness: she would not have criticized. But David's visit was not social. He was full of his own purposes, nothing to do with me, eyes went straight through me again to the messages he wanted to bring.

'How are you, Susan? You look well.' The liar.

'Sebastian in?' The question was loaded.

'Not yet.'

'Ah well, doesn't matter; you I wanted to see, but I'm sorry, this is all a bit difficult . . . Don't quite know how to put . . .'

Really, David, not like you to beat about the bush, not even for the thirty seconds' beating taken so far. I asked if there was a problem, aware of the highness of my voice, more falsetto as a foil to the mess of my appearance, my pale face in a room which is horribly stuffy. David has a permanent tan, which is a mystery to me; one of those faces turned to the sun and immediately kissed.

'I'm afraid we're going to have to stop the arrangements with the Harrisons and the children. Katherine's job has come to a rather sudden end, you see, the shop where she works closing down, but she'll still do some work from home, importing things, she thinks. Which means she can spend more time with the children and we can't have them coming here on a part-time basis, one day here, one day with us, far too disruptive. So we thought it best to call it off completely. There's also the sad fact that my boy is allergic to your dog.'

Patsy Labrador was in the room, her great heavy head raised briefly from floor level at the mention of herself, an uncanny habit revealed before anyone even mentions her name. She did not get up in greeting for David Allendale, a strange fact suddenly apparent to me in one of the few reactions sharpened by the evening's gin consumption, me realizing idly at the same time how she never goes near him in the street, an indifference quite at odds with her character. Anyway, he smiled at dog to show no offence and she shuffled closer to me, one ear cocked. 'So you want to take the children back home,' said I, never fast on the uptake. Wanting to offer him a drink since I needed one myself but knowing the tonic was downstairs, gin itself on the desk, very obvious to all. He was sitting uncomfortably on the shoebox, which he moved to one side without examination, his eye flicking over the mess of the room, flicking back to me with his warm smile, the one which unhinges me somewhat, far too well mannered to comment on the manners of my dog. He is so desperately charming when he tries; I could feel in myself the dying of resentment.

'I do realize,' he was saying earnestly, already in command, 'how short notice this is.'

'How short?'

'Well, Monday, actually.' Friday today: short wasn't the word, no notice at all. '. . . But I'm sure they won't lose touch. Only this allergy of Jeremy's has been getting worse. Not the dog's fault; simply anything hairy. He isn't a strong child. Difficult pregnancy, poor Katherine.'

'I see, yes I see,' not seeing at all, but asking inconsequential questions to cover the feeling, this awful sense of abandonment as if I had ever taken much notice of his children, knowing I would actually miss them. Even they found my house poisonous.

'Mrs Harrison won't like this. She's very fond of your kids.'

'I thought I'd give her a bonus, a generous bonus, for all

she's done. And pay you as normal for the next quarter since we're being so inconsiderate, not giving any notice. Will that be acceptable?' Perfectly acceptable, over-generous, in fact, apart from me being incredibly hurt: fiscal honour is desperately important and Mrs Harrison not immune to filthy lucre either. He was making himself look anxious, a man striving not to offend or over-personalize what was still the ending of a contract. 'I don't want any hard feelings,' he was adding for good measure. 'We're so lucky to have you as neighbours; we both value the friendship.'

At that moment I valued theirs, wanted to tell, confess our true circumstances, rather wanted to say, would you please ask Katherine if she would step round and see me? Both to explain and let me howl on her shoulder, forgetting all I had ever thought of her. But the words would not come out. I mouthed like a fish, pride at war with need.

Therefore he left with no more than mutual protestations of goodwill, the manly kind with which that brave sex comfort each other and which have the same effect on me, but as soon as he had seen himself out, the anger rose, subdued by his physical presence but still in force, my mind jumping back to the questions which had prefaced his visit. Fingers, nervous for exercise, back inside the shoebox he had moved to one side, offended by his touching and his casual glance at the contents. Patsy Labrador shuffled beside me: she had growled at his back retreating downstairs, my damned dog making my comments for me, like an *alter ego*, but very rude all the same. 'Naughty girl' I tapped her nose. Repercussions could surface later: for the time, I could do nothing else but continue to search for the necklace. Even while wondering how to break all the news to Mrs Harrison.

No, don't call for Mrs Harrison; she is the real ruler of this house, so I go downstairs, carrying the gin to wed to the tonic and thus acquire a little more courage. She waddles upstairs to our kitchen as I waddle down, moving more and more like my dog but feeling a touch of hysteria.

There is no finesse in me: let alone diplomacy, and besides, these days, words happen in gulps, rude announcements to hide the things I cannot say, brusqueness the only tone.

'The Allendale children are not coming round here any more. He just told me. Their mother is going to do a hand's turn for once because she's lost her silly little job, going to be a full-time mum. Also Jeremy's delicate and allergic to our dog, another factor, I believe. Did you ever notice him being delicate?'

'I thought he had hay fever.'

I've never before seen her nonplussed, but dear Mrs H was ashen-faced, recovering slowly. 'What about Jeanetta?' she was whispering, lowering large rump into kitchen chair as she spoke. 'What about Jeanetta, oh, poor little girl . . .'

'What about her? Nothing we can do, is there?'

She was turning her grey head from side to side like a dog trying to get at a fly, 'Oh poor little girl, shame, really, shame . . .'

'Why poor? They're bloody well off.'

I couldn't have Mrs Harrison out of control and any more emotion of any sort was going to shatter my nerves. 'Shame,' she kept repeating, 'shame.'

'Don't go on so, really, doesn't help.' Me, not quite snapping. 'Bet they'll keep on coming round all the time. And you still get paid the same, for less work. Mr Allendale says he's very grateful, wants to give you some kind of bonus, and it won't be small.'

If I thought that would bring a smile to her face, I was wrong. One forgets, you see, with Mrs Harrison, the lumbering humanity beneath the pinafore, the bit of her which makes her a child's delight even as a disciplinarian. As ever with servants I was sorry for my words, awkward without being able to change tack, caught in my own breeze.

'Have a drink, Mrs Harrison, please. Whatever you like.'

'Do you know, I think I shall. Whisky.'

She's welcome: Harrison pinches it all the time but I loathe the stuff. Sloshed some in a glass and we sat for a moment, nursing different sorrows in silence. She drank the amber like a good 'un, took a little more. All conscience is soluble in . . . I remembered, watched her face pinken by the second, and my single-track mind reverted to course.

'Mrs Harrison, sorry to mention this just at the moment, but I seem to be missing a necklace.'

174

She finished the drink abruptly, refused more. Settled back further in her chair and became portentous, one arm resting on the kitchen table, looking like a boxer between rounds.

'Oh, Mrs Pearson, what a pity, oh dear, oh dear, I wonder . . . No, nothing.' She looked at me sideways, an uncomfortable look.

'Something you want to tell me, Mrs H?'

'Don't like to, ma'am, really I don't . . . Telling tales, and I've no way of knowing, not really . . .'

'Oh what is it? Listen, in case it should have crossed your mind, don't imagine I think either you or Harrison could ever be involved, don't think that for a moment, but I know very well I left a gold necklace in a shoebox in my study and since Harrison's known to carry a duster in there, he might have seen it. Did anyone come in, you know, non regular? You know, butcher, baker, candlestick maker, plumber, anyone?'

She smiled at the nursery rhyme references, but there was palpable hesitation. 'No one,' she said, 'today or yesterday.' Another hesitation. 'Except Mrs Allendale, of course. Came in for tea, early home she was.'

'Upstairs?' I was examining my hands.

'Downstairs, with us.' She pointed with her finger stabbing towards the floor. 'But I was worried, ma'am, she did go up, to the loo, while I was making tea. Gone a long time, she was, ever so strange when she came back, couldn't wait to go. And Jeanetta, she does sometimes run off with toys . . . You don't think . . .? No, she wouldn't, not Mrs Allendale, she wouldn't . . .'

'No,' I said firmly. 'She wouldn't.' Silence surrounded the two of us.

'No, of course not,' murmured the lady. 'Well I don't know, Mrs Pearson, I just don't know.'

And after that, the evening chuntered into dark. The way these long, long evenings do, all the emotions joining force in the darkness, dancing round like fireflies. Back and forth across the kitchen floor with muted footsteps, what did I do wrong, what did I do right, the picture of life cracked, all defences half gone, another drink, please. Face staring into the garden while tongue gags on a piece of cheese: my feet going upstairs to

175

Sebastian's study looking for clues; back to my own lair, no longer looking for the necklace and all the childhood which went with it. Across the landings, into the rooms of sleeping children, looking and looking, coming away and going back, afraid to leave them alone or disturb such fragile peace.

I would rather think about the necklace than think about the rest if you see what I mean. Quite obvious, really, why dear David is making revisions to his regime, keeping her at home, obvious as a lighthouse beacon. Must be hard to have a thief for a wife as well as one for a father, so hard I must find it in my superstitious self to be generous. Besides, things matter so much less than they did, I don't know why. She can have the bloody thing: she is not Sebastian's mistress, that role is given to another. Words, words, words, what's the good of them. I never liked that necklace anyway: I simply wanted to know. One more for the road. I have no idea which road but it seems to be going downhill. I can only remember the jokes. Silly of me to think of confiding in Katherine, wasn't it? Did I say I'd thought of that? But you can't, can you? Not with someone you know is a thief.

14

When she had set out that morning, her resolution had been firm. She would explain everything to Mary, who would tell her if her life was normal, but all resolution faded in the face of food. Almost two weeks at home with Jeanetta made everything hinge on food. Katherine sat at a prominent table in the restaurant next to the Academy, waiting for Mary. There were times when she saw the whole of her life as a series of sitting at tables, waiting, landmarks to existence the culinary details of which she could always remember. Every last bit of food, but not always the company: recalling three-dimensional details and even the taste of whatever she had consumed on dozens of occasions, but the faces opposite or alongside were blurred. Facing her now was a woman eating a piece of cold chicken, picking at the bones with her knife and fork, her face rapt with concentration as she removed the flaccid flesh from the bones and placed small morsels into her mouth. Katherine shuddered, began to forget the words she was going to use to explain.

Mary was late, a bizarre condition for Mary, who would sooner be caught naked than delayed. At least that was as Katherine remembered, but Mary might have changed over the last years or the last week; you never knew. People did, she noticed: they changed colour all the time. Katherine looked at a book she was carrying. She always carried a book for camouflage, but her reading was minimal unless of magazines printed on shiny paper, full of coveted things as well as platitudes, advice columns and illustrations, especially pictures alongside articles which offered some reassurance. She copied ideas from periodicals, read articles on child care which she forgot when faced with Jeanetta, shamefully reflecting how she had never applied any of them to Jeremy. She seemed to have done an awful lot of living to learn so little.

Pausing in her nervous handling, she pinned back a centre page with a column title of 'How to deal with the two-year-old tantrums', smiling for a moment at the ambiguity of the heading – how could a tantrum last for two years? – then scanning the writing with one eye, the other still looking out for Mary. There was a picture of a bawling infant, mouth wide open in toothless protest. 'These tantrums do not last,' the article stated. But they did: in Jeanetta's case they had persevered longer than that. Which was surely why Jeanetta was at home at the moment, locked in the playroom. 'Best to ignore the outbursts of tempestuous tots,' said the article. Katherine squinted at the page and turned on. Perhaps they were right. Children are very hardy. It was nice to know.

Jeanetta had been relatively undisturbed by one night in the playroom, or so it had seemed. When David, with Katherine hovering, opened the door in the morning, they had found her truculent, sitting amid a pile of clothes. She had peed in her pants and on to one of Katherine's old evening skirts: there was the sharp smell of ammonia. The small face was blotched red and white and her hair was flopping over a pale forehead. There were obvious traces of tears but a quiet defiance: she had always been a stubborn child. 'Go and get washed,' David had said to her. Mother and daughter had walked upstairs, Jeanetta crying then over the business of cleaning teeth, snuffling slightly and without words, stiffening at first when Katherine tried to hug her with all the usual awkwardness, trying to include in that embrace some apology without expressing approval. Then child had relented and hugged back, still speechless as they descended again to breakfast. Bread and butter had been placed on Jeanetta's plate: she ate like a small and quiet wolf, never querying the absence of the cornflakes which were locked away out of sight. By contrast, and to Katherine's intense relief, Jeremy banged his tray, threw himself hither and thither and would not eat at all. Under cover of this distraction, Katherine tried to supply a little more of the bread to her daughter. 'No,' David had said, without even turning his head. 'She's so fat.' Jeanetta did not insist. Nor did her mama, breathing an outward sigh of relief. Everything would be all right after all: everything was under control. There was just the little question of how they would spend their days.

But of course such tranquillity could not last, broke into a rash of the opposite many days before this meeting with childless Mary, who would regard the whole débâcle as part of Katherine's incompetence and renew the accusations about never doing anything useful. Katherine hoped Mary would make the usual suggestion of charitable works: she needed work other than housework and she could bring Jeanetta with her. Giving extra attention to her daughter did not make her biddable: it rendered both of them irritated. Jeanetta's temper had not survived the gradual realization that she was not going back to the Harrisons. One day after the first spell in the playroom, dressed with hope, trailing downstairs with Donald Duck, the red cloak and all the impedimenta she was used to drag next door with her, Jeanetta had sat at table and asked, loudly, when were they going across to Mrs Harry. 'And Sammy, and Mark,' she added for good measure. The question was addressed to the ceiling, Jeanetta's body pointed in David's direction, but keeping her distance.

'Mrs Harrison is away,' he said shortly, spooning food into Jeremy's willing mouth.

'No she's not, she's not, she's not. I seen her from the window, outside, I did, saw her, saw her . . .' The voice was rising to a scream, swelled with her knowledge of being told a lie.

'Be quiet, Jeanetta: eat your bread.'

'Hate bread. Want cornflakes.'

'No. You make a mess. Tuck your shirt in.' His voice was cold.

'Please, can we go to Mrs Harry, please?' A change in tactic, a wheedling tone.

'No.'

Jeanetta took a slice of sticky granary bread, spread thinly with butter, and placed it face down on the table beyond the limits of the plastic cover which protected her place. Then she struck the slice repeatedly, first with the heel of her hand and then with her fist. The table was polished and solid, beyond damaging, but the cutlery and glass of orange juice next to her plate rattled. 'Want to go, want to go, want to go,' Jeanetta chanted, grinding the bread into the surface of the wood, '. . . want to go now.' Jeremy gaped, wide-eyed with interest, then blew the food off the spoon held near his face. A muscle in David's neck had begun to twitch. Katherine said nothing and removed the bread fragments quickly. Jeanetta reached for more.

Sitting in the vaulted room with the paintings on the walls, waiting for Mary, looking at the others either talking or eating, Katherine pictured David's hand instead of any one of theirs, reaching out and removing the bread, his voice ordering silence. Jeanetta, sitting, pulling faces while the rest of them ate, denied food herself, determined to choke on silence rather than complain. Then when Katherine was sent out, Jeanetta being placed in the playroom with the door locked and herself just beginning to understand the makings of the regime. 'You cannot spend all day in the house, darling,' pleasantly said by David. 'The less people know about your job the better. Go out, meet the girls, meet Mary, go and do something cultural. Here, take the phone and do something, go to the gym. I like you here, but you don't need to stay all the time. People will think it odd.' So her days would be thus: spent with Jeanetta in front of the television, or if not, Jeanetta to be in the playroom out of harm's way while the boy stayed glued to his father, passive in any event and further pacified by constant music and conversation, happy in company. Whether the sojourns in the playroom were imprisonment or safekeeping made no difference: he would see to her needs, he said, do go, Katherine, you're getting on my nerves. Her own silence on the subject, her agreement with the new order, was assumed. 'Look, it does her good,' he said. After days without Harrison titbits, Jeanetta was noticeably thinner. Katherine understood that in David's eyes, this proved some kind of point. A child being streamlined and subdued to go with the rest of the house.

Let it go for now: life would improve, life always did. She

turned back to the magazine. 'This is only a phase,' said the article. 'Things are bound to get better.' If only he did not put her there at night. He never struck her, did he, never abused her, never slapped her face. She had read of those things, they were serious. Cruel fathers did that. Jeanetta was in the play-room now. She had been in and out of the playroom for days. Katherine began to count on her fingers the numbers of days, and stopped.

David was not cruel: he was kind. She closed her eyes, and in the absence of sight, the voices around her were suddenly enlarged while she remembered her Italian honeymoon with darling David, trying in the memory to call up the foolproof mantra of happy reminiscence. But all she could remember was the coupling before breakfast, lunch, dinner, post-midnight, the incessant fucking like a cat marking territory. Imprints all over herself as if he had never been there before: Mine, mine, mine; and her, glad to be owned. She wished she could go back to that point without the morning sickness: the disbelief of his which had grown in the few years since that apparently premature birth. Grown at the same time as the house was becoming so perfect around them, the end of him treating her like gold dust. The end of being allowed her own childishness. Panic rose again. Whatever defeat was involved, she must tell Mary.

'For God's sake, Katherine, wake up. You do look silly with your eyes shut. Sorry I'm late.'

Katherine jumped.

'I wasn't shutting my eyes,' she lied. 'I was looking at the ceiling.'

'Oh. Why?'

Mary settled bags around herself without more greeting. She was always restless, an examiner of the masculine watch too prominent on one thin wrist, reminding Katherine and everyone else how busy she was, what a favour this interlude of her time. Since she was looking for signs of guilt in her little sister, she was more restless than usual, her cursory examination closer. Katherine was as slender as ever, possibly more so but, since this was a characteristic Mary shared and therefore could not envy, she passed to other features. It was Katherine's softness which always intrigued and escaped her, a kind of fluffiness she coveted but scorned.

'So why the culture shock today?' Mary asked rudely. 'Haven't seen you for ages. So kind of you to phone. Of course, I forgot, we do this every year. God knows why. Do we eat first or look at the pictures?' The woman opposite them on the next table was shredding the last of the chicken from the carcass. The flesh near the bone was pink. Katherine grabbed her handbag.

'Look at the pictures, I think.'

They wandered into the hall of the Royal Academy, paid their money, Katherine nervously. The allowance for an afternoon out was exact; never enough to pay for a phone call. She thought of asking Mary for change, but Mary's abruptness silenced her and in the quietness of the place, the old pride was returning. Then they moved up the stairway and began in gallery one. Katherine had an eye for pictures: she chose to look at them in the way others might have gone to see films, perceiving shapes in nothing, without any particular preference, but drawn to a series of colours, mooning round galleries as if drawn on a string, forgetting everything else, wanted to stay in the galleries for the simple absorption of swivelling eyes. The summer exhibition was a ritual, followed by Katherine out of love; Mary because Mary thought it a proper thing to do. Katherine never looked here for excellence, only for oblivion, hypnotized by the vast rooms. Thinking at the back of her mind, anything good, David said every year, write down the name, put a sticker on it and note the painter. Art to David was also investment, requiring his wife's eye. Katherine paused, rapt before a Tuscan landscape of vivid blues and ochre fields, shimmering with heat as if the canvas was on fire. 'Oh, lovely,' she breathed.

'Was it like that on your honeymoon?' Mary asked inconsequentially, still watching, waiting for something.

'I can't remember,' said Katherine. They were used to brief conversations. Mary found them stranger today, a series of *non sequiturs* which signified something. She usually only came to the summer show on sufferance: today she had come to watch her sister, full of resentment at Katherine's reservations, her

182

sullen self-satisfaction, Mary's own head stuffed with nameless jealousy. Claud had not phoned; she was completely alone. Katherine was selfishly surrounded. Mary's frustration pinpointed itself in Claud, who was not the real cause, but enough to render her irrational self quite out of control and sharp as ice.

In the room of abstracts, all the paintings were unsold. Mary preferred these lines and distortions to the literal depictions of what she privately considered rather frivolous themes. They moved further: she was hungry and impatient, hated to see her sister with this religious concentration, captivated by the eye. She paused deliberately in front of a large canvas, not abstract but allegory, she guessed, something more in the style of the surreal. There were two red bodies twisted together obscenely to form the bulk of the painting. In the background was a luminous woman in white, the foreground littered with teardrops of shiny blue. The painting bore the large title 'Adultery', written in the left-hand corner of the canvas in the same colour as the tears. 'I like that,' said Mary, inspired by sudden malice. 'I think it's wonderful. Don't you?'

Mary was excited: she felt they had been led to this spot, divine intervention in her search for clues and there were all the leads, a woman in white hovering in the background with copulation in the front, reminiscent of Katherine in white, lingering in a wine bar waiting for Claud, but really Katherine in the forefront, one of the twisted red bodies. But the surreal quality, the lack of any prettiness, upset Katherine, who hated ugliness, shook slightly in emotional disapproval. Mary saw a distorted vision of Claud: Katherine saw David, Monica and a monstrous legend of treachery. 'I hate it, absolutely hate it,' she muttered, clicking on to the next gallery, a smaller room full of miniatures. No wonder you hate it, Mary crowed: no bloody wonder. Guilt writ large in letters of your own adultery. You just don't like it painted in red, can't bear the spotlight. She could read once promiscuous Katherine like a book, could she, but in the heart within heart, she did not really believe her sister would be such a fool. She did not believe anything, but through her own red-rimmed eyes, the theft felt entirely true.

Oh yes, she had her answers now. No word from Claud, a

deafening silence in which he came to mean more and more, so that even the phone bell rang in her ears. Look at her, all the answers so obvious in Kath's uneven movements. There had been no word from Claud, Katherine so jumpy, not once but twice, guilt tingling in her, something she was dying to tell. Mary felt a rising tide of anger, part hunger, part several kinds of frustration, present in her fingers as she dug into a bowl of murky salad back in the restaurant. Everything for Katherine and a dish of herbs for me. 'Well,' she said brightly as they sat where they had sat before. 'That was fun. Going to buy anything, what's the news and how's the job?'

Katherine jumped again, her seat leaving the wooden chair. 'Oh fine, absolutely fine.' A vague response, rearranging her food. Nothing carnivorous or substantial today: salad with feta cheese. She must tell Mary about the playroom. Mary thought, guilt, again: see, she cannot even eat, and felt a greater rush of impatience.

'I went to Mr Isaacs' shop,' she said pointedly. 'This morning. Thought I might meet you there. But you weren't at work.'

'No,' said Katherine, 'not today.'

'I see,' said Mary, seeing it all. The p⌐   ⌐⌐ job, Katherine setting out in the morning, waving goodbye to dear David, pitching up at some little hotel in the vicinity, or maybe a service flat, Katherine could afford a service flat. So could Claud, arriving with flowers or gifts. Katherine would take off her white dress in front of a window. It did not matter if this was not quite the way it was, but whichever way it was, Katherine was not telling the truth, assuming her sister was a fool. Or so she felt, all of her raw from real and imagined rejection.

'So you still have that job?' Mary inquired casually. Not according to Mr Isaacs, not as Mary had understood from his waving of arms, and his hesitant words such as sad, very sad, not reliable. *En route* to no real explanation at all, he had added that he was sorry for the lady's husband, such a gentleman. Why, Mary had asked. Embarrassing, Mr Isaacs had muttered: she cheats all this time and I could never tell him. What kind of cheat, Mary had asked then. Mr Isaacs had rubbed his nose, refused to specify: Mary's imagination, acting overtime, hazarded more than one guess.

'You're lying to me, Katherine, I know you are,' Mary said out loud putting a piece of salami into her mouth as soon as she had spoken. Food had lost appeal. Katherine jumped yet again, higher than ever.

'Pardon?'

'You're lying,' Mary repeated, satisfied with the reaction.

'No, no, no . . .'

'Yes you are. I know you are. I've been talking to people.'

Katherine settled back nervously. Mary had been talking to David. They used to talk more often before than now: Katherine often had the uncomfortable feeling that Mary had arranged her whole marriage like a broker, and maybe kept her feelers on it through visiting Sophie. But in any event, it struck her that the competent people in her life often talked to one another, with herself the occasional subject. What shall we do with Katherine: she had heard that sentiment whispered, knew the subject of herself was often a conversational parcel. Never really minded since it absolved her from decisions, and even the shame of that carried relief. At least she might explain to Mary now, about the necklace, since clearly, Mary already knew.

'So, I suppose you know, all about it,' she said at last, thinking of Mr Isaacs and the numdah rugs, but thinking more of the diamond and gold necklace, burning a hole in some locked drawer in the studio. Jeanetta in the playroom, sharing the same punishment. Mary nodded wisely, thinking of nothing but Claud, people stealing things, people in bed together.

'It wasn't my fault,' Katherine rushed on. 'It just happened. I couldn't help it.'

Mary leaned forward, her face twisted in anger. 'No, you couldn't, could you? You never could resist, could you? You're an absolute sucker for the sparkle in any man's eye.' But while she spoke, Katherine was choking and beginning to cough. The brown bread she had nibbled was stuck to the roof of her mouth creating nausea: something else stuck to the grains, and in the relief of being able to share some worry with Mary, she had swallowed backwards. 'Can I tell you about it?' she said, tears from the choking standing in her eyes. 'It's so awful at home. David's so angry all the time . . . Jeanetta . . . what can I do, if I could just explain, you could tell me what to do . . . Oh I do wish you would come home. Could you come now?'

But Mary's tolerance was completely gone. The overdue invitation, issued like a plea, rose like bile in her throat and jealousy was twisting her spine.

'No you can't explain,' she shouted. 'Not now, not ever. What on earth makes you think I'd ever understand. You're a disgraceful little slut. If he throws you out, don't come running to me.'

Katherine moved forward in her uncomfortable chair, watching the iron rod of Mary's back as Mary strode out of the room. Then she looked up at the ceiling again. To keep in place the tears of confusion. She had wanted to tell, but no one would let her tell, better not to try. She had knocked to speak to Susan Pearson, seen her and been told she was not there. Tried the Harrisons, knew others she dare not try, like Monica and Jenny, in it together, laughing at her. Even Sophie never phoned any more. No one was going to listen.

Tap, tap, tap. Mary's flat heels, steel tipped for economy, were tripping down the spiral stairs into the underground, the whole of her tense with irritation. The rest of the day was programmed, each appointment dovetailing into the next, and she was on her way to the next. Hot as fire and cold as ice, looking at the men on the other side of the compartment, hungrily. Looking for the new Claud, looking for satisfaction, abandoning Katherine wholesale. That's told her: that's set her right. No good thinking she can run to me when she's up to her old tricks; picks me up and drops me; let her stew: who does she think she is? And more of the same righteous rage, tripping over the first. Pictures, looking at pictures, can't bear people wasting my time, she can look at pictures with Claud, thinking I have nothing better to do, idle cow. Mary looked at the large dial of her watch. She was early for the next appointment. Busy, busy, busy, they would have to take her early. She was too highly charged to stop.

186

Still tap-tapping, up a West End back street to Child Action Volunteers, premises awaiting her inspection, their scruffy offices above the headquarters of some manufacturers of maternity clothes and next door to a private family clinic, very apt and very droll to Mary's mind. Mission: take a look at the place to discuss the allocation of funds and see those volunteers who were supposed to qualify for awards. Damn, damn, damn: then go home to nothing, or another, similar appointment. Mary was trustee of a charity melting-pot, filled periodically by the sort of bequests which said, 'All to charity' without specifying which, leaving her and her kind the discretion which Mary herself much enjoyed to exercise over other people's money. For the moment, because of some knock-on effect of her own moaning hormones and the meeting with Katherine, Mary was rather off the whole idea of children. Monsters in miniature forms: mainly it was the adults who needed protection.

Two cramped rooms were approached by creaking stairs, and the tenure of the place was only possible because most of the few staff were out at any given time. For committee meetings, they were forced to convene in the pub: otherwise two desks and five chairs were occupied in shifts. The furniture bore traces of defeat and there was a patched hole in the ceiling. The heat of the city outside had risen into the trap of the roof, stirred by one electric fan as old as it was inadequate. As Mary trod upstairs, she could hear a plaintive male voice, talking insistently but slowly.

'Oh come on, I'm sure you can manage a kitten. Just the one. Come and see them at least: I can watch them for hours. You'll be sold as soon as you look. They are quite, unbelievably beautiful.' The voice contained an edge of adoration.

'Why do you want to get rid of them, then?'

'Well I don't if you want to know, but I've got to be realistic. There's five of them you see, and they're beginning to run up the walls. I'm only trying to find good homes; if I don't I shall have to keep them. My favourite's a perfect tabby . . .'

Mary stood outside the open door at the top of the stairs without being seen herself, watching and listening.

'. . . And of all things, a black and white one, with a sort of tabby stripe. I think Kat had a wild evening, straight from one to another.' There was a giggle from the secretary. 'Promiscuous puss,' the male voice added.

Mary saw a tall, spare man, sitting on the edge of a battered desk, talking to a faded-looking woman of about fifty tired summers. The persistent twitch in the visible corner of the man's face rendered his smile, even in profile, slightly foolish. Cats, Mary thought furiously; a paid charity worker sitting on a desk and wasting an afternoon talking about cats. Mary hated cats, which reminded her of Katherine at her kittenish worst. John Mills rose in the same moment of Mary's grimace of disgust and saw her lingering behind the door, lurched towards her in a series of utterly graceless shuffles. 'Hallo, hallo, hallo,' he said in a mimic of a suspicious policeman, 'who the hell are you?'

The secretary at the desk touched his arm in warning, anxiety present on her good-natured features. 'This is Miss Fox,' she hissed, 'come to look us over.' 'Oh,' said John, unabashed, his face breaking into a grin which Mary found worse than the twitching seriousness, 'I don't suppose you want a kitten either, do you?'

With one hand extended, he rose to full, awkward height, towering above Mary like a crooked obelisk. His colouring reminded her of Claud, but there the resemblance ended, with this shambling body sloping downwards from thin shoulders towards a small stomach and stick-like thighs, every feature in a man she did not like. A little, round underbelly, worse than a big, taut one, the sort which would at least go with a bon viveur, nothing tight about him, all of it slipping slightly out of control. While Mary spoke with her usual brisk politeness, he in turn took in the clothes which made her look like a traffic warden, the clipped accents, the air of an official, felt prejudice rise like a tide breaking into the foam of instant irritation. Dislike of this instant kind always made him act like a fool: he was as uncomfortable as a schoolboy with a hated master, showed her round the offices in a series of silly, defensive flourishes, giggly with every second phrase.

'Oh yes. The equipment. Here we have the filing cabinets.

Out there is the loo, would you like to go, ladies and gents for the use of. Here is our Miss Moneypenny, who knows everything. This is the telephone. Here is another chair, broken. I'm not at all sure what it is you're here to inspect, but this is all there is. Don't ask where are the staff. There aren't many and they're out.'

The secretary watched, embarrassment buried in the business of making tea, escaping down three flights to the shop next door for sugar which none of them wanted, pouring from a cracked pot as all of them perched round the desk, brittle with tension.

'Do you find,' said Mary, clearing her throat, calmer now, dislike chilled by her own inquiring smile, 'that your work involves a racial and social mix?' This question came from a questionnaire and she addressed the secretary, who began to open her mouth as John answered brusquely.

'Racial yes, social, no. You must know very well that most of society's disorders are confined to the poor. The dross, you might say.' He emphasized 'You'. Mary considered her own background briefly before shutting it out, recalled that she had never been given to understand that poverty had been much of a factor in her own parents' dreadful lives, let alone the cause of her abandonment. Memories of Claud and Katherine had long receded and she was busy disliking John Mills entirely in his own right. For the twitch, the underbelly and the bloody-minded arrogance. 'Not necessarily so,' she murmured. He looked at her with ill-concealed contempt. 'If this kind of abuse really went across the board,' he said, enunciating each word clearly as if lecturing the hard of hearing, 'It would be a very rare social disorder indeed. Only the most specialized diseases reach epidemic proportions in the good old middle and upper classes. A good analogy, I think.' He waved his arm expansively and Mary backed away. 'The rich generally look after themselves, don't you find? Immune from most things after all.'

'You can't generalize . . .' Mary began.

'After fifteen years of this, yes I can,' said John rudely. They all sipped tea in uncomfortable silence, Mary examining the contents of her cup with suspicion, knowing full well he had deliberately handed her the one with the cracks and brown rings inside. When the telephone rang, the secretary leapt towards it as if the receiver could announce salvation.

Tap-tapping downstairs again, a mere half-hour after entry, Mary was still too early for the next appointment, cancelled the day in her mind. She did not believe what she had just been told, about how she had hit these offices at the only slack time in weeks, something to do with summer holidays, factors she chose to ignore. Cats and prejudices, silly men with big feet and shoulders only large enough to cater for chips resting on them. One thing was certain sure: nobody in this little outfit was going to get one of the bloody awards. Or a pay rise out of charitable funds. Or recognition.

Mrs Harrison saw John Mills walking home on the opposite side of the road, looking up at the house. He reminded her of a tortoise, the way his head slid out from his shoulders with such suspicion. She waved to him from the window of Mrs Pearson Thorpe's study, but since the outside of the glass was so pristine clean from the ministrations of the early morning window cleaner, all John saw of her wave was a black reflection. Mrs Harrison had been dusting, removing *en route* the odd bottle and sticky glass from behind the small sofa which still held the shoebox of the family jewels, making her tut-tut in disapproval. So careless. Harrison, the better half, was downstairs watching Tee Vee with the children, boring stuff of which she disapproved, either cricket or cartoons, she couldn't remember which, suitable stuff for a stifling late afternoon. Jeanetta wouldn't have put up with that kind of sop: she would have played merry hell with all the sitting still – why had she been so fat? Mrs Harrison punched the cushions on the sofa, hammering them into shape with her fists and then losing interest, going back to the window, full of unexplained restlessness, stoked with anger. Poor little brute, Jeanetta, hidden for two whole weeks, you would have thought they would have let her come round to play, just to get used to the idea, bad for children, all these abrupt changes of regime. Mrs Harrison had knocked at next door twice, offered to take the pair of the kids to the park. Were they grateful? No. The refusal from

David what's-his-face had been distantly polite, cheesy grin all over the place, so kind, so very kind, but she's off with someone; maybe another time. She knew her place: knew her own version of her own station well enough to recognize repeated asking as being impolitic. She would, though: she bloody would. There was nothing inconsistent in the fact of her refusing to let Katherine in when she had come to the door. Harrison had done the same. She didn't want the mother: she only wanted the kids.

Pausing still by the study windows, Mrs Harrison fished in her pocket and found her cigarettes. Bugger it, room was stuffy enough and Madam would never notice the smell. Nevertheless, she took the precaution of opening the window, then thought for a moment, dragged up a chair and put her feet on the ledge, why not. Convenient, this: in the absence of a saucer, the ash could be flicked into the street. She coughed loudly. There was heavy dust in the green damask curtains. Shake these, she thought, and I'd suffocate in dead flies, but if Mrs P can't care less, no reason why I should either. Then she leant forward sharply. Drifting upwards, her keen ear had detected the voice of young Jeremy Allendale, his words unclear, but the high, questioning treble quite unmistakable. She pushed her bosom over the ledge to watch father and child crossing from left to right and approaching his car, perfect companions, walking close without touching. Then her heart stopped, oh dear God Almighty, there was that bloody beggar, lurking on the driver's side of the shiny vehicle, the same dirty man who had been inside this house like a magpie on legs, pathetic little creature, all wrinkled, tree-bark brown. Mrs Harrison leant further out of the window, ready to shout stop thief, stop him, Jerry boy, don't you see it's the same one, same little runt, grab the bastard and call the cops, before she checked herself in time and drew back beyond the distance where they might see her face, shaking her head in sudden self-congratulation. Then she sat back in her chair and threw the half-finished fag out of the window in a gesture of impatience. No way would little Jerry point out this thief: she knew what the memory of a two-year-old was like, nothing more exciting than the last two minutes, but wasn't she a fool, wanting to shout.

'Can't do that now, can I? Oh, shouldn't tell fibs . . .' She wagged one admonishing finger in front of her own face. 'Now, now,' she hummed to herself. One further thought crossed her mind, making her venture another bending forward with the bosom out of the window. Father and son had reached the car, but the vagrant man had moved beyond it. As she watched, he crossed the street at a gallop and in one fluid movement, picked up the cigarette she had jettisoned. He flicked at the end which had been lit with one experienced forefinger, put it in his pocket and moved quickly out of sight. Damn, said Mrs Harrison loudly, damn, blast and bloody, bloody hell.

When he had walked towards home up the street, John Mills had seen the tramp sitting on the pavement by the car and thought for one glorious minute he was guarding it, having heard of such things. Being very credulous about everything he read and never having owned a car, he thought a large BMW might be worth the guard, cheaper, probably, than any mechanical alarm. A body did not activate and embarrass the neighbours with yelping whoops simply because of the vibration of passing traffic, far more efficient. The man he saw squatting had eyes which were vivid pink against his ageless face. John's observations were brief and superficial: he was thinking of the kittens and how to find them new homes although his heart wanted to break at the very idea. His face twitched into a smile as he passed the car, grinning at the man for no reason while the plastic bag full of Kit-e-kat tins, stretched by the weight, bumped painfully on to his shins.

Matilda Mills was home one whole long half-hour since, all because of a little tiff. The man had called – the man, elderly and adoring, who had courted her for weeks – waited while Matilda's supervisor tutted and stood close by with a lot of heavy breathing, sniffing disapproval while Matilda spoke. As a result, Matilda had been terse, the man, who had wanted to arrange another jolly session in an even jollier bar, even terser in the space of a three-minute conversation which ended up in no arrangement at all. The resulting vacuum in herself left

Matilda frightened: she wanted to shout about how she did not deserve yet to lose this promised escape route, so she had hurried home in order to phone him from there, maybe get back out of doors before John came home. But the impulse had somehow died along with the panic, the sense of going to prison increasing as she plodded from the bus and over to her own front door. The image of the smiling, slightly plump seducer was receding like the Cheshire cat she remembered from *Alice in Wonderland*, a vision disappearing only to return in a clearer sky. Tomorrow would have to do. She felt some hope in that, but in the meantime, the all too familiar paralysis.

Friday evening, early. For the last month or more she had celebrated the end of the week with the other man. Outside the takeaway, where one of the Asians took down the shutters, Ahmed with the grin was unloading the van. He opened the back doors and whistled. Matilda watched in amazement, thinking of a childish joke heard in the shop, between children, one she had heard before. How do you fit six elephants into a Mini? Easy, three in the front and three in the back. From the back of the once white van, there emerged one enormous black and tan dog, the size of a small pony. It stepped out with delicacy, showing a soft black muzzle and drooping jowls, eyes of liquid brown which regarded the owner with complete trust while the leash was clipped to the collar round the neck. The doors of this mobile kennel were slammed shut: the dog flinched at the noise while Ahmed noticed Matilda and smiled his automatic smile, showing very white teeth and pink gums. ''Lo, missis. You like our doggy? This,' he patted the black and tan head, 'is our Rotty.'

Matilda did like, after a fashion. She waited behind them as Ahmed unlocked the side door which led through the building and on to her stairs. Following man and dog inside, she was fascinated by the swagger of the dog's rump, with a pair of enormous testicles swaying between the muscular legs. This impedimenta disgusted her, but she admired the rest, extended one hand to pat the rump before she departed upstairs. Ahmed turned and saw the beginnings of the gesture, jerked the leash so the animal sprang forward out of reach.

'Don't do so, missis. He is not quite knowing you, yet.'

'He's very handsome,' Matilda said warmly, withdrawing her hand all the same. 'I thought you said he was friendly.' Ahmed shifted from one foot to the other. 'Oh, yes, yes, yes. Very friendly, liking everyone, everything. Excepting cats.' He laughed uproariously. 'But only when he is knowing you better, you see. Then you pat him, take him for walking if you like. Very friendly dog. We take him home tonight. Back again, always Saturday. Busy then.'

His grin flashed in the dark corridor and he walked round the dog, which remained entirely still. Matilda watched as the door beyond was opened, revealing one square of the weedy, paved yard, stacked with boxes, still brilliant with sunlight. Then she went upstairs in the airless darkness, nostrils twitching, remembering the scent of cat litter, the cupboards full of muesli which looked the same, all the tins, accumulating over a week, waiting for the smell of feline life, the noise of hungry kittens and the feeling of venom which would overtake her.

Not entirely by coincidence, since it was Katherine who had taken them there the year before, Monica and Jenny went to the Royal Academy on their own. Monica had proved so difficult to pin down, but somehow she fell in with this idea. Jenny suggested they invite Katherine too, but Monica said, don't bother: she's at home today, leaving Jenny to wonder how she knew, not deigning to ask but relieved that they had spoken. Katherine's friendship was something she wanted to share, never mind dilute, and she was not going to ask any unnecessary questions or do anything at all to increase Monica's tetchiness. Neither had an eye for a picture, but people talked about this exhibition, like the American couple they both knew well: you had to say you had been or be dismissed as a Philistine. In any event, Monica fancied something big and modern for her house, she said. Anything halfway decent will be bought already, Jenny said. I don't want anything decent, said Monica. OK, don't argue. Jenny would settle for something small and pretty or nothing at all. She was becoming impatient with what she took to be sulks, wished in a way Katherine was with them after all. At least in her dreamy way she would have enthused and Jenny knew she would never buy a picture without her approval.

No chance of that anyway. Canvases of landscapes, pretty bowls of flowers, pictorial beauties and anonymous portraits of gorgeous women were all gone. Jenny shuddered at the nudes which Monica pretended to like while Monica poohooed pictures of children which Jenny adored. By the time they reached abstracts and simply non-figurative, their steps were getting quicker, breaking into a canter towards the general direction of the exit and restaurant. 'Right,' said Monica. 'I think I've had enough of culture. Oh, Christ, look at that.'

She slewed to a halt before the lurid depiction of adultery, taking in the lewd shapes without reading the title. 'Great, isn't it?'

'You must be kidding,' said Jenny. 'What's happening anyway? Has that poor woman given birth to twins? Oh, I see. They're at it.' She peered at the title. 'I can't understand what on earth that's got to do with it.'

'Neither can I,' Monica responded grimly. 'How much does it cost?'

Jenny looked up a price list on the wall. 'Five thousand pounds. Katherine might say it was a masterpiece.'

'I doubt it. Unsold, I see. Colin would love it on the living-room wall.' Monica put a hand over her mouth and snorted with laughter, a look of misery in her eyes which was misunderstood. 'I like the frame,' Jenny contributed, pleased to see at least the laughter. Something in the picture stirred an entirely unconnected guilt. She must, absolutely must, telephone Katherine, but Monica, awkward, troubled Monica, came first, and for reasons she could not fathom, Monica would not like it. Jenny was hungry and thristy: the day was hot even in these vaulted halls. She no longer wanted to buy. Monica was preoccupied and selfish. What about me, Jack, Jenny wanted to say: please listen to me.

'Hungy, thirsty. What about you, Jack?'

Jack be nimble, Jack be quick: Jack jumped over a candlestick. Jeanetta played with Jack, quite unable to remember the chance rhyme which had brought him into existence in her head. Jack also climbed a beanstalk out of the roof. He had come to live in the playroom since ever she had spent so much time in there alone: he was hungry too, but very, very clever. Jack sat still and pretended to eat, sitting solemnly with his legs crossed in the corner, a knife and fork in his hands, cutting at the floor very tidily, putting bits into his mouth and saying, 'Mmmm, mmm, very nice.' She followed suit, juggling the cutlery with great expertise and making the same noises. 'I think I'll have ice cream now,' she told Jack aloud. No you won't, he said: There's none left. Jeanetta stared wide-eyed and vacant towards a space on the wall. 'Greedy Jack. What's for me? Oh, nothing much. Yogot and cornflakes and a few biscuits. Goody goody, I'll have the biscuits.' She picked them tidily off the floor, the small mouth working and the whole of her swallowing, desperate to feel the solidity, imagining the sweetness. But all the swallowing made her thirsty: she was getting tired of this game. Jack was even cleverer. Yesterday, whenever was yesterday, or another day anyway, she followed Jack on top of the chest to reach up to the window. Together they had licked off the moisture from the pane until she fell from craning too high, but then he showed her how to dabble her fingers in a small pool of condensation on the ledge and transfer dirty water into her mouth. She did not mind the inclusion of dust. Dust was funny: she had never seen it before except in Mrs Harry's house, not here, except when Daddy built things. The little pool of water was vaguely grey but the colour hardly mattered.

'Come on, Jack.' She blundered over to the window, coughing.

Swallowing did that too. No, she really was getting fed up of this game. She stopped importantly to pull up her shorts, which tended to waggle down over her behind. Since they were soiled and tended to get in the way of clambering on to the chest, she took them off instead. Every ounce of energy was needed for climbing the chest: something about it got higher and higher, the ascent harder and harder, but she finally got there, winded, coughing again. The sun was sharp. No water. She shut her eyes and counted one, two, three. Sometimes there was water, sometimes not. Pretending made her weary. 'Not enough for you, Jack,' she called down. Not enough for anyone. She searched the wood along the edge of the pane, picking at the paint. Then slithered back to the floor, trying not to cry. Be good, be good. Her throat hurt. You lied to me, Jack, you fibber: you did. She wanted to be sorrowful but instead was angry, weakly angry, and wanting to pull things apart. Jack disappeared whenever she was cross.

From outside in the kitchen, she heard the downstairs telephone. Daddy's voice.

'No, I'm sorry, not today. She's not in. How are you?' No screaming, she remembered, and the throat was too dry for such protest, her face all squeezed up and her hands clenched with the effort not to cry. Where are you, Jack? Where've you gone, come back, please. He would, she supposed. Someone had to come back. In the meantime she was still angry, still remembering not to scream.

Jeanetta, feeble yet furious, looked round for something to tear with her teeth.

15

Katherine lay spreadeagled on the bed, aching in every limb, listening for the sounds of his breathing and the sounds of the night. How wrong, she thought, in a burst of perspiration, a sweat of panic, how wrong can a person be? Controlling herself, keeping her being as calm as she could, imagining that the only threat was against herself, letting it all get out of control. Imagining she was the only one who might be at risk: thinking that if she was good, everything would be all right. In the bathroom mirror, she had seen this evening older and wiser eyes, known, unbelievably for the first time, where the real threat lay and who might be the victim. The belief was tenuous: she did not want it, but it would not go away.

She was aware of hurting without being able to tell the source of the pain, smoothed one inner thigh to relieve the sensation of bruising and distract the nausea. She had been dry as a bone, the sexual exercise forced without protest and without response. One floor above the playroom, she could no longer hear what might have been Jeanetta's screaming, or the talking, or the singing, or the strange, keening noises she made, all of the childish sounds faded into merciful oblivion, drifting downwind when David had half helped, half lifted her upstairs, she leaning on to his arm like an old lady.

Jeanetta had not eaten today, nor yesterday. Virtually nothing on all the days since Katherine's meeting with Mary, confused to find on her return those fractious howls filling the kitchen air, sure sign of a presence beyond the door. The same each day since. Jeremy had been asleep, siesta-ing quietly away from the noise which tended to make him shriek in symphony. David had emerged from his studio, infuriated by Katherine's interruption, hearing her protests with calm indifference.

'Of course she screams, darling. She's been naughty. It's guilt, that's all.'

'Hunger, that's all. She hasn't had any food since . . . when? Why did you keep her in? She could have stayed with you.'

He shrugged.

'She's too fat to eat.'

'David . . .'

'Leave her.' He had closed the door on himself and the playroom key.

That day, she seemed to remember, they had let the child out for cold supper, a fragment of the bread, but for the days since she had now spent far more time inside the playroom than elsewhere although there had been one or two spells in the garden. She had tried to eat some leaves: next door's dog did that, she said. As well as grass. Today Katherine had looked at her and experienced some difficulty in perceiving this as her own, fat child. The clothes on the body were standing away and the arms which emerged from the sleeves of the stained cotton blouse were no longer plump; surely she was slender enough now for this streamlined house. Mother always imagined David had in mind a sort of enforced diet, simply to make her appearance more amenable. Katherine had moved to embrace child, but child screamed, leant backwards, the scream releasing spittle from her mouth which landed on the pristine white of Katherine's skirt. David was ignoring the sound and looking over the child's head into the carnage of the playroom. 'Christ Almighty,' he said. 'Look what the little bitch has done now.'

Jeanetta had made a good few hours' work. The playroom contained two large cupboards and one oak chest. On the evening when she had been letting rip with her granny in charge, Jeanetta had learned for the first time the strength and skill to raise or lower the heavy lid of the chest which contained her mother's ancient frocks, a red cloak, a long purple gown, and now the floor was festooned with evening clothes, the mess accentuated by the variety of colours. One of the blouses, frilly, georgette, was torn to shreds. From the cupboard, Jeanetta had dragged her toys along with all those which were Jeremy's least favourite and kept separately from the store in his room. It had proved impossible to smash all these toys, but she had tried without discrimination, looking for something to break the window, then looking for distraction. Soft toys were minus eyes: a large horse, big enough to wheel around and once the right size for her to sit astride, present from Granny, was now minus tail and ears, while on the floor, eyes looking skywards in mute appeal, lay a doll with teeth marks in the pink forehead. One arm of the corpse rested on the window-ledge where the paintwork was scratched along the bottom of the pane. David turned back the door of the room, finding identical scratch marks, tut-tutted loudly. Jeanetta shrank back from his discovery. It occurred to Katherine, very dimly and not in a way she could begin to articulate, that Jeanetta was growing like herself, all notions of what was right and what was wrong entirely dependent on his reaction, however irrational: the severity of the wrong never marked by anything as obvious as a blow.

'Jack did it,' Jeanetta shouted, pointing at the doll. 'Jack did, he did, he did.'

David ignored her, stepped into the playroom and began to retrieve toys which belonged to his son. At the other end of the kitchen, Katherine stood by the sink, alongside three portions of fresh cheeses on the draining board, unidentifiable outside the delicatessen wrappings in which he had carried them home. She pushed one of the portions into her handbag, then moved towards her daughter with some hesitation. Since Jeanetta did not rush to her side, but stared with dark, suspicious eyes, Katherine did not venture to touch. 'I'll take her for a wash,' mother murmured to the back of David's head, and led the way upstairs. 'Come on, sweetheart.'

'I'm bringing Jack.'

'Yes, I know.'

The child followed, slowly, without looking back, breathing with deep and noisy breaths. She had developed a cough. Katherine had heard it, dry, polite and painful.

I should have known, I should have thought . . . Cheese is

too rich. Twitching in the heat, feeling warmth radiate from the body beside her, finding the touch of even one, thin sheet unbearable. Katherine placed a hand over her mouth to stifle her own retching. Hidden in the bathroom earlier with stinking Jeanetta, watching her wolf down four ounces of fresh soft cheese, grimacing at the taste she disliked but nevertheless swallowing without chewing. I should have known. Back down to the supper table praying all would be well; David these days preparing even that as if he expected to be poisoned, leaving Katherine nothing but the incessant cleaning. Jeanetta trailing behind silent but fresh in clean shorts and top, green around the gills, behaving to perfection. Until, gazing furtively into the now immaculate playroom, staying at the other end of the room, watching Papa as if transfixed and drawn to his side on a thread, she had been violently sick almost at his feet. The cheese, yellowish, scarcely digested, deposited on the shiny floor as vivid as egg yolk. Child stumbled towards the windows out to the garden, unable to run fast. He had followed without rushing, caught her easily, picked her up and put her back in the playroom without a word. Punishment; still out of control. This time she had not screamed.

In the silence after the locked door, Katherine watched not David's face, but his hands as he replaced the key in the pocket of his trousers and resumed his swift and efficient preparations. Wash lettuce, not iceberg, tasteless stuff, preferred a good cos every time. Bash two fillets of veal with a small wooden mallet, coat them in fresh breadcrumbs. A few new potatoes, very few, tossed when hot in a tablespoon of soured cream with finely chopped chives, flavoured further with sea salt. As he cooked and as they ate, the silence beyond the playroom door was ominous. Katherine guessed Jeanetta was crying. David spoke as if nothing had happened, planning out loud the arrangements for the birthday party which was now becoming imminent. He loved to plan: they had not entertained for weeks. Katherine listened, part incredulous, slowly beginning to grow calmer as the other silence persisted. Her head was bowed. The prospect of a houseful of people was suddenly welcome. Jeanetta's absence on that occasion would be very pleasant, a thought she dismissed but still gave room.

'A very gourmet, very simple meal, I think,' he was saying cheerfully. Only ten to feed, shouldn't be so difficult. You'll have Monica and Jenny for company, plus husbands, Susan thing next door and hers if he's around, don't blame him if she isn't. Oh and I asked the American couple. Quid pro quo for the glamours of their thrash.' He grinned at her meaningfully. 'All forgotten now, honestly. Glass of wine, darling? Try this, you usually like Chardonnay. No? I agree, a bit heavy, this one.'

He ate the veal, and some of hers which was left unfinished, economizing with his movements, always quiet and perfect with a knife and fork, a quick eater, even in company. 'We'll take drinks outside, especially if it's like this. Cooler.' She was silent, blessing the apple tree which spread some of itself across the window of the playroom, shading half the interior until evening when the branches stepped aside for the sun to come streaming through. There were always wasps around the tree, as if booking space long before the autumn apples which never grew to fruition, remaining hard little marbles suitable only for scavengers. She forbore to mention the wasps to her husband: he would take the mere suggestion of a nest as a personal insult. Katherine ate the lettuce with the same enthusiasm she might have eaten porridge on this night of heatwave. It tasted of dust, spiced with the biting crystals of sea salt.

Then in the quietude of the post-prandial cigar, the one unhealthy indulgence allowed by the master of the house to himself, with David eyeing his wife like a man contemplating dessert, there came the scratching sound from the direction of the playroom. Scratch, scratch; then blows, more of a tapping than the kicking which had been the earlier noises. Jeanetta beyond, destroying the new tidiness of her little cell, weaker than she had been, hitting at the door with the dismembered arm of the doll which had fat fingers spread into a fan. The noise was slight, insistent, almost rhythmic. Katherine stiffened, alarmed but also irritated. Didn't she know by now what was good for her, good for all of them? Peace was so fragile.

David reached back behind his chair and turned on the radio.

'Let her out, please. Please, darling.' Katherine's voice emerged from a stranger.

He smiled at her, the devastating smile which creased his eyes, revealing teeth cleaned and flossed to white perfection. 'Later, darling. I think we have better things to do.' The words filled her with despair, the formula familiar. Food, wine, sex, a familiar cycle. She had been feeling sick all day.

'No.' Her own, sharp protest startled herself.

'What do you mean, No?' She shook her head.

'I want more babies,' he said suddenly, apropos of nothing. 'More sons. You were right never to cut your hair. Beautiful, handsome sons, with hair like yours. Lots of them.' Then he lifted her upstairs.

Such an old face in the mirror. The face of someone old enough to know better. Even if she was mad, so possible a fact she was prepared to embrace it, she could abdicate no longer, could not lie here and lie to herself in silence. Silence. A deafening silence one floor above the ground in a quiet, polished house. David's lean and muscular torso turned away from the window. In the stillness, the hum of traffic, a tangible sound, quite inhuman and without any comfort. Her eyes, stiff with sweat and tears, thinking of Jeanetta downstairs, talking to Jack and frightened of the dark, her own intermittent anger at the child another source of unease. Inch by inch, Katherine stole from the bed, moving with precise steps towards the chair where his clothing lay folded. She held her breath as she sidled to the chair, felt in the pocket of the trousers and closed her fingers over the key, the sensation of the metal feeling like a scald of hot water in her palm, jumping as the belt, still looped round the waist of the garment, clicked against the wood of the chair. David turned slightly in his sleep, a ten-degree movement of his broad shoulders, twisting his neck with his hand sliding under the pillow. Beneath the dark head, his neck looked vulnerable: at once she understood an impulse to take the pillow next to his face, blot out that springy hair, subdue that strong profile into a mass of white linen for it to remain still, without breathing for ever, but the passing thought fled without tempting action. She felt momentary triumph in her possession of the key, lost as she fumbled downstairs. Light from the landing windows reflected on the mahogany stair-rail she had polished to perfection this morning: she clung to the warm surface like a guiding rope, lowering herself by degrees into the bowels of the house, paying out the banister, reluctant to leave it. You must not shout or scream, Jeanetta: you must not make a noise, this is our secret: this will be over soon. Wait till he notices how thin you are, be quiet, darling, please: say nothing, do nothing. I'll get you cornflakes at least. No key on the fridge and one locked cupboard yielded to Katherine. The one containing dry food, rice, cereals, ugh, all foods to stick to the lips, but there was fruit on the table. None of your favourites, Jeanetta: no biscuits, they make a person fat.

In the kitchen, the silence was profound, the room insulated from the traffic sounds just discernible upstairs. There was a slight, tick-ticking sound from the boiler hidden in the cupboard by the playroom door. As Katherine placed the key in the lock, one hand gripping the cool brass handle of the door, the ticking sound seemed to exaggerate, move closer. She imagined a booby trap, a time bomb triggered to the latch, but the hands with a will of their own, remained functional, the ticking regular. Shhhhhh, she breathed into the keyhole. Shhhhh, Jeanetta, me, shhhh, for heaven's sake. Her whisper cut through the silence like a knife, horribly loud like the staccato shufflings on the other side of the wall. Katherine paused, then pushed open the door, seeing the brilliant blonde of Jeanetta's head emerging from the cloth of the evening dress she was using as a blanket. It was cooler on this floor, but Katherine sweated beneath the cotton nightdress she had dragged over her head. The clash of colours inside the room was so vivid, Katherine held her breath for a second, expelled it in one gasp. There was a fleeting impression of how pretty the child looked swathed in this adult satin, lit by the moon; pretty and almost comic, rubbing her brilliant eyes, then staring without smiling. She began to scrabble out of the material, one arm stuck in one sleeve of the dress. Her hand came free with a small tearing sound; Katherine put one finger over her mouth. 'Shhhhhh,' she said again.

'Mummy,' said Jeanetta, 'Mummy, Mummy, Mummy.

Help me, Mummy. I'se so hungry. Very hungry. I'll be good.'
She was wobbling slightly as she stood, not a shade of the
truculence left, no pride, frightened baby. She stretched out
her arms and Katherine held her briefly, aware that there were
tears coursing down her own cheeks, blinding her, making her
shake. Already, as they swayed together for a moment, her
plans were changing. Food first, then get out. Anywhere, just
out, even in the dark, dressed as they were, out. Away. It was
suddenly obvious there would be no end to this, no finale apart
from a fading away and in that brief embrace, of desperate love
and affection, Katherine could feel the sharp edge of a rib-
cage, more poignant and revealing than any tears. The child
was thin, horribly thin, and the cough a rasp of accusation.

Softly, she closed the door of the kitchen. The pair of them,
Katherine in particular, suffering from the peculiar desire to
laugh, the kind of giggles accompanying a midnight feast,
although, despite her still persisting nausea, Katherine had
found from nowhere a clear head and considerable authority.
Jeanetta clutched her skirt, refusing to move from her side.
'Now,' she whispered to Jeanetta, 'eat as slowly as you can:
you don't want to be sick, we haven't time.' Katherine had
always been vague about food suitable for her children, gave
them whatever she had, but in the 2.00 a.m. clarity, saw how
cornflakes were the best she could offer in all their digestible
blandness. With even more uncharacteristic forethought, she
placed two apples in the handbag she had left earlier in the
kitchen, thinking ahead with furious planning. There was a
thin summer coat on the hallstand outside, a pair of espadrilles,
enough to cover her modesty. There was no money in the
handbag, nowhere to go, but none of that mattered, not any
longer. All they had to do was get out, knock at the next-door
house, hammer as long as it took for one of the inmates to
answer, didn't matter if they were resentful. Nobody would
listen, but someone had to listen. Perhaps she could encourage
response by yelling 'Police' through the letter box, or ask
Jeanetta to create one of her truly piercing screams, but they
were wasting time. Katherine watched: Jeanetta shovelling a
small portion of cornflakes in so tidy a fashion she was clearly
cured of the habit of mashing all food to pulp, one thin arm

transferring the spoon to her mouth with well-mannered speed as if she had only just realized this was the most efficient way to consume, eyeing her mother over the bowl. Slowly, darling, please. Katherine wanted to stop the eating process, flee the house without delay, but she did not have the heart to curtail a tiny meal. In the mind's frantic calculations lay the knowledge that in real terms, the child had been subsisting on crumbs. She had been on the verge of lunacy, distracted, out of her mind, thinking all the time that it was herself who was the most vulnerable. For a brief moment, she felt as strong as a lion.

'More, Mummy. Please.' Dear God, the manners were perfect. So was the obedience.

'No, darling, not yet. We're going now.'

'Where?'

'Mrs Harrison.'

'Ohhh, yes.' There was a long sigh of sheer relief. Jeanetta had been kneeling on the chair, twisted off it and made for the kitchen door. 'I'm bringing Jack.'

'Wait. Got to be very, very quiet.' Oh why had she mentioned a destination causing this noisy excitement, when all the time the front door was locked, how could she have forgotten? 'Come back, darling, come back, not that way. By the window.' Katherine's head was clearer than it had ever been, her words showing no shadow of the usual hesitation. Jeanetta obeyed her.

The kitchen window, security locked, but not with a key. On either side the window was fastened against intruders by bolts in the frame, easily unscrewed from the inside. What had once been a steep basement well a few feet below had been boarded over by David to save it being filled with litter from passers-by, strong enough boards for a safe landing even if they jumped. They were both such light people. Sudden movements, she noticed, made Jeanetta stagger, issue her polite little cough: her small feet unsteady as she smothered the sound, while Katherine was finding yet more energy, removing the bolts with deft fingers. She had cleaned the inside of the glass yesterday morning, noted the position of the locks even then, but as she opened the sash window, her eyes registered another problem. Once out on the boards above the basement, they would still have to surmount the railings, but all would be possible once they had placed both feet into the outside world. Pad the top of the railings, climb over.

'Sweetheart, fetch one of the dresses from the playroom.'

'No, Mummy, please: You go.' Jeanetta could not bear to retreat back in that direction. Katherine smiled at her, ran back across the floor, pulled out the red cloak from the pile of clothes on the floor, ran back, forgetting now the need for shoes or coat, she would do as she was rather than risk opening the door into the hall. 'I'll go out first, darling, then you can land on me. Jack will manage.' Jeanetta smiled weakly, her face strained.

The stone window-ledge barked Katherine's shins and the height of the ledge from the boards was greater than she had imagined. At first she tried to lever herself down, then she jumped, still carrying the red cloak, landed with a thud and a searing pain in one foot. Hurriedly she threw the cape over the railings, turned back to the window. 'Jeanetta?' a loud whisper, full of exhilaration. 'Come on, darling, quickly.' There was silence. No small head appeared above the window, no sign, no voice. The rustling of the fine trees in the street was deafening, the sluggish breeze in the air deliciously cool after the confines of the house. I'm wrong, I'm wrong, Katherine thinking, all wrong, suddenly quite terrified of the dark: I could have simply taken her out through the garden, over the wall at the back, into next door, we could have waited there, just as we were, until morning. She looked briefly at the railings which surrounded her, the height of her shoulder, huge, but not insurmountable. Then called again, 'Come on, Jeanetta, come quick, just climb over, I'll catch you. Don't be frightened.' There was more silence. Katherine gripped the stone ledge, jumped up to look into the kitchen, saw nothing but the yawning gap of window, unable to see far into the room. Had child gone back for food perhaps? For Jack? Katherine stood irresolute, ready to risk a shout, or climb in again to fetch her daughter, and standing, was aware of a prickling in the scalp. As she held on to the ledge, ready to go back upwards, swearing under her breath, she turned her head to one side, stopped. The front door of the house was standing open. David lounged on the top step, shaking his head. He held in his hand the old key to the gate in the railings, and the new key to the door of the house.

'Are you looking for burglars?' he asked. 'Or were they looking for you?'

Her headband fluttered to the floor. As if it had controlled the inside of her skull, something in her mind snapped and darkness closed round her.

Sophie Allendale had always known it would happen some day, and now it had. To her own surprise, she had been the soul of calm, but then she had not caught them in action. The other fears set in later. Her life for the last few years had been geared to fear of this breed, burglars, that was: people she always envisaged from her local paper as being large, fat, working in gangs armed with axes, the scourge of anyone over sixty, all hell-bent on pursuit of her possessions. But she had been talked out of the usual vigilance by one of her friends, who said you can only die once, and the way you carry on, death will be from heatstroke. Don't be so silly-billy, Sophie, Mary Fox had added cosily; even burglars get lazy in the heatwave like this and you'll shrivel up if you don't open the windows. They had been eating tea the other day, or at least, Sophie eating, Mary pacing up and down in an irritating manner, bitching about her sister and also about the heat. Today is August, Granny, do open the windows, there's a dear: having them shut all the time is bad for your skin. This last remark was the deciding factor. Sophie considered her own skin quite remarkable for her age, while Mary considered the panoply of pots necessary to sustain the bloom quite excessive. They prevented access to the bathroom basin. So Sophie, if only to justify the expense of the pots and lotions, had opened the French windows of her living room to find the effect such a relief she forgot to close them again as often as not. Somehow the burglars, or the survival of her furniture, or the prospect of rape, were not as important as they had been and the neurosis of a lifetime slipped sideways. She had other things on her mind.

Such as being barred from the house of son and grand-children. Distressing was not an adequate word to describe the sense of rejection. She could not begin to explain herself to the coven when she met them for coffee in Luigi's; could find no formula to reply to the question 'And how's the lovely babies, then?' without the lie or the equally telling lack of detail becoming transparent. None of them was born yesterday: they relished family conflict and Sophie had lorded over them a little too long. 'Wonderful,' she would say. 'Growing so tall, eating so much,' none of this news anything compared to the fulsome details she was accustomed to provide even though her contact with son and grandchildren had never been as frequent or consistent as she had pretended. No contact at all was not a difference of degree; more like a body blow which left her wheezing and gasping for air, a humiliation so acute she could not mention it. Mary said Katherine was to blame, and although Sophie had not been strictly truthful in her account of the last evening's babysitting, she tended to agree, since it was, in the last analysis, Katherine who had barred her from the house.

When the burglars struck, she had been wandering in a street, which street mattered not, provided there were shop windows and nothing was far from home. She liked looking at antiques if there were any to be seen and was particularly fond of masquerading as a buyer, well aware that her general appear-ance, her clipped accent and the deceptive appearance of being a lady of means, instead of one who had had her pocket money regulated by her son since ever he was twelve, made the sellers inclined to listen and answer questions for twenty minutes at a time. She was looking, vaguely, for pieces of furniture she had once possessed and lost, little tables, chairs, all gone, sold or taken; she had been looking for years, never finding. But in one of these delightful interludes, so frequent now, when she felt the need to chat was even greater than the need to eat, the burglars had found the living room and stepped through it. Unnecessary, she thought, to break one pane of glass: the window was open already.

Oh what a mess. Dearie, dearie me. The room was always one kind of mess in the form of clutter, but this was a different type of mess. She did not find the fact of only the minimum of things being missing to be any sort of comfort. In the course of removing one precious television, a radio not quite so indispensable and two or three ornaments which happened to be recognizably silver, they had invaded every drawer, every cupboard, despite the flimsy locks which Sophie used for the safe keeping of almost everything she owned. The contents appeared to have been tipped on the living-room floor. Looking with quick, bird-like eyes at what was left, Sophie knew a feeling of pique. How dare they imagine that her Staffordshire dogs, her ornaments, the cups of David's which were nickel, not silver, or the lace antimacassars were not worth the bother of stealing? Cheek, ignorant pigs, the indignation soared through her, granting a feeling of superiority which arrested the cold sensation for a minute. She supposed she could call the police, but only wanted to call her son, and in the dilemma of what to do next, she sat on the floor once she had established there was no one left in the flat and the windows were firmly closed, made tea and began to examine the piles of things on the carpet. No, she would not call the police; she had enough to do with them once, great big brutes. There on the floor was Daddy's death certificate, medical reports citing malnutrition. Oh, he had been so fat and fair once. Fractured skull from falling downstairs, falling, it said. Everything scattered about now, along with his indictment for embezzlement and fraud, his convictions for theft. Sophie shuffled away papers, merely examined the objects, preferring to find things the existence of which she had forgotten. The forced, slow turning over of items which had been locked away was a voyage of discovery, accompanied by a great jumble of memories and confusions, all far more disturbing than the burglars themselves.

For a start, there she had been for something like weeks, ever since her banishment, hating her daughter-in-law with the sort of poisonous hatred which would have made her stick pins in her wax effigy if only she could have found the wax and the hair she believed necessary, but here, on the floor, released from some place of safe keeping, were all those lovely things Katherine had given her in the past. Yes, she pictured it now, this same flat when son David was courting, bless him, that gorgeous girl arriving armed with flowers, chocolates, assorted goodies, clothes. Oh and a care in the choices too, a pink silk scarf so precious that Sophie saved it only for best until she forgot where she had put it, then, saucy girl, some camiknickers which had been the most flattering thing of all, a recognition of being not just any old woman, but a pretty old woman, you know, the age usually the recipient of beastly thermal underwear, delighted to receive something fit for a sexy lady. Sophie had saved those to look at, tried them on sometimes, giggled and decided that she did not dare, but in looking at them now, remembered she had worn the frilly blouses and used the exquisite lace handkerchiefs provided from the same source, and not with David's money either, not as far as she knew, no definitely not. David had been as surprised by the perspicacity of the choices, even a little annoyed, so he certainly had not paid. Oh dearie, dearie me, oh my ears and whiskers. Sophie was scratching at her head, feeling the curls damp with the heat, Katherine even used to take me to the hairdresser. Katherine loved me, she really did. Whatever Mary says.

The evening had come down like a curtain over a short act, surprising her into dusk. Suddenly she was too exhausted to bother with anything and what did it matter, none of all this had anything to do with Daddy. Tomorrow would do. Nor could she cope with any one of the coven, or Katherine's sister, who would have come round like a shot at the merest hint of disaster. It was only after she went to bed, leaving the mess, only shutting the drawers in the bedroom so as not to be alarmed by different shadows on the walls, that she began to shake and imagine whoever they were would come back. Despite the metal grilles across the broken window frame, piece of nothing to such a team. She could not envisage this as the work of one teenage boy (which it was), lay there quaking and listening for any sound not instantly familiar, got up to fetch the radio at midnight before she remembered it had gone. She made tea, drifted to and fro to the lavatory and sat there for an hour, the bathroom feeling secure since it appeared to have escaped invasion, ah there was a trick to recall for the future, put the silver in there. She tried to think of insurance, the bonus of money back on what was stolen, but could not think straight. All the time she wanted to call her son, strangely wanted to call Katherine. Pride forbade, but she could not stop the wish. Then a squirt of anger intervened. This is my son, my only son: she is my daughter-in-law. I am an old lady. Why the devil does it matter if I call in the middle of the night? At 2.00 a.m., according to the clock too old to be worth the burglars' appropriation, she dialled, but put down the phone after three rings. She imagined it, by the side of their marital bed, oh no, supposing Katherine did not love her after all, put down the phone as soon as someone at the other end picked up their receiver. Then the anger took hold after yet more tea. She dialled again at three. This time she waited for an answer.

Sophie, hand shaking on one end of the telephone, waiting to speak to a son while hoping the spouse of the son would answer. David had been wrong: Katherine would not mind the mess, Katherine never had. Sophie, receiving, after a very long pause, how many rings, she lost track, determined this time to hang on to the receiver as if it were a lifeline, a voice out of the wilderness. David, speaking with a suspicion in his tone which sounded a little like guilt. 'Hallo . . . Who's that?' Not the aggression she might have expected.

'Mummy,' she mumbled.

There was an exclamation. 'Mummy who?'

'Your mother,' Sophie yelled, angry with him for sounding such a stranger.

'Oh.'

'You took long enough to answer. What on earth do you think you were doing? I hope you weren't having a nightmare.'

'I'm not doing anything, but I was trying to sleep. It's the middle of the night. What do you want, Mother, are you drunk?'

'I've been burgled.'

'When? Now?'

She was aware she might achieve more by exaggeration of both timing and scale, but could not bring herself to lie.

'No, this afternoon.'

'Did you call the police?'

'Well, no.'

'Are you all right?' The question sounded bored.

'Sound in mind and limb if that's what you mean. I only needed to talk. Could I speak to Katherine?' The hesitation was palpable.

'No, you can't: she's asleep. And she hasn't been well.'

'I'm sure she won't mind if you ask her. I'm not very well either, as it happens.'

He laughed, a little uncertainly. 'Not like Katherine, Mama. Different kind of sickness. We think she may be pregnant. Not sure yet.'

'Ohhhh!' All Sophie's fears, angers and alarms melted in the face of one sensation of delight. The burglars were forgotten in David's master stroke. Surely her son would need her now. 'Ohhh, darling David, you are so clever . . . Ohh, I'll leave her in peace.'

'Listen, Ma, it's 3.00 a.m. I can't come over now and leave the children. I'll drift across in the morning.'

'You're forty in a few days,' Sophie remarked in one of her *non sequiturs* which only meant she was not anxious to relinquish the phone.

'I know, Mother, I know. Go back to sleep.'

She was completely mollified, suddenly weary. 'I haven't been to sleep, oh all right then, sleep tight. Give Katherine a kiss for me. Bye-bye.'

David replaced the phone on the bedside table. The mattress beside him was empty. He was marginally grateful to his mother for the earlier interruption, not for the later. His house was now secure, because of her, all his possessions safely housed. Jeremy slept; there was never such a sleeper as Jeremy. Jeanetta was back where she belonged, out of earshot, while he could imagine the faint sounds of Katherine in the attic, walking up and down, down and up, her frantic rattling of the lock suspended now. She should have known better: such a pity she always had to be taught all over again just as soon as she appeared to have learned. As he drifted into sleep, he remembered the red cloak still on the railings outside and reminded himself to remove it in the morning.

So many tasks.

16

'Do you love me?' My husband asked me that, once, in another life, two years ago.

'Don't be so damned stupid. Go to sleep.'

Something like that, was what I said, something derisory. I remembered, wide awake somewhere about four o'clock this morning, and into these ghastly hours comes every single depressing thought, everything I never wanted to know or think, conclusions I have never made.

Then there's a count of everything drunk the evening before in a vain attempt to prove that these broken slumbers and the consumption of alchohol are not related, a piece of mathematics which invariably fails after three gins, half-bottle wine, three more of the same . . . Not much, not much at all, of course not, the old lie turning into that sickly sweet taste in the mouth which tells the truth and makes water into nectar. Sometimes, the deepest sleep follows the waking, but in the small hours, I admit defeat and I miss him. The warm back mostly, the shreds of conversation. The brief intrusion from the front. Did you love me, did you ever love me?

He wasn't always so perfunctory, you see. It was me who started the rot. Bored, grumpy, can't be bothered to go out and I hate this house, pushing him off while thinking instead of sums or clients and taxes, ignoring the children the way I had been ever so nicely, ignored. Such a tidy house of servants, the one of my childhood and the one I created, no responsibilities for mother. Perhaps privilege does this, I do not know, made me so frightened of intimacy through lack of practice, keeping life as formal as possible, but I begin to see how modern man wants more, suffering the same as us from a rising of expectations. They want cuddles and a warm kitchen as well as brain; want us to civilize them with talk, comfort and wallpaper so that pure marriages of equal minds and equal duties may not work. Mine was always treated like a deal, Sebastian and I like directors on the Board and if we disagreed, he was outvoted. Less said the better, mine was the only way, never a hint of democracy here and precious little sentiment either. Something there was I missed or I would not be missing him now. Would not consider, in the purgatory of the early morning, begging him to come back, and if pride was once my backbone, it has a curvature. In my own loneliness, I now see, his.

Backache, heartache, headache. Yesterday morning I had all three as well as the peculiar conviction of being woken by something other than the pre-dawn nausea, opted for pillow over head until daylight, gave up towards six and wobbled towards the study for some pretence at work. And God, the heat. Weeks of this constant sweat, making everything grey, an open window carrying the mockery of a breeze as fetid as a cow's breath, the air so thick you could cut it with a knife. Not a sound in the street when I look out to check if anything else is alive, blinking downwards to something like a flag on the railings flanking the Allendales' house, so startling I squint and look again, very quietly. Thick red material on top of the blunt spikes near the front window, a sort of red carpet for a burglar's bottom. Pretty and pretty odd: half asleep, I tried harder for the imperfect view which misses their front windows and the recess of the door, nothing visible, no sight or sound apart from the red material, hanging there like a signal while I feel absurdly disappointed to see nothing more malicious.

They weigh on one now, if you can understand, a family like that, so bloody self-contained, and they treat me as if I did not exist, the first humiliators of the deserted wife. I can't approach them, knowing what I know, but I wanted one of them to approach me with the hand of friendship we're supposed to have, but neither of them will. To think I liked them once after my own fashion while now I tend to despise them for despising me: you would think their children had never spent the greater part of two years in my house because in the few weeks since they left, there's been scarcely a word. Oh I know David gave Mrs Harrison a large sweetener, but it doesn't follow that the kids should have disappeared so completely. Mark may have found Jeanetta a pain, but now he sulks, so does Samantha. They are a little confused by the absence of Daddy, however little they saw of him: having those Allendale brutes around the place would have helped since what seems to control children most is the presence of other children. Oh damn, damn, damn. All right, Sebastian, you've made your point. I can't bring myself to call you darling, but OK, you did help: you actually did far more than I, and I miss you.

Did you love me, my husband? Did I try? It was me, wasn't it? And you in spirit, sitting on that park bench, lonely as a day in hell.

I shouted last time we met, but my heart wasn't in the noise I was making and when he had his turn he spoke with more authority than I'd ever remembered. He has fine eyes and his hair was untidy, I wanted to touch while I capitulated so much, thought so much, realizing things I never knew, and if suffering ennobles the human spirit, I would prefer to remain base. There is no black and white to life any more, only shades of grey like dirty washing. He looked leaner and fitter, which irked me into the shouting and also drinking more, watching him watch me and seeing through his eyes what it did to my speech. Oh for the luxury of drunkenness instead of the confusion, the vulgar cracks, occasional obscenities and sharp memory for irrelevant jokes which float to the surface of my wine, making me less and less able to get what I want. As if I knew any longer what that was. I drink therefore I digress, and in that process, acceded to all demands. The end-result is that later this evening, Sebastian will come to the door and take Mark away for a couple of days. They will have their own holiday while my spouse and I continue to deliberate, ha, ha. The men of the household seem to be winning.

On that dull thought I was finishing his packing, most of it done by Mrs Harrison since I do not even know where my children keep their clothes. Such miniature things for a miniature Sebastian, me putting them in a bag and wanting him to come in and say he preferred my company to his father's but knowing he wouldn't, and wishing I did not deserve it; when in the middle of what threatened to be tears, Mrs Harrison, more tight-lipped these days than ever, came to see if I was in control. Not of myself, of the packing. And also to 'have a word'. Her presence was an unwelcome echo of my own redundancy: 'a word' is never brief and she never chooses the right time. I wanted Sebastian to come and go: I did not want to listen.

'Mrs Pearson,' she said, picking things up and putting them down, 'Mr Harrison suggested I have a word . . .'

'What's the matter with him, cat got his tongue?' She ignored that. Harrison is a man of few words.

'About next door,' she said firmly. I remembered the red flag on the railings, remembered at the same time that the silence with our neighbours would soon have to be breached. David Allendale's birthday party. Social obligation, some time soon.

She cleared her throat. 'Mrs Pearson, have you seen Jeanetta? I mean, anywhere? Only I got to wondering if Mrs Allendale had been in to see you. When we was busy, that is. Recently, I mean. Some evening, perhaps? Maybe said how she was.' The voice trailed away. She knows very well that no one comes into this house without her knowledge, noted by her eagle eye and their dimensions measured. Or lack of dimensions, in Katherine's case.

'No, not either of them.' (Not as far as I know: the days are so blurred.) 'Oh, yes, I have. No, wait a minute. I've seen her going out, both of them. And him coming in. With Jeremy. Yes I've seen them all. I think.'

She sagged with relief. 'Are you sure, the little girl, I mean, Jeanetta?' standing there, doggedly persistent in the face of indifferent replies.

'No, not completely sure. Why the hell does it matter?'

'I'm worried about her,' said Mrs Harrison, limp before bursting forth again. 'I mean, very worried. Nothing. Not a word. She's just gone. You can't keep a child in a street like this and make it invisible. S'posing she's sick or something? I've knocked and said I'll take her out and he says she's out

217

already, thank you, but why don't I ever see her go? Don't even ask me to babysit like they used. You'd have thought . . .'

'You mustn't spy on them. They're none of our business. Can't you see they're probably keeping out of the way because of that business with the necklace?' I was stuffing a toy inside Mark's kit with all my strengh. She flapped her hands, running short of words, looking anguished, opening her mouth but not speaking. Then Mark sidled into the room, peeped from behind her back. I could sense in him a desire to be gone, wanting these few days with his father as a woman might crave diamonds or a lover, impatient desire written all over him, and so hurtful it took away my breath, but I could see I had not devoted enough to him to warrant anything more. But all the same, the harshness of the ache made me angry with him. In retrospect, I was at my worst.

'I seen her,' he said. 'Me and Sammy saw.'

'Who?' All so irrelevant I'd forgotten already, Katherine, Jeanetta, indifferent to both, my eyes on my son. 'Where?' said Mrs Harrison, pouncing on him, holding his shoulders. This annoyed me more. Unhand my son who does not touch me, afraid I might spoil his treat. He twisted, shrugged her off, sure indication of something shameful. They had secrets, those two.

'In the garden,' he muttered finally. 'Dreaming.'

Mrs H took him by the arms again: he was frightened, but I didn't know why, her yelling and I didn't know why either. 'What do you mean, dreaming? And how did you see? When? You been poking in their garden, have you? How d'you get in? I've told you not to climb that wall at the end, it isn't safe . . .'

I said, yes, yes, automatically. She glared at me and we both waited for Mark. Watched him put on his best mulish and defensive face like his father, thinking of the imminence of Daddy and wanting to avoid trouble.

'Sitting on the steps. Their steps. You can just see, only just, from the bottom. I was looking for puss, she's been sick again. I put my head through the fence thing.' He meant the trellis with the half-dead creeper.

'Talk to her?' Mrs Harrison barked. 'What's she look like then?'

He kicked the floor, pawing the carpet with his feet, sulking and anxious. 'She was dreaming,' he repeated. 'She didn't take any notice when I shouted at her. Sitting on those steps what go up to their kitchen, I think.'

'Which go up to their kitchen,' I said.

The interruption made him hurry. Mrs Harrison added hers, angry. 'Was she playing then, was she? What was she doing? And how long since?'

He wrinkled his forehead. 'Oh, a day or two. Or three or four, I don't know, don't look at me like that . . . Oh, when's Daddy coming? All right then, I shouted at her, hallo or something, but she wouldn't listen or didn't hear, didn't want to. I thought she was being snotty. Just sitting there in the sun, on the steps, wearing this funny long dress all over. Singing. Only for a minute. Then her daddy came out and she stopped and I went aways. He doesn't like peoples in his garden. Or looking at him.'

'Sounds perfectly fine,' I said crossly. 'Dressing up again. Always was fond of other people's clothes, that girl.' He shook his head, wanting to say something more, not daring.

'Mrs Pearson,' said our Mrs Harrison, sizing up to me like a fighter with her fists clenched. 'Mrs Pearson . . . ma'am, the reason I'm mentioning this is 'cos Samantha saw Jeanetta, last week, I think, she doesn't really know, you know how vague she is. These scamps,' she gestured to Mark, who blushed. 'have been trying to get in next door. Their own garden not good enough, see. Only Sam says Jeanetta was poorly. Not like she was, you know, not fat any more. Says she was as thin as a lizard. Like a little rat. It's no good, Mrs Pearson, you've just got to go and ask what's happened to her. I can't: I've tried. Something's gone wrong. You've got to go. When will you go?'

Well, things never go wrong singly, do they?' It was the tone of the order in her voice which hit that large part of me already primed with a sort of grief, anger, disappointment, Mark, Sebastian, sleepless nights of new recrimination, and terrible dawns. I had nothing left, not even the authority of the mistress of the house, standing there, receiving commands while I listen to these blatant and alarmist exaggerations. Blood rose in my face: she stepped away from me, spontaneous regret, and into that tiny vacuum of silence, the doorbell rang. Mark dashed past us both, hurling himself downstairs, yelling, 'Daddy, Daddy, Daddy,' leaving me and the rebellious servant, both with a hand on the half-closed case. My son would have gone naked with his father, and that was all I knew. I regretted it while almost understanding in one fell moment, greater than other regrets, blotting out anything more. Had I wept in her arms, Mrs Harrison might have liked me, but I did not, could not. Instead I followed downstairs, found Mark struggling with the door like a demented animal, only partially calmed by Harrison, who opened with the butler's dignity, a smile on his face.

I never saw it before, only dreamed it now in the wake of the dawns, the love Sebastian inspires in anyone else. Without counting the days since he left, I know how long they have been, how rudderless the household, how genuine that great grin of pleasure on Harrison's face. I never knew, I never knew, and ignorance was bliss in the old arrogance of never caring. They all adore him. He was framed in the doorway, a handsome man for all that, whose life I have left as a blank, never asking what he did with it or wanted to do. Apart from keep me in the style I could afford, cater for my carelessness and stay away when the drunken going was rough. He did not come in: I mounted the stairs, becoming the servant, to fetch the incomplete bag belonging to the son, carried it down with me, handed them over to one another as if neither had ever been mine, smiling, smiling, smiling. Not in front of the children. No weeping please. Nothing, but wishing well. Seeing my failures. Furious, impotent, sadder than age, weak at the knees. Smiling. Have fun, Oh, when are you coming back? I don't suppose, no, no, never mind. 'What was it?' he asked, Sebastian speaking, holding Mark by the hand. I kicked the carpet on the floor, the same way Mark kicks carpet to hide embarrassment. 'We . . . ell nothing. The Allendales' party . . . will you be back?' He has a memory for dates which is like an instinct, the same, I remember, as the instinct which never wanted to hurt. 'Of course,' he said. 'Not long, is it? Perhaps we'll go?' 'Please,' I said. 'We'll be back, won't we?' Mark looked up. 'I suppose so.' He took his turn at kicking the carpet. 'Don't do that, Mark,' I said, wishing I had not spoken. 'All right. See you.'

I can't remember who closed the door.

There was worse, of course. There is always worse whenever you think you've hit the bottom. Such as Samantha flying downstairs in her nightie, a ghost with a red and angry face. A mistake perhaps to keep the fleeting visit of her father such a secret: I was consulted on the subject, could not remember. Think I said we could do without both the jealousy or excitement. Thinking her turn would come, if I thought at all. We might as well not have bothered: the decision was not good. Democracy applies to children too. 'Was Daddy,' she shrieked. 'Daddy. I heard him, I did, I did, I did . . .'

'Come on, sweetheart: back to bed. Late,' said Mrs Harrison grimly. Samantha turned to me. She is like me in so many ways while Mark resembles his father. Samantha has none of their mildness, a will of iron and a fog-horn voice.

'You didn't tell me. Was Daddy, it was . . .' No one denied it. '. . . You didn't tell me. You never said he was coming here. I want Daddy. Daddy, Daddy, Daddy . . .'

'All right, all right,' I moved to touch her, watched her leap away from my infection. 'Why?' she wailed. 'Why?'

'Because . . .'

'I hate you, Mummy. Piggy, piggy cow. Bastard, bottoms.' Oh where do they get the words? She stood there trembling, the little face contorted with tears of fury, the whole of her concentrated on producing the worst insult she could summons, the most hurtful thing she could imagine.

'Fat legs!' finally spat from her. 'Big bums. Stupid ole witch. Hate you.'

Laughable, yes, this pocket-battleship rage, comic in any other set of eyes but mine. She fled upstairs, unnerved by her own hysteria, sobbing. Even without energy, I should have followed, but the stiff upper lip was well in place, not self-ishness exactly, only guilt. So instead, Mrs Harrison went after her and knew she would be the most welcome.

Drink, drink, drink. Not in the kitchen, Harrisons have eyes, melting into the back of their bloody heads when they go downstairs, X-ray eyes like antennae. Confused: now what exactly do I want, bottles hugged to bosom, still clanking up the stairs. Tonic for the gin supply hidden in the study desk. Somewhere, long after ten o'clock, I was aware of Harrison's deferential knock at the door. And did not answer. Even later, the pinging of the phone. The servants, using the line downstairs, running my house. I went to sleep in the chair. Finally, in the dawn, I cried. For the mess I had made.

Please help me, please. I want to do better: I have learned so much too quickly and I did not see. There is nothing more salutary than being left alone. More than anything else, I want all those children back. So I can start again.

17

'I don't believe you. You've lost your mind to do such a thing ... How did you do such a thing?'

'Easy enough. Don't know really. But it won't last, I shouldn't worry. He more or less said so, and I agreed. Besides, it simply isn't practical. Fun though.' At the moment, Monica did not look entirely sure. Jenny thought she looked more dispirited than illuminated. The whole effect was disappointing.

'Practical? Never mind practical, it isn't fair either,' she spluttered. 'In fact, completely unfair. How would you feel, oh, sorry, I forgot you sort of know how it feels, but poor Katherine. You shouldn't, not to a friend. For Christ's sake we were all going to their party next week: I won't know where to put my face.'

'You won't know? What about me?'

'If you go,' said Jenny rudely, 'that'll be your problem. Mess on your own doorstep and then you have to clean up. Or at least sidestep. Colin will notice. You can't go.'

'Yes I shall go and no, he won't notice. Don't be such a prig for God's sake. Besides you're forgetting she messed first. Ogling my husband as if men were newly invented ...'

'But she didn't, Monica, not exactly. I'm sorry, but I thought it was the other way round.'

'I don't care which way round it started. He still got a chest full of lipstick, cigarettes crunched in his back pocket, grass bits in the turn-ups of his trendy trousers. Loves the great outdoors, but you don't collect that kind of litter without an element of participation. Don't pity Katherine. Not the first time. Past master at the game. Mistress, I mean.' The voice was suddenly vicious.

'Oh I don't think so, surely not. She'd be too . . .'

'Well, he told me so himself, David, I mean. David told me lots and lots about Katherine. She's a slut. Paternity of one child seriously in doubt. Always the quiet ones, isn't it?' They were sitting in Jenny's garden. Monica drew on her cigarette and threw away the end so the lit stub glowed for a full minute on the lawn. Jenny was silent. None of this equated with her own experience of a sheltered life and she was not sure quite what she believed. On several occasions in a long acquaintance, Monica had been careless with the truth, creating exaggerations. Jenny bracketed this last news along with similar examples of the same syndrome and refrained from comment. Katherine had been weighing on her conscience, lightly but unaccountably, and although she would have liked some scandal to prove Katherine was horrid and absolve herself from that niggling guilt, Monica's revelations were not providing any such reassurance. Rather the opposite, and, on the underside of disgust at the bad behaviour of a friend, there was a prurient curiosity yearning to be satisfied. Hardly a moral question, but what did he do, she wanted to know: exactly how did he get you into bed or on to the floor, feet first or what? And what did he do next? Give me the details, please, without me having to ask. Instead, she sidestepped.

'I don't understand,' she said slowly. 'Not quite, anyway. You spent the whole afternoon at their house, but where the hell were the rest of them, such as Katherine and the kids?'

Monica stretched and yawned. Jenny caught a whiff of fresh perfume from one exposed underarm, was embarrassed. Did people wash after such adulterous assignations? She supposed they did.

'Katherine was out. Always out whenever she can, gym or some such self-indulgent thing, such as spending the hard-earned cash: how awful, our conservatory might go to pay for her clothes. Probably creating or preserving the body beautiful. I wonder why he liked mine? No real comparison, is there?' She made an attempt to laugh which was far from the usual full-bellied sound. 'Anyway, Jeremy, the boy, he'd been left at some playschool David's found, sort of trial run for the after-noon, and Jeanetta wasn't there. Empty house. Perfect.' She paused, reached for the wine on the table between them, frowned. 'Well, he said it was an empty house. No disturbances, no knocks, no tradesmen at the door, but when we were upstairs, in his studio place – no, not their bedroom, he didn't suggest it and I couldn't have done it – I kept feeling as if someone was there.'

'Ghosts. Or conscience,' Jenny snorted. 'Serve you right.' Monica shrugged. 'Probably. There were sounds from the attic, or at least I think it was the attic. Above the studio, something like a mouse or a cat creeping round. I mentioned it and he laughed at me, said it was nothing if not birds in the roof-space. The rooms above us were always empty. We'll go and look if you like, he said, but I said no. I didn't want to creep around her house more than I needed. I'm not quite a natural for this game, you see.' She shivered and reached for the multicoloured cardigan on the back of her chair.

'Monica,' said Jenny, 'tell me something . . . Is he . . . Is he a fantastic lover? Is that what it is?'

Monica fiddled with the buttons on the dreamcoat. She could not have worn such a comfortable garment to any meeting with David because she knew he would never have liked it. Too bright and fussy. Looking for these small compensations, she paused, considering the question.

'Yes, he is as a matter of fact. Very strong, very dominant . . All male. Doesn't ask, but knows what to do. Knows where everything is. If you see what I mean.' Jenny saw perfectly well.

'And is it worth it? On that account?'

'No,' said Monica, hugging her arms to her chest and finger-ing a small bruise below the sleeve of the dreamcoat. 'No, I don't really think it is.' She turned to Jenny, her face flushed. 'Which is why we've all got to go to this party and you've got to help me. There's only a few others; we've got to go. It's quite all right, Jenny darling, the whole little escapade has finished. If I don't finish it, he will. He loves his life and he loves Katherine, you see. Loves everything in his house too much to risk a thing. So we'll go on, all of us, just as we did before, as if nothing ever happened. Like real grown-ups.' Her eyes were shining, tears or determination Jenny could not tell in her own sensation of acute relief. She felt inclined to keep the conversation neutral.

'In that case, I'll do what I was going to do anyway. Because I was a bit worried about her. Have the kids over to play with ours one weekend. This weekend. Give Katherine a break.'

Sympathy for Katherine was still not what Monica wanted to hear. 'Count me out. You can try, though. I seem to remember him saying Jeanetta was going to stay with her granny. Or she's already gone. If you want to be useful, you'd better check first. I think we need another bottle of wine.'

His footsteps came upstairs soon after midnight. He was trotting noisily on the last, uncarpeted flight, his leather mules clicking on the wood. 'When I've made a sitting room up here,' he had once told her, 'I want green carpet up these steps, with brass stair-rods to catch the light and show off the wood. Nice.' He had looked at the stairs with the satisfaction he reserved for new territory waiting to be tamed. 'There's a fortune in attics,' he had added. 'All that space, hidden away.'

Hidden away in the attic room at the back for over twenty hours, Katherine had stopped counting time since late afternoon. Pieces of her watch lay on the floor from her efforts to concentrate her mind and hands by taking the thing apart with the aid of a hair-slide and a nail which had worked up from the floorboards. Destroying any knowledge of time seemed important. He had showed her in there with her one plastic bowl and a thin blanket: the bowl smelled in the corner and the blanket was damp with sweat, although she had only covered herself briefly since the night before. That was in the afternoon, when she tried to smother the sounds she had heard from the room below.

Long before that, after the key first turned, she had deafened herself with her own screaming. Hitting the door, pounding the lock and screaming for Jeanetta. Put her with me, David, please, please, please, until the voice had trailed into a dry shout, coughing the way the child had coughed, the futility of such racket painfully obvious. Something returned; a remnant of the realism which had got her out of the kitchen window to escape, shoved back down into the recesses of logical thought because she could no longer afford logical conclusions. Such as the fact that no one could hear unless they were David, who could sleep through a storm and did not wish to respond. Exhaustion won, so she slept herself in a crazed kind of way, dozing into nightmares as the shadows of the moon through the high window danced in the corners and grew enormous. They were static, but moved when she watched them, black figures advancing until she whimpered against the wall.

He had been so cunning, doing this. David knew her weakness, knew very well her horrors, the imprisonments and escapes of the past. Katherine counted on her fingers all the times she had ever been locked away. That time with Mary, when they were found in the coal hole and given flannel pyjamas: then another time with foster parents, not in the dark, a benign punishment for bad behaviour. Then being told to remain quiet in a room while the favourite foster parent died, or being shut in a room to defray the amorous attentions of the last borrowed daddy of them all, before return to the hostel with the rigid curfew from which Mary had plucked her, still wilful, impetuous, high-spirited, into the liberal regime of Mary's bossiness. There was one corollary in all of these imprisonments which loomed largest now. If she was good, without protest, darkness was always followed by light, hugs, apologies, attention, sometimes treats. They were always sorry when they shut you up; so much so there had been a part of her which even grew to like it, see in each episode an anticipation of what would follow. They would expect to see her helpless, cherish her like a baby doll, every time. Being let out was like having a birthday, all over again.

Some dim resentment stirred in the blackness of the attic room. There had been no treats, no being allowed to be a child like that ever since she had given birth to one. It wasn't fair, it was all too much, what about me, me, me?

Somebody hug me, please: I can't cope. Like the aftermath of all those other times, not at his hand. David would be sorry for locking her away. And when he was sorry, he was nice.

When he was sorry, she became as precious as a tiny little child. She was loved when he was sorry and she had been good, treated like the fragile crystal they displayed with their food, shining and admirable, touched gently.

Then the shadows touched her skin: she could feel tendrils of darkness stroking her cheek, wrapping themselves around her throat, creeping between her legs, extensions of familiar nightmares, but if she screamed, she would stay here for ever. Or as the last alternative, she could be put outside in the dark, where the shadows would become hands, tearing her apart with sharp nails, forcing her to run and run and run. Even in the depths of nightmare, cringing towards the window, she could perceive at least the solidity of the wall behind which shadows could not creep, while the fate beyond the door of the house might be worse. Better in here than out, far better. There was logic in this punishment, not quite the worst she had known since there was still a surface to clutch as darkness paled into light. She remembered what silent obedience brought; embraces, sweeties, kisses, protection. All the bravery of the evening before, the logic, the realism, died. Katherine simply waited and endured, forgetting everything.

Dawn had been short-lived relief as time sped forward, the comfort of light short-lived as the sun rose and eleven o'clock heat raised the room to an oven, so warm she could not have shouted without water. Then, in the middle of her fit of strangled coughing, he had come back, standing clean and polished in the doorway, holding a jug of water. For the liquid, she would have crawled, but she stayed as she was, knees clutched to chest, her fingers twisting her hair with little movements. He put the jug by the door, finger on his lips.

'You've been very naughty. You've got to be good. For a little while.' There was a promise in that, the beginnings in him of the guilt for which she watched and hoped, made herself smaller in the belief he would notice. Be good, sweet child, and let who will be clever. So she was good. Monstrously good. Picking up the tiny particles of dust and fluff which dwelt on the floor, rolling the fluff into balls and making a neat, housewifely pile of miniature rubbish. Busy until she heard them in the studio below. Shocked into stillness by

228

Monica's voice, the loud, braying laugh cutting a line through her forehead, the noise of it absorbed through her eyes and skin. Katherine opened her own mouth to shout, remembered, placed one finger over her teeth and bit her knuckle. Don't say a word: don't speak: be good, and something nice will happen. Familiar enough sounds from him: the same noises he had made so lately without a wall between them, and from the woman, a crescendo of moaning, but Katherine had the blanket over her head and stuck into her ears as she began, stealthily, to dismember her watch. The bracelet was gold. In the daylight hours left, using her teeth, she had prised apart seven of the links. She added them to the little pile of fluff. As long as he came back.

The key turned in the lock and he was framed in the electric light from the hallway, hurrying towards her, pulling her upright and wrapping his arms around her. 'Darling, darling, darling . . . I'm sorry. All right now, not your fault, was it?'

She stood limp with her arms by her sides as he embraced, pressing the back of her head into the shoulder which was soft and warm. A river of perspiration ran down into the valley of her bosom, stuck to the nightdress which was grubby from the floor. She had thought that another night would have made her die, but she had waited for this, had known he would be like this. The heat of her body ended in arms icy cold, the rich cashmere of his sweater soothing. He adjusted her arms so they rested round his waist and she left them there, fingers touching lifelessly. Comfort was comfort, nothing registered but the end of the nightmare, the reward.

Downstairs, from the studio, there was a tinkling of music from the radio.

'You must be hungry,' he said with infinite gentleness, 'poor little thing. A bath first. Then bed. I'll bring you up some supper. Something simple. Glass of wine. You'd like that.' She shuddered violently in the return of memory, only semi-free from the mesmerizing darkness, dug her fingers into his haunches, spoke the first words. 'Jeanetta. Netta . . . What have you done?'

'Shhh, shhh. Don't worry. All over now.'

'What have you done?' The repetition was dry, a voice

which had to ask but did not really want to know. Knowing
would ruin the treat.

'Taken her to stay with Sophie. She wanted to go. Sophie
wanted to have her. Give us a break. Naughty girl, trying to
get out. Leading you astray. It's all her fault, you know that,
don't you? She's always doing that, making you naughty. No
good for the two of us, is she? Always been her, spoils things.
Should have been a boy.' He stroked the back of her hair,
feeling the tangles made by hours of twisting. 'Anyway, she's
fine, absolutely fine. They'll be eating biscuits. Sort of holiday.
Just you and I, darling. I'll look after you.'

'Not my fault,' she repeated in a babyish voice. Disinterest
in Jeremy was evident, as complete as his in her. Rippling
waves of physical relief moved from her feet to her head and
she slumped against him, her fingers locking behind his back.
She did not ask why this, why the other: she had been schooled
for years not to ask why; it did not matter. What mattered was
belief in safety, belief in him, flooding back like a tide, washing
before it all the scum of incredulity.

'Come downstairs, with me. Just for a minute. I want to
show you something.'

'What?' Fresh fear gripped her lungs.

'Something.'

The elegant stairs seemed to number a hundred steps: she
held back, but he nudged her on with one arm round her and
guiding her all the way down to the grand front door. Opened
it, simply stood there with her in the doorway, both of their
feet on the step. The kitchen door was shut on her left and she
could hear the comforting sound of the boiler humming in the
background. She shivered in the nightdress and pushed her
hair behind her ears.

'Listen,' he said softly, both of them facing the wide road,
'you can go whenever you want. There it is, all yours. Go now,
if you like. I'll get you some shoes. And a coat.'

Over the road, a chestnut tree stirred into life, rustling and
hissing in a warm breeze. The noise was sudden and fierce,
announcing a storm. One street lamp shone level with the
lowest branches of the tree, twigs smacking against the glass,
and a single moth, drawn by the light from their own home,

blundered into Katherine's face so she covered her eyes. Apart from the lamp and two lights from the house opposite obscured by heavy curtains, the street was as empty as desert, the heatwave finished. Katherine regarded the view with unspeakable horror, a flood of panic hitting her as her bare feet scratched on the cold step. She leant back against her husband, felt his warmth, watched as he crushed the moth in one palm. Katherine clung to the other arm and they retreated indoors.

Sleep, after bath, after food. Sleep with her hair sweet and wet from water she wanted to drink. Curled like a foetus, safe. Sleep; as gorgeous as any hallucination. Fingering a swollen stomach, sleep. Jeanetta with her granny, sleeping both. She had been good and everything was going to be all right.

When John Mills failed to get his award, he began to cry. He knew the failure on the Saturday morning when nothing arrived in the post and a colleague from the NSPCC phoned in anticipation of sharing his own good news. If both had won recognition instead of only one of them, they would have joked and said how ridiculous was the whole idea: as if it mattered, such silly condescension, stick the thing in the lavatory. A certificate and a piece of silver sculpture from a posh shop, only fit to be pawned, but best placed all the same in the bathroom's insulting obscurity where every visitor would be bound to see it. But it did matter. Nothing was any longer all right.

John found these days he cried often and with ease, quickly moved to tears by either affectionate gestures or frustration, but mostly by animals, real ones as well as creatures in pictures. He even considered changing his allegiance away from human beings entirely. The award, however silly, would have been a marker on the last years, made them look worthwhile although he doubted they were, as well as giving him some incentive either to carry on, or retire with laurels. So it mattered, desperately. Matilda found him with three of the kittens on his knee, stroking them one by one while they dug experimental claws into his thighs. He was talking, ostensibly to the animals, really to himself, but in any event the chat was exclusive.

Half of her wished this was madness while the rest of her

recognized it was not. Nothing wrong but a man without company and capable of receiving none. Matilda was confused and the confusion floated on top of a cocktail of rage. There was this other man, extending on each of their emotional meetings the invitation of alternative life. A house in the suburbs, not only all paid, but entirely free of cats; even with all the fussiness attached, an attractive prospect. Bugger true love: she'd done all that, but as the delicious spectre of such an untried existence grew into sharper prospect, so did the ultimatums. Matilda had determined to abandon her own stinking ship, at some time to coincide with this bloody award: leaving John stronger, but instead of jubilation, she was here, encountering a husband talking to his cats. Their cats, almost their only common property, symbolizing everything she did not want.

She regarded John with all of herself sinking into despair, looked at the animals with loathing. One of them played with her feet and the impulse to kick it out of the window was almost irresistible.

'Pussy, pussy, pussy: Give daddy a kiss.'

The hidden obscenity might have been laughable if she had not overheard John's telephone conversation with the half-known colleague, all that talk conducted in tones of forced jollity, quite different to the voice reserved for cats, a silly, childish voice. She looked at that pale face of sunny gentleness, big hands holding horrible kittens fast growing beyond the reach of a palm. Ignoring the vacancy of his expression, she centred on the animals. John removed them from his knees one by one without ever looking at her, his face alive with concern for the movement of all those flailing little legs. In one awful gulp of a conclusion she knew yet again that she could not leave him here. Not today, even if it was the last chance of several, similar days to this, with her tenure on the alternative weakening with every procrastination.

'I'd better go to work,' was all he said.

'Don't,' she said, surprised by the sound of her own voice.

'I must.'

'No, you mustn't.'

'What else should I do?' He did not seek comfort, never

sought second opinions or even asked what she might have suggested. He had sprung a lifetime's trap without any kind of permission. Frustration boiled inside her, a quiet, white heat. He never consulted, never even canvassed opinion, and the quiet adoration was not enough.

'Go then,' she said turning away. 'Enjoy yourself.'

He placed all the kittens in the box where Kat slept, a larger box by now, with an even larger and cleaner version waiting to accommodate them tomorrow after the same early morning running up the walls which had woken them that morning. Kittens settled with satisfaction, sucking mother like little pigs although they had already eaten solid food. The cat litter in one enormous tray was fresh, but the scent of urine still lingered.

After the door shut on her departing husband, Matilda completed the business of dressing. Then walked up and down, her steps going quicker and quicker in the confinement of the small living room. She cried briefly, but reverted to the white anger, hatred for everything about her existence, especially the cowardice and the cats. When the frantic pacing stopped, the stillness of the whole place was unnerving. She pulled on a jacket since the night's rain still chilled the upper stories; found the new cardboard box and inverted it over the kittens' bed. With them imprisoned and her handbag over one shoulder, she lifted the double box and went out of the door, closing it but ignoring the double lock. By the time she carried the large burden downstairs, juggling the load to open the door to the back yard, she was out of breath. She set the box down against the far wall. Next to the heap of old newspaper and the rug which formed the makeshift bed for Rotty the Rottweiler's rump, whenever he arrived. Matilda intended no real harm, did not suspect animals of malice, but it seemed appropriate to put them all together. This would be the first place John would look: he would simply be shocked out of his lethargy and that was the full extent of his wife's conscious desires.

'Quick, quick, Eric. Quick. There's someone outside.'

Eileen Harrison panted upstairs. Harrison panted down. 'Quick,' hissed Eileen. 'Quick, while she's out to the shops, for God's sake.'

They pattered back towards basement level. 'Sammy, you stay there,' Mrs Harrison ordered. 'Just for a minute, good girl.' She closed the upstairs kitchen door and Samantha began to howl. 'Shut up this minute you hear me?' The crying stopped. 'Eric, it's that little beggar, I'm sure it is. Knocking at our back door. What's the matter with him? I'm frightened, Eric, I am. What's he want, must be mad, isn't he? Mad as a hatter, coming back in here. What the hell . . .?' They paused in the half-light of the stairwell. The innocence of Saturday morning going on all around them, patter-patter outside, did nothing to alter the tension of conspiracy. The tapping at the door went on. Both of them were panting.

'What if he's come back with that bloody necklace?' Eileen whispered, grabbing Eric's arm.

'Don't be so stupid. He wouldn't do that. No one'd do that, you silly cow.'

'What does he want then? He's knocking at our kitchen window as if he was crazy. He's gone nuts.' Harrison thought for thirty seconds, the strain puckering his eyebrows.

'Call the police. Quickest way to get rid of him before Mrs P comes home from the shops. We'll all be for the high jump if anyone knows he's been in here before. Specially me. Can't take being lied to, can she? You know what she's like. About things.'

'He'll tell them, and they'll tell her, what's the difference. Get rid of him. He can talk, can't he?'

'Maybe not. So what if he does? Never seen him before in my life, nor anyone else either. Call them buggers, go on. I'll see what he wants. Go on. You can shut her up an' all.' Samantha's wails were resumed.

The vagrant had overslept. Huddled in a red cloak, he had waited outside a semi-familiar house for most of the afternoon and then he started to explore, ending up in the park. Drugged by the sun and betrayed by the heat's failure to recede with the light, he remained where he was, dead to the world. So soundly he slept under the bushes, the vigilant park-keepers did not find him. He slumbered without sound, helped by a quart of cider. Stiffly he sidled out of the park, back towards where his billet was, but he could not remember precisely where to go, sidestepped up and down the right-looking road, disorientated and confused. Everywhere looked the same and everywhere was so black he began to feel giddy. Even equipped with the red cloak he had found over a railing the morning before, he was not equipped for nights and besides, was afraid of the dark. He was superstitious, easily alarmed; and as his friend had noticed, beginning to go a little crazy.

So he wandered manfully up and down, down and up in ever decreasing circles, pausing against parked cars, bored, frightened and wakeful after a long sleep, but still craving the oblivion of more. More than sleep, he needed a place of safety, even one of the hostels if he knew the nearest. About midnight, a police car caught him mid-roadway: the driver slowed the vehicle and looked at him closely. He stuck his nose in the air and began to walk with exaggerated purpose, half stepping, half running, a comic movement down an alley at the end of a road, as if he knew where he was going. Once out of sight he scaled a wall far higher than the scope of his normal efforts, found himself in a small garden, unkempt and empty, so empty he felt the opposite of safe, so climbed another high wall on the opposite side. Reckless by now, he simply wanted a place to rest where he could see lights and know there was someone there, even though he planned to have moved long before they saw him. He wanted to look at lit windows to relieve his own isolation whatever the risk: the sight of people was better than empty sky, kept at bay the threatening ghost which had begun to torture his dreams. By the time he reached the third garden, he had no choice but staying put since the energy which had driven him so far so fast died in his skinny chest to the tune of loud panting and a pain over his heart. In any event, this garden was nicest on account of lights burning safely in far upstairs windows of the house to which it belonged. He had settled into a hidden area beneath elegant steps which he only admired for the shelter they offered. Put the red cloak round himself and slept without caring when the rain began to fall.

Sleep proved treacherous for the second time, carrying his oblivion well over dawn and into the hours when life was busy around him. Cars in the street beyond, a drain gurgling close to his ear, flies buzzing and the whole world wide awake, tickling his grubby skin with a very slight awareness of danger. Despite all that, he still could not find a sense of urgency. Everything about him was blunt and his feet were wet, nor could he remember the route he had taken to get where he was. After standing and shaking himself, he climbed beyond the steps up into the garden, noticing the blank French windows and on one side a projecting wall with a narrow window at his own head height. Something drew him to the cosy little window, jammed open for a crack at the top, familiar temptation of a man who was not really a thief, but still an opportunist, reassured by the silence of the building despite all the noises right and left. He crept close, raised his head slowly until his eyes were level with the pane and his nose was pressed to the glass. Then he clutched his own throat to stifle his own scream, his heart hurting his chest in one giant convulsion. Immediately opposite his own eyes, separated only by the thickness of a centimetre, was another face also pressed against the glass. A wild, miniature face, distorted by the contact, grubby with tears, hollow-cheeked and luminous pale. The flattened orb was surrounded by a tangled halo of gold, the eyes china blue, the pink mouth opening and closing like a fish, mouthing words. Slightly above the ledge of the window, higher than the head, there were small hands each side of the staring eyes, clawing at the window with bitten nails. The face began to disappear as if drawing back, breath left on the window from the mouthing of words. 'Mine,' the soundless voice appeared to be saying, 'Mine, Mine, Mine,' while the fingers clawed and pointed. His jaw hung slack for a minute: he noticed the nails, chewed to the quick like his own, as his eyes remained locked, fixed on the other hands, smearing the pane, helpless. Transfixed only for the moment, the terror then reached his feet: he staggered, stumbled wildly to the extreme end of the garden, not the way he had come in, but crashing over a medium wall and a flimsy trellis on the other side, stumbling forward to another building, down some steps to collide with a basement door, knocking at it and gibbering like an animal while he hit at the window in the top, all caution lost in an agony of terror.

The vagrant needed humankind: if they put one arm up his back or stabbed at him or beat him, he still needed them more: could not control his tongue or his own brown and bitten fingers which rapped for attention. He gibbered in his baby language, gibbered more like the child, wanting nothing else than they should let him in.

After the police had come and gone with more indifference than efficiency, carrying away with them this small, filthy adult suffering from dementia, Mrs Harrison made a cup of tea. Thick and strong with plenty of sugar the way they liked, even more sugar than usual because it was good for shock. Samantha's yelling had added to the distraction and speed of the officers and for this service she was being rewarded with chocolate biscuits. On account of the row, the officials had required minimal information, nor had any of them waited for tea, such a disappointment to one and all in finding nothing more than yet another vagrant in a neighbourhood populated with such. 'Talks a lot, didn't he?' said Harrison, feeling braver and far more confident in the aftermath. Mrs Harrison was simply relieved for the continued absence of the mistress. That old lie about the necklace lay heavy, although what with Mrs P caring nothing for anything, might not have mattered any longer, but then again, could have been trouble: you never could tell; and besides, second nature dictated she lied at least a little of the time. Keep them in the dark about everything except your own perfections, a habit maintained over years of service for which she never considered herself properly rewarded. Too late to confess now, although, thinking as she did so frequently of Jeanetta, she bitterly regretted the dis-honesty imposed on Katherine Allendale, felt profound unease.

'He was just jibbering,' she said slowly, 'that beggar, talking like a monkey. Must have been frightened by something, I don't know. Kept trying to pull the blighters into the garden, but there wasn't anything there. All that fiddling, pointing with his fingers and waving his hands round his head. Bit touched, poor devil. But he must have seen something, or why knock?'

237

'He must have wanted catching. Comfortable inside, isn't it? Better than being out in the rain. Must have been the rain that did it. He was talking foreign, I thought, in bits.'

'How would you know?' she jeered at him.

'I don't know, but I couldn't make it out, so it can't have been English, can it?'

'Probably saying thank you to you for letting him in. Like you did last time. Here, open the windows, it stinks in here.'

Harrison ignored the jibe and sank into the chair which was the oldest, aged entirely by his own behind, took a sip from the tea mug, shuffling. 'What's this, then?' His behind was disturbed by an extra crease, uncomfortable, since he was familiar with every nuance of his favourite chair. 'Here, look,' he said, retrieving the red shawl from under his behind; 'he's gone and left this.' The red cloak emerged, filthy and crumpled. 'What's he think he is?' Harrison chuckled. 'Batman?' Mrs Harrison grabbed the garment.

'Put it down, you daft man sitting on it, you don't know where it's been.' She held the cloak aloft with suspicion, tempered with puzzlement and a *frisson* of familiarity. 'Might have been a nice thing once,' she remarked moving towards the fire with the thing held between two fingers. Then she appeared to think again and shoved it in the bin which contained the rubbish. A number of stranded memories were struggling for connection: she began to take the cloak out of the bin again when the upstairs door banged so loudly the house shook.

'It's Her,' said Harrison, 'back from the shops. Got herself the usual supplies, by the sounds of it.' There was a thump of shopping hitting floor. 'Did you have another go at her, after I did, about next door? You said you would?' He knew she had from the way the face clouded. 'Shut up,' said Mrs Harrison, 'just shut up a minute. Let me think.'

The day was so fresh after rain, and her mind so clear she did not want to think. Katherine had slept a sleep which was free of all dreams and even the alarms which followed waking were not disturbing. Such as finding the clothes in her wardrobe had been pruned of almost everything she had acquired without David's guidance, including the suit she had exchanged in the boutique he most frequently preferred. All that remained in the scaled-down collection were clothes which reflected his preferences, severely classical or tarty. Since he had slept late, hugged her without any demands before rising to see amiable Jeremy, putting her first, she was more than disposed to forgive, did not really consider there was anything to forgive although she vaguely regretted the hiding of a pair of jeans. There was nothing nicer in the whole wide world than knowing that she did not have to get up, could stay, if she wished, in the cocoon of that bed, safe.

Tranquillity bloomed through the house with Jeanetta absent from it: Katherine set her mind away from anything which could possibly disturb that precious status quo, let herself be fussed over, an exquisite pleasure. Going down to the kitchen, dressed in a neat skirt and favourite cashmere, she found the tidy crumbs which signified their breakfast, wondered where the men had gone, feeling absurdly cosseted and happy. The basement, perhaps: Jeremy adored the workshop below stairs. Katherine looked inside the fridge, found sliced cold beef, and suppressing the hurt which arrived with the knowledge of how well he had looked after himself the day before, took two slices. She could have her own way today; anything she wanted was hers. Eleven o'clock: a sandwich as good as anything, and she began, with gaiety, to construct one. Oh what to do with the day, nothing for preference: exhaustion was still lurking despite the refreshment of such a calm and blissful morning. From the garden end of the kitchen, the radio was playing softly. Surprising for such a self-sufficient man to need so much music, but he said the sound soothed the boy. Her handbag was still on the kitchen floor, nasty little memory of some time ago, the sight occasioning a guilty memory, only subdued by her recovering from inside the apples she had placed there, washing them and returning them to the fruit bowl. So tired still, so very tried. She walked to a mirror on the wall by the windows to the garden, examined her hair: what a mess, a frightful bush full of wisps and sticking-up tufts, must remember never to sleep with damp hair. He would never make her cut it now. Using both hands, she pulled back the mane, looking round for something to tie it, sighing. It was only then, close to the playroom door, she could hear an echoing sigh, absorbed in a sound which seemed to come from a great distance, a kind of singing.

'Rainy, rainy rattlestones. Go away . . . and break his bones . . .' A pause for breath in the tuneless droning, immediately resumed. 'Pussy-cat, pussy-cat . . . Where you been? He's been up to London to . . . something the Queen. Miaow . . .' the line and the subdued voice trailing away into a cough. The cough was politely subdued, as if not part of the repertoire.

Katherine moved like a marionette legs refusing to bend. She jerked back to the table where her beef sandwich sat on a plate. Jeanetta with Sophie, gone to stay with silly Granny, oh good, he had said, he wouldn't lie, would have left the door to the playroom locked whatever, he always did, all the doors. This was imagination, rain playing tricks, spoiling everything and spoiling her turn to be spoiled. She looked at the sandwich, granary bread, beef and a little mustard to spice the taste in her mouth. Reached in an unlocked drawer for a piece of polythene, wrapped her breakfast and put it in the handbag. Rose from this stooping to the floor and jerked back across the room, not looking at the playroom door, and turned up the volume of the radio.

18

Sophie had found the cat on Sunday morning. Marshalling her energies, although these seemed to lack direction whatever she did, she had travelled on the threatening tube line and alighted at the wrong stop for the house of her son. Knowledge of the losses in her burglary made her abstemious enough for public transport: otherwise she could not tolerate less than a taxi or walking, which was her preference provided she need go no more than half a mile without a little rest. In the whole of her dependent life, she had never arrived on the doorstep of her son unannounced: the sheer temerity of her expedition made her nervous. Then the lack of consideration showed by a train driver in depositing her so deliberately at the wrong stop, especially after she had waited in surroundings of sublime ugliness for the thing to arrive, angered her to the extent she walked away from the wrong station muttering something along the lines of how she would never darken their doors again. Only two stops wrong, so small a space on that map on the wall of the tunnel. Looked as if you only walked in a straight line, no distance at all. But she came out of the station and lost her bearings, encountered a main road leading to another road twice as busy. Looking for a quieter street, she fell into a small Sunday market where music played from stalls and clothes of all colours were for sale. This was the cause of half an hour's distraction and a total expenditure of three pounds sterling. Parting with the money in those small, bright coins which always reminded her of chocolate currency consumed at Christmas, she refused to think of how closely the sum approximated to a taxi fare between her own violated house and that of her grandchildren.

Such a notion could hardly count when she had just purchased for them both a pair of luminous socks, also a pair for David. He would scoff, of course: but it would show she had remembered his birthday. The only hope was that the mellowness of that occasion would have leaked into this weekend before the event, enough to make her welcome although she was breaking all the rules. Enough to allow him to admit her unannounced, or make him explain why her last cry for help, in the middle of the night for heaven's sake, had met with so little response. Well, no response. Which would be the problem to face if only she could begin to discover exactly where she was. At the moment she saw the cat, she wanted to sit down and howl; repeating howlings of all their names in order to bring them to her side and scold them for putting her old body to such trouble, and also because she was lost.

She had set out so bravely, muttering all the evening before, 'Now listen here, David: what d'you think you're up to, old tricks again, mmm? I'm your mother, just you listen to me . . .' All of this bravado might have faded on his doorstep, but she could not find his doorstep. Somewhere in a mass of flyovers, underpasses, a pedestrian in a jungle of cars, the courage faded sooner. She was sat by the side of the road, counting her money and weeping, and the cat came and rubbed against her legs, keening in tune with her own, quiet moaning.

Since the burglary, she had been brave and organized, but occasionally found all her senses slipping, everything changing as she watched some of her instincts undergo a kind of metamorphosis. The nondescript animal at her feet was nothing she would ever have adopted normally. Far too dirty, scarred by a fight, limping, with matted ears and one malfunctioning eye, ugly as sin even taking misadventure into account. Sophie looked at it, remembered she was alive, and who she was. 'Go away,' she said, 'get off, you dreadful thing. Ugh.' the ringing tones of her carrying voice would have graced a military parade ground, but there was no one to appreciate the evidence of command. 'Go A-way,' she repeated, then looking down at the matted ear, speaking in an even greater confusion of memory, added, 'Please, oh do get off, please.' The cat arched round her ankles as a lorry thundered by. 'You shouldn't be here, really you shouldn't,' Sophie went on, rubbing her shins, quite liking the sensation. Then the thing began to move towards the road and she noticed how small it was. Not a cat proper, a kitten, mangled by fortune and even more bereft of street wisdom than herself, scuttling towards the traffic. Perhaps it had thought she was going to kick it, oh my dear, what a thought, as if she would. 'Stop,' she commanded, 'stop at once.' The small rump wobbled in response to a draught raised by a passing car. Sophie leapt forward, dropping the socks and her handbag, scuttled back to the safety of the wall with one bundle of fur. She stuffed it in the front of her best jacket and picked up her bag, noticing the dirt on her hands and the lace of her cuffs. She felt the bizarre elevation of having stolen something, and somehow, what with that and the filth, it was not quite possible to carry on to David's house.

'An absolute dice with death, my dear. Really, I didn't know I had it in me. Practically under the wheels of a juggernaut. Isn't that right, pussy? Nice taxi-man brought us home.'

'For nothing?' Mary asked caustically, doubting with her usual consistency any act which even smelled of philanthropy. So far the saga of all these events had taken longer than planned. She had only intended a passing visit, an interlude in the desert of Sunday afternoon, which was even worse than Saturday. If there had been a point to this story, other than one disgusting animal lying on a hearthrug, she had begun to forget, as the teller intended.

'We paid the man, of course.' Sophie was not about to repeat the episode of offering him the luminous socks in lieu. 'Anyway, that's why I never got to David's.'

'Why were you going?' Mary asked. 'Did they ask you? Shouldn't you phone and explain why you never got there? It's three o'clock. You know how they are about Sunday lunch. Or any lunch.'

'They didn't ask me, as it happens,' Sophie stated after some hesitation. 'I was just going to go. Time that boy was sorted out. Really. Never coming to see me after I was burgled, appalling behaviour. Not Katherine either.'

'Oh, Sophie, sweetheart, I am sorry. And about your burglary. How absolutely awful. You should have phoned me.'

'I didn't want you,' said Sophie with devastating dignity. 'I wanted Katherine.'

Mary was shocked into silence, standing to one side of Sophie's chair with her fists clenched. 'Not at first,' Sophie continued artlessly, 'I wanted David, of course. And the children, more than anything. Something to hug.' Her brow wrinkled in the effort of concentration. 'I haven't seen my own grandchildren for weeks. But then I wanted Katherine nice, sweet Katherine. She's always been nice to me. She understands me, you see.'

'Katherine didn't come either, though,' Mary snapped. 'Shows how sweet, how kind, doesn't it?' She had not meant to sound so waspish. Guilt and rejection hardened her.

'I wouldn't really expect her to come over here,' said Sophie. 'They'll be having a party next week, I expect, for his birthday. They usually do. She'll be busy, and anyway, she should rest, in her condition.'

'What condition?'

'Why, another baby of course, David thinks. That's why I had to go today, not really because of the burglary. But then I got lost and then this kitten and then, oh, I don't know, I came home. I'll go tomorrow. They don't answer the phone. Always engaged or always out. Busy, I suppose.'

'Which indicates sound health all round.' Mary was still sharp, but the beginning of a familiar worry was nagging. She was beset with visions she could not quite understand: Katherine, pale as a ghost in a restaurant, wanting to confess. Katherine in front of the depiction of adultery, blushing and sweating. A Katherine pregnant not quite equating with the same person rolling round with a lover on hot afternoons. Not the Lover she knew, every inch the pragmatic Frenchman, he was, every single inch: careful with passion, but passionately careful. She knew all about him, and also how sick pregnancy was like to make her sister. The worry grew.

'Sound health?' Sophie repeated. 'What's that got to do with anything?' She bent to tickle the cat, which was entirely at home. 'Something's wrong in that house. Something terribly wrong.'

'Oh, surely not . . . too much luxury . . .'

'Yes, yes,' Sophie insisted, not without relish. 'I know there is. David may be having a bad patch.'

'Rubbish, I'm sure he's fine: they've got plenty of money.'

'I don't mean that kind of patch. He has turns, you see. Locks himself up and broods. Oh not violent or anything, not really. The psychiatrist said it was all something to do with anxiety.'

'Which psychiatrist?' Mary almost shouted. The thought of psychiatrists made her ill. Sophie turned pale-blue eyes on her. The dislike in them was veiled by a vagueness only half deliberate. 'Oh, long, long time ago. When he was a teenager and finally got Daddy sent to prison. Daddy stole all his things, so he locked Daddy up and when Daddy came out he went on the rampage. David didn't hit him first of course, he never hits anyone first. But then,' she added with apparent irrelevancy, 'Daddy was very untidy. He'd always taken away everything David and I had and David didn't like that. He was a bully, Daddy. I'm glad he's dead.' This was said with prim precision.

'A long time ago,' Mary echoed, letting Sophie hear the disbelief in her voice. 'Nothing to do with the present. Katherine's causing the trouble. I know she is, not David. Katherine always causes trouble. I can't tell you how, but she does.'

Sophie turned eyes back to the cat, hiding the impatience, privately wishing to be left alone with the newer and less demanding friend. She should have thought of a cat long ago. 'Katherine never meant harm to anyone in her life,' she said with finality. 'Would you like some tea?' The invitation was not enthusiastic.

'No thank you. I must dash. Will you go again tomorrow?'

'Yes, of course. Unless they phone.' She hid from Mary an expression of fear. Of the roads and the train and the confusion, as well as the reception she might have at the other end. Resolution was waning and Mary could not follow the undertones. 'Certainly I shall. Or perhaps the day after. I'll have to look after this baby creature won't I? Why don't you go?'

Well, why not? The rain began as Mary tap-tapped home. Her steps were even and determined. Katherine had once told her she walked with the same-sized steps all the time as if trying to avoid the cracks in the pavement. Or trouble of the kind created by superstitions, the past and every colour of emotion. The steps were systematic but agitated. Maybe she had got everything wrong, but Mary knew she was never mistaken, not ever, and most of what she thought on the subject of her sister's family was still subsumed in anger, licking round colder thought processes like a flame. Silly Sophie wanted Katherine; so. Dear David adored Katherine to distraction, as had, and did, Claud; so. David had a muddy past, so. Weren't they all made for each other, so what. Mary stopped at a corner shop for food, comforting carbohydrate, tea cakes, biscuits, rubbishy company for the last of the afternoon. Thinking and munching butter and sweet things to clear the mind and add to the guilt. There was nowhere on Sunday to take tea: luxury should begin at home. She added to her purchases three bunches of half-dead flowers, the kind reserved for sale on the sabbath to people with more money than sense, but enough to alleviate the white of her unmarked walls. The white reminded her of duty, and all the institutions which had ever spelt security; she wanted to blot it out. She thought of Katherine in hospital, white walls. Another baby, well, well, well. Three for you and none for me: let Sophie help you: I shan't.

It was only later, after that strange phone call, that she thought of the best trick of all. No good keeping quiet and pretending she was not worried: worry about Katherine was an ingrained habit and telling herself she had no responsibility at all to prevent the silly little creature from mucking up her life and not contacting her mother-in-law, was a repetition which palled and was fading fast. There was a compromise in there somewhere, which would fulfil the duty and avoid all contact with a sister she could not bring herself to see. More than one compromise, but first things first. So she telephoned Susan Pearson Thorpe.

Mary's black telephone book was not quite comprehensive enough to contain the numbers of her sister's neighbours, although it did include on the well-thumbed pages, so many of Katherine's friends and every kind of professional contact under the sun, all the charities, plumbers and doctors active in central London. The name of Pearson Thorpe rang a bell, large person, mentioned by Katherine as the next-door neighbour where the children resorted every day, and there could not be so many Pearson Thorpes in the book. Mary rehearsed her inquiries, 'I'm so sorry to bother you on a Sunday evening but I can't raise my sister, would you happen to know if they've gone away?' No, not raise my sister, sounded like something coming up out of a tomb. That thought was suddenly frightening, equally soon dismissed as nonsense, if only she could control the images in her mind instead of thinking like a child, thinking in colours and pictures as Katherine always had, crippled by imagination. There, she had found and dialled the number. She had even got halfway through the spiel in her authoritative voice before she sensed the hostility. Or the fact that the woman on the other end of the line was not quite following anything which was said.

'K'thrine A'dale? Sister, who she? Oh, yes, yes, yes yes. Got you. Whatchyou phoning me for?'

'Being a bit of nuisance, I'm afraid . . .'

'Not a bit of it. Nobody ever calls me. Pity. Whatcha want, again? No, I don't think they're away. Who was it? Oh dear, sorry.'

There was a muffled thump, as if someone, or something heavy had fallen to the ground. Mary held the phone away from her ear. There was a very loud clearing of the throat. 'Whoopsy daisy,' said the voice, slipping into a short giggle, curtailed by a hand across the mouth.

'Perhaps Mr Pearson Thorpe could help,' said Mary in her best voice of endless patience. The smothered giggle turned into a snort.

'You betcha he could. He could help a lot. He's gone off, though.'

'Well anybody who might have seen my sister, really. I'm sorry to ask, but their phone doesn't seem to work . . .'

'Ah.' There was the heavy breathing of laboured thinking. This woman is drunk, Mary thought: God help Katherine with her neighbours and what the hell is going on with the kids. 'Tell you what,' said the voice, gathering speed and clarity. 'You wan' Mrs Harr-is-on, not me. She always knows allll about nex' door. All about it.'

247

'About what?'

'Nothing. She thinks a lot. I'll get her. Now. Wait a minute. I couldn't give a toss about nex' door. Nor a fart. Wait a minute . . .'

By this means, with patience worn thinner than a thread, Mary came to speak on a Sunday evening to Mrs Harrison, total stranger, and they came to reassure one another. It was all very simple. Mrs Harrison poured forth into the ear of Mary Fox all the worries she had never succeeded in imparting to her employer, who would not listen. The worries had been incubated into a state of incoherence, and the television boomed in the background. She talked long and excitedly about not seeing the eldest child, Katherine's first-born, in as many weeks as the child had years. She gabbled about the little boy, fine, oh yes perfectly fine, out with Daddy. Then she accelerated into children's tales about a thinner version of little Jeanetta sitting in the garden, singing to herself, thereby giving, quite inadvertently, the impression, that this had been yesterday. Then there was news of a party the Allendales were having on Tuesday or was it Wednesday, all information spewed forth in a rush and an irritating accent. Mrs Pearson Thorpe would see everyone then, said Mrs Harrison. She would be able to check. Mary doubted Mrs Thorpe's powers of observation in any context, and was aware that she had not been invited to any party. Lastly, there was something incomprehensible about a man coming to the door with a cloak which this Mrs Harrison had seen before.

'Jeanetta loved to dress up,' she explained.

'Just like her mama,' Mary added into a split-second silence.

She was beginning to think the whole household was mad, regretting the phone call in earnest. Nothing she had heard was raising alarm bells too loud to ignore, but the woman would not stop, even when Mary started to pity her sister for living adjacent to a pair of harridans. The very word came to mind, and with it something which was expedient as well as a practical joke. She remembered Sophie's dreadful new pet, was reminded of cats and charity workers, oh what a joke. In another frame of mind, less sharpened by rejection and less irritated, Mary would never have thought of what she considered now. She would never wilfully waste anyone's time.

'Listen, Mrs Harrison, I'll tell you what I'll do. You say you've been round and they don't let you take the child out, never mind. But if you're seriously worried about the children, have you considered phoning the authorities?'

'Oh, no, I couldn't do that, really I couldn't. What would people say? I just couldn't.'

'Well, I could. Better than any of us, wouldn't it? Someone to check? Then we'd certainly know if there was anything up. I know just the chap to ask.'

'Oh no, it's not that bad ...' Mrs Harrison was back-tracking, embarrassment oozing from every pore. '... I'm sure everything's all right really. I've tried to get Mrs Pearson Thorpe to go but ...'

'I quite understand,' said Mary smoothly. 'Well, we'll send the chap, shall we? Then we'll know for certain sure and you won't need to worry ever again.'

'Yes,' said Mrs Harrison, after a long pause to weigh up all the pros and cons. 'Yes, that would be for the best. Oh, thank you.'

'Tomorrow,' said Mary. 'Today's Sunday.'

'I know,' said Mrs Harrison. 'I don't like it, but I'll sleep easy now.'

'Goodnight, then,' said Mary. The official, reassuring voice was all Mrs Harrison heard.

The reassuring voice gave itself a little more to eat, marvelling that food was such a good, if temporary panacea. Laughing to itself for such a coup of an idea. Good old Child Action Volunteers, the perfect people, with John Mills the very perfect sort of pest to inflict on that perfect household. He would lean on a nest of tables and splinter the wood: he would mar the perfection: he would offend Katherine with his shambling presence and he would infuriate David with his persistence. And Mary would have done her duty, just in case there was anything really wrong. He was certainly best for the task; if there was anything wrong, he would find it. Had a reputation after all, as well as perfect, utterly reliable reports. A sweet combination for maximum effectiveness, and a very large element of revenge. Tomorrow would do. Sunday was a day of rest. It wasn't as if, on the basis of all these flapping old women, there was any panic at all. Like Mrs Harrison, Mary slept easy.

John Mills had almost forgotten what it was like to sleep by the time he recognized the presence of Monday morning. When he had returned home from a mild day's work on the Saturday evening, to find his flat bereft of animal life, he had panicked before he went back out to look for them, pacing the streets, stopping people and asking questions. Many of those interrogated *en route* for Saturday night pleasures resented the interruption while bowing to his insistence since he was clever at making an 'excuse me' feel like a blow. 'Excuse me, but have you seen a stray cat? Or one, or two, or three?' his face illuminated with urgency and the twitch below the eye working overtime. Responses varied between, Yes, seventeen cats, Don't think so, Pardon? and No, I fucking haven't, piss off. The irritation would have been less if he had not always repeated his question, were they quite sure they had not seen stray cats, I mean, absolutely sure. He asked similar questions in shops and pubs like a man repeating a litany of prayers and in between said little else but oh dear, oh dear, or made strange noises towards the alleys between houses and even towards drains. With rare logic, he did not take his questions to the takeaway downstairs from the flat. They were busy and besides friendly enough to have returned his properties had they found them. 'I don't understand,' he kept repeating on his return; 'I just don't understand. Why would anyone come in just for kittens? No stereo this time, no telly, just cats, I can't work it out.' Matilda had been silent and restless, jumping each time he spoke although he did not notice. 'Other people might love them as much as you,' was the last she had snapped, turning away. Because of his tossing, turning and mumbling, or so he presumed, she went to sleep on the sofa reserved for their rare guests, and early in the following morning, went out. For the day, her note stated, not unkindly. Will be back. In the normal event, such a missive would have distressed him. As it was, he did not care for company.

The thought gradually occurred that no one deliberate enough to steal a crate of kittens would be likely to leave them around in the locality for the owners to find at leisure. Whatever had been the purpose of so odd and tidy a piece of burglary, via roof or door, he knew not, he hoped the motives were benign. Visits to terrible estates had once forced him to witness cats being stoned: cats being coated with paraffin and . . . But by evening, he had persuaded such images out of his mind and made himself imagine the whole furry collection assembled elsewhere, in front of a fire, perhaps, a better home than this. Matilda's silence on any subject was a matter of indifference. On Sunday, he slept better, still fitful; waking at dawn to curse himself for his failures and his own stupidity.

For God's sake, going round the houses and never looking at his own. The nether regions other than the roof formed areas he had never explored, go to it. At this bright suggestion, Matilda shot out of the flat two hours early for work, muttering something about errands, and he went downstairs. He was still heavy with grief, not optimistic for anything at all when he found the back door to the yard, not locked, resigned himself to nothing, whistling as he went out in pursuit of one, last chance. Oh, dear God, what God, there never was a God. Only a devil with an army.

Such a pathetic amount of blood in that confined space amongst the weeds, plenty enough to indicate death as well as agony. Scratched on to the remains of two cardboard boxes moist from the rain which had fallen overnight, gore in spots dark against the broken concrete of the ground. In one corner, Kat, her long body described in one ugly arc defined by her dead fur, each limb reduced to bone by the wet. The legs were stretched, the teeth bared and her back broken in a sharp angle. By the bowl still full of water for an absent dog, John found one of the kittens, neck snapped and distended, the little abdomen punctured in one massive wound, and against one wall, amid drifting balls of fur, another corpse, curled peacefully but without the fluffy tail he had often stroked. Half of a head; so little blood. He closed his eyes against the screaming, yowling, shrieking episode, the tornado of sight and sound which had made this carnage, heard and saw it all the same, driving his face against a cold brick wall to graze his skin. He moved slowly, edged dead Kat gently with the toe of his shoe before lifting her off the ground, imagined as he did so the sound of cracking bones. Then he was sick into the bowl belonging to the dog, and stood there, holding the wet bundle of fur, not crying, but howling like a beast, the blood on his own face not yet congealed.

'Sorry, very sorry: he's out at the moment . . .' Oh shit where is he? When the indispensable man arrived for work, he was a whole hour later than expected. His steps up the stairs were audible, the same pace as an old man. When he opened the door and showed them his scratched face, grey but washed, no one noticed the difference and the phone began to ring.

There was something Mrs Harrison loved about Mondays, any Mondays, but especially this Monday. Madam upstairs went to work for a start, didn't she, so the world started going round again as per normal, thank you. The air was fresh, these silly rainfalls the signal for autumn and the winter she preferred with all those snug evenings with the Tee Vee and no need to pretend to be busy because the light was still there. And yes, Mr Pearson Thorpe was bringing Mark home today and no need to worry about anything else, not perfect, this status quo, but perfectly workable. She sat on the step with her cigarette and surveyed the street. Nice, until him next door came out with all the reminders of other anxieties and daft things said. Looking carefully, but keeping her pose studiedly casual, Mrs Harrison watched David Allendale coming down the steps, carrying Jeremy like the Crown Jewels in one arm, a pushchair in the other. Because she found it so difficult to forgive him for his response to her own visits to the same front door from which he emerged, Mrs Harrison did not emit any large hallos, or expect him to either talk or notice her presence, simply looked the other way while watching out of the corner of her eye. That boy was too big for a pushchair, make him walk, toughen him up a bit, could see dad's point if they were going to a supermarket, all walking kids a bloody liability. Where were they going, never mind, probably shops, nowhere else on

Monday. They trundled away uphill, the child chirping like a sparrow, pointing and twisting in his father's arms, Oh for Christ's sake look at them, why had she ever worried about the whole damned family. Your eyes, said husband Harrison, are bigger than your brain.

In the confidence of Monday morning, another idea occurred amid the sunshine and the everything all right with the world sensations. Mrs Harrison suffered one last stab of guilt which spurred her into action. She checked that the key to the house was in her pocket, clambered down the steps, minced up the street while throwing away the fag and went up the steps to the Allendales, all of this done with a bit of puff and a rhyme itching inside her head from Samantha's repetition of this morning. Bugger rhymes: sometimes she wished she knew fewer, but could never resist the singing. Nothing else to say, Harrison said: you never got out of the nursery. How did it go, easy.

> Miss Polly had a dolly which was sick, sick, sick,
> She sent for the doctor to come quick, quick, quick;
> The doctor came with his bag and his hat
> And knocked on the door with a rat-a-tat-tat.

'Tick, tick, tick,' said Samantha.

No, no, Mrs Harrison had scolded, wrong bits of words, thinking like this while she knocked at the door with a rat-a-tat-a-tat, ignoring the brilliant polish of the bell. She waited for a response, wishing she had not thrown away the cigarette half done, slightly nervous in case the master should return all of a sudden and find her there. There was a lengthy delay before the door was opened, slowly and far from wide like you would if you intended a welcome. In the small space through which Mrs Harrison peered, her own face obscured by the sun behind her but nevertheless transfixed in an artificial grin, Mrs Harrison saw Katherine. Even at 10.00 a.m. in her own home, hair brushed, pressed camel slacks in cool gabardine, a white blouse and a tiny row of pearls soothing the neck. None of these accoutrements prevented Mrs Harrison from noticing that the other was extremely pale and apparently thinner than ever, but then again, clothes were terribly deceptive. Nothing worth any kind of remark.

'Hallo, Mrs Allendale. Lovely morning. How are you? Listen, I was just wondering: I was going to be taking Samantha up the park, you know, to the swings . . . Shall we take Jeanetta too? Might give you a break if you want. Lovely day,' she repeated.

Katherine opened the door a trifle wider, looked anxiously up the street in the direction her husband had taken, took a step back. She seemed to struggle for composure, put her hand over her mouth and coughed painfully, then straightened her narrow spine and smiled.

'Excuse me, got a cough.'

'Oh dear,' clucked Mrs Harrison automatically, 'Nasty.'

'Both of us, actually,' Katherine continued. 'Jenny and me. Flu or something, but she can't come to the park, Mrs Harrison. She's gone off, you see, to stay with her granny. You've met Granny, I'm sure.'

'Can't say I did,' Mrs Harrison replied.

'Oh, I thought you must have done.' Katherine thrust a strand of hair behind one ear. 'She lives out of town, in the country. Jeanetta loves it there, she gets so spoiled, she won't want to come back. They eat nothing but biscuits.' Both of them stood there smiling at one another.

'Well, that's all right then,' said Mrs Harrison. 'Very nice for them, I'm sure.'

'Yes,' said Katherine. 'It is, actually. I miss her.'

'Well, yes. I expect you do. Nice, though, the peace and all that.'

'Yes, very nice. Ever so nice.'

There were a few other words about days being lovely before Mrs Harrison, still missing the cigarette, scurried home. Oh dear, oh dear, how silly she had been, her tongue sticking to the roof of her mouth in one great scolding of herself; I don't know, I really don't.

Embarrassing, all of it, really. ''S all right,' she yelled to Harrison as she came indoors, 'everything all right,' as if he had even asked to know. No response, which made her crosser. Everything all right and every bugger should need to know. What a fool. She wished she had found the sense to take the number of that sister woman, whose voice had been so bossy, that one, last night, how stupid not to take down something like they always did on the Tee Vee, in offices. Then she could have called her back before the woman phoned her tomorrow like she promised, told her not to bother with whatever it was she was about to bother with. No one should worry at all, nor should they. All that stuff we watch, she said to Harrison, makes us think too much; we imagine things. What things? Things which bump in the night.

The front door closed behind him. Katherine did not ask where he had been, what constitutional he had taken with Jeremy by his side like a guardian angel, the one to the other. When he arrived in the kitchen, she was standing at the business end with her hands in the kitchen sink, and as he breezed into the room with arms full of food shopping, he did not cease to smile when he saw the direction of her gaze. Placed his packages on the table and came across to her side for one, brief hug. She did not respond.

'Mrs Harrison came,' she said dully. 'I told her you-know-who had gone to stay with her granny. Like you told me.' Without comment, both had ceased to mention the name which had dropped entirely from any conversation.

'That's right,' he said cheerfully. 'So she has. Having a great time.'

'But it isn't right. You know exactly where she is. Here. You lied, David.' She pointed with one trembling arm in the direction of the silent playroom door. He placed his hands on her shoulders.

'Katherine, my sweet, be sensible. Why don't you change your clothes and go out for a while, hey? The gym? Shopping? Nothing too strong, darling: You're not so well. Plenty pocket money, big treat. Lovely outfit for you to collect. For tomorrow night. My birthday present to you.'

Katherine stared, the eyes in the middle distance, a puzzlement crease developing over her forehead.

'But she isn't staying with Granny. She's there, you-know-who, behind that door. Not with Sophie. We should get her out. Why doesn't Sophie ever phone any more? She never phones like she used to phone, does she, David?'

His voice sank to a level she could perceive as dangerous. His hands were full of warning.

'Katherine, listen. There'd be so much trouble if you let her out. Prison and everything, I promise you. No one would recognize her. You'd be locked up, like I told you, how many times?' Katherine shrank back, hugging her arms to her chest and whispered.

'Did you look today?'

There was very slight hesitation. 'Yes. No, of course not. Why would I do that? How silly you are. It's very simple. You know very well she's gone to stay with Sophie. Granny. Repeat that after me. Then go out and say it again, only louder. Go on, say it now. So I can hear you.'

'She's gone to stay with her granny. She's gone to stay with her granny. She's gone to stay with her granny.'

'Good, good girl. Very good girl. Now don't forget collecting that dress. I'm going to start with the stuff for tomorrow evening. You could always buy me something for my birthday. I shall make myself a cake, with candles.' He beamed on her, his face containing all the innocent pleasure of a schoolboy while her face was held in the spotlight of his smile.

'Will you give her some?' The smile faded.

'I can't, Katherine, you know I can't. Say it again, what I told you.'

She tussled with memory and then her brow cleared. She raised her hands as if to conduct an orchestra, waved them level with her shoulders in the effort to repeat, carefully controlling the words.

'I know, I know, I know. Now I know. She's gone to stay with Granny.'

'That's right,' he said. 'Absolutely right. Now we all know. You're a good baby and I love you to pieces. Who's a good little girl then?'

'I am. She's gone to stay with Granny.'

He tapped the underneath of her chin lightly and playfully. 'Very good girl. Look, I've bought us sweeties . . .'

19

Glory, glory, alleluia. Nothing ever stays the same. Because I thought this was not the case, I thought there was nowhere else to go but down and anyway, looking up hurt the head more than somewhat. I'm so sorry, though, about that poor woman with the officious voice who phoned last night: Oh, dear, I have always been rude, abrupt and indifferent, but slopping drink and words down the phone in equal proportions excelled most other efforts in that line. Not a matter for self-congratulation. Nothing about me worthy of praise: *in vino veritas*, a slug, a worm, a nasty piece of goods. I was stoking up and well lit up, preparing for another onslaught on another week, another bit of my life which looked set to slip away and I wanted Sebastian so much the whole of me screamed. The thought of his returning on the Monday evening, saying his goodbyes, agreeing perhaps, for the sake of form and my fallen face, to come to the neighbours' party with me, was all too much. So I practically took the gin through a straw. Then I fell over. When I woke up, I wanted to die.

Monday morning, dawn, was thus the very end of the world. There was rain in the air, better than all the heat which created the wet, but dark rain, an unspoken storm making the sky bleak and I could not believe it was seven in the morning and cold as ice. There is a tautness to the face which comes from drink. In a way, it flatters my looks, smooths out the skin suffused from all that fluid, the same plumping out of a baby in tears, soft, flushed skin and the true state of health only showing in the pink whites of the eyes, as if one had swum in chlorine for half the night. All I had to do was reconstruct the visage with all those expensive cosmetics bought in one optimistic day, stagger to work via the well-known route, blind as a bat. Despite the investment of my life in the whole business of work, My career, My office, My everything, bolstered by the loyalty of clients as abrasive as me, I am well aware that my sacking is on the agenda. I should have been aware far sooner than this, having sacked others for lesser crimes than indifference and pink, babyish, early morning faces. I have sacked them for devotion to their families, God help me: work and selfishness came first, emotional impoverishment or the quality of life not my concern. It is now. We old soaks, you see, need to have an element of insight forced upon us and we resist to the last ditch. I do not think I have noticed a single thing about the life of anyone around me for months, possibly years, but, as I said, God is good when he is not a bastard: things change.

Sitting in the office, doing nothing but nursing the head, I could hear noises off, like a whispering behind scenes in a play which is going wrong. Regular whispering: just like home: Mrs Harrison, Mr Harrison, Samantha, Mark, chuntering behind the door, saying, 'Shall we go in?' Sebastian, too, saying out of earshot, shall I go home: will she talk to me this evening, no, better to stay: there will be no food, no comfort, no nothing at home, and could I ever make love to her any other time but early morning when she does not even notice ...? I am so used to whispers behind my back, whisperings reminiscent of some hated head prefect at school, talked about from a good distance in case the bully should hear. I should have listened to the whispers, not merely shouted back, but I've started now. Perhaps I can learn a little sensitivity after all.

Mark did it, seven-year-old Mark, that child of charm brought up mainly by others. They went off to the sea, my husband, whom everybody loves and I had ceased to notice, and Mark, joyous son, to look at waves and do manly things like play pin-ball machines in arcades and have fun. Consume fish and chips like starving creatures and make entertainments together, I don't know what, I didn't ask. But Mark fell over some spike in the sand, and cut open the soft calf of his leg, first thing Monday morning, I gather. That was what the whisperings in the office were about, should we tell her he phoned before she got in here? With a garbled story about a little boy, oh so small (all those little things in a suitcase), hurt badly, Mrs Pearson Thorpe, don't know how bad. Your husband phoned from hospital. They think they'll be coming home in the afternoon. Don't worry.

Worry? Not for a minute. All these defences going into overdrive, me being brisk and saying, Well what about that, silly little sod, what'd he do that for, and where did you say they were? Don't rightly know, to be precise, they said: somewhere on some coast, coming back later. How badly hurt? Don't know either: can't be so bad or they'd keep him in hospital, wouldn't they? But he's broke his leg, as well as cut it, your husband said don't fret, kids is strong and doctors know what to do. Knowing as I do the level of sheer incompetence in all worlds including my own, I doubted all the time who would know what, but I never doubted Sebastian acting for the best. Apart from being such an incompetent ass, such a fool, to let this happen in the first place, I at least understood complete relief about the company my son kept while hurting himself. Sebastian is built to ensure survival. I made my excuses, went home, making myself slow down.

I was only going home to wait, it was better not to hurry. Coming down the street as I was coming up, I ran into Katherine Allendale. Running was not quite the word, since I was running, she, I seem to recall, jerking from one paving stone to the next, carrying a carrier bag, don't know why I could bear to stop. Memories of her sister on the phone the night before, whatever that was about, memories of a number of things, including my lost qualities of politeness, made me hesitate enough to speak. How's things, Katherine? I remembered children, I thought of nothing but children, and how were hers, not wanting to know, but for once, wanting to ask. She said it three times if she said it once; everything fine, do you know, Jeanetta has gone to stay with her granny. Yes, I heard you, I said, how nice for them both. Yes it is, actually, she answered. And where are you going? Me, driven by the same politeness, trying to postpone the news from home. I'm going to the gym, she said. I looked at her, forgetting she was a thief, my rival, my glamorous and pathetic neighbour with the husband I once fancied and the house Sebastian coveted and it crossed my mind she might be a bit mad. Taking that insect figure to that dreadful gymnasium for further refinement. See you tomorrow, she said. What, I said. David's birthday, she said. Dinner. I did not say, Oh no; I simply wanted to say it.

Everything changes. We had all enjoyed health, my family, never thought of health as something one actually enjoyed, simply a condition of life which nothing ever seemed to affect, along with money, property and all that, an automatic assumption of continuance. Our children, like my parents' children, never suffered any accident bar scratches and all this had kept me in a state of innocence, helped me to take it all for granted. So when I sat in the study, waiting the return of the wounded, I admired the insouciance of my soldier father, wished I had seen blood and been able to say, rubbish, only a cut and a boy's a boy. I phoned every hospital on the east coast roughly in the area where I knew they had gone before I drew blanks on five and stopped. No one had said where they were, or I had not listened. I remembered how no one ever tells me the truth. Perhaps they had been trying to avoid telling me the boy was dead.

'Dead: I do hope he isn't dead,' such a politely expressed thought crashing into the light like a train out of a tunnel, huge and incapable of being shoved back. So all of a sudden I was winded, had to sit down, fighting back nausea even though I couldn't sit, made little running forays into all corners of the room, a headless chicken skittering backwards. Not the ague of drink but the blow to the solar plexus, that sudden vision of his never again being there, nothing more terrible to contemplate than his absence and I cannot begin to describe the horror of this. I may have learned words for feelings while learning a whole new range of the feelings themselves in the few weeks before this, but never enough words to describe these sensations. No Mark: never to see him again, hear him, no child in that seat, no small man espied forever in the corner of my eye, no backdrop to existence. But you scarcely saw him, I told myself: you gave birth crossly and put him to bed, but it does not follow that mothers as indifferent as I could fail to panic at the prospect of such loss. Late realization of love, call it what you will, but how any woman, even a monster, suffers such a death and survives I do not know. I thought of TV news, children lost in fires or kidnapped, all of this stuff dismissed by me as parental carelessness, and I wanted to weep.

To forestall weeping, I called Mrs Harrison, gabbled the news. Gabble was right, a turkey rather than a chicken. 'Hush,' she said, 'hush now, don't fret. Nothing to worry . . .' calmer than I but still unable to finish words and twisting her hands in an effort to keep them still. I want to scream, I told her: I just want to scream. Why doesn't Sebastian phone? 'I know, I know,' she murmured, then brightened. 'I know why he doesn't phone,' she said. 'It's 'cos they're driving home.'

This vision worked, I don't know why, simply the thought that you can't drive and telephone at the same time without one of those bloody machines in the car. 'They went all the way to Norfolk,' Mrs Harrison said. 'I remember, it's a long way, Norfolk. I went there once when I was younger.' She laughed nervously at the memory of the distance and probably something else. 'Oh, yes, a very long drive.' Then she consoled herself cunningly with action, squared her jaw and offered me the same panacea, clever by instinct.

'Listen, Mrs Pearson, there's things to do. Being as they are on their way home . . .' she stressed the certainty of this, '. . . I've got to do the rooms. Harrison left it all to the last minute, didn't he? All spick and span, we want to be, don't we now?' Her nose wrinkled in distaste as her eyes travelled round my study. 'I left Mark's as was, better clear it since he's not so well' (another, clever dismissal of the seriousness). '. . . But you could do in here, if you liked.' The old diffidence returning, '. . . Oh, and you could keep Samantha with you, leaves my hands free.' In quiet acceptance of her hands being more effective and therefore more important, I took my orders, obeyed without question.

Therapy in action, mustn't fall down, must we, things to do, wise old bird. Giving me chubby Samantha as my companion, so adult, she, so forgiving. How absolutely perverse it was that I should be cleaning and dusting with the clumsiness of no real practice, Samantha equally inept, obeying instructions to be good and telling me jokes, both of us actually enjoying ourselves. It was bizarre to have such a completely happy couple of hours, anxious but completely absorbed.

'Mummee . . . Here's a good one . . . Why can't you play cards in the jungle?'

'Don't know, darling. You tell me.' I was packing surplus paper into a polythene sack.

'Too many cheetahs!' She rolled around on the floor, clutching her sides and laughing like a chimpanzee, though I'm quite sure she has no idea what a real cheater is. 'Another?' she said, gasping. 'OK, go on, do.'

'What's a crocodile's favourite game?'

'I don't know.'

'Go on, guess.'

'I can't, that's far too hard for me.'

'Snap!' She would shout, jumping on the sofa and kicking her legs in the air, while I laughed too, both of us like that, we love jokes, only I never realized. 'Come on,' I said, 'this is work. Carry this stuff downstairs.' 'Why, what is it?' She peered inside a sack replete with bottles, old letters and dead flies, some of the bottles not quite empty. 'Rubbish,' I stated firmly. 'I like rubbish,' said my daughter.

Still bleak outside, you could forget it was summer, a preternaturally dark day, autumn striding rather than creeping into central London like a colossus and the trees shaking their heads in wild disapproval. Sammy and I crashing sacks down the steps to place by the railings the detritus of two rooms, Mark's and mine, and Sammy insisting on adding hers, but abandoning all labour to run up the street on her stubby legs in order to examine the far more interesting rubbish of everyone else. Monday is rubbish day in this stretch of London, but like many a Monday, they had forgotten to collect. On this day in every seven, the street takes on a polythene life with sacks and bins and God knows what appearing from all over the place, oh what work you could do investigating the lives if you looked inside. Be you never so rich, you still have to take out your trash, only I had never done it before. I kept mine indoors, in my mind.

'Look, look, look . . .' Samantha was ten steps away up the pavement, examining a bag outside the Allendales'. 'Mummy, look,' a strangled stage whisper louder than a prompt.

'Darling, you shouldn't look at other people's rubbish, not nice, come away.'

'Look,' she insisted, standing ground, she of the iron will and bossy tendencies so refined in her mama. So I ambled up with studied innocence in my walk, and looked: anything to continue this conspiracy with my suddenly gorgeous daughter. 'Doggy must have bit the bag,' she said importantly. How observant she is, picking the one bag with a large split.

And I could see why she was interested. No mouldy old foodstuffs here. A grey plastic sack (the Allendales would, wouldn't they? – designer rubbish, not put inside ordinary black), split open down one side. Flanked by other grey bags, up-market rubbish, I bet, fish-bones and empty caviar jars, my own bitchy guess, but in the torn bag, colours dripping on the ground, nothing but clothes. My eye was caught and held like a bur on a yellow thing with pink spots, diminutive garment sandwiched in between other smaller garments and a pair of striped pyjamas. I should have stopped Sammy, but she pulled at the things, bringing more of them on to the pavement. 'This is a nice one, Mummy; why is they throwing it away?' Only the colours danced in her eyes, but I saw more. A swathe, there was, of Jeanetta's clothing, little favourites I recognized out of the new clothes Katherine had bought for Jeanetta that one time weeks before, and stranger still, in the same heap, I thought I saw the dustier, more sophisticated pink of a summer suit I had seen that mother wear when we met not long ago. A new suit, I thought, as well as those striped pyjamas, either a replica of the same or a pair of Mark's: I had never checked to see if they had all been returned. 'Don't,' I repeated to Sammy, 'Don't. Put them all back, they'll see us.'

'Who will?'

'They will.'

She was fascinated like a dog determined to pursue a smell, while I felt the strangest sensation in my bones, so strange, a paralysis worse even than that fear for Mark, a sweeping chill which rooted me to the spot, powerless to stop her while goose-pimples raised on the back of my neck and my mind struggled for thoughts. I was shaking with cold but my arms were rigid with shock: then the light went out: I heard the trees again, and Samantha, screaming in whoops of excitement, howling with joy. And slipping into the kerb with noiseless efficiency, Sebastian's Mercedes with a small, white face peering out from the rear window. White and triumphant, trying to look solemn but really smiling like the hero coming home, my son, never more alive.

Sometimes since, I have wondered, without being at all wistful about it, what it is like to be a child. The son and heir was indeed injured: he had fifteen stitches in one calf and a broken ankle, must have hurt like hell, but all he could see by the time the stitches were inserted, was all the compensations which his little mind understood as bound to follow. Such as, 'I won't have to go back to school quite at the beginning of term, will I?' or 'Do you think people will want to sign this?' pointing to the modest amount of plaster which decorated his skinny shank. That plaster, such pride: he produced it from the car like a film starlet might produce one high-heeled leg, slowly and with great aplomb, waiting for the whistles and the applause, even enjoying the fact that Samantha, initially so full of welcome and gabbled news, was rapidly filled with jealousy.

'Mummy, will I be able to have some crutches?' Sweet, dozy questions from Mark's bed, where I simply sat and watched him.

'Anything you want,' I said. And I meant what I spoke. Anything he wanted, anything within my power either of them wanted. Watching him, without thinking too much, I knew I had hit the bottom only to rise a little. There was nothing more important, nothing to begin to put into the same scale, as this boy, this precious life. Oh, I did not weep: I was even bustling but I knew it well. I love my children. Oh Christ I love them all.

Equally well I knew how sensitive was my husband, delivering back the son and heir and letting me take over, even knowing how clumsy I was. Of course he could have bedded the child, washed him with greater efficiency and skill, done all those things better and quicker than I, but they stood back,

the Harrisons and Sebastian. He soothed Sammy with attention, left me to direct the comfort of the patient, guided by his
instructions. 'No, Mummy, mustn't get it wet, this plaster
stuff. Can I have a biscuit? No, a chocolate biscuit, please.
And some apple juice? Can I get Adam' (a friend from school,
another stranger to me) 'to come round and see my leg tomorrow?' Yes, yes, yes, until he was drowsy, some drug in him
other than trauma making him slip away although he was
fighting to stay awake, muttering as his eyes closed, desperate
to inform and receive anything he might have missed in his
small world, his questions following no sequence.

'Did the beggar come back?' he asked suddenly from the
depths of the pillow.

'Which beggar? A man in a book?'

'You know, the dirty man who got in here and got upstairs
when Harrison was watching the cricket. Sammy said he came
back.' Sammy and Mark had conversed in whispers through
the door of the loo, before she was shooed away. '. . . And the
police came, Sammy said. I think the beggar took Jeanetta,
that's what I think, and that's what Sammy says. Is that why
the police came? I missed it . . . ow, that hurts. Jeanetta could
have come and seen my plaster . . .'

'What man, darling?'

'That one, you know, you must know. But I wasn't supposed
to tell you until Mrs Harry told you. Or they would take us
away, other beggarmen, we'd be kidnapped, she said,' he
added with sleepy relish.

'Of course you wouldn't. You are a silly-billy.'

'But Sammy says they took Jeanetta. Jeanetta isn't there any
more. She was so thin, Mummy.'

'Jeanetta's coming back, darling. She's only gone to stay
with her granny. I expect she'll be back very soon. She'll be
able to write on your plaster.' Why the hell was he thinking
such irrelevant things? Sickness makes for nonsense: I couldn't
remember him mentioning next door's lot for weeks. But then,
I had not been paying attention: for all I knew, they may have
been discussed *ad nauseam*. Sitting there in the quiet comfort
of his newly tidied room, I got back an almost imperceptible
hint of that peculiar coldness I had felt in the street. Mark's

beautiful dark eyes were gradually closing and his face was rosily pink. The dog snored in the corner, another indulgence for the patient.

'No, she won't come back. Netta. Anyway, she won't write on my plaster, 'cos she can't write . . .'

'Can't write, night-night. Nice dreams.'

'It was ever such a big spike, Mummy . . .'

On my soft way downstairs, treading quietly although there was no need, dizzy with relief and the mind still in overdrive, I wondered about this beggar, but there were too many other things of greater importance, just then. Besides, he was a secret, whoever he was, and in my new humility, I was prepared to let them have their secrets, as many as they liked, Mrs Harrison and all: I could not afford jealousy. The house was warm: the tranquillity too precious to disturb. Tomorrow would do. Tomorrow would do for everything except whatever was going to happen next.

The face my husband turned to me was lined with incredible weariness, and in it, I saw all the reflected features of our son. Sebastian had not sat in that chair for so long, the mere sight of him, slightly dishevelled, open-necked shirt, all of him creased from the head to the shoes, reminded me suddenly of the man on the park bench. Lonely. Like me, I suppose, making my first admission. I did not feel tension since there was no emotion left: I did not feel awkward because I was more grateful to see him there, and if there ever had been another woman for him to run to (which I knew very well there was not: he never tells lies), I had lost all power for indignation.

'Would you like a drink?' My request, noticing he had made no move to find his own.

'Please.' I disinterred the whisky, the hated whisky which I loathe, quite proud to present it still full. Then I poured a very small gin, put it ever so slightly beyond the reach of my own hand. That way, I would have to reach every time I wished to sip. I cannot reform all at once; I cannot pretend that I would, any more than I can pretend about anything. Dishonesty, like the jealousy, is not a commodity I could afford.

'Are you going to work tomorrow?' A casually loaded question from him.

'No. I thought I'd take a few days off and amuse the boy. Are you?'

'No.'

One sip of the gin, this part required some courage. He was opening his mouth to say something which I interrupted with my words first. I could not let him ask first.

'Will you stay here then? Please.'

'Yes.'

We did not touch. You do not rush across a room and embrace the spouse who has left you, even if you left him first, or you do not if you are me. I saw the father of my children, not a new-found lover with nothing at all to reconcile. But I touched his shoulder as I passed to the kitchen, briskly, a very passing gesture which he might have thought was a mistake if he had cared to notice, which I thought he might. It cost me, that little touching, but I did touch first. Then I made some supper for us both, like wives are supposed to do, once in a while. Mrs Harrison might be proud of me.

20

'Don't snap at us, John. We're all busy and you aren't the only
one with a head for God's sake. You moody bastard,' fondly
said. 'What's the matter with you today? You drank too much,
or something?'

'Nope. I . . .' Somehow he could never finish the sentences,
tore his eyes from the blank sky of the windows and smiled.
The lethargy was becoming overpowering. '. . . Only all . . .
day, I haven't been able to fathom this bloody message. Why
didn't she phone again?'

'It's that woman. A mogul. They don't repeat themselves.
But she is a relative and did say it was urgent. I didn't ask why
she couldn't intervene, not wise to ask, you told me so. Accept
what they say at face value and act on it, no other way; hope
they're wrong. You jus' gotta go.'

He shuffled, awkward. 'Not enough,' he muttered, 'not
enough to justify . . .' fumbled again, '. . . I mean, no screams,
no yells, bruises. Simply innuendoes. Parents disbarring relatives from house, maybe all relatives a pain in the neck, often
are. Mother neurotic, often is. Twentieth-century disease . . .
enlarged groins, enlarged consciences . . . to say nothing of the
expectations . . . what's different?'

'Nothing. As much as we usually get. Sort of message starts,
nothing wrong and what there is I'm sure as hell not going to
tell you. They're all ambiguous, you know they are. Nobody
says what they mean, quite; they put out signals, little screams
for help, and that's our strength, recognizing the code.
What's the matter? . . . Just because you didn't get that bloody
award. Well, we didn't either. I thought you were bigger than

that. OK. I'll send someone else.' John stirred, outraged.

'Don't be stupid. Of course I'll go. Have you seen the address?'

'What's that got to do with it? I don't suppose you could possibly give us some sort of report by tomorrow?' she added, knowing she was pushing her luck. 'That woman, you know. The complainant. Think of the funding.'

He wandered up the street, his favourite and yet most unfavourite street, later on the Monday evening. Or at least the hour felt late, technically well into daylight, but dark with the rainy cloud, full of threats; the sky was distended, releasing nothing, and the sun was dead. John felt little but a dull hatred pulsing against his temples as he plodded along one side of the perfectly maintained pavement, the sweeties in his pocket scratching against his thigh through the thin fabric of cotton, his right hand missing the usual plastic carrier of tins. Nothing in this street which was not subdued to man's most prodigal taste: nothing strictly utilitarian at all. Proceeding in a westerly direction, looking left and right with his arms now linked behind his back like a policeman on patrol, he noted the cars. Mercedes, BMW, tiny new Renault, small enough for the wife's runabout or a toy for the servant. Bastards. John knew this street so exactly from his daily passage, he was always surprised to notice more, disgusted himself by the ignorance which never read numbers and had never given him to understand that his destination was right next door to Mrs Harrison. He looked in the street for the familiar vagrant, saw no one guarding the cars, stopped short of the Harrison house. This was ridiculous, quite ridiculous.

All he could recall for the moment was that woman's casual remarks about the affluence of them next door and the fat child of theirs he had once seen. Bitterness rose like bile, the heartburn of anger. Affluence, inexact anagram of flatulence, diminishes, ruins, desensitizes all those in possession, but above all else, protected them from evil, Amen. There could be nothing wrong with this house. He passed the Pearson Thorpes' slowly. Lights in each window, no need to worry about the quarterly bills, not they, what with no one in sight but, sitting like a king, one grand and perfect Persian cat slightly above the level of his eye, fitting height for his majesty occupying the whole of a windowstill. The indifference of the cat basking in good fortune and obscene health stung John like a whip, bringing treacherous tears to his eyes while the animal neither blinked nor stirred under his scrutiny. A pedigree purring. John moved on.

The seven o'clock sky was even darker and those ominous trees flanking the large houses were respectfully still. Fifteen self-conscious steps (turning back only once to look at the cat), until he was level with another window affording a better view. Inside here, a glowing kitchen, the same place where he had once been surprised by a senior lady dressed in lace, sipping sherry while inviting him to bow to her regal wave. But currently in her place, a small, bright, dark-haired boy with damson eyes, sitting in a high chair. Flowers on the table, big, fat, Michaelmas daisies. A man, so patently the father, cooked while the boy watched for the next meal, and a blonde woman was setting their places, her face turned half to the light and a frown of concentration marring the features. You get to look old by doing that, John heard his own jeering words: watch for the frown lines, lady. There was a door at the far end beyond, only partially in sight, and greenery visible through large French windows beside. The boy at the table swayed to the sound of some music, waving a spoon in time to an orchestra which John, mere onlooker, could not hear.

He could not see the colours or the elegance, only the distance between these and other lives. Sod them. Sod the informer as well as this mother and child waiting like baby birds with ever open mouths. Sod them all. Bastards. Filthy rich, plutocratic, patrician, sound-proofed against youth and age, bastards. Deliberately he leaned over the railings, not so much careless of being seen as indifferent to their indifference, spat into the well of the basement, twice. He could write the fucking report blindfold; could describe in words stinking with authenticity each detail of every magnificent floor of this house, borrowing details, dimly remembered but still exact, from Mrs Harrison's accounts of the house next door. 'All them stairs, Mr Mills,' her words taking him from room to room. He looked back once more towards the cat, so sure of its own survival, imagined the blonde woman dressed in a fur coat. Threw the sweeties out of his pocket. Walked slowly and seething to an empty home.

The evening of the party posed all the normal problems. 'What are you wearing?' Monica was asking Jenny, suspiciously bright with the evening of Tuesday.

'I don't know yet. Haven't finished putting the kids down. Can't think.' She did not say the call was an intrusion, but her voice implied as much along with apology for her own irritation.

'Oh, that reminds me,' Monica said, oblivious to the hint. 'Did you have Katherine's kids at the weekend, like you said?'

'What? Oh, no, the older one had gone to stay with her grandmother. Another time, I suppose. I was rather relieved, to tell the truth. Place is bedlam as it is. So I haven't thought of what to wear. It's only a few people for supper for God's sake.'

'Well, I just wondered. Do we dress up or down, casual or smart?'

'Oh, I see what you mean. I'd dress up if I were you. Might prove a point. I will, I suppose, if you do. Besides, when have you ever seen Katherine casual at any kind of party?'

'Right. Out with the shoulder pads, heigh-ho. A total reconstruct in ten minutes. Should we take a present?'

'Yes. For Katherine, not for him. A not very exciting houseplant, I thought.' Jenny laughed, a guilty sharing of the undertone of malice which went against conscience but was worth the friendship resuming an even keel. If there were any question about division of loyalty, she was Monica's second and had been anxious about the whole evening. Then she remembered to telephone the American couple who had asked for directions, since last time they had lost themselves on the way, as they would this time, directions or not. For that purpose alone, they set out early.

Inside the Allendale kitchen, David put the finishing touches to the table. The surface of the wood was covered with an antique linen cloth (they had debated about that, Katherine

271

preferring the texture of the wood but he preferring dignified protection), the cutlery heavy silver, similarly old, bishop's pattern, and on each elaborate plate setting was a matching linen napkin, white embroidery on white, stiff as sails. In the centre was a round dish of flowers, late blooming garden roses cut short to crowd against each other in a shallow pyramid of red and cream, dark-green foliage spilling on to the cloth. David loathed arrangements which ebbed and swayed, obscuring one person from another like the wispy ferns of restaurants. The lilies Katherine had arranged stood on one side, illuminated by two broad candles which would be placed with the final flourish on the table. The door to the garden stood open, the lawn smelling sweetly of the earlier rain which curtailed the idea of outdoor play since he could not have borne to see high heels sinking in the grass, but in the living room, drinks were ranged in the old and priceless tantalus, bottles gleaming in rows on either side. Katherine stayed there, out of the kitchen, hearing from where she stood the music playing as David worked, compact-disc music lifted from the studio to replace the workaday radio. Jeremy slept. Husband and wife were casually dressed, Katherine downstated in khaki skirt and blouse with no ornament other than a gold collar, broader than the wedding band on her finger but soft and comfortable, a new gift. She stayed in the drawing room because of the cool and the absence of rich smells, and besides in the living room, her room, she could survey her own work with a modicum of pride. Such high polish there was in here, such a multitude of colours in harmony. Sitting on the extreme edge of the striped sofa, she longed for the oblivion of sleep while her mouth craved soft-boiled eggs and bread soldiers, childish food with heavily sugared tea.

No such simple fare visible in the kitchen; basic ingredients and pans out of sight as all eight guests arrived with gratifying punctuality. They drank Tanqueray gin laced with minimal tonic and wedges of lemon, Glenfiddich whisky with nothing, Sancerre or dry fino, each couple perversely varying their favourite tipple, all generously administered to accompany smoked oysters on ivory cocktail sticks and tiny rounds of red-roe covered pastry. While Sebastian Pearson Thorpe fascinated

272

the American wife with his sandy Anglo-Saxon looks and artless public-school accent, Monica, splendid as a peacock in pink and black, made very merry with Jenny's husband, and Jenny spoke to Colin with similar animation. Both women were ceasing to notice how, in comparison to their hostess, they were somewhat overdressed and forgetting that fact was going to take far more of the white wine. Jenny observed without anxiety the passing of a lingering glance from Colin across the large room, over the bold stripes and colourful cushions she so admired, towards the armchair where Katherine sat, sipping fruit juice, as delicately fragile as David, incongruously perched on the arm, was solid. Monica had taken the second glass before they all moved across the hall to ooh and aah the table: Susan Pearson Thorpe merely her first since they were late; David inconspicuously drank his small, but third whisky. Merely imagining the tension of hosting, from which her own sufferings were always extreme, Jenny allowed a moment's sympathy. Her eyes were drawn to his hard body: she found it impossible not to imagine him *in flagrante*, naked as a baby but rampant as a bull, wondered what shape he was, turned away in embarrassment and watched the rest. All of them vaguely familiar from similar occasions, in this house or other houses, weeks or months since, plenty enough acquaintance to justify them all greeting with loud familiarity. As if they were friends. That was the conspiracy. They were bound, seduced and easily persuaded to applaud one another: mutual approval the purpose of the evening with which all present willingly complied. But the small element so vital to such an occasion, a sort of spontaneous burst of relaxation, goodwill or whatever ingredient, was missing. There was in progress during those initial stages, too much of watching and impressing, too many darting eyes.

By the time all sat at table and the candles were lit, they were noisy perforce and some sense of genuine celebration took over. It was the table itself, so beautiful, an aesthetic appetizer for the food to follow. Each was supplied with a battery of glasses. Small portions of cold artichoke soup, served with a little sherry. 'No, we did not grow the artichokes,' David apologizing manfully, 'did we, darling? I'm afraid to admit this is a tribute to the delicatessen. One simply adds the cream.' Who is *one*? Monica wondered: I would have thought Katherine did all the cooking, remembering at the same time he was no mean hand with a pot or pan: even for a lunch of cold roast beef with fresh horseradish sauce. Good God, he might have done it all: so why had she ended up married to Colin, who did so much less and did not always do it well. She felt a little bitter, ate more swiftly than the soup deserved. Susan Pearson Thorpe, far more muted than Jenny remembered, but charming, perfectly charming to the Americans, spooned the creamy mixture into her mouth with what seemed genuine hunger while the rest were more delicate. At the same time she had swallowed the alcoholic accompaniment in a single gulp, looked at the empty glass in mild surprise. David talked about food. In fact, they all talked about food. Sebastian recollected some uncle of his saying that the brandy and cigars formed the more spiritual part of the meal and he was glad to reflect that the two temporal ingredients were bound to be forthcoming, and discussion of grub was bound to cease. Susan and he should do more of this. He ventured a smile in her direction, noticed she was trying so hard part of him melted. The day had not been easy: she might have wished to see herself transformed, but he really did not want her like a Katherine. Depending on this evening's restraint, he would tell her so.

'You really need to go to the eastern seaboard if you guys really like to eat,' said the American, eyeing the next course, noting with great approval a dish of sole véronique. 'If you like fish,' he added. 'I just happen to love fish, any kind of fish.' 'Especially lobster,' his wife added. 'He goes crazy over lobster.' 'Have you had any oysters this year?' said Sebastian so politely he sounded like an advertisement. 'Season just begun, I believe.' 'Oh, oh,' joked the American wife, 'fun and games in the shires, I guess. I just couldn't let him eat oysters. Is it really true, I mean, what they're supposed to do to you?' She addressed the question to her host, enjoying herself. David winked roguishly. Katherine cleared plates with delicate and almost noiseless efficiency.

Schools: they were on to schools. Sebastian liked this better than food or furnishings, both of which might have offended his wife, but he still looked forward to something else. Which schools and where, horses for coarses, a loud pun from Monica which made him wince. At least Susan and he were in agreement on this front; knew which paths were surfaced for their children, added them into the conversation. 'What about Jeanetta?' Jenny asked, a question over her shoulder in a polite attempt to include monosyllabic Katherine and make her belong. 'Where will she go?'

'What? Oh . . .' A plate dropped from her hands and crashed to the floor, followed by a chorus of cheers, sympathies and offers to help. 'Oh, don't worry,' said David, 'always happens. Wasn't a very special plate, no, no, sit down. Darling, can you pass me the serving spoon?' 'Will you look at that,' said Jenny, the wonder again so genuine she was pointing with one finger as if the rest could not see exactly what she saw. Slices of duck, overlapping in a rich circle on a dish, stewed cranberries as centrepiece and the table full of the scent of both. 'How do you get a duck to behave like that?' said the American, impressed. 'My, oh my,' said his wife, sitting on David's right as David transferred slices on to plates and she passed them along with the aid of her linen napkin. Katherine fussed with a dish of tiny French beans and a platter of duchesse potatoes which other hands took from hers. On the sideboard by the lilies, a magnificent glass bowl of salad had appeared, radicchio glowing purple, Monica noticed, lifted from the fridge early to remove the chill. The next course settled as they ate the last. Inevitably, the conversation returned to food.

Where do you buy cranberries, how do you cook like this, where do you get the best fish, poultry, game, questions all smothered in sauce. The compact-disc player had stopped in reverence as mouths filled in preparation for a further round of compliments and questions, leaving one whole minute of masticating silence. Two glasses were empty, the quiet not uncomfortable since all bar Katherine were eating with concentration. Monica began to talk again first, but as David passed round the back of the high-backed chairs with the wine, his hand brushed her shoulder and she forgot what she wanted to say. Colin knew: it was something about the duck, part of an old argument, but he remembered not to speak when his mouth was full. And then into the continuing semi-silence, each of them in turn heard the sound of scratching.

Colin noticed first and turned his head. Monica looked at him inquiringly, taking the direction of his gaze. Then Jenny and then the American wife. Sebastian took no notice, concentrating on his food, and Susan Pearson Thorpe, finding the whole evening desperate, was raising her glass. The scratching came from beyond the playroom door at the far end of the room, a slight but regular sound, almost like the sawing of wood heard from a distance. Monica thought immediately of the similar sound made by a puppy she once had which would scrape at a door, scrape, scrape, pause to wait for some sort of reply, surprised that the door would not shift, repeat the process, scrape, scrape, sit back on haunches. 'What on earth is that, David?' she asked casually, none of them in any sense alarmed, merely curious. 'Sounds like a dog.'

He had put down the wine and crossed the room to the compact-disc player, flicked one or two switches so the music recommenced, slightly louder, putting his napkin to his mouth. 'Pardon?'

'I said it sounded like a dog. In there.' He laughed easily. 'No, no, no. Not a dog. Kittens, actually, for the children. We keep them in the . . .' he flourished with his hand, still holding the napkin. 'In the playroom,' Monica finished for him. She had the habit of finishing sentences for others, a trick Colin loathed. Now he looked at her curiously. He had not known the Allendales had anything designated as a playroom: it was somehow out of character. 'Kittens!' The American wife clapped her hands. The sound was friendly but sudden and as she stopped, the same scratching sound was still slightly audible. 'Oh, I love them, the darlings, can we see? Oh, come on, David, give us a peek.'

'No, not now. They run up the walls, you see . . .' He began on longer explanations, but the words were not finished. With an indelicate choking sound, Katherine had half risen, pushed herself back from the table, and was suddenly, monstrously sick. She was sitting at one end of the table, opposite David, and the hands, gripping each corner within reach, clutched at

276

the edges, her fingers so white the rings glowed against the cloth, while highly coloured, undigested, viscous food splashed to the floor, the remnants dribbling from her mouth. All of them watched her head thrown forward, the bright-blue eyes staring at the playroom door beyond. Then all eyes turned to the mess on the floor, a solid fluid of brilliant colours. Until David moved, nimble as a fighter round a ring, lifted her bodily out of her chair and lightly flicked his fingers across her cheek. Lacking the brutality of a slap, the effect was the same and she closed her drooping mouth abruptly, beginning to cough. Tears had sprung to her eyes. 'Shh, darling, shh. It's all right.' She leant into him, taking the support of his arms, but rigid. Like a ballerina, Jenny thought later, held tense by a partner in a *pas de deux*. David flashed his disarming smile on the assembly, who faced the tableau of himself and his wife with varying expressions of horror. 'Excuse us,' he said. 'I'll explain in a minute. Please, carry on.' Both left the room. Susan Pearson Thorpe heard them going upstairs, David's soothing tones floating back.

'Katherine never did like cats,' she observed. Monica sniffed nervously, slightly comforted by the remark which none could regard as anything but poor taste. It made her want to giggle. She and Jenny quickly found cloths and scooped the mess off the floor, both used to dealing with children, pragmatic while the men looked on, dumbly. All of them had lost appetite, but there was nothing else to do but finish the food. At least the food on the plates. No one would have wanted to ask for more.

They were all waiting for the return of the host, all privately planning when they should leave.

'Listen,' said Jenny, 'I think I should go and help, really.'

'Perhaps not,' said Monica. 'I'm sure David knows what to do. It seems to have happened before.' Colin nodded agreement. Jenny put down her napkin. 'Well, in that case he can tell me to mind my own business.' She rose. Monica rose too. 'I'll come as well.' 'I won't,' said Susan, 'I would be *de trop*.' They went upstairs, neither sure of where to go, looking inside two rooms before they found the third, signalled by David leaving, pulling the door to behind him. 'She's all right,' he said reassuringly. Jenny pushed past him, suddenly determined. 'Well could I just say goodnight then? Perhaps a woman could help, you know.' He hesitated, nodded to let them go in, but hovered at the door. Katherine lay on one side of the double bed, covered with a quilt, one knuckle in her mouth and her eyes open. 'What is it, Kath, what is it? Better now?' Jenny murmured as she would to the youngest of her children suffering from a scratch. Katherine was trying to speak, touched Jenny's hand with the fingers taken from her own mouth, damp with saliva, an unpleasant touch, but the words were incoherent.

'Please,' said David from the door, 'please don't. You'll only get her excited.' Monica felt pity rise, along with a tinge of revulsion. 'I've got some valium,' she said. 'Would that help?' David looked at them both as if towards saviours. 'Oh yes,' he said, 'it would. She usually has some, but forgot to get more. She's pregnant, you see: it does this . . .'

'No valium, then,' said Jenny firmly. 'Oh no, the doc says it's fine . . . It was for me,' said Monica, fumbling in the handbag which accompanied her everywhere. The news of pregnancy had a strange effect on her, like a slap or a sharp punch. 'Half of that, then,' Jenny insisted. 'She's only small.' The eyes on the bed followed their movements, drank water, looking towards Monica in something akin to fear, towards Jenny in a plea she refused to register. The mouth stopped mumbling and swallowed without resisting. After five minutes, they went downstairs, leaving the door open. In the kitchen the men had begun to smoke. They presumed they were not going to reach the spiritual part to the meal.

David resumed the role of host, pressed them to eat. She would want this, he said: she was so looking forward, please do. I'm afraid this sometimes happens with Katherine, her nerves. And she is in a certain condition, worries her so, the other two were not easy. Better in the morning. The men nodded wisely, full of sympathy, moved to kindness but feeling their own impotence and their own immunity. Susan Pearson Thorpe was silent, her glass half full but treated with indifference instead of the customary anxiety, while her look expressed extreme puzzlement as if she were working out a sum in her head. They accepted coffee, all of them, black please, without sugar, and were glad to go home. Monica Neill and Colin were breathing evenly as they got into their car, neither able to confess to the other how they had been worried for anything Katherine *in extremis* might have said. How good, they agreed, is David, what a shame for his birthday, pity. The Pearson Thorpes walked home. Jenny drove, and the Americans got lost *en route*, following them so far. All couples, still sober and in need of comfort, made love in their different, broadly similar fashions. They tried to forget the scratching and the shining, vomit-filled face in an exercise which lasted from five to thirty minutes, depending on who they were.

Equally occupied, but with a far greater degree of concentration, Mary Fox arched and crouched over the recumbent form of brown Claud, seeking the solace of sex for longer than all the rest of her sister's guests put together. They had wasted, after all, one whole hour before she had been convinced of his explanations, Katherine's total lack of involvement, which she already believed, only established after a very lengthy row. Ending inevitably in bed, him with licence to play until 11.30 in the evening. Claud did not tell the whole truth: Claud never did any more often than she expected and only then on subjects of no personal interest, but the half-truth he told was both recognizable as such and sufficient for her purpose. Wife ill, children ill, holiday postponed: don't be such a fool, if I'd been with anyone, if would not be anyone so near to you. You know me better than that. While she hardly did, she felt convinced and above everything else in her life, Claud, in all his anonymity, gave her hope. She forgot all her boredom, the sense of desperation which had dogged his absence, made her own version of love like an Amazon. You are thinner, darling, said in admiration: he liked his women skinny, such words easy on her ear, they made love again. The voracity of it all made him slightly relieved to go home and Mary, for once in weeks, relieved to be alone. She smoked a rare cigarette, drank the last of the wine Claud had brought as a peace offering and found herself satisfied, warm and only a trifle broody. Thinking could wait until the morning, tomorrow was not going to feature much by way of work. This was after all the way she liked it best. After they went home, provided she knew they would return. Her sister, misjudged Katherine, came swimming into focus as Mary brushed her teeth, swam out again as she applied her avocado nightcream. All that could also wait until tomorrow.

Katherine staggered out to the bathroom mirror. The huge eyes which stared back at her were the eyes of a stranger, a very old woman. Not the child she had seen reflected in the morning: there would never be a child reflected in this face. All an illusion, this sense of safety. She was an old woman, not allowed to go back in time. Downstairs was the child and the man who was murdering them both.

'Well, why should she behave like that, why?' Jenny had attempted to debate the Allendale behaviour patterns with her husband on the way home and then again in bed. The first attempt had been futile: the second met with better response since he was mellow but tired enough to fall into sleep after the second paragraph. Compassion, such as it was, remained Jenny's contribution to family life along with concern and neighbourly kindness: he wanted no part of either and besides, there was work tomorrow. Stupid idea to have a dinner party on a Tuesday: you could tell how many people never really worked or they would know that Wednesday followed. Jenny was accustomed to such shutting off and could not argue with a man who was to all intents and purposes, bar the breathing, dead. She courted the same state in self-defence, thinking ahead to the day after and the few after that. But almost as soon as sleep intervened, the little one, Emily, came to wake her. Their bedroom door was shut and in reaching for the handle, Emily bumped and scraped on the bottom panel with the doll she carried. Jenny hardly registered the sound until the child stood by the bed, feigning distress but really wanting to play, pursuing no nightmare but lack of company. Theirs was a big bed: she could never see why she should not share. Jenny knew she should follow the books, get up herself and make the child resettle to ensure herself an easier long-term life, but she let Emily clamber beneath the duvet instead, sure

that the other half, whose objections were always more strenuous, was in no position to notice until morning. Dolly was
abandoned on the floor. As child fell back into sleep, Jenny
remembered the scraping at the door, the dyspeptic duck and
the kittens which had heralded the dinner party fiasco. The
memory, along with indigestion, was profoundly disturbing.
She hugged Emily close for comfort and vowed to do something tomorrow.

David cleared the kitchen systematically to the sound of the
1812 overture, suitably triumphant for the time of night. First
he assembled all the glasses and washed these in soapy liquid,
rinsed them in clear, hot water and stood them on towels.
Neither glasses nor silverware could be entrusted to the dishwasher and Katherine would polish tomorrow. All other crock-
ery was rinsed and stacked in the machine. He left behind him
on the table a tray with all the bishop's pattern cutlery. Although slightly angry at the early demise of his evening, the
irritation was gone and he regarded it as more of a success than
failure, whistled idly as he worked, not in tune with the music
which moved from one crescendo to another. Mechanical tasks,
conducted with precision, pleased him: he could subdue to
these the whole of his concentration, filling the sink with more
hot, soapy water for the remaining silver. Wash, rinse, stand
upright like the glasses, no short-cuts to the final shine. What
mollified him most about the evening was the way the table
had glowed, the gasps of admiration almost orgasmic: David
had liked that, a seal of approval for all those lovely things,
arranged with care. He had never wanted anything which
other people did not envy: there was no point. Nothing ugly
after Daddy, nothing fat, nothing unsafe. Daddy tidying up
like this after a bout of rage was something which had long
since passed from mind. Turning to the table to fetch the last
cutlery, he was pleased to notice out of the corner of one eye
that the cloth had not been stained, only rumpled. More so
than before.

By Katherine's hand, bunching a corner of heavy cloth into
her left fist. She was paler than the colour of the material: her
other hand held a carving knife and she had been moving on

her bare feet towards his back, the right hand raised, her face serene with determination, the thin body still dressed in crumpled skirt and blouse, the gold collar twisted round her neck. Two feet, three feet, progress steady, dragging the cloth after herself. 'Now, now, darling, don't be silly.' Cutlery clattered to the floor, released from the cloth which she seemed quite unable to relinquish. 'Now, now,' he repeated carefully, but she still came on with an even pace. The knife was sticky with the grease from the duck: the dirt offended him. David retreated almost into the sink, risked turning his back for one whole second. He lifted the half-full washing bowl, flung the contents in her direction.

The *1812* crashed to a finale.

21

Sophie was learning cunning from her cat, a creature with many other advantages. Kitten kept at bay all those vast wastes of insomnia which had led to such exhaustion, and because he, she, or it appeared to grow by the minute, mimicking the antics of a lion at play with a lot of delightful running and snarling, Sophie had convinced herself that the presence of the cat would deter any burglar who was not a giant. 'You just growl at him, dear,' she said in admiration. 'You know, the way you do when I pretend to take away your food. Oh, look at that, kitty, you were spitting. Ever so fearsome. Was your mother a tiger, then, must have been. Funny colour, though.' Sophie giggled, watching the kitten stalking a ball of wool. 'No sense of smell,' Sophie scolded. 'You can't tell pink from white.'

Granny was aware that she talked to herself and the cat more than to anyone alive, pushed the thought out of her mind. There was no one else more thoroughly disposed to listen when she was frightened much of the time, and the cat seemed so fearless, as well as providing every excuse to delay her departures from the house and hasten her own return. This morning she had contemplated taking kitty to the hair-dresser; she could not see why on earth they should mind, but some dull instinct told her that they would. So she stayed at home, becoming vague on the subject of the hour, even vaguer than she was on what day of the week. Her memory slipped out of gear with such ease, as it had done for more than a year. Nobody seemed to notice or mind while she dwelt for much of the time in a tunnel of apprehension she could not confess, but beginning with the brainstorm which had made her pick up the cat, the selectivity of her recollection no longer dismayed her.

She concentrated on doing as she pleased, shedding onerous tasks whenever she wished. David's face, David's figure, never quite became blurred, but the thought of him and his wife and his children was a profound pain in her chest which was only cured by picking up the cat and cradling it. She did so now. 'Should have gone,' she said to the cat, 'should have gone, you know, for his birthday. Only he wouldn't have you indoors, you should see what he does to cats.' She pointed to the wall with her spare hand and held the fingers as if they were a gun. 'Bang, bang. And anyway, he didn't ask, so he doesn't get a present. Lovely socks, silly boy.' The luminous pink socks were sitting on the sofa beside her, along with a number of other items, only the socks garishly wrapped with the sellotape very prominent, making the whole parcel gleam stickily. 'But Jeanetta would like you, she would so. We'll go tomorrow.'

When the phone rang, she was reluctant to move. The afternoon sun was so pretty through the window and the kitten had gone to sleep on her lap. With a slight start, she realized she was not wearing a skirt, only an underslip, which was why the kitten felt particularly warm and tactile and the juvenile claws so sharp. The thought of being caught thus, in a state of *déshabillé*, made her move. Remembering the phone was only the phone, not attached to a television, slowed her down again and she did not answer with the alacrity which had once been her hallmark.

'Sophie? Is that you?' Sophie turned and grimaced at the cat, which sat at her feet, discomfited and looking for entertainment.

'Course it's me. Who else would it be?' Sophie smoothed the pieces of fur from the underskirt, noticing without caring that the fabric was grubby. The sight of her own hair in the hallway mirror over the phone was not encouraging either, so she simply moved away. There was a little difficulty remembering the voice on the other end of the line which was overfamiliar and one she did not like.

'How are you, dear?'

284

'I'm not dear. I'm cheap. And I'm fine. Thank you.' Mary Fox, never the most sensitive, began to appreciate the call was not entirely welcome. 'Oh, good,' she said, lost for words. 'Listen, won't keep you, you must be busy . . .' Sophie nearly spat down the phone. Of course I'm busy.

'. . . Did you go and see David and Katherine? Like you said?' The voice always assumed this sort of wooing she had never realized she could not abide. Not at all like Katherine, who listened rather than spoke, although you wished all the time she would.

'No. I spec they had a party, they usually do. I didn't go round. They'd be clearing up. Changing the towels. I know I said I would go, but then I thought I wouldn't. Mustn't impose,' she added meaningfully. My word, the wits were sharp today, she'd cut herself. There were no cares left in the world: only annoyances. 'Just checking,' said the voice. 'Any other news?' Sophie hesitated, not yet immune from the desire to speak. 'We . . . ell, I didn't get my hair done. They wouldn't let me bring the cat.' Mary paused at the other end of the phone, breathed out slowly. Another one for the social services. 'All right,' she cooed, 'see you soon.'

Sophie went into her bedroom and put on a skirt, the brightest she could find, covered in mossy roses and flimsy for the time of year. Then she turned on the radio and settled down.

Right, right, action stations. Mary was not used to guilt, found the sensation acutely uncomfortable. It was all after waking with that unaccustomed stiffness of limbs which created the sensation she had spent half her life avoiding: introspection rampant as she rolled out of bed very carefully and very late, one foot moving after the other in slow motion to the bathroom. No conscience about the lovely sex which had created such complaints among the joints, the removal of the sticky diaphragm from between her thighs a positive pleasure, but guilt on the subject of sisterhood, suspended from the night before to return like a hangover and play havoc with breakfast. Mary phoned Child Action Volunteers. There was no real anxiety about Katherine's children: there never had been on her part.

285

Yes, they had had the report since Tuesday afternoon and could say now there was nothing wrong, absolutely nothing: Mr Mills had been quite emphatic. Would she like to enlarge, for the record, why she had thought there was? No she would not. Mary felt guilty about asking for that shabby man. Not a serious guilt on that score. Any bossy intervention minimized guilt, but somehow it had returned in dragon shape the next morning. So in the afternoon, having failed to digest the beast, she phoned first Sophie and then David. She was mildly alarmed by the first call, infinitely more so by the second.

'Hallo, David. Mary here. Happy birthday for yesterday.' She could not resist a small hint about being excluded from any celebration. Duty had dictated she send him a card, which he did not mention.

'Thank you,' he said.

'Katherine there?'

'No, as it happens. Gone to the gym.'

'Should she?' Mary bit her tongue, not wishing him to guess any secondhand knowledge she might have about Katherine's alleged condition since she sensed David would not approve this clandestine contact with his mother. 'Why not?' said David. 'She finds it helps with the tiredness. I made her go. Such a lovely day.'

Made her go. This caused Mary to bristle: so did the fact he did not say, How are you, not seen you in ages, so bloody impersonal as befits a mere spinster sister. They would see: her blood was up. 'Kids OK?' she persisted.

'Fine, fine. Jeanetta's staying with her granny.'

The last information was dispensed without any great enthusiasm, a piece of news often repeated, so much so that Mary almost took the statement at conversational face value, until her heart missed a beat and her hand clutched the receiver in mute recognition of a downright lie. Instinct forbade her to contradict. 'Oh. What time is Kath due back?'

'Don't know really. Five-ish. I'm spring-cleaning just now.'

'I'll be round then.' To leave no possible chance for an excuse she replaced the phone as soon as she spoke, stood there, shaking with anger, then looked at her watch. Three-ish. Go now.

*

Mary always knew the way to everything: Katherine did not, but the route she followed that afternoon was followed blindly. She had been told to go out so she was going out. There was no hope for anything unless she did exactly as she was told and she had no will to do anything else. Down road, cross road at zebra crossing one hundred yards on left, take train at one of two possible tube stops, or not if she fancied waiting for the bus, which she did not since movement was a must and standing still for all that uncertain time absolutely impossible, so she walked to Edgware. Got on one train then another, led by the same familiarity, clutching the bag which contained all the things for the gym, ready packed as ever. Went down the steps to the place, changed for mid-afternoon class half an hour early, smiling the same smile at mostly the same people. But all that precious orientation went when she started to move: the music's pulsation seemed not to reach the ears or if it did, to enter each orifice out of sequence in order to jumble in the middle, her mind fixed on sounds more rhythmic than heavy beat. In the studio mirror, she noticed her hair was lank, dulled by washing-up water which would not quite dry, patted and soothed her own locks with one uncertain hand while the others shook their legs. Then she participated as best she could. Stretch, flop, obey orders, at first roughly following the routine but gradually slipping further and further away, lagging behind or speeding in front. The class went on, each of them staring fixedly in the mirror to avoid looking at her, preternaturally pale, thin girl in the front corner, lacking any sense of coordination whatever. A newcomer smiled secretly to her friend, eyes raised to ceiling with a Look at that, we aren't so bad after all, who does she think she is? The friend shhhed her. Classes were slightly sacred, interruptions not popular, and if anyone could not take the pace they usually left and besides the occasional weirdo was not unknown. Classes included manic anorexics, hyperactive fatties and others more obviously in a world of their own.

Only when Katherine began to dance all by herself with a particular if clumsy grace, skittering across the floor with her arms in the air and her ballerina legs all over the place, did serious alarm set in. She sidestepped the barre, flung one ankle across with agile ease and lowered her chest to her knee with such abandon they could hear the sinews creak, removed the offending leg, replaced the other, removed that and danced on into high kicks, the rest jogging on the spot in time to the music, goggling with embarrassment. Then she twisted and fell heavily, stayed where she was. The beat was drowned in the sharp intake of breath, the sudden paralysis which was not broken until the teacher turned off the music and called for help.

They put a dressing gown round her shoulders and led her away. Babies, she kept on saying, I must have more babies. 'But you already have two, Katherine, don't bother about it for now,' said one of the mothers who knew the vague background details from changing-room chat where all mothers at least remembered the names and ages of each other's children as well as remembering to compliment each other on any loss of weight. 'Babies,' repeated Katherine; 'I've only got one.' 'Two,' the mother corrected. 'You always told me you had two. 'One,' Katherine repeated vehemently. 'Only one. Just one. I want to go back to the class.' Spoken while the remnants of the class stood around her in a group of leotarded dummies, gaping at the code of words which only the mother could begin to understand. When Katherine was finally beyond her burbling speech, they decided the blanket was not enough and called for a doctor. Someone looked in her purse, surprised to find no money bar one fifty-pence piece, no trace of an address and nothing to define this woman at all.

David was indeed spring-cleaning. Mary could see that at once since she recognized all the symptoms and they were difficult to miss. He had led her into the kitchen only when her insistence on the doorstep grew louder and louder, having tried to shut the door on her with politeness: with equal insistence she had repositioned one foot and remained as she was, repeating how she would come in and wait. All right, he grudged, not long though, I'm busy. Shut the door behind you. Intent on following the sound of a radio speaking a play, Mary merely pushed the front door with one foot, the leg behind the foot still stiff. Katherine would be home soon, no matter if the door did not actually slam and some half-formed feeling in her preferred it not to be tightly shut.

She noticed on first sight how the contents of the cupboards were out on the floor and surfaces were covered with detritus from other regions of the house. Three grey plastic sacks were stacked by the sink: protruding from one were the heads of lilies, browned to imperfection but far from dead. 'Why are you chucking these?' Mary asked. 'Plenty of life in them yet.'

'Past their best,' David said cheerfully, the smile on his face masking visible irritation. 'Look, I'm in the middle of this . . . sorry about the mess. Do you want to come back later, when my wife, Katherine, I mean . . .'

'I'll wait,' said Mary. 'I'll help if you like. I'm good at this.'

'No,' he said violently.

'Well you can make me a cup of tea then and I'll watch.' She was mildly surprised when he complied. Not even mere compliance but a fury of fuss with a china teapot, tea left to infuse while lovely Italian china mugs were banged out of a cupboard which he had to unlock. 'Why lock it?' she asked, but he smiled the vacant smile of a polite and busy man. 'Oh, children, you know.' She imagined she could detect a slightly demonic gleam in his eye and for the moment she was frightened, but only for a moment. Fortified by tea and harmless chat on the subject of spring-cleaning, the brink of autumn, the weather, the removal of beetles from carpets and so forth, all of which he debated with animation. 'Leaves drift indoors, and we must beware of harvest mice too,' she finished ironically, determined to keep the upper hand and also to tease him. 'Anyway, I thought Katherine would have done all this.' 'Sometimes,' he replied vaguely. She took the plunge. There were several things she did not wish to say but felt obliged to say, all of them in private before Katherine came home.

'David. Where's Jeanetta?'

'Jeanetta?' His head turned on his neck towards hers as if he had difficulty placing the name. 'Oh, Jeanetta. Staying with her grandmother. For the moment.'

'Sophie?'

'Yes of course.'

'Since when?' He looked at the table and passed his hands over the steam rising from his mug, at the same time pulling a mat beneath it to protect the table surface. 'Only yesterday. We had a birthday party, you see.' Mary felt her shoulders lift in relief; only since yesterday and Sophie this morning had forgotten to say, naughty Sophie. The relief was short-lived: Sophie would have said, even Sophie on the brink of senility would have burst forth with such tidings. Mary held her tongue and sipped her tea.

'Not your favourite child, is she?' she asked. David's eyes travelled to the open French windows. Outside on a small patio, Jeremy played with bricks, a study in childish concentration so acute he had neither noticed nor greeted his aunt.

'Jeanetta?' said David. He seemed unable to speak other than one-word questions, betraying an uncertainty, a man needing a prompt in the corner of his stage. 'Jeanetta isn't mine, you know. Katherine's concern, that child.' Ah, so that was it, an excuse for a dislike which might have nothing to do with what anyone would call real reasons, such as ugliness, lack of control, all features which Mary's casual and just occasionally acute perception had only now borne downwind, less the result of direct observation than the sum total of Katherine's offhand remarks. 'Don't be such an absolute bloody fool,' Mary shouted. 'Of course she's yours, you crapulous idiot.' Then she was quieter. People, even male people, were supposed to be amenable to reason and he was, after all, short on information. She was ready to inform but he went on, 'She had this blond man, this lover when she met me. She saw him once or twice, you know, after she met me; she told me, she tells me everything. He was there, after we met, I know he was. After she was born, I kept waiting for Jeanetta to go dark, like Jeremy did, so soon, like me, but of course, you know who stayed pale and fat, like an albino. Of course she wasn't mine. Too ugly. Like a little pig. Blond pig.'

Mary drew breath slowly and spoke with emphasis, as if speaking to an idiot. 'Katherine had several lovers, which you must know very well.' She was extremely precise to keep her temper and control the heat of her face. '. . . Including the last, one with the impossible name of Claud, a man inherited by me. In all senses. Claud is a man with a ten-year old vasectomy if you must know, and you clearly must. He couldn't have produced a child if he'd tried. And he still tries. Are you listening?'

'Well, well, well.' He was smiling and this time, she was more than slightly afraid but again the feeling passed. He shrugged and spoke with deliberation. 'What a slut you are, Mary, must be in the family. Fancy screwing a man who can't make babies, I shall never understand women. Well, well. Too late now. Nothing to do with us, really, nothing at all. You-know-who was simply disgusting. She had to go. She was . . . Oh I don't know.'

Was, was, was. The words registered like hammers, each striking a blow of different magnitude.

'She, you-know-who, Jeanetta, is not disgusting. You pig.' Mary did not know she was screaming. 'And anyway, where is she? Not with your mother.' He did not respond to the scream. 'Look,' he said with exaggerated patience, 'look, I'm having this spring-clean and I've got to finish, you've got to go. Must clear the mess, can't stand it, Katherine can't stand it, such a heap . . .'

She leapt from the table and slapped him very hard. The combined force of guilt and rising hysteria were behind the slap, so sharp the imprint of her fingers remained on his face like a birthmark. Towering above him she stared down and watched a vague and dreamy look come into his eyes as he put one hand to his flushed cheek. 'Don't,' he said pleadingly, 'don't, please.'

'Where is your fucking daughter?' Mary said, her voice descending to a low hiss, her sharp face thrust into his. His glance drifted beyond her, over the grey sacks by the sink and swivelling round to the French windows and the playroom door. 'Tell her, Jeremy boy,' he said. 'She wants to know.' The boy, bored at last, staggered through from the garden with a broad smile on his face. He brought for his aunty three of the bricks and a key. On a key-ring, the jangling sound a source of better delight than any rattle. He did not want to let go.

'Show me,' said Mary.

22

I thought I was good at sums. Another joke. As it happens I
have been quite incapable of the most simple factual additions.
So I think now. Tuesday night, prelude to a slow and unevent-
ful Wednesday morning, was one of the first when I have
retired to bed with only a modicum of alcohol aboard and I
was not entirely sure I liked the result. Not with dear Sebastian,
I mean: that was nice and waking up to find him, my feelings
as uncertain as they are, is at least a qualified delight. Sometimes it is better not to think and taking refuge in the depressed
jumble which weighs on post-alcoholic dawns might be preferable to the sharper focus of sobriety. At least when suffering
from an overdose one never thought of anyone else; there was
no room. But I woke today with other worries, a sort of
indigestion from everything I had seen.

We should not have gone to the damned dinner party,
would not have gone except for the guilt created by an invitation sent so long in advance and the knowledge of a small
gathering where we would be missed: I have not quite lost my
manners yet and some of them are returning. Then there was
Mark, of course, insisting he would be all right because he
wanted a break from his parents for the privilege of watching
TV later than they would allow, with the Harrisons. And
Sebastian saying we ought, you know. Me fishing out a dress,
such a novelty going anywhere with a husband and remembering how often I had refused in the past, grateful for the chance
to redress and determined not to overdo the drink. I had not
told Sebastian all about Katherine and our distrust: not about
the necklace, for instance. There was a portcullis over my

tongue which stayed down all evening and after we came home. So that two things haunted me well into today's sober dawn. Not her being sick like that, revolting though it was: I don't know why, horrific without being too surprising, but the necklace she wore, as solid a piece of gold as ever I saw, so why the hell did she need mine? Oh I know a thief is not selective on the basis of need, but why, when she could never wear the damn thing with one already. Unless of course, she took mine to sell. A gold collar like a prize slave-girl: poor Katherine: I found it in me to pity her even before she vomited all that lovely food. But more insistent than that, I was haunted by the scraping at the door, the funny sound which seemed to trigger the explosion, scraping and scratching by kittens. In that house, temple of cleanliness and germ free, with baby Jeremy allergic and her always trying to poison our cats? Impossible to believe whatever he said: they would never spend good money on kittens and I've never known any cat make a noise like that. I said as much to Sebastian and he said they probably kept monkeys. Without elaborating, he seems to have changed his favourable opinion of David Allendale. Never mind, said my spouse: none of our business. I wondered: remembered all those clothes outside and felt another chill in my bones. I don't often confide in Mrs Harrison, but I told her about the party because she asked and I couldn't just say everything was fine. Hearing about the hysteria, she simply stared and shuffled, then burst forth. 'We was so worried, Mrs P, we got the NSPCC round to them . . .'

'You what?'

'We was worried about Jeanetta,' she said defensively. 'I did tell you.' 'Yes,' I said shamefacedly, 'you did. But the NSPCC . . . Really! Did they go?' Her face was full of relief but she did not want to elaborate: the whole episode was obviously hideously embarrassing as far as she was concerned. 'So I gather,' she mumbled. 'I spoke to Mrs Al'dale's sister: a man went about it. Nothing wrong. Anyway, Jeanetta's with her granny, so it was all a false alarm.' I let it go at that, all of it festering in the same chill.

Oh well, Samantha's turn for treats today, to mollify the jealousy (this child is so like her mother), which is now

293

extreme. She went out with her father alone for a heavy-duty tea, leaving Mark and I alone with the Junior Scrabble, him with the leg irritating like a scratch. Not exactly a treat for him, but I'm ashamed to say, one for me since so novel is this spending time with them, I'm still enthralled by it and I hope the feeling passes after a while or I might never go back to work. So clever this boy at games, he could almost let me win, but as if the distractions in my mind were infectious, he could not concentrate either. The Allendales were still percolating on the brain and I could not persuade them to take a graceful exit. When the dog scraped at the door to join us in the study, I jumped. Thought of trivial, unconnected things. Mark spelled out T H I E F with triumph. Memory does strange things, but I had forgotten his sleepy confessions.

'Mark, you remember telling me about the strange man, and Sammy saying he'd come back when you were away with Daddy?' He nodded. 'I shouldn't . . .' he began. 'Course you should, darling. Don't worry, I know all about it, but if he came last week, when was it he came the first time?' He saw no contradictions in these statements of my knowledge, frowned in an effort to remember.

'Oh, ages and ages. I know, yes I know. Jus' before Jeanetta and Jemmy stopped coming and stayed at home, then. I think. He came in when Mr Harry and me was watching the cricket and Mr Harry was telling me about cricket. Did you know, Mummy, a cricket ball can break your head?' 'The vagrant man, darling,' I reminded, picking up my Scrabble pieces. 'Oh yes. We chased him out, Mr Harry and me. He got in upstairs, then Mr Harry heard him moving about so we chased him out. I wasn't scared 'cos I'd seen him before anyway. With you, out of the window, and another time.' His voice went down to whispering level. 'Mr Harry thought he took something. He was worried, but the man hadn't done nothing. Sammy says when he came back, he wanted to get in.'

I am beyond anger these days, or that would have been uppermost in my mind, might have been, had I been more interested in control of my house than I was currently in the Allendales'. I had always known, after all, that the honesty of Mrs Harrison is selective. A simple connection of memory hastened by the ever present picture of Katherine with gold collar. An intruder in our house, not confessed to me, on or about the day that bloody necklace went adrift. Oh, poor Katherine: I could have misjudged so much more than I thought.

'Daddy'll be home soon,' I said smoothly. (Nice, actually, to be able to say that.) 'Then I'll go next door and see if Jeanetta's back. She might come in and play with you.' And I make some kind of peace with her mother, I did not add. Mark's face lit up. 'You could go now,' he suggested helpfully. In the eyes of an almost eight-year-old, adult company cannot compete with another child, even a far younger child. I laughed at him. 'All right. Mr Harrison will come up. Don't get into mischief.' 'I can't move,' he sighed.

Neither could I, or at least not with any speed. I have ever been reluctant to enter the perfect portals of next door, because they put me to shame and my reaction to shame has always been resentment. In daylight or darkness, I do not like that house despite admiration, which is not the same thing. Which is why I paused to put lipstick on mouth and comb hair before leaving: sometimes these boosters have an effect, not always and not really today. So sunny and warm this street, an Indian summer now, merged with the last of the proper season, the trees shedding first and giving the only hint of future darkness. Mark says he can never believe it will get dark again, why should it, and I tend to agree. I still did not want to go and knock next door, even when I had made up my mind and got out into the road, I walked slowly like a sightseer. I went up the steps to their door; rehearsing a few words about thanking them for dinner and found as I raised a hand to the bell, that the door was just open. Oh good, that would break any ice: I could joke about our vagrants (there was a new one hanging round in the street) and warn them to be more careful. Hate it when the door is on the latch like that: one never knows what to do. You can't push it open and go in unless you know the family well and otherwise you simply wait like a lemon or shout. I was trying to decide but I did not have the chance.

Screams, screams, more screams, emanating from the womb of that building, cutting round the door from the dark hole of the hallway and into my ears like knives. Katherine's screams, I thought: I had been imagining screams in my head for almost twenty-four hours, hated the reverberation which would not leave me alone, paralysed me all over again. You cannot analyse screams, say on first hearing if they are anger, terror, fear, but they must always be fear, there is little else which matters in a scream. My God, these were endless and I was a coward. Mind your own business: you owe nothing: simply her pregnant nerves, their affair not yours. And then, it could be murder, might not be safe to go in there, you fool, you have children of your own and you want to live. Standing on the doorstep, looking round for help and seeing none: children in there too. You would kill a person who left one of yours in a house with screams like that. And you owe Katherine: she might be hurt: she's having a baby, she's fallen: go in, go in, you ghastly, drunken coward. Into the kitchen, following the path of the sound, so easy, no mistaking, first room off the hall, you were there not long ago. More screams in disharmony with the rest: a child, that boy Jeremy screaming with his mother. I ran the last few steps.

At first I thought it must have been murder, a fight of massive proportions, the pristine kitchen I had sat in and admired through their window a heap of junk, bags, bits everywhere, everything in comparative chaos, not the place of entertainment I had known. After his impression of violence, the next thing I registered was the howling face of the boy, standing by the French window unattended, his face red with shrieking, holding a blue brick in one hand, frightened. I looked for Katherine, the source of the barking screams so different from those of the boy, saw what I took to be her until I realized in the same split second it was not, struggling with David in the door of the playroom. Sunlight streamed through, blurring his features, making her, this woman, a silhouette merged with his: they were not so much struggling as holding on to each other, he preventing either of them moving, pushing her back away from the opening. Her face was turned to the sun: the struggle seemed absurd but still she screamed. They did not notice me and he pushed her clear of the door, saying something, his voice guttural with panic. The next thought of mine was relief: no one hurt yet, no blood, me interfering; nothing but noise: an argument and a terrified child, but then on a peculiar instinct less brave than curious, I slipped between the distracted adults and into the sunny alcove where the children played: their room, blinded by sunlight, seeking out each corner.

Such colours in there, such hideous, hideous mess. Clothes and dismembered toys, little teddy bear legs, broken cars and torn posters, but mostly clothes, shiny fabric, a large expanse of vivid purple cloth. Beyond that, a cloud of pale-blonde hair, obscenely coloured against the material, a half of a face visible and one small hand with huge knuckles. From the other end of the purple cloth there stuck a thin calf with a foot simply and pathetically adorned with one white sock. She did not move.

It was then they noticed me, the adults, or it may have been then he slapped her to stop the screaming, not a flick of the fingers this time, a slap. I knew by then she was not Katherine but I did not care, whoever she was did not matter. She appeared to subside in the brief glance I gave her, looking to David for some sort of explanation. But he shouted, was all: my eyes, still adjusting to the contrast of light and dark, only noticed a contortion of his face into a shout of furious warning, one fist clenched towards me, the other holding her. Only the threat went home, the danger. I turned back, instinct again, stopped, bent down, tucked the purple round the child on the floor, scooped her up and ran. Not running as I scarcely know how to run: running like Sammy did when she learned to walk, a drunken stagger, ungainly, effective, determined. Crashing through the front door into the street, up to our door, pressing the bell with my chin, the limbs of the thing I was carrying flapping round my waist, arms and legs free, the one white sock left on the pavement. A brittle, septic-smelling, bundle, damp against my blouse. Into our house past whoever opened the door, shouting myself, get this, get that, phone, phone, I can't remember, but I know it was coherent. Breathless, upstairs, shouting some more. He was behind me in the street, I know he was, that man: he will try to get in. My voice screaming. Get Mark out of the way, and for Christ's sake, phone.

We sit with her in the study. I shall be sitting here for ever

297

in my mind. I thought my own trembling might communicate some movement, but not yet. Downstairs there is someone hammering on the door, voices raised, but too soon for all the help. I know who you are, my sweet: I knew as soon as I saw your hair and I sit here weeping for all my blindness while those around me organize. There is nothing more important than a little life, my own child or anyone else's, even if it were a life I ignored; why didn't I know, why didn't I see. What wickedness, what terrible stupidity. Bring the doctor, yes, yes. If I hold on to this child, I shall warm her. Don't do this to me, God, you bastard, can't you see I was learning already? There was never a more hapless, futile weeping, such harsh initiation into priorities. I must stop crying and hold still: tears fall chilly on this shiny cloth and God she needs the warmth. The face of her is familiar, but very, very old. I think in some weird flash of the futility of face-cream. I must hold her tightly, so that she feels the radiant heat of me. Our silly adult lives do not matter, may she please have the choices we have got. Why didn't I see? He is shouting at the door, Give her back, she's mine, she's mine. I shall never give her back.

Sebastian will be here soon. They will all be here soon.

She is very cold.

23

Mary got up from her chair and closed the casement window of her bedroom with noisy efficiency. What had once been a bare boudoir was now cluttered, overfurnished with an armchair, clothes strewn carelessly but with some sense of order. Not a tip, to use Mary's own phrase, but not tidy either. Katherine was curled in the armchair, wearing a track suit of great antiquity, Mary's from more energetic days. The shiny magazine she was reading fell to the floor as she raised one hand to tuck hair behind her ear. The smile she gave Mary was dutiful, automatic, not quite reaching the eyes, but an attempt nevertheless. Mary was grateful for anything, felt the rising in her of a protection so fierce she wanted to place barriers on the door. Any expression, any concession to life, was preferable to the catatonic state of her sister when first she had walked upstairs. Katherine squinted towards the sunlight from the window, rattled by a gust of autumn wind outside. Her face became anxious and Mary felt alarm.

'What's the matter, Kath?'

'Those curtains need mending. The hems have all frayed. Can't have been very good cotton.'

'Or very good sewing,' said Mary tartly. 'You made them, remember?'

'Did I? Oh yes. Liberty cotton. Remnants in the sale. You didn't like them. You wanted blinds.'

'I love them,' said Mary, stepping up on to a stool by the window and unhooking the material from the rail overhead, 'so you'd better mend them, OK?'

'All right.'

Now there was a triumph: little sister presented with a sewing box, looking into the contents as if they were not entirely unfamiliar. Slowly, with all the deliberate movements of a drunk, finding a needle and the wrong-coloured cotton reel, threading the eye with enormous concentration. Picking up the first curtain, turning up the hem again and making great, clumsy tacking stitches. Really, Mary thought, it does not matter how they look.

'I made a whole bedspread once,' Katherine said inconsequentially.

'So you did. Do you want something to eat, Kath? We never had any lunch.' She ignored the shudder which shook her sister from neck to feet, the pale face impossibly paler as her head shook a faint negative. 'Come on,' Mary coaxed, 'I mean, nothing much. Toast or something. Eggs and toast soldiers. You know very well that's the limit of my culinary skills.'

'Bad for you', said Katherine automatically, 'all that cholesterol. Just toast, if you're really making some.'

'Milky tea?'

'Please.' The hands were becoming more certain over their work and the tacking stitches were smaller and more precise. Thank God. Not out of the woods, Mary thought, but perhaps beginning to recognize the trees. She sat on the bed, wanting to fold the pyjamas which were Katherine's apparel for most of the day. Striped and flannelette, Mary's again since Mary never threw anything away, resurrected and worn uncomfortably, Katherine's insistence. Katherine saw her sister looking at the pyjamas and looking away.

'I know they make me look like a convict,' she said calmly, biting the end of the thread. 'All they need is little arrows on them. Don't worry, I'll soon be what I look like when I'm wearing those. Convict.'

'Oh, Kath, stoppit. The lawyer said, well he said, he doubted if . . .'

'I know what he said. I do have ears, you know.' There was no shade of reproof in the tone. 'He said it would depend on the charge, and whatever happens, they don't always put you away. And on what He says, of course.' He. There were names they could neither of them mention, not even Mary in her newfound courage, her anxious, uncritical, guilty care. There had been a daughter and a father: now there was neither who could be described by forename, although their faces swam into focus with every passing thought. Confused, swollen, poisoned, hungry faces which made Katherine scream in the middle of the night. Mary, awake in unison, the two of them embracing in a way they had never before embraced, even as frightened children. 'I love you, Kath, here lean on me, I'll try to do better,' brushing away the lack of response, meaning every word. So humbling, to see how you had thought you knew someone, to find you had never known them at all.

'Oh well, I'll make this toast.' Mary roused herself.

'If they do put me away,' Katherine continued, determined to avoid the end of the subject which Mary so wished to block, 'I shan't mind, you know, and you mustn't either. It would feel like paying a debt.'

'That's no way to pay a debt. And I don't know how punishment comes into it. And we don't know yet if Jeanetta . . .'

'They'll be howling for my blood,' said Katherine. 'I know what people think. I read these magazines. I sometimes read your paper. There has to be punishment.'

'You don't mean you won't even fight . . .'

'No,' said Katherine, picking up the curtain again, stitching faster. 'No, I don't mean that.'

'Why, Kath, why? How did you let him?' Mary burst out.

'I wanted to go back,' Katherine said. 'Back to being little.'

Mary left the room. She went into the kitchen to prepare some food. Katherine seemed to refuse eating in principle, but she could be persuaded towards the nibbling consumption of scraps. There were stocks of biscuits, sponge cake, cereal, bland carbohydrate, nothing fancier than eggs and Cheddar cheese, nothing which required the heating of a pan of oil or the scent of frying. The cheese was eaten with biscuits, the eggs were boiled, soup came out of a tin. Sophie's rations were on display, ready for a visit the same afternoon, acting as both a relief and a trial, bringing the kitten in a special basket, the other arm holding a pint of milk and all conversation consistent of nothing but the rigours of her progress from her own house to this. In her merciful unawareness of all but unimportant detail,

301

Sophie was even funny. Ha, ha, not much to laugh at at all, but then Mary's sense of humour had always been grim. Forbore even the visit of Mrs Harrison with some of Katherine's clothes. Oh God, the quality of human kindness, like cruelty, was so strange, so completely unexpected. She had never known.

Katherine sat sewing, streamlining the pain of her thoughts by furious concentration on the stitches, stopping to look round the room. Spartan white walls, awful furniture, none of it as it had once been, offensive. The sort of semi-institutionalized room which was now synonymous with safety, devoid of character and containing nothing other than standard issue, brought in at a discount without thought of taste. She looked down at the cotton of the flimsy curtains. Some of it had made cushions too, she seemed to recall, pretty. Cushions like the sort you shoved down the front of your smock when you where about six, pretending to have a baby. Those were the days. Something from nothing. These were the days to follow. The room was hot, making a tiny trickle of perspiration escape from the line of her hair, forcing her to rise reluctantly and open the window cold-blooded Mary preferred closed. The flat was over a garden, with a road running along the side. Further down the road was a school and in the distance, newly released, childish voices were raised in screams, distant footsteps, distant taunts flying and thundering. Katherine closed the window, moved like an automatic toy back to the armchair, sat with eyes closed and heart pounding.

Something from nothing: nothing from something.

Sophie tiptoed in, still dressed in her coat, eyes alight with anticipation of tea and company. Seeing the eyes closed, she carefully placed the cat into Katherine's lap and stood back with satisfaction. She might know nothing else, but cats did things to people, look how. The thing mewed in protest, then simply accommodated itself to a new source of warmth. With a will all of their own, Katherine's fingers stroked the tabby fur. The cat began to purr and the sounds of the children began to recede from her mind.

'So you aren't dead then?' yelled Sophie. 'Ah, curtains.'

'No,' Katherine said, kneading her hands gently in the neck of the animal on her knee. 'Not dead. Not yet.'

'Any news?' Sophie yelled again.

'No.'

'Oh dear, dear me. Still, no news is good news.'

The long fingers paused, tensed. 'Why did you never warn me, Granny? About what he was like?'

Sophie shuffled. 'He was only doing what was sort of done to us, dear. I didn't know he would. Don't let's talk about it now.'

Mary came in with a tray of tea, weak to be laced with sugar.

'Where there's life there's hope,' intoned Sophie, repossessing the cat. Katherine moved with a greater briskness, picked up the curtain again. 'I knew a woman once,' Sophie went on, 'made her living out of sewing curtains.' For the first time in the days of their resumed life, Mary saw on her sister's white face the ghost of determination.

'Well,' murmured Katherine, 'you may have just met another.'

Then she began to cry, holding the printed cloth up to her eyes, a silent, soaking weeping.

Sophie turned away, hiding her distress. 'I say,' she hissed to Mary in a stage whisper, 'they can't make her, you know get rid of . . . it? Can they?'

'No, they can't.' Katherine surprised them all by a loud voice, tremulous but almost shouting, petulant but determined. 'They can't. I want it.'

Wisely the woman kept silent. Mary smiled. They were safe here. Waiting.